THE LAST BOAT FROM DANZIG

by

J. Alexander

from a true story

Red'n'Ritten Ltd.

Editor: Joan Stanley

Published by Red'n'Ritten Ltd,
17 Kings Barn Lane,
Steyning,
West Sussex
BN44 3YR
© Red'n'Ritten Ltd. 2007

ISBN 9781904278528

A CIP Catalogue record for this book is available from the British Library.

Printed by Marston Book Services Ltd.

Cover Artwork by Mike Avery.

Editor Joan Stanley

THE LAST BOAT FROM DANZIG

by

J. Alexander

This powerful and moving story takes us to Germany in the early 1930's. Nina and her two sisters grow up in a traditional, upper-middle-class, professional, Christian, German family, with Jewish friends and strong ties to England. But when the Nazis take power life-changing decisions have to be made.

Nina and friends develop an escape line for Jews, risking their lives in one daring event after another. Claudia is also involved, but her other sister Anna marries a Nazi officer…

When World War Two breaks out one by one members of the family are arrested or disappear. Towards the end of the war, Nina and Claudia are trapped in East Prussia as the Russian army closes their escape routes.

Ships have been leaving the Bay of Danzig, but can Nina and her refugees survive the gruelling weather and cross the frozen waters in time to board *The Last Boat from Danzig*…?

Based on first hand, real life events revealed to the author, this book gives a fresh insight into the lives of the German people, themselves caught up in the Nazi oppression.

Dedicated to

Karen

whose story

it started out to be.

Thanks

My grateful thanks go to Don and John who have not only lived with the story for many years, but have given me enormous encouragement and help when I faltered or lost heart.

I must also thank my editor and publisher, Joan Stanley, without whom this story might still be mouldering in a bottom drawer somewhere in the cellar. She had the insight to see through the original naïve writing and guide me with some useful advice, which helped me become at least a jobbing writer.

Then I must thank Dr. Ian Crammond, who was acting Dean of History at University College, Chichester, when I asked him if he would read the story for historical accuracy. He gave me one or two priceless pieces of advice without which I might have made a schoolgirl howler or two. If I missed out on something you said, Ian, put it down to my innate ability to ignore expert advice and carry on regardless.

And, most importantly, I have to thank Karen who told me her personal history many years ago. I added a family you may not recognize and events, which happened to others and not to you. I hope you won't mind too much.

To any living relatives of those I used as models for certain characters I would like to say that where I have done so, I researched painstakingly so I would neither hurt nor embarrass them, nor demean their memory. I hope their heroism, for that is what it was, has come through in the characters in the book. My main hope was to show that men and women find the courage to fight tyranny in many different ways, often in the certain knowledge that when it is finally brought down their part in its downfall will be glossed over or forgotten. Perhaps the time has come to think of the heroism shown by civilians in all wars, whichever side they are on.

And, lastly, my greatest concern was that in writing such a story I would somehow justify or excuse what the Nazis did: I hope I have not done so in any way. I thoroughly abhor and condemn all such tyranny and stress that the people I have written about also condemned it. But, like most people, they were powerless to change things except within their immediate circles. And there, they did what they could.

J. Alexander
2007

One

"Nina? Come along child, you must do your duty. Take that dreamy look off your face. And don't get your new white dress dirty against the window."

"Oh, but I just wanted to watch..."

"No buts, dear."

Nina heard the slightest note of command in her mother's voice, sighed, and turned back to the ballroom. "Yes, Mama."

She rejoined her family as they waited in the doorway for their guests. Otto and Hildegard von Luden, and their other two daughters, Anna and Claudia, already stood in line. She took her place thoughtfully at the end of the row, while her parents greeted each guest with the casual elegance and authority that came from centuries of position and gracious living.

Hildegard von Luden, born Hildegard Will, came from an old East Prussian family whose ancestors had owned a limestone quarry deep in East Prussia, and a small amber mine near Königsberg, from which the Will family had made their considerable fortune.

A forbidding woman to many of the locals, to her family Hildegard was the doyenne, the linchpin around whom the whole extended family revolved. Her solid frame had been acquired after years of sampling Black Forest gateaux and Viennese chocolate cake, with some assistance from Belgian whipped cream and Parisian chocolates. She had, she confessed, a sweet tooth. The expansion in her girth was reflected a little in her face, which was unlined, if a little puffed around the chins.

According to her husband Otto she was as lovely as ever, and indeed her face still retained some of its former beauty, though he thought now she might best be described as striking, rather than beautiful.

He remained as slender as he had been during the Great War, but his face was etched by harrowing memories into a picture of quiet unhappiness, sometimes of real anguish.

Otto came from a Prussian military family, rising to the rank of general in the army. He had been invalided out of the war after a gas attack had gone badly wrong, catching even the generals by surprise. It had been only a moment before he donned a gas mask, but it had been enough to damage the delicate lining of his lungs, and he was to suffer with breathing difficulties for the rest of his life.

Shortly after the end of the Great War he had expounded to his brother, "War should be outlawed, it's become barbaric. You used to know where you stood; even the enemy stuck to the rules of warfare. But now we have gas, barbed wire, flames, tanks... anything goes, it isn't clear any more. That's no way to fight."

A central street in Nordberg, the nearest town of any size to their estate, had been renamed Otto von Luden Strasse after him, and a newly built bridge had also been given his name in a lavish ceremony marking the end of his distinguished career. Strategically, it was a small, fairly unimportant bridge, but the honour indicated the measure of his importance within the East Prussian community.

Thin and gangling, all arms and legs, Nina stood with her back straight, and her left hand loosely clasping her right forefinger. Her head was tilted a little sideways, always an indication that she was listening and thinking intently; yet her youthful face expressed a mind far away in some inner world. Most of the family enjoyed greeting their guests as they arrived for their Christmas party, but not Nina. She used her prolific imagination to invent all manner of unusual excuses to avoid such boring rituals.

Anna whispered quietly, but firmly, in her younger sister's ear, "At least try to look as though you're interested, Nina."

"I do, Anna, but..."

"Then you must try harder. It's only once a year. Come on! Put a smile on your face at least."

"But that's hypocritical. I don't feel like smiling."

"Oh, for goodness sake, Nina! This is for Mama and Papa."

"All right. But I'm not enjoying myself."

Anna turned away and scanned the room for the only person who captured her imagination, Captain Peter Richter.

As the guests came through the ballroom door they accepted champagne and petit fours from smiling maids before polarising into two groups. An elderly landowner quickly drained his glass and looked around for a refill. "Of course I've heard of Hitler," he said to his companions. "Who hasn't? But what does he stand for?"

"You've been out of the country too long, Georg. He stands for our interests; he says what we all want to hear. Mind you, I don't much care for some of his ideas, but if he can stabilise the economy he's got my vote."

"Big business is backing him to the hilt, so I hear, Reinhard. I suppose they wouldn't support him if he didn't give them what they want."

"I agree. He goes off the rails a bit when he talks about the Jews. They're some of my best customers; I don't want to upset them too much. But he's a strong leader. The country needs someone to get rid of the Communists. And he's the only man right now capable of stamping them out."

"Absolutely! They're far too powerful, and if they take over the government they'll start confiscating our property. We can trace our lineage back several centuries. I'm certainly not prepared to allow a bunch of jumped up, so-called workers to take over my estates after hundreds of years of my family's hard work."

"We need someone to get us out of this mess. Who else is there? Von Papen's a weak, old aristocratic type. Hitler at least has backbone. And if he gets out of line, we can always have him replaced."

Nina, struggling to understand their discussion, left her place in the family line to listen to the women's gossip instead. One diverted a conversation with her friends from fashion to politics. "Yes, I wore the new tweed suit when we went to one of Hitler's meetings. He ranted a lot, but what a hypnotic speaker he is! He got the crowd really worked up."

"I felt awfully threatened by his guards, though. Didn't you?"

"He makes me feel proud again to be German. And if you listen to what he says you begin to understand the need for his storm troopers."

"What about his right-hand man, what's his name? Goebbels? I heard he's a bit of a womaniser."

"He's a funny-looking, little dwarf, isn't he? I can't see women falling for him."

"I rather like Goering, the one with the splendid uniforms. He reminds me of a mediaeval king, covered in medals, bags of self-confidence. What about their wives? They aren't very chic, are they? They wear all kinds of drab clothes. And their hair! The less said the better. Very lower middle class, if you ask me." The women smiled disdainfully at the visual images.

Nina tried to absorb and evaluate everything she heard.

As Frau Elisabeth Braun and her family shook hands formally with each of the von Ludens, she gushed unconvincingly, "Otto! Hilde! How kind of you to invite us all."

When the Brauns moved out of earshot, Hildegard whispered disparagingly to her husband, "Nouveau riche!"

"Yes, I've heard her talking. She behaves as though she was our equal, just because she doled out soup during the Great War. Her husband told me she was quite steamed up about it. Kept the country going on her own she did, apparently."

Hildegard was quite scathing about some of the middle classes who thought they had earned the right to equal social treatment by the von Ludens simply as a result of their war work. "What nonsense! She only came along when the photographers appeared. When they went, so did she! She wouldn't dirty her hands, yet she thinks she deserves her place at our table. I can tell you she wouldn't have been allowed through the door if it wasn't for the hard work her husband puts in as Chief of Police."

Herr Braun and his wife entered the ballroom as Nina rejoined her family, and as they passed, Frau Braun stared at her and said, "They all put on airs, the whole bunch of them."

Nina was fourteen this year and she felt very grown up, even though she was wearing a girlish, short, white dress and had her long, blonde hair tied back in a neat plait, with a huge red bow at the end. Her mother expected her to make a slight curtsey to each guest as they passed: a sign that she was not yet their equal. Yet Nina was beginning to think she was too old for that, and it was a little demeaning.

Although Claudia was allowed to wear a longer evening gown, she had decided on a fashionably short, peach-coloured dress that gave her more freedom of movement. With a string of real pearls around her neck and a pretty peach headband, threaded through with smaller pearls, adorning her golden mane, she looked very different from her sisters.

Anna, the traditionalist of the three sisters, had her hair carefully styled in the short, clipped bob of Clara Bow, the striking American silent-film star. She was unaware that she looked the height of fashion, simply accepting her hairdresser's assurance that it suited her bone structure. Her couturier always made her 'what Madam looks best in,' and she had created a long cream coloured silk dress for Anna, which clung to her slender, nineteen year old frame and emphasised her youth. Yet Anna had the maturity of a woman of forty: constant attention to her two younger sisters had brought out her mothering instinct and matured her prematurely.

Both the hairdresser and the couturier were guests at the party, as were many of their regular tradespeople. When they compiled the guest list, Hildegard had advised Anna, "If you want the best attention from them, you must make them feel special."

This was the first Christmas party in which Nina had taken an active interest. In past years, after only a couple of hours she had disappeared, with Nanny, up to the bedrooms in the children's area at the top of the house. But she had always longed to be grown up, to be a part of the exciting world downstairs.

She and Claudia had often talked and dreamed of what the future would hold, of what they would become when they grew up. "I should like to be influential ..." Claudia's confidence was boundless.

"Papa said we would all be leaders one day. But why would people follow you? What will you do?"

"I should steer them into the right way of doing things, like defending Dreyfus or someone like him when no one else was capable of getting him free. Something glorious and noble. A grand gesture like giving my life so that others may live; that's what I'll do!"

Claudia was too absorbed in her idealistic dream to ask Nina about her ambitions, but she told her anyway. "I don't know what I'm going to be yet. I should like to make life happier for everyone, somehow. I don't know how, though. You don't see many smiling faces, do you? Will you become a lawyer?"

Claudia had not answered Nina's question, it was too specific for a dreamer, and grand gestures seemed possible and desirable then. Both girls saw themselves as the pioneers of social fashion, not the followers, and whatever they did would be emulated by others around them.

The thoughts whirled through Nina's head as she automatically curtsied, smiled and spoke to her parents' friends and neighbours. This year her emotions were in turmoil. One moment she imagined being captivated by one of the handsome, youthful officers her father had invited, and captivating him so he had eyes for her alone. The next she was being relentlessly sensible, chastising herself for such nonsense and insisting that she was not at all attractive. Anyway, what's so important about romance? I shall be like Aunt Alice; I shall live alone and do what I want.

While they waited for the next guests, she nudged Claudia and whispered, "Why do women always have to do what men want?"

Claudia held out her hand to a gallant, elderly gentleman who politely pretended to kiss the back of her peach glove, clicked his heels and moved on to Nina, to whom he attempted to do the same. Nina was startled by what seemed to be so intimate an act, and began to pull her hand back. But a nudge and a frown from her sister stopped her and she submitted, unwillingly.

After he had moved into the ballroom, Claudia whispered, "Because men are in charge of the world, so they can do what they want, including telling us what to do. And that was father's bank manager you were nearly rude to!"

"But why? That's not fair!"

"Life isn't fair." Claudia was sardonic, impatient with Nina for still being a child, while she was now grown up and knew everything.

"Oh, Claudia! I've just thought. Do you remember you always wanted to make a grand gesture? Can't you make one about this? Do something to make men see that it isn't right? Like that lady in England who was killed by a horse so women could get the vote?"

Claudia had moved into a cynical phase. "Not according to that English teacher we met last time we were in London. He said it was the war that got them the vote."

"Yes, but he was a man." Nina protested lamely, knowing what she meant to imply, but not knowing quite how to say it.

They were interrupted by their mother remonstrating with their father, "For goodness sake, Otto, can't we have just one evening in the year without politics spoiling it?" Hildegard spat out the word 'politics' as she would spit out something foreign in her food, something foul tasting and ill-placed. In her opinion it was the fount of all that was wrong with the world these days and those who became embroiled in it brought trouble upon their own heads and upon their families.

Christmas for Hildegard was, above all, a religious occasion, a time to think of God and His good works, to thank Him for all His big and small mercies, not an excuse for all the men to get their heads together and argue endlessly.

"You'll have plenty of time in the New Year for that." She lovingly dusted an imaginary hair from the lapel of Otto's evening suit. He still looked smart, very suave and handsome, and she found it easy to forgive him.

"Come on, Hilde, politics is the stuff of life. Most of the guests are going to want to discuss Hitler and the elections. It's a momentous time historically. You're the history graduate in the family you should know that. How can I stop them?"

Hildegard pursed her lips ominously, "You shouldn't encourage them. Ah! Ruth! At last." She smiled her sweet welcoming smile at Otto's brother Franz and his wife Ruth, and their four children.

"Hilde! I'm so sorry we're late. We'd have been here this morning, but I felt so drained. We had to stop in Danzig for me to recover. Usual problem, you know. What a pain I am, aren't I? You're looking well. You've put on some weight, haven't you?"

"You know I can't burn it off the way I used to. And before you say 'You should take more exercise,' with the family to bring up and the house to run I don't have the time."

While talking animatedly with them all, Hildegard forgot her irritation with Otto.

With a huge hug, she reassured Ruth, "I'm glad you're here now and feeling better. And you look so well. And so do you, Franz."

Releasing her brother-in-law, she hugged the twins, then stepped back and held them at arms length, "My word, Susanna, aren't you growing up? And Wilhelm, too. Look at you! What a size you both are!"

The ten-year-old twins looked at each other and giggled, their eyes rolled heavenwards. They heard the same words every time they visited their Aunt Hildegard; it was tiresome, but they loved their aunt dearly and always looked forward to their visits to East Prussia.

"Hans and Christina, it's been too long. Goodness me, don't you look healthy? I feel quite pale and uninteresting alongside all of you. It's that Baltic air, isn't it - it's so good for you."

Hildegard prattled on, looking round for her youngest daughter who was eagerly awaiting her turn to greet them. "You two run along with Nina."

Grateful to be active, Nina threw her arms around her aunt and uncle, and whispered in their ears, "I'm so glad you're here. It isn't half as much fun without you." Ruth and Franz looked at each other in surprise; Nina had never been that open before.

She steered the twins over to where Nanny and Aunt Alice were sitting with the other children. Nanny Watson sat upright in the shadow of one of the four marble pillars - two at each end of the room - surrounded by the young children in what had become known as the children's corner.

"Mother told me to go back, Nanny."

Nanny eyed Nina suspiciously, but she held her tongue; it was a party, after all.

Nina quietly informed Susanna, "I'll be back soon, then we can enjoy ourselves talking about everyone."

The close relationship she had with the twins was maintained despite the distance between East Prussia and Pomerania. They spent the Christmas parties gossiping together about the guests, who Nina mimicked; though she was beginning to feel that it was not a nice thing to do, and she ought not to be setting a bad example to her cousins. The child was becoming the mother of the woman. Nina was growing up.

Two

Hildegard had been married for twenty-two years and she had never regretted a single moment. Her sister Alice had made an unfortunate match: her husband gambled away their capital until she had eventually been driven to divorce him, before he lost the roof over their heads.

Hildegard felt that even in those circumstances divorce was not quite proper. After all, Alice had promised to remain with him through all the vicissitudes of life, and until death alone parted them. And a divorced woman was, somehow, tainted, to be avoided by both sexes. Alice had ignored the gossip as beneath her contempt and happily moved to Königsberg with their mother, from whom she would eventually inherit the family home.

Childless herself, she always treated Hildegard's three girls as her own and her will was made out in their favour. "Not that there will be much to leave you, but this old house will be yours one day, and all my jewellery. I'm going to give you some of it now, before my accountants and solicitors use it to pay themselves."

She had handed all three sisters several pieces of her very large jewellery collection. It was Alice's pearls that Claudia was wearing around her neck and in her headband; Alice's amber brooch and necklace, which Anna wore; and Alice's gold cross with a discreet diamond at its intersection, which Nina fingered tenderly.

Alice arrived two days before Christmas and entertained the three girls with her tales of life in Königsberg. Claudia loved to hear her aunt's stories of her rebellious youth. She, too, had been like the 'lady in England,' an early suffragette fighting for the rights of all females. Claudia wanted to follow in her aunt's footsteps. But any such 'grand ideas' had become very personal, an inner ambition too precious to air before anyone, even Nina.

Nina's best friend Eva Rosenthal, who was the only child of a half-Jewish professor of mathematics, was also staying with the von Ludens. They shared a dormitory at their private school in Danzig, and during their long vacations they were in and out of each other's homes. The two girls had grown up together and Nina had never been discouraged from befriending her.

The fact that Eva was a quarter Jewish had begun to come between the two friends. Not that either of the two girls were any less friendly towards each other, but the atmosphere generated around them by adults had begun to make them aware that there were differences between them.

Eva did not look Jewish; neither did she have any of the characteristics associated with Jewish people. She could easily have passed as an ordinary, dark haired German girl. Her teachers were drawn by the warmth and charm of her character, but they were also constrained by political expediency, so they kept her at a polite distance. If Hitler gained power soon it would not be wise to befriend any Jews.

People were already beginning to acquiesce to the course Hitler had mapped out for them, jostling for positions in each of the social layers; seeking ways to make their lives better, more prosperous; some making a stand politically, morally, or ethically for or against him. The von Luden family disliked the 'bumptious corporal', as they called him, and were waiting to see the election result before taking a stand against him.

Regardless of the consequences, Alice refused to sit back and remain passive. Her activities had already marked her out as a supporter of some of the Jewish shop owners in Königsberg. As she sat watching the proud young Nazi officers, shamelessly flaunting themselves in front of the young ladies at the Christmas party, she expounded her views to Franz who had wandered over to the children's corner to be with the twins.

She held her slim body upright, her shoulders back, her head instinctively held high, giving her a haughty air. "I don't care what people say, I will never accept that upstart. As you well know, I take people as I find them, and if I see anyone being unjust or unfair, I'll tell them. And what Hitler is saying about Jews is simply not on. I won't stand for it. Young Eva here was just explaining her situation at school. She expects to be expelled when Hitler gains power. For heaven's sake, what are they thinking about? And her father's position at the university has been undermined. Now perhaps you see what I mean by the poison of anti-Semitism spreading throughout the education system. It will spread into most other areas before they've finished."

Franz patted her fondly on the shoulder: "I think you've probably exaggerated, as you usually do, Alice."

She winced noticeably at his touch. "You don't live where I do, Franz. You're quite unaware of the grip they already have on some of your own compatriots. And it isn't just anti-Semitism, which endangers our society. Positions of considerable power are being given to quite unsuitable people who have no experience of it and will undoubtedly misuse it."

"No one has experience of leadership until it's given to them, do they? You have to start somewhere..."

"Don't be so woolly, Franz, you know what I'm trying to say! He's giving authority to people with no vision, no humanity. Put power in the hands of that sort of person and... We'll see what happens in due course. But the way they're treating Eva and others like her is a national disgrace."

Eva was encouraged to know that someone understood and believed in her. She loved her schooling, especially her language lessons. Now she and Nina spoke together in Italian, a language they knew few of the other children within earshot understood sufficiently to follow their conversation.

"You know Anneliese's coming, don't you?"

"Yes, you told me. Has she been here before?"

Nina did not want to admit that Anneliese's Jewishness was an embarrassment to her family. "No. I said I'd take her round the house when she arrives. Will you come, too?"

Eva nodded her assent.

"If you see her before I do, let me know. I promised Mama I'd take care of her as soon as she arrives and she'll never forgive me for not being there to greet her. Mama says she's uncouth."

"Papa calls her unpolished, but he always gives people the benefit of the doubt."

"I know. I've never heard him say anything unkind about anyone. If I didn't have such a lovely father, I'd wish I had yours."

Eva smiled at the compliment. "I wish I had your mother, no one would dare upset her. It's hard being even part Jewish. Nina, you're the only friend I have who never mentions it, ever."

"It isn't important." Nina had a dawning comprehension that life outside her social background was different, and she had a naïve certainty that it was her duty to change things, to bring people together, so they could understand each other better. She loved her friends for whom and what they were, not for what others said they should be.

She waited patiently for Anneliese, spending some of her time asking her aunt questions. "Aunt Alice, what does 'putting on airs' mean?"

"Getting above your station in life, Nina dear, the status and place in your community, which God gave you at birth."

"Ours is to be at the top, isn't it? How can we get above it?"

"That only applies in this area. In Berlin, for example, there are many families higher than ours. If we tried to be in their set, so to speak, we'd be in trouble. Whatever made you think of that?"

"Frau Braun. I heard her say it after we'd greeted her at the door. I think she meant us."

"Did she indeed! If anyone gets above herself, it's she! If Hitler wins the election next year, you'll see what it really means."

"Women don't have the same rank as men, do they, so if they try to be like them, are they getting above themselves?"

Alice was quite adamant, "Good heavens, no, dear! That's men's doing, they put us in this lowly position, not God."

24

"But Adam was made before Eve, doesn't that make us lower than men?"

Alice stole a quizzical look at Nina's serious face. "Goodness me, you are doing a lot of thinking tonight, Nina. I've always seen that as man's interpretation of the Bible."

"Do you think I'd be going too far if I take philosophy or religious studies at university?"

"Ah! I begin to see where this is taking us. No, I don't think so. More and more girls are pursuing what used to be seen as unsuitable studies for females. Your main duty is to gain as good an education as you can, in whatever field you choose. Then you can pass on your enlightenment and your high moral values to those you employ. The world is changing. Women are changing. You'll have a responsible position some day, perhaps even a powerful one." Alice leaned back and turned her head to lower her voice so only Nina would hear, "I have a hunch, little one, that you might be one of our first female politicians."

"Oh, no! I'm sure I won't."

"If, *when* you do, you will have responsibilities towards your work force. They must be loyal to you, but so must you be in return. Look after them when they're sick, defend them, even when they're wrong."

"Why when they're wrong?"

"Everyone makes mistakes. Parents defend their children even when they're naughty. Servants and employees are family, and must be treated as such. Now, I really do think that's enough. Go and enjoy yourself with your cousins and friends, Nina. We'll talk more tomorrow."

Three

Otto was becoming impatient with having to stand still for so long, and his mind wandered to the young officers he had invited. As he surveyed them, strutting around self-importantly, he dismissed any idea that he had been like them at their age.

'Today's youth is a different breed. Life has evolved beyond anything I remember, and the young have changed with it. Old-fashioned virtues are almost unknown to them. These young whippersnappers accept nothing of value any more. Their obedience and duty seem to be only towards Hitler.' He lamented the sad fate of German youth, but kept his thoughts to himself.

His idle musing was rudely interrupted by Hildegard's annoying tap on his arm. She motioned towards the Rosenthals.

"Otto! Do listen to what I'm saying. Would you keep an eye on Ruby and Jakob? I'll look out for Leon and Berthe Steiner. With any luck they won't come."

Otto stared at his wife, startled. It was unlike Hilde to be so negative, yet he could understand her trepidation. There had been some heart searching by them both prior to issuing an invitation. Otto had suggested they send one, and, if their visit were unsuccessful, they would not be invited again. Hildegard was simply against the whole idea.

The Steiners were not liked either in Elbing, where they owned two shops, or in the nearby town of Nordberg, where they had one more. Local people did not approve of them, because they were Jews. They were also prosperous and that led to envy, especially amongst those families who had been hit by hyperinflation, which Germany had suffered a few years back. Hitler was making suggestions that the Jews were responsible for all the troubles in Germany, economic and political. It seemed to many East Prussians at the party that there was a lot of truth in the idea of a great Jewish conspiracy, when they considered the Steiners as an example.

"Oh, dear! Here they come. Leon thinks he'll be accepted into the community after coming here. People like that never understand..."

Hildegard stiffened, then nervously leaned over to Ruth and whispered behind her fan, "Stand by me, Ruth dear, won't you?" She fanned herself vigorously, summoning up courage for the potential ordeal.

"Don't worry so, Hilde. Your guests will have to accept them, because it's your party. And if they don't, let them leave..."

Hildegard broke away from Ruth and greeted the Steiners and their two children as though there was no other family she would rather have met. Her effusive greeting completely disarmed Berthe and Leon, who received no warning of the welcome in store for them from the other guests.

Hildegard was still greeting them when Nina tripped up and cannoned into them. "Nina! How many times have I told you not to run in the ballroom?"

Nina blushed; she had only meant to walk quickly, but her wayward feet had a life of their own these days. "I'm sorry, Mother."

"The apology is owed to our guests."

Hildegard was unbending in her insistence on good manners, Christmas party or not.

The contrite Nina apologised to Leon and Berthe Steiner, shaking their hands in greeting, and curtseying slightly. She could not explain in front of them that she had intended to take their daughter Anneliese under her wing immediately she arrived. Neither did she see the consternation and condemnation that her small, automatic curtsey caused amongst many of the congregation in the room, who noted the Steiners' arrival with great alarm.

Anneliese was overwhelmed by the ballroom and stared goggle-eyed at the walls and ceiling until Nina and Eva were becoming embarrassed.

"Did your family do all this?"

The girls looked at each other amazed and taken aback by their friend's

28

ignorance. "Good heavens, no! This was built centuries ago. Father employed people to revarnish the wood, that's all. It's antique!"

Anneliese's attitude was understandable. The elegant late eighteenth-century mansion had been part of Otto's heritage, handed down through the eldest son for generations, and much of their inheritance had been spent on its upkeep.

The huge ballroom covered most of the first floor. French windows led out to the black, iron-balustraded balcony running the full length of the building. Guests could stand on the balcony, enjoy the well kept garden below, sip their champagne and be soothed by the gentle cascade of water from the fountain almost underneath.

Three long, diamond shaped chandeliers hung from the ceiling of the ballroom, the central one dominating the other two in size and radiance. When alight, as they were now, their flickering reflections dappled the varnish on the recently renovated wooden ceiling. They reproduced themselves in the oblong mirrors, each decorated with delicate, gilt, mock-rococo flowers and fruit, and lazy cherubs draped along the tops. When the room was overflowing with colourful, cheerful, resplendent guests, the atmosphere became charged with brilliance and gaiety: a dazzling tableau of rich privilege.

The von Ludens disliked the decadent social class that the ornate ballroom represented, even though they were Otto's ancestors, but could not bring themselves to vandalize the expensive, exquisite decorations by having them removed. The room represented part of their country's history and should be preserved as a reminder to future generations. And, on occasions such as the present one, it served its purpose.

Anneliese could find no words to describe how she felt. At school, she had gained no idea of Nina's privileged background. She was torn between admiration for the house, pride at having Nina as a friend, and envy of her family's position and power. Her own family could buy a mansion to rival this one. They could make money and become as rich as the von Ludens. But, however hard they worked, however charitable they were, however well they treated their employees, they could never be accepted into this community. From this enclosed, élitist society, she and her Jewish family were excluded. She envied Nina's family with a childish passion that was almost hatred.

Losing patience with her friend who still hung back, staring around her, Nina commanded in an unexpectedly threatening tone, "Liese, come on, I'll take you round the rest of the house." Nina saw her mother heading their way with a grimly determined look on her face. "*Now*, Anneliese!"

Anxious to remove her friend and save the family's face, she escorted Anneliese out through the back door of the ballroom, unaware of the brazen hostility being openly directed at them.

Leon Steiner, a self-important man, could not resist the chance to speak to Otto and Franz. "Well, Otto?"

It was an inauspicious start. Leon had never before addressed Herr von Luden by his Christian name. Despite his respect for all humanity, Otto found himself bridling at Leon's intimacy.

For his part, Leon felt that by being invited to the von Luden's Christmas party, they were now, at long last, accepted by their society and on equal terms with most of them. After all, Otto was the community. Although Leon could see that the von Ludens and other established families had more status than he enjoyed.

Herr Steiner announced approvingly, "So, we're going to have Hitler at the helm, after all."

Hildegard looked over at him sharply, directing a pointed stare at Otto.

Otto arched his eyebrows defensively and his eyes asked, 'How can I not answer one of our guests? I know it's politics, but it would be rude not to reply.'

He only conceded unwillingly, "I'm very much afraid that we are, Herr Steiner."

Hildegard huffed and pushed herself between them. "Herr Steiner, Leon - may I call you Leon? Why don't you and Berthe come and meet some of the other guests?"

She took their arms forcibly and, with something approaching a triumphant side glance at Otto, steered them away from the frying pan of his politics and into the fire of ostracism from the other guests.

Franz, standing next to his older brother - one arm casually leaning on the marble mantelpiece, the other hand languidly lighting an expensive Havana cigar - gazed at the two Steiners as they were taken around by Hildegard and Ruth.

Although their attire was the equal of any in the room, the Steiners looked awkward and undignified, plunged into an environment for which they were not fitted. Berthe kept glancing nervously at her husband, as if for reassurance.

Living in Pomerania, cut off from his brother in East Prussia by the Polish Corridor, Franz could not keep up to date with all their news. "How come Nina is friendly with their daughter? They're not exactly cultured, are they?"

"Not at all, not at all. He's the kind of person who gives Jews a bad name. This year, the girls all found themselves in the same dormitory at school. Under those circumstances you become more attached than you might wish. You know what it's like, living in the same Mess. Nina couldn't invite Eva without inviting the other one: difficult situation. Why they put Nina in with Jews I don't know, but Nina wouldn't have it changed. You know what she's like, stubborn as a mule if one of her precious principles is at stake."

Some vestiges of anti-Semitism briefly stirred within him as he appraised the Steiner family.

"Still, I'd have found some way to exclude them. Without being rude, of course," Franz added, thinking Otto had been very unwise to invite them.

Franz and Ruth, who were more politically aware, were quicker to note the dark and sinister side of the guests' reactions. Franz made a mental note to speak to Otto about the family's future behaviour if Hitler finally gained control of the Reichstag.

But Otto saw only what he wanted to see and heard only what he wanted to hear.

Four

By eight o'clock all the guests had arrived. The six handsome young men Otto had invited were being examined constantly by the pink-faced young ladies fanning themselves energetically after dancing. They laughed merrily with one another as they eyed the officers over their fans. One of the girls blushed deeply as the others chided, "We saw you making eyes at that captain, what's his name?"

"Peter Richter."

"He's spoken for. That's Anna's beau. They've been going out together for months, now."

"Yes. Hands off, or you won't be invited back here next year!"

"I didn't like him much, anyway. Too intense for me."

"He's so political. He doesn't stop talking about the Nazi party."

"Anna doesn't seem to mind."

"Well, she's different, isn't she? Like the rest of her family. And Claudia and Nina are weird; they talk politics all the time. Most unladylike, my mother says."

Captain Peter Richter and his friends were diametrically opposed to the views of the von Luden family. They promoted the cause of the National Socialist Movement, which was poised to take over total control of the country. They entertained no doubts that this was a welcome new spirit that would sweep away the Old World. In their enthusiasm for the new order they cared nothing for the hurt they caused those, like Otto, who had worked all their lives to maintain the values of their immutable way of life.

Otto noticed Anna smiling at her captain, and turned to his sister-in-law. "I've tried everything I can think of to thwart Anna's relationship with him, Ruth, but nothing's worked. It will only bring her misery."

33

"Love will out, Otto. You can't stop her, if she's really determined to marry him."

"You know, Ruth, I'm extremely loath to give up the traditions of our society. Fathers controlling daughters has been the way of things in the past, not just here, but all over Europe. We've produced generation after generation of like-minded adults, because we've never changed our ways, and it's served us well as a nation. Time was when I could have laid down the law and forbidden her to see him again."

"She certainly wouldn't stand for that."

"If I'd known democracy was going to bring so much freedom to my daughters I might not have supported it so willingly."

"Why shouldn't women make their own choices, Otto? You talk as though you need to be in control of them, as if they were some kind of domesticated stock on one of your farms. Even women are above animals. Dogs lick your hand, because you train them and feed them. Perhaps it's time for a change, Otto. Why not look upon it as a good thing for them? If you've done your job properly they'll already have those values. You've got to let them make their own mistakes."

"Were you given carte blanche to choose?"

"Yes, I was. I come from very enlightened stock. And I don't think I've made a mess of it, have I, Otto?"

"Not you, Ruth, no. You have children you can be proud of, as I am of mine."

"So you should be."

"Yes, I suppose you're right. I'm reluctant to admit they're almost grown up."

"Anna already is."

Otto stood quietly surveying the ballroom, watching his wife directing the servants to take a drink here or remove an empty plate there, checking the guests to see who might need a glass refilled or extra food. He studied his daughters for a while. Everything about them was a source of great pride to him: their shining, eager faces, crowned with halos of flaxen hair;

their earnest participation in the life of the community; their devotion to the family and the way they were now cheerfully helping their mother make a success of the party. He observed Anna charming the female matrons, sticklers for old fashioned virtues; and carefree Claudia spreading sunshine and laughter all around her; and little Nina, thoughtfully studying her mother, trying to follow in her footsteps.

Just then Anna danced past in the arms of Captain Richter and Otto wondered where the last twenty years had gone. He remembered her birth, their firstborn. Hers had been a protracted birth, as though she had been unwilling to enrol in the human race. She had always shown perplexity, and a reticence that had infuriated Claudia, who burst into the world late in nineteen-fourteen with a vigour she would maintain throughout her life. And lastly, Nina had been born with calmness and little fuss, as though she already understood her lowly position as the last born. Their childhood had always been full of such promise. He wondered which path in life's rich pageant each of them would follow.

He was brought back to the present with a jolt as Anna reached out to touch him, and smiled as she was swept by. Captain Richter jerked his head formally, acknowledging Otto's presence and social superiority.

Ah! Otto remembered there was still the problem of Captain Richter. All he could do was to ensure she understood what her Captain stood for, and the values and customs of her own family.

Anna was not beautiful, but at nineteen she had radiant rosy skin and attentive eyes that carefully took in everything around her, from Captain Richter's immaculate appearance to her younger sister's disorderly hair. Before the dancing began, when Captain Richter had caught her eye yet again, she blushed and gave herself up to rearranging Nina's plait and straightening out the bright red bow. When she had finished, Captain Richter was still surveying her with a presumptuous grin on his face. Anna smiled her acknowledgement of his presence and reluctantly returned to the trivial conversations that she usually found quite bearable, but she was deaf to what her younger sister had been saying; all she heard was the Captain's invitation to dance. Bathed in the warmth of his dark eyes she felt the strength of his protective arms encircling her as she was literally swept off her feet.

Claudia, scornful of Anna's Captain, noted his expression, "He thinks he owns her!"

There was a chorus of approval at Claudia's remark from her two friends, Magda and Ulrike. "It's up to us to show them that we're independent."

"Are there any men around who think as we do?"

Claudia's eyes twinkled mysteriously, "One, but he lives over in Pomerania."

"Do I hear wedding bells, Claudia?"

"Not yet! But you never know. I have to get through university first."

"What if he won't wait?"

"If he means what he says about female independence, he'll wait. And if he doesn't, I don't want him."

"I don't think Captain Richter has female independence in mind for Anna, do you?"

Whereas Claudia and Nina questioned the tenets from which the Nazis would build their new thousand-year-Reich, and their right to impose it on the country, Anna only wanted to know what the new laws would be and how to observe them to the letter.

Subconsciously recognizing that the new regime would bring changes to her family, she looked to Peter to answer her questions. What will be expected of me under the new regime? Will my life change fundamentally? Will I still be able to practice my religion? Will my family be at risk?

Peter's rather stiff and formal exterior suggested order and adherence to rules and she saw in him someone who would not only keep her abreast of them, but also protect her and her family from them.

She was unaware just how deep the division of political thought between them was, for her life had been, in the main, repressively conservative. She had followed the formalised rituals with forbearance, and once their meaning and importance were understood, she followed them from choice. Her strict Prussian upbringing instilled correctness, formality, justice and obedience into her compliant nature, and these were the very attributes that had first attracted Captain Richter to her. She was endowed with pride and reserve, which made her appear difficult to approach, but in their circle that was considered to be the mark of a lady.

She had none of Claudia's sense of fun and only a little of Nina's humanity. Left to herself she would have busied her way through life without ever asking fundamental questions like why am I here or what is the purpose of life? She knew they were unanswerable. Her time could be more usefully spent on the physical necessities around her. She was there, because God had willed it so, and the purpose of her life was to look after her family and the running of her home. Beyond that, she floundered.

Otto understood his daughter's limitations very well. When he voiced his doubts about Captain Richter, Franz suggested a different approach. "She may have a good influence on him."

"I don't think so, Franz. You know Anna, she can be easily led when it comes to things like politics."

"But she has a stubborn streak a mile wide. Like her aunt. And don't forget she has a very strict moral code. Once he goes against her on that you'll see the sparks fly. She understands how our family feels about Hitler, Otto. You'll see; she'll change his views, not the other way around."

"I hope so. I expect to hear from him soon. It's about time he spoke out about his intentions." Otto tried to convince himself that Franz was right, that Anna had what it took to contain the wayward enthusiasm of the Captain. At this time Otto felt no immediate cause for alarm for the future of either his family or of his country, and if Anna married a Nazi sympathiser perhaps it would bring some degree of safety into the family.

37

Five

By ten o'clock in the evening there were signs that some of the older guests were tiring. All of the chairs were filled with exhausted parents fanning themselves, whilst their more energetic children dominated the dance floor. People drifted between the ballroom and the buffet, quietly chatting while they chose their food. When they had eaten their fill they began to look around at the other guests, to smile at their neighbours, discuss them, or criticise them.

Those who had been impoverished by the financial crash were wearing fake jewels made to resemble the genuine diamonds they were known to possess, but which were now in the hands of a pawnbroker. Beneath the glittering surface there were dozens of unhappy stories of misery and struggle; of well-loved family heirlooms pawned in towns where they were unknown for goodness only knew how long before they could be redeemed or sold off forever.

The surfeit of pride that did not allow their poverty to be seen spawned imaginative clothing repairs. Women shared intimate conversations, revealing their innermost thoughts on explosive subjects like politics, or even private topics such as their bedroom habits. But they never let anyone know they had insufficient funds to buy new clothes. Personal wealth was a most unsuitable topic of conversation in polite society.

On the pretext of moving nearer to a middle-aged, buxom lady in order to hear better, one noble matron rearranged her own silk skirt to hide a tiny stitched-over hole near the hem. "My dear, did you see the Steiner girl's dress? It has a huge patch on it!"

"I saw it! And they charge the earth for their dresses in Elbing. They must be making a fortune."

"Enough to buy her a new one. You see how these people treat their own daughter?"

The Steiners became the main targets of gossip.

Frau Braun intervened spitefully, "I think Otto and Hilde have taken leave of their senses. How dare they even think of inviting such pariahs? I would have left immediately they arrived, but it would have been too rude." The fear of appearing rude had never stopped Frau Braun doing anything; rather, she flinched from social exclusion.

Otto was the social leader within their small community, and his friends obtained the best positions. If she appeared to snub any of his guests, she might blight her husband's chances of keeping his post as Police Chief.

"Wait till we take power, then we'll show him how to treat the likes of them."

The von Luden family's liberal attitude was seen by the coming political élite as dangerous, but while he had a title, money and property, Otto was the legitimate ruler of their area, even though he did not display what they considered to be proper nationalism.

All around the room the Steiners were being branded as troublemakers, money-grubbers, ill-bred foreigners, and Otto and Hildegard as foolish and politically naïve. Yet the upright matrons of Nordberg were delighted to see the daughter of their most prestigious family obviously entranced by Captain Richter. In many minds they were already husband and wife. "Yes, that's true, Otto is liberal, yet look how well Anna has turned out. What a nice girl she is. She and Peter Richter make a fine couple, don't they?"

"Capital fellow!" Berthold Braun agreed with his wife, "Good to see the young taking over the reins and steering us along the right road again. We got lost there for a while with all that democracy nonsense."

His largely female audience nodded sagely and approvingly. The Brauns were clearly going to be something important in the new regime: it was unwise to be seen disagreeing with them.

Vexed with everyone, Nina stood with her friends behind Nanny Watson and Aunt Alice; she was annoyed with her mother for publicly humiliating her for something as trivial as bumping into someone, and with herself for feeling obliged to protect her Jewish friends. But, above all, she was angry because she took everything to heart so much. Jealous of the huge smile on her sister's normally serious face, she wondered why she felt so gloomy when everyone else was enjoying the party so much. She stole a look at Eva and Anneliese, and detected something in their manner that she did not notice in anyone else: uneasiness, wariness in the way they were looking around.

Eva caught her eye and smiled. Nina felt guilty; she had not been attending to her duties. "Are you all right?" She asked them both. Seeing Claudia appear in the doorway of the anteroom, holding a drink and eating a roll, she added, "Do you want something to eat?"

"I am a bit hungry," Eva admitted, "but I didn't like to go and help myself." She was a cultured, intelligent young woman who understood the reality of her situation, but had not plucked up the courage to face the formidable women alone.

"I'm starving," Anneliese declared frankly, "we haven't eaten since this morning." Nina and Eva both looked at her, surprised more at her indelicacy than at the length of time she had gone hungry.

In the anteroom long tables, covered with white cloths and decorated with fir cones and sprigs of holly, were groaning under the weight of food laid out on them. Nina gathered the children in her charge and supervised their buffet. "Wilhelm, don't be so greedy. You'll spill that lot on the floor!"

"I'll eat some of it now, then." Wilhelm grinned cheekily, and crammed two slices of sausage into his mouth. Free from parental influence, he reverted to childish instinct, the veneer of civilisation cast aside.

Nina didn't feel in the mood to remonstrate any further and looked around for her other charge. "Where's Susanna? Anyone seen her?"

"There she is, dancing with Uncle Franz." Claudia pointed to the edge of the ballroom where Franz was holding his daughter at arm's length, prancing around in what seemed to be a polka. "At least, I think they're dancing!"

"They look absolutely stupid," Wilhelm said.

"That's disrespectful, Wilhelm. You shouldn't say things like that about your sister." Claudia gently cuffed his shoulder, "Mind you, they do look a bit odd."

"No, not Sue. Them! The Brauns!"

Claudia and Nina saw that he was gaping not at his twin sister and father, but over their heads across the room at the redoubtable, rotund Frau Braun and her acquiescent, fawning husband, shorter than his wife by almost a head, and half her width.

Claudia grinned maliciously, "They look like cartoon characters from *Simplicissimus,* you know, the satirical magazine."

"I don't like her, do you, Nina?" Wilhelm asked. "She frightens me."

Nina saw the Brauns settle themselves amongst a group of fat, comfortable ladies on the opposite side of the room. "No."

She stared in discomfort at the seething, noisy dance floor, with its laughing, gyrating couples. With newly discovered introspection, she questioned why she was the odd one out: why don't I like dancing? When I was a child I loved parties. Why am I different now? She could find no answers. The others went back to the children's corner while Nina stayed, grumpily surveying the scene.

"You look as though you're at a funeral, Nina," Claudia chided her.

Nina squinted at her happy, smiling sister. "Claudia? What do the Brauns have against Anneliese and her family? They've been very rude to them. Why does being a Jew mean everyone dislikes you?"

"That's a daft remark. Go and ask Anna to explain it to you, or better still, Captain Richter. He'll give you the official reasons." Claudia turned her back on her irritating younger sister and walked away, into the social whirl. She was in her element, she loved parties, and she was certainly not going to allow a moody, rebellious sister to spoil her evening.

Nina became aware of the undercurrent, the hidden menace of prejudice in all the corners of the room. She was beginning to understand Alice's earlier remarks about the poison of anti-Semitism being there in their own home. So hating Jews was what anti-Semitism was! It was her political awakening, and it shocked her to think that their guests were talking disparagingly about her friends, and even about her.

On her way to rejoin the children, she tried to discover why they felt that way, but Claudia had not listened, Anna was engrossed in playing the piano, and Hildegard was too busy with her duties. She looked for her father and found him in conversation with Eva's father, Jakob Rosenthal, and Leon Steiner.

"Otto, I don't understand you," Leon was saying. "Here you are, a big business man. I know you don't see yourself as one, but you are. You're a landowner, a farmer, you own mines and you're anti-Communist. You were a soldier so you understand the need for law and order. Yet, despite all that, you won't support Hitler?"

Jakob interrupted him, "Leon, you're letting yourself be fooled by this man, Hitler. He changes his promises to fit his audience."

"For an intelligent man you can be quite stupid sometimes, Jakob."

Nina looked at Eva's father in astonishment, expecting him to be outraged at the insult, but he simply raised his eyebrows and rolled his head gently from side to side to express his disagreement.

"Who is causing all the trouble?" Leon did not wait for an answer. "Everybody knows it's the Communists. Who has proved himself to be the only person capable of cleaning up the streets and getting rid of them? Hitler!" He folded his arms and stood staring at Jakob, defying him to think of anyone better qualified for the job.

Jakob shook his head sadly in disbelief. "In the first place, Hitler, himself, is causing trouble…"

"You have to use tough methods to stamp out ruffians! And don't forget, Hitler is backed by big business. They know he'll get rid of the troublemakers and business will prosper. These Marxists want to nationalise everything. I'd have nothing left if they took over."

"Under a National Socialist regime you wouldn't be there to run it. You would be killed, deported or enslaved." Jakob waved a finger at Leon as though he were one of his more backward students. "Don't make the mistake of believing Hitler will overlook the fact that you're a Jew even though you fought for your country in the Great War. If he gets into power your days are numbered my friend, just as mine are."

"What will you do, Jakob?" Otto asked, sympathetically.

"I'm already making arrangements to move to America, Otto. Probably in the spring. Even if he doesn't become Chancellor, we shall go. New York has offered me a chair at the university. America will be an education for the family, though Eva will be sad to leave her school here." He glanced down at Nina kindly, understanding what effect their move might have on the two friends.

Eva had not told her anything about leaving Germany, but perhaps she did not know. Nina understood the deference that people paid to Eva's father. As a professor, he was looked up to as a man of intellect and high standing, yet even he was being affected by events over which he had no control.

What on earth was happening in the world? Why was Hitler having such an impact on everyone around her? She puzzled her way back to the others.

"Eva?" She beckoned her friend and they slipped away quietly down to the library where Nina confronted her.

"I knew we would go if Hitler became the new Chancellor, but I didn't know we were going anyway." Eva welcomed the move.

"Father made it quite clear what we could expect if we stay in Germany: he would lose his job, I would lose my education, and we would soon exhaust our savings simply trying to survive. We would only have a life of poverty to look forward to. America doesn't seem to be anti-Jewish, so it will be better for us all."

"You'll have to write to me in English... American."

"Oh, I will, every week, I promise."

"I don't suppose Anneliese's family will go. Her father seems to like Hitler."

"What? How can he?"

Nina had no answer.

Back in the ballroom, Nina stood silently as Frau Braun swept by carrying a plate of food and a glass of wine. Nina nudged Eva and, in a sudden rush of embarrassment for her friend, blurted out, "I wish I hadn't asked you to come, Eva."

"It's been all right, Nina, really."

"No, it hasn't! You're too nice to say anything, but I know what those old harridans have been saying and I won't be polite to them in future. Look at them, all vying with each other to say the nastiest things. They're horrible!" Nina felt like bursting into tears at the thought that neighbours she had known all her life could behave with so little kindness.

Wilhelm and Susanna were giggling together over Nanny Watson, who was increasingly listing towards the arm of the settee on which she sat, her eyes closed, while Alice tried to explain to Nina why such gatherings were necessary.

"You see, Nina, it's all part of belonging to a community and these parties and balls are one way of introducing you children to your peers, and your elders. You get to know who is in which position, and Otto will tell you that it's whom you know in life that counts. And it's a lot of fun, too."

A fearsome voice suddenly interrupted, "Don't lean over the seat like that, Nina. Remember, straight back at all times." Out of the corner of one hooded eye, Nanny had seen her slump. The twins jumped back, startled, and stared at her, their eyes round and huge in astonishment. Wilhelm whispered to Susanna, "I thought she was dead!"

Nina stepped back obediently, straightened up and stood quietly between Eva and Anneliese trying to discuss current affairs, but Anneliese torpedoed their discussion by saying, "My father doesn't believe any of it.

He says it's all Communist propaganda. They're trying to make Hitler out to be an evil man, because they want control."

Nina thought there might be some truth in that, but Eva was adamant. "Absolutely not! My father read Hitler's own book and I tried to read parts of it, too. Hitler's going to kill all the Jews if he gains power."

The thought filled Nina with horror. "But that's dreadful, awful! We have to do something. Why isn't everyone shouting in the streets about it?"

Anneliese answered cynically, "Because they don't care what happens to us, that's why."

In a voice loud enough for all the children to hear, Frau Braun spoke boldly to her husband as they passed by again, their plates and glasses refilled for the umpteenth time, "I tell you, Berthold, it can't be soon enough for me. Some of these Jews think they're as good as we are. He'll put them in their place. And those who make friends or do business with them." She stared at Nina as she haughtily sauntered back to her group of acolytes.

Downtrodden Berthold tried to remonstrate over her last remark; he respected Otto and the von Luden family and did not want his wife's remarks to reach Otto's ears. "Really, you go too far sometimes…"

But Nina barely heard him. She stood stock-still, her eyes widened in astonishment as she instantly grasped the frightening significance of the words. The scales of political naïveté fell from her mind: most of these so-called friends were supporters of Hitler.

Looking at Anneliese and Eva, she realised that they had both heard and she flushed scarlet, staring down at her feet, ashamed of her neighbours for the first time.

"Old cow! I don't care what she thinks," Anneliese protested loudly to Frau Braun's back. Frau Braun turned her head and gave the children a malevolent look that said she thought it beneath her dignity to respond.

Nina urgently needed to discuss what she had discovered about their neighbours with someone, but she felt obligated to stay with Eva and Anneliese. She had already bothered Alice too much, so she stood quietly mulling over what she had heard, trying to see all sides of the man who was creating such a stir in her society. Eventually she agreed with her parents that Hitler was not a good man. The officers, Frau Braun and the rest, were wrong.

Anneliese flounced off to where her parents sat stiffly, her mother's eyes downcast. Caught between an understanding of political reality and the necessity of supporting her father's views, she didn't know which way to turn. She envied Nina's safe and stable position, but all the excitement of being invited to her friend's house had evaporated.

Claudia was tapping her foot impatiently in time to the music, aggrieved at being a wallflower. Franz had been watching his nieces whilst talking with Otto and now offered himself as a partner to Claudia, who signalled her relief to him with a dazzling smile.

Like her youngest sister, Anna had also struggled with the concept of National Socialism, but her feelings for Peter Richter were too strong and she pushed any doubts aside. Conversely to Nina, she argued to herself that if Hitler were such a bad person, Peter would not support him.

Searching the room, she found Peter engrossed in conversation with her father and uncle. "I understand your hesitation, sir, but if you had read Mein Kampf you would perhaps have more understanding of the reasons and motives..."

Otto interrupted the gushing Captain rather curtly, "I'm probably one of the very few people who have read it, and the motives seem to be pure revenge. But the policies! Well..." He could not bring himself to dignify what he had read by speaking about them.

"But there are always plans in any political programme that one does not go along with, and which party, when it finally attains power, is ever allowed to implement all of its ideas? They're voted out before they have time to do everything they want."

At that moment, Anna felt his enthusiasm draw her to him, but instinctively she felt it would need to be channelled in the right direction.

He broke off his conversation as Anna approached and, with a courteous apology and bow to Otto and Franz, he whisked her onto the dance floor before she could refuse him, leaving Otto's discomfiture somewhat relieved.

"Are his ideas so modern?" Hildegard temporarily ignored her own injunction to not discuss politics. "I wonder. I seem to recall in the nineteenth-century, someone called Bismarck. Didn't he have a policy of blood and iron? I think Hitler is only continuing an attitude that threads throughout our past. It's really only the Weimar Republic that is modern in Germany, not Hitler."

Otto rebuked her mildly, "Just because you read history at university you think you have all the answers."

Franz agreed with his sister-in-law. "No, I think Hilde's right. Hitler would never have risen to such heights if we'd won the war. He touched a nerve in the Prussian psyche, in the German heart. Such a common little man would never have gained a high place in society if there hadn't been enormous support for his ideas already; that's our trouble."

As Otto slowly waltzed her away, Hildegard looked over her shoulder at Franz and sadly responded, "That's our tragedy."

Anna only heard the excitement in Peter's voice. "Was that so important to you?" She would have to learn to accept his views, but try to restrain them a little.

"Yes, of course! This is the last waltz and I shall have no further chance to dance with you."

"It isn't the last waltz, and there's still plenty of time left. I meant what you were talking to my father about." She smiled back at him happily, pleased that he had wanted to dance with her so much.

"We all have the same views. He gives us such hope for the future. Don't you sense it, too?" Anna felt his fervour gather her up and carry her along with him. Later she would apply herself to what he meant, but not now.

Up in her bedroom, Nina sat at her window, peering out over the dark garden. Her satin dress and shoes were neatly put away in the wardrobe, and her mind was at long last at rest. Next door, the twins were already asleep from sheer exhaustion and excitement. Her friends had either left for their own homes or were in rooms along the corridor. Her duty done, her presence no longer required, she had gladly retired early, to be alone with her thoughts and her God, to pray for help and guidance for the day to come and to give thanks for the day just finishing. However busy she was, however tired or unhappy, she'd always find time to be with Him.

She felt contented for her sisters and at peace with herself. The muted, joyful sounds wafted up to her as she knelt, unaware her childhood had almost gone and she had embarked on the great metamorphosis that would transform her into an adult.

Below, the wearied gathering stood around the Christmas tree in the darkened ballroom. The servants hovered nervously with candlesnuffers and jugs of water, ready to stifle any flame that accidentally caught the dampened fir needles above it.

Listening to their carols and the music of the very last waltz, played by tiring musicians, Nina smiled as she imagined Claudia whirling around, torn between joy at dancing and sadness that the evening was nearly over, and Anna in the arms of her Captain, stars in her eyes.

When the music stopped, and the noises of feet crunching on gravel, car engines revving up, and echoing voices of departing guests had ended, Nina was sound asleep.

Six

"Hope?" Hildegard raised her eyebrows when Anna repeated Captain Richter's words to the family next day. "Hope for what? For whom? For the German people or just the chosen few? You should tell your young man to speak to the Rosenthals. They don't talk of hope... quite the opposite in fact. They can see what's happening and they're leaving Germany. Did you know that?"

Hildegard swung round, staring fiercely at her daughter as though she alone was responsible for their untimely flight. "The trouble in the streets is getting worse, not better, and Hitler's henchmen are always in the thick of it. Heaven only knows what will happen if they attain total domination!"

It was clear to Anna that any further comment would only arouse her mother against her, and despite her maturity, she was a childlike coward in the face of Hildegard's wrath.

"It's far too early for this kind of conversation." Hildegard was still angry with the young officers whose social graces and manners left much to be desired. "The hall's in an unbearable state after the party. It's a disgrace! Suppose anyone arrives? Where are the servants?"

Hildegard would usually have noticed that the servants were doing their jobs quietly and competently, but her daughter's infatuation with one of Hitler's supporters had touched a raw nerve. She was troubled by their relationship, uneasy about the National Socialist movement. Her friends and acquaintances kept telling her how good it would be for Germany, how life would now finally change for the better after their disastrous flirtation with democracy and republicanism, but she couldn't see it that way. She would speak to Alice some time; Alice was a political animal. If anyone understood this new breed, Alice would.

Long ago Otto had learned to hold his tongue when Hildegard was clucking around like a demented hen. His father had once said, "Never argue with them, m'boy, especially when they're involved in their housework," advice he had stuck to ever since.

Alice, a formidable woman like her younger sister, and braver than Otto, suggested, "Aren't you being a bit hard on the girl, Hilde? After all, it isn't Anna's fault, is it?"

Anna jumped in quickly, hurrying to capitalise on her aunt's endorsement, and perhaps swing her mother's anger onto Alice instead. "He does have a point, doesn't he? Perhaps he's right; perhaps we do need an old style dictator."

Claudia bent down and ruffled the hair on their old red setter, Bismarck. "But we've never had one like Hitler before. Has anyone read his book? It's absolutely awful!" Claudia had draped herself comfortably along the grey velvet sofa, her feet - still shod in outdoor shoes from an early walk with the dog - propped up casually on the arm, mud clearly visible in the treads.

Hildegard said nothing, but moved stolidly past her daughter who had unwisely brought herself to Hildegard's attention. And with a curt, "Off!" she flipped Claudia's legs from the end of the sofa.

She gave her father a wry smile. They shared the same feelings. Now she held her tongue, refusing to respond to Hildegard's bait. They knew she was spoiling for an argument over something, but neither of them would be the willing proponent.

Bismarck barked loudly, looking at Hildegard as though to say, 'What was all that about?'

"Quiet, Bismarck!" Claudia commanded, not wanting her mother's ire to fall on the dog.

Anna countered her sister's rebuke defensively. "Do we need to read it? He's reported frequently enough for us to know what he stands for. And after all, what you say in a book isn't necessarily what you'll do in practice."

Claudia was impatient with Anna, "You're just saying what Peter said!"

"No, Claudia, Anna's right."

Alice had seen the Hitler Youth and the brown shirts out on the streets, whipping up hatred for Jewish shop owners. What was actually happening was obvious to anyone with eyes, though the propaganda tried to suggest otherwise. But here in the country the family was cushioned within their small, cosy community. They didn't see the riots, beatings, and humiliations Jewish people were subjected to, or the hatred and terror. Alice did, she had seen her own friends humiliated by louts. And what was worse, she had watched other people stand by and say and do nothing. When she had tried to intervene, she, too, had been roughly manhandled and called names.

"What you say in a book isn't always what gets put into practice. Most politicians don't get a chance to do that, thank goodness. But I think in his case it is what he will strive to achieve. And if he succeeds, heaven help us all."

"He's just a bully!"

Alice patted Claudia's arm. "Yes, dear, I do believe he is. But not just a bully, Claudia. Let me show you what they did to me. It was, incidentally, the reason why I wasn't able to get here two weeks ago as I'd hoped."

Alice stood up and unhooked the top buttons at the back of her high-necked cotton blouse. Slipping it towards her left shoulder, she revealed the top of a long scar down the back of her shoulder blade. "They were outside my favourite jewellers in Königsberg, barring the entrance, trying to stop me from going in. Of all the cheek! I've been going there for years and I wasn't going to submit to some jumped up youth in a smart new uniform, trying to prove he was important. Which he wasn't! So in I went, pushing him out of my way. He didn't tackle me on his own, he had to find some colleagues; it took three of them to get me out of the shop. One hit me with something."

Hildegard and the family were deeply shocked. "Good heavens, Alice! Why didn't you tell us about this before?"

"Oh, don't fuss, Hilde. It would have spoilt the party. And, anyway, I don't remember much after that. They stitched me up in hospital and I had a call from the local Party leader. He came round in person to apologize, would you believe! I sent him away with a flea in his ear, I can tell you."

"Why did he apologize?" Claudia asked.

"They're not in power yet. They're still not strong enough to take chances with the landed gentry. I've been treated very well since then and the shop has been left alone, they don't have a guard now. But that won't last. As soon as they take over..."

Otto was unable to appreciate how far the values of his old society had changed under the influence of the Nazis. "What kind of people are they, to hit a defenceless woman? What is the world coming to?"

Some of Hildegard's impatience returned. "Why on earth didn't you tell us yesterday? We could have given the Brauns a thing or two to think about!" She rang for the servants. "Where is that girl?" She held up the remains of an expensive crystal glass. "Look at this – broken!"

Bismarck prudently lay down on the floor out of Hildegard's way and watched her soulfully, ready to lope out of the room at the first sign of trouble. Hildegard's personal maid, Irmgard, appeared at the door. "I'm sorry, Madam. Gertrud isn't feeling well this morning. I told her to stay in bed. We're trying to catch up with the work, Madam."

Hildegard scrutinized the maid's face. "Hum! In bed? Well, take this and be careful with it. Don't cut yourself or we'll have you off work as well." She put the glass down. "And finish cleaning up in here, I'm still finding bits and pieces on the floor and under the sideboard. Can't expect Bismarck to eat everything. I'll go and see how Gertrud is."

Hildegard stomped off to the servants' quarters in the basement. She always insisted on looking after them herself and would bring in the family doctor if they needed him. Irmgard was a sensible woman, capable of organizing the whole household. If she said Gertrud were ill enough to be in bed then there must be something the matter with her. Irmgard had been with the family before Anna was born, from the time Hildegard's previous personal maid, Frieda, had killed herself.

Down in the meadow, visible from the children's bedrooms, stood a huge, spreading Ilex oak, darkly green and thriving in its dominance over the surrounding meadow. Frieda was an impressionable young girl, rather emotional, as Hildegard had noted when Frieda's fiancé was called away to the front line. On receiving the news of his death, Frieda was hysterical, inconsolable. One evening shortly afterwards, the head gardener found her body swinging from the lowest branch of the oak, which ever afterwards was known as Frieda's tree.

From that day Hildegard had kept more in touch with her servants' lives. It was the memory of Frieda's desperate act that led Hildegard to go off in search of the young Gertrud. It also gave her a well-needed chance to reflect. It seemed from Alice's experience that the violence was not only aimed at the Jews; even family members might become targets. Hildegard needed to address her own feelings. Would she and the children be strong enough to stand up to them as Alice had? Once she began thinking along those lines she would weaken, and they had to remain strong. They had to be able to take what was coming.

After Hildegard left the room, Alice continued, "Since the storm troopers became more visible, shall we say, I've attended a few meetings in the town hall. There are one or two women's political groups, which are anti-Hitler." She looked pointedly at Claudia. "You ought to join one, Claudia. They don't meet in halls any more, they aren't safe, and they're always attended by Hitler Youth or the storm troopers. We tend to meet in our friends' homes, nowadays."

Otto rapidly intervened. Alice's fearlessness sometimes made her unthinking. "That isn't a good idea. I believe he's a man to hold a grudge. He'll be taking note of who joins. I'd beware if I were you, Alice. And, Claudia," he turned and faced his daughter sternly, "I absolutely forbid you to join any political organisation. Openly or officially." One part of him knew that Claudia would do just as she wanted despite anything he said.

Claudia was bored with the conversation. "Why are we all talking about such solemn ideas? It's Christmas! Let's go for a walk and enjoy ourselves. Come on Bismarck. Coming, Nina?"

Nina, who had been listening with interest whilst feeding scraps of leftovers to Bismarck, felt the hairs on the back of her neck stand up. Long ago she had learned to listen to those hairs; they always indicated something of importance. But now, for the life of her, she could not see anything significant in her father's words. She was still angry and sad alternately at the imminent loss of her friends, the Rosenthals, and gave no more thought to his words.

"Hello, who's this arriving round the back?" Otto asked as he observed a car approaching the rear of the house. Anna left her aunt's side and peered over his shoulder.

"Oh!" She coloured and immediately strode out of the room towards the hallway.

"Well? Who is it?" Alice commanded. "Though from Anna's reaction I can guess."

"Yes," Otto answered her absently, "it seems to be young Richter. I wonder what he wants on Christmas morning."

"I'll give you one guess, Otto. You said yourself it was time he made his intentions clear. Mind you, I think all that folly should be done away with. Anachronistic in this day and age, if you ask me. Why does the young man need you to give him Anna's hand in marriage? She's a grown woman who can make up her own mind. It should be their decision not ours."

"It's always been done that way, Alice."

"Stuff and nonsense! It's time some of your precious traditions were got rid of. If it were me, I'd simply elope, get married somewhere, and inform you later."

"Yes, you would, but Anna's an old-fashioned girl. She likes our quaint, courteous customs, and adhering to the conventions."

"She's a man's woman, all right." Alice suddenly gave a low, throaty chuckle. "I can't wait to see your face when Claudia comes in one day and informs you she's just got married. She's her own woman. You'll soon find out how much social manners have progressed since your day."

"Our day."

"Yes. But I was always ahead of my time. Shouldn't you be finding out what he wants?"

Anna dismissed the maid in the hall and opened the door herself. "Good morning, Peter. Happy Christmas." She smiled cordially, her heart thumping as she offered her face for a greeting. She was certain of why he had come. He kissed her on both cheeks, holding her close to him. She shivered. "Your coat's freezing!"

"It's frosty outside. I need to be warmed up as quickly as possible."

Embarrassed by her flushed face and their exposed position in the hallway, she extricated herself from his embrace and ushered him into the library, quickly closing the door behind them. The hall was far too public and the servants were still in and out clearing things up. And she was aware they gossiped about the family when they were in the kitchen.

"I wasn't sure if you'd all be at church, so I came round the back way, but I couldn't see your car in the church yard."

"We're not going until this evening. Half the family are still exhausted after yesterday, so everything's behind schedule."

"It was a rather special evening, wasn't it?" Peter took her hands and held them, steadily surveying her from under his black brows, his eyes twinkling. "Anna, there's something I have to ask you and I won't take no for an answer." He reached into his pocket and drew out a small dark red box. Snapping it open, he revealed an engagement ring, a small round sapphire surrounded by six smaller diamonds.

"Oh! It's gorgeous, so elegant," she gasped, admiring not just its blue flashing beauty, but Peter's good taste.

He refrained from confessing that he had sought out her jeweller to ascertain which stones she liked best and what size ring to buy.

Gently slipping it onto her finger, he urged, "You will marry me, won't you?"

Anna collapsed in a peal of laughter. "You're supposed to ask, not insist."

"Then, will you?"

For a second Anna kept him in suspense, but could not sustain the pretence. "You already know the answer, don't you?" And for the first time in her life Anna took the initiative with a man and, slipping her arms around him, she kissed him warmly on the lips.

They were still clasped in their passionate embrace when Otto pushed open the door, clearing his throat loudly. "Anna, your aunt requires your assistance," he motioned with his hand for her to leave the room.

She flashed a quick knowing smile at Peter and left them to their discussion. But she hid the ring on her finger from her father's gaze; he would want to preserve the old-fashioned niceties and would not be pleased that Peter had asked her first.

"Good morning, Captain Richter. I trust you enjoyed yesterday's party?"

"Very much, Herr von Luden." Peter addressed Otto as Anna's father, not as an army general. "I wanted to formally thank you for inviting us all. It was a very generous gesture." He bowed, clicking his heels noisily.

Otto gritted his teeth. What had seemed well mannered in his day now appeared vulgar and ostentatious.

"I also wanted to speak to you about Anna."

"I rather expected you might."

"As you know, sir, we have been seeing each other a great deal and I believe Anna feels about me the way I do about her. I ... would you do me the very great honour of giving me Anna's hand in marriage?"

As Otto remained silent, Peter continued as though he had not noticed the slight. "She will want for nothing materially. My parents are giving me their house in the country together with its resident servants. And, as my wife, Anna will have a high position in society."

"What hopes do you entertain in terms of your career?"

"I can only aspire to the position you yourself attained, sir, but that will not be for some time yet."

"You believe you can attain the rank of general?"

"I've been given to understand that my future is extremely bright, especially when Hitler becomes Chancellor..."

"If Hitler becomes Chancellor."

"He will, sir. We're all convinced of that. He will give us a forceful government, not a weak one like the recent republic."

"A strong system can wreck a country just as easily as a feeble one."

"But ours has made us decadent."

"I can't say that I see many decadent people around me, other than a few who are clearly self-indulgent with food, shall we say? And they seem to be supporters of Hitler rather than of a democracy." Otto pursed his lips, eyeing Peter shrewdly. "Wouldn't it be better to wait until we recover fully from the effects of the Wall Street Crash and then go to the electorate again? Then we'd know which system they prefer."

"How long will we have to wait to recover fully? Hitler will make up for the shame of Versailles and turn us back into a proud nation."

"That sounds like revenge. That only makes men bitter."

"No, not revenge, but it was wrong. They hit us when we were down and out, but we only went to war because of the treaties with our allies. What they did to us at Versailles showed there was a new spirit of hatred abroad long before Hitler rose to power. Apart from his enthusiasm, Hitler encapsulates the ideas we already believe. Isn't that quite democratic? To do what the people want?"

Otto was nonplussed, wondering how it was that Peter had succeeded in not only lecturing him in his own home, but also in making him feel that Hitler might actually have a point. He turned to the side cabinet,

59

taking out two glasses and a bottle of brandy. "It's a little early in the day, but in the circumstances, we ought to drink a toast."

"I understand your hesitation about Hitler, Herr von Luden..." Peter began as Otto poured them drinks, but Otto cut him off.

"Here's to you and Anna. May you both be happy and healthy and have a long life together, and let's forget everything else for now."

Peter clicked his heels and bowed formally, understanding that Otto had at last accepted him as a future member of the von Luden family.

Otto later admitted to his brother, "He's right. Hitler didn't start all the hatred. Communism and capitalism were fighting it out on the streets before he rose to any position, above the rank of corporal, that is. I'm not so sure democracy is such a wonderful thing."

"Not for us, perhaps, we're simply not used to it, unlike England, France or America. Our culture seems to lend itself to dictators."

Otto's pent up anger over the ending of the Great War spilled out unexpectedly. "We were all supposed to have a say in our own futures. The Czechs, the Slovaks, the Poles did. But we weren't even allowed to have representatives listening to what they were deciding about Germany's future, let alone participating in it. We were outcasts. And The Corridor! It's made us strangers in our own land. How could they have expected a solid new country to rise out of that beginning? If that's what the Captain meant, then I'm right behind him." He added after a reflective pause, "Though it wouldn't be good for him to see that."

Franz studied his brother with a curious sideways glance. "You can't believe that might and force will gain us our lost territories?"

"I'm sure they would. I'm quite convinced we could physically take back The Corridor before anyone realised what was happening. Who's going to try and remove it from us? The League of Nations has no teeth; the Poles have no army to speak of. But doing that wouldn't gain us credence in the eyes of the world. If Germany is to gain international status the government has to allow secret ballots with no guns at their backs. You and I know what war is like and we don't want any more of it. But the young people of today think differently."

"Take care, Otto. If Hitler gets in, men like Braun and Peter will be given much greater power. Braun and his wife could be very dangerous foes in the new order. And Peter may prove to be a little too close to home for comfort."

Seven

Over the months, between the election and Hitler's eventual attainment of complete power, far-sighted and wealthy Jews sold their property at a loss and began life again in a more friendly country. There was no future for them in Germany.

The Rosenthals left for America, but the Steiners remained, buying up businesses and small farms cheaply, believing that by so doing they were amassing the small fortune for which they had worked so hard. They accepted a certain amount of harassment as something that they must get used to, never believing for one moment that any of the wild rumours could be true.

Leon thought the Nazis saw lazy, unemployed or poor Jews as the problem, not Jews as a race. He believed that once he was rich, his money and property would buy the position and treatment due to them. The Nazis would see he was on their side, and he and his family would be left alone and unmolested.

Nina was uncharacteristically petulant, flaring up over trivial remarks. She had lost her best friend, with whom she had shared everything, and it was hard to adjust. She wrote frequently to Eva and was never happier than when she received a reply.

That summer she spent much of her time in the meadow below the house, beyond Frieda's tree. Past the little stream, hidden in a thick copse of bamboo, sheltered from the bitter northern winds, was an old wooden hut, which had once been used by the estate workers.

Further away from the house, Otto had erected a new brick building for the workers' tools and as somewhere to shelter from bad weather. Nina now took possession of the disused building, sitting inside on windy or showery days to write her letters, dream, or prepare her homework. It became her summerhouse, a place to be on her own. Everyone became used to seeing her, pens and pad in hand, a white cotton sun hat perched on her head, wending her way purposefully down through the meadow.

Summer was usually the time to go to Uncle Franz's home on the Baltic coast in Pomerania, near Kösslin, but this summer Franz and Ruth would be coming to them instead, for Anna's wedding.

Hildegard was driving the family into a frenzy of organisation: there were all the clothes to be made, especially Anna's gown and the bridesmaids' dresses, and all the fittings that entailed. Curtains and carpets had to be cleaned; new bed linen on which the family crest needed to be embroidered, and a new dinner service had to be bought. All of this would require countless trips to Danzig. The house was in turmoil for weeks. "I don't know where we're going to fit everyone in."

"Nonsense, Hilde! We've had lots more than this. The girls will have to go in together, the twins, Hans and Christina…"

"Hans and Christina are far too old to go in together, Otto! Whatever are you thinking of?"

"Oh, does it matter? The Richters will be in the West Wing. We are family and it's only for a short time. Stop worrying, it'll work out."

Hildegard knew the Richters had very high standards and, for Anna's sake, she wanted to present the best possible image. In the past people had tried to live up to the von Ludens and the land-owning aristocracy, but Hildegard was aware that since Hitler came to power, the National Socialist image was beginning to dominate. Now, what the Richters thought and did was more important. They had become the litmus test for Hildegard of how well the von Ludens fitted in to the new social order. But their biggest problem was that they were known to be anti-Hitler. She understood only too well that they would have to move some way towards what Hitler stood for, publicly at least, if they were all to survive under his new Reich.

The local church was densely packed for Anna's wedding. Every possible space inside was occupied, with people standing at the back, whilst those unable to enter the building were jostled by Peter's friends, wearing uniforms and Swastikas.

"Why ever did Anna choose to be married here rather than in the cathedral in Danzig?" Ruth asked Hildegard. "There's barely room to swing a cat."

"I did tell her, dear, but she wouldn't listen. I said that once Peter had invited all his friends the church would be packed. But she would have it here. Something to do with romantic charm. She isn't at all practical when it comes to religion. She said she loves the cosiness of it when all the candles are lit, and the sun streams in through the stained-glass windows."

"I can see what she means. If you can ignore the crowd, the church would be quite a divine place. And the stained glass is stunning, what glorious colours! Are they the windows Otto donated?"

"Yes. Too modern for my taste, but once the sun hits them it's a bit like sitting under a rainbow. Anna was adamant and she's probably right. This is a proper family wedding. Anyway, it's what she wanted."

The Richters were seated opposite the von Ludens' family pew unable to hide their disappointment at the venue. They had wanted their only son to be married with all the pomp and circumstance that their money could buy, but could not persuade the two young people from their romantic ceremony. Now, as their eyes fixed on Peter, standing waiting at the altar with his best man Captain Schulz, they wished they had insisted on the cathedral.

Hildegard could see the unhappiness on Irene Richter's face, but knew that once Anna appeared with Otto and the two girls she would forget where she was and concentrate on the ceremony. She smiled across the aisle, trying to make them both feel more at ease. We must make bridges between the old and the new if we are to accept their ways, she decided.

She settled back into her pew, satisfied that she had arranged everything as well as she could and forgotten nothing, and closed her eyes. She allowed the music from the small organ to flow through her, listening with rapt attention to the local choirboys, most of whom she knew. One tiny voice soared above the others in a solo performance, exquisite in its perfect pitch. Hildegard opened one eye sufficiently to see the singer, and noted not only ten-year-old Roland, but also the Brauns, sitting on the other side of the aisle, smiling with justified pride at their grandson.

Alice leaned across and whispered in Hildegard's ear. "A pity someone who can sing like that has such philistines for a family!"

Hildegard nodded in agreement, closed her eyes again and sank back into her euphoric state. She forgot the people around her, forgot those left outside, and relaxed for the first time in weeks.

Outside, the crowd had built up. Locals wanting to see what was going on, friends of the von Luden family unable to get into the church, and Peter's friends all vied with each other for the best viewing positions. Someone commented in a loud voice, "Look at those Nazi thugs, pushing their weight around," and immediately a minor scuffle broke out between a few local youths and the officers.

Inside, as they waited for Anna and her father, unaware of the ugly confrontation developing, Hildegard scrutinized the congregation. "Look at that, Franz, Peter and his friends, all wearing Swastikas on their arms, in the House of God. It really is insupportable."

With a sigh of resignation, Franz almost apologized for their unsociable behaviour. "They have to, Hilde. Hitler decreed it should be so, and it is so."

"Don't blaspheme, Franz! I know you're not a great believer, but you should take it seriously."

"I'm sorry, Hilde, but whatever that man says the great German folk seem to take as gospel, they look upon him almost as a God."

Alice almost snorted in disbelief. "God indeed! I cannot imagine anyone further away from God. He creates such mischief I could almost believe he's the Devil."

"We don't all have your strong will, Alice; some are easily swayed. I think our family and friends will take it as a sign that they're right to hate what Hitler stands for and the Richters will see nothing wrong with wearing them in church. There isn't much we can do, unless you want a spell in prison."

"Your backbone is bending with the wind, Franz. That isn't like you."

"I'm simply realistic, Alice. If we were involved in a fight with those hooligans who would be arrested – them, or us?"

"Oh, you're right there, Franz. We would, without a doubt."

A distant cousin leaned over between them from the pew behind, where he was sitting with the younger members of the family. The smell of alcohol hung in the air. "I have journalist friends from overseas who I see in Berlin. They think we've all gone mad, putting Hitler in charge. They all say he's a warmonger…"

"Keep your voice down, please! Remember where you are."

"You've picked up their drinking habits, I see," Alice said drily, with the slightest of smiles, as though she knew what was coming and was going to enjoy it.

"They can't hear us over the other side of the aisle, Hilde…" Franz was cut off in mid-sentence by his son.

"Then we'd better make sure they can." Hans raised his voice and looked across at the uniformed men, pointedly. "Who invited them, anyway?"

"Hans!"

"If people realize what scoundrels they are, we can get rid of them. But if no-one speaks out…"

"That's enough, Hans, and you, too, Seb. I won't have Anna's wedding turned into a brawl." Hildegard awoke from her reverie, her peace shattered. "For goodness sake! You're in a church."

"They don't care about that," Hans grumbled, "They don't believe in God."

Another friend of Hans appeared at the doorway, a blood spotted handkerchief pressed to his cheek, diverting Hans from baiting the Nazis.

"Whatever happened to you, Michel?"

"They're practically fighting each other out there. I had a job to get through. I got caught in the middle. If Anna hadn't arrived I think it would have been pistols at dawn."

He and Hans glared across the aisle, Michel dabbing at his cheek. The officers muttered to each other. One looked as though he was about to jump up, but the organ struck up the wedding march.

The congregation turned to the entrance where Anna stood in her elegant, form-fitting white dress, at her father's side. Behind her the two bridesmaids, Claudia and Nina, in identical lemon dresses, carried posies of white carnations and cornflowers. Each had a ring of cornflowers in their hair to mirror the headband that held Anna's veil.

Hildegard dabbed her eyes discretely, tears welling up unexpectedly, "She looks lovely, doesn't she?"

Alice patted her arm fondly, "The perfect picture."

"Beautiful!" Ruth added, "And don't Claudia and Nina look demure?"

"That won't last long," Alice muttered to herself.

As Hildegard wiped her eyes gently, she looked across and saw that Irene Richter was doing the same. They smiled at each other with pride as Anna and Otto slowly walked by. As Otto handed his radiant daughter over to Peter, standing proudly tall in his uniform, he forgot his reservations and allowed himself a measure of satisfaction at his wife's planning and joy for his daughter's sake.

Peter had a few words with his friends and the reception at the house went off without a hitch. The only moment, which threatened to get out of hand was when his colleagues, merry with drink, were singing their regimental songs rather too loudly in the ante-room, threatening to overwhelm the other guests. In a twinkling, Otto's dotty Aunt Griselda saved the day by quietly taking over the piano and playing and singing one of their most patriotic songs. She had been a trained opera singer in her day, if only in the chorus, and her soprano voice, high and still on key despite her age, drew the attention of the company to the song, and soon Hildegard and Alice joined her.

Otto's deep baritone dominated the room, and then other guests began singing until everyone in the ballroom was involved. Otto knew Peter's colleagues would be unable to resist joining in since they could not contemplate being accused of being unpatriotic. And, sure enough, their rowdy behaviour soon ended and they gathered around Griselda, with gusto, lifting their glasses and praising Germany's greatness through the song. Otto was able to retreat with dignity without any incident evolving. And Aunt Griselda went up in the family's estimation.

As Anna and Peter left for their honeymoon, there was no hint of any further trouble. On their way to the station in the open horse drawn carriage, the newlyweds threw traditional bread rolls to the cheering crowds lining the route who in return showered the couple with rice. Peter's friends used the occasion to show support for the new regime by issuing Swastika flags to local children who waved them enthusiastically, abandoning them only to scramble for the rolls.

The Richters later left for their home further east, full of praise for Anna and their son, proud that he had married into such a lofty and obviously well respected family. They dismissed the fighting outside the church as a mere trifle and nothing to do with either family.

Just as Otto said it would be, Anna's wedding was a triumph, a spectacle for the locals who, sensing such traditions would soon be a thing of the past, wanted to enjoy the occasion while they still could.

Eight

In the summer of nineteen thirty-four, while Alice and Hildegard remained at home to look after the expectant Anna, Otto took Nanny Watson and Nina on a tour of some of the capitals of Europe. They flew to Berlin where they collected Claudia from university, and then spent a week in Brussels before travelling on to Paris for a second week, practising their French in both capital cities.

They were then to stay in a Park Lane hotel in London for three or four weeks in order to update their already perfect English. Nanny believed that though grammatical correctness was extremely important, it was also useful for the girls to hear the current idiomatic use of the language.

Edith Watson had been born in England, as had Hildegard's mother. It was she who had chosen Edith as her children's Nanny partly to reinforce the London connection, and to ensure that they spoke perfect English. Hildegard and Alice became bilingual, and Hildegard's three girls were trilingual, talking English to Nanny, Italian to their governess and German to their parents.

In the course of the tour Otto intermittently suffered from his persistent lung problem and doctors in more than one capital city ordered him to rest. One day, while Otto remained behind to see his Harley Street doctor, Nanny took the girls to see where she had once lived, walking slowly down from Hyde Park, with one girl on each arm. They knew London well, but they had never been to Edith's house. "It's further than I remember," she peered ahead trying to focus on her old home.

"We'll get a taxi back," the ever-solicitous Nina responded, concerned that the walk would prove too strenuous for Nanny.

The house had four-storeys, with splendid Doric columns supporting the arch over the doorway. Nanny had lived in the spacious ground floor flat

71

with her parents. Steps winding down to a basement door, hidden below the main steps, were cordoned off by spick and span black railings and a locked gate.

Although it was the rich centre of London, the Watsons had not been well off. They had inherited the property and let the other flats out to business people who paid well, but most of the money had been gambled away by Edith's profligate father who was always chasing the big win. "This is the one," he would say as he put the last of the family's weekly money on the next horse. "I got it from the trainer himself. It's a certainty!" But it never was and Edith, at age sixteen, had found herself in the unenviable position of having to find work for which she had not been trained.

Through friends, she had learned that the von Ludens were looking for someone to take back with them to East Prussia, to be ready to act as Nanny and English instructor to their expected children. Hildegard was born within two months of Edith arriving, and Alice was born two years later. She had lovingly watched the two girls grow from babies: they were the children she was never to have. Later she became Nanny to Hildegard's three daughters and hardly had time to miss having a family of her own. They were her family, her own babies. She came from stout English stock, and though in her sixties, with a family of other servants to help her she still had plenty of strength to cope with the three girls, and she took it all in her stride.

Now Anna was to have her own baby, and Nanny would start all over again. She was torn between love of small children and desire for a well-earned rest. She stared up at the white painted house, memories of her long distant family flooding back. There had been no rectangular bronze plaque on the wall in the shadow of the porch when she had lived there.

"Nina, dear, run up the steps and tell me what it says."

She tapped Claudia's arm, motioning for her to hold on tighter.

To Nina, obedience to requests from Nanny was second nature, and she immediately ran with alacrity up the flight of stone stairs. She tripped over the top step and fell noisily against the solid black timber door in a painful, self-conscious heap.

"Oh, my goodness, gracious me!" Nanny fluttered her free hand back and forth as though trying to dry it. "I remember that step! I ought to have warned her."

The door opened and a tall, slim, blond young man appeared in the doorway, and Nina's life was changed forever. He caught hold of her with one strong hand, brushing dust from her light summer coat with the other as he pulled her to her feet. "Are you hurt?" he enquired apprehensively, his face a picture of genuine concern.

"I don't think so. At least," she ruefully rubbed her left wrist and elbow, "it seems to be mostly my pride, which can easily be dispensed with." She smiled shyly and looked at him directly. "I hadn't realized; you spoke in German. How did you know I was German?"

He whispered in her ear, "Your grandmother was asking for God's help in fluent German, so I guessed!"

"But she's English!" Nina laughed, looking directly into his eyes. They were green, with flecks of grey and hidden depths, and they were looking at her curiously as he considered her words.

Nina was studying him intensely, wondering what he was thinking. There was something about him that she liked immediately: perhaps it's his discretion in whispering in my ear in case he said anything to make me feel awkward in front of the others, or, perhaps, because he didn't stand aside and let me get myself up. Nina knew little about love at first sight. She had heard of it, but had no idea what it really meant. The chemistry between them was instantaneous. And in their eyes there was some deeper understanding. They briefly, silently stared at each other, a gentle smile on each of their faces, as though recognising dearly loved friends.

"Oh!" Nina remembered Nanny and Claudia and introduced them.

"And I am Erik Larsson. I work here for the Swedish Embassy in a temporary capacity," he indicated Nanny's old home.

When it was explained to him what their mission had been, they were invited inside. "It's perfectly all right. There are no secrets here," he smiled, answering Nanny's suggestion that it would not be right for them to enter. "We've just spilled over from the main embassy building. All we do here is stamp papers, sort them out, file them, that sort of thing. They're all locked away, don't worry!"

Nanny spent some time explaining what each room had been used for when it had been her home. Sometimes she sat silently remembering her past life, and then Erik would diplomatically inform them what now went on there, or ask them about their lives in Germany.

Claudia warmed to him when she discovered he liked horses. Whenever Claudia could not be found at home she was either in the stables assisting the groom, or out riding by herself. She loved nothing better than to jump ditches and hedges, the more excitement and danger the better.

"At home in Sweden my mother has a stable, but we only have two horses left now. It was rather a lot for her to handle." Erik felt a little in awe of Claudia's bravery. He preferred watching horses to riding them.

Nina in her usual fashion sat quietly studying him, listening to his conversation with Claudia, now and then probing tactfully into his background. He was, she learned, torn between the diplomatic world and becoming a preacher. At the moment, a career in diplomacy was winning, in view of the menacing European situation.

In the warm atmosphere and with a small glass of sherry inside her, Nanny had nodded off.

"What threat?" Nina asked ingenuously, after Erik suggested the new Germany was a menace to European security. She knew exactly what he meant, but wanted to keep him talking, to be with him for longer.

Erik thoughtfully studied the two girls. "You know about the Night of the Long Knives, don't you?"

"Yes, Hitler had the storm troopers killed, but how does that threaten Europe?"

"It doesn't, not directly. But it shows us that Hitler wants power and will stop at nothing to make sure all his rivals are eliminated. In a democracy you simply don't do it that way. Hitler has not only thrown away the old Germany and put a totalitarian state in its place; he's also made sure the German army is no danger to him."

"By making them take an oath of allegiance to him?" Claudia asked, briefly revealing her political knowledge.

"Yes, that's absolutely right. They can't break their personal oath, it wouldn't be honourable."

Nina knew what her family felt and was pleased to think that Erik also had the same attitude. They chatted on without noticing the time, and all the while her affection for him was growing.

Never usually so open and free with details of his personal life to anyone, he found it easy to talk to Nina and was at home in her presence.

'I feel comfortable with her,' he admitted to himself as he later took the tea tray from his secretary. 'The older one is like a spirited horse, she needs someone to hold onto the reigns tightly or you'll lose your seat as she pulls you over the jumps.

'But the younger one is enchanting! She doesn't say much, but you can almost hear her mind working. And when she does speak, she does so softly, with so much reflection in her questions; there's passion behind that gentle façade! What a fire there'll be in a year or two!'

He mused to himself as he held the teapot, waving away Nanny and Nina's proffered hands. In East Prussia that was the work of women, and they found it unsettling to allow a man to pour their tea for them. Claudia leaned back in her chair, hands clasped behind her neck, that was anybody else's work, not hers.

"I think you would make a good preacher," Nina told him candidly, not fully understanding what was involved in the role of a diplomat. "You seem to care deeply about people and that's what's really important, isn't it?"

Nina was astonished to hear herself speaking so intimately about someone she had only just met. She knew instinctively that this tall, green-eyed young man, whose face came alive with vitality when he smiled at her, was going to be important in her life, that their destinies were linked. His very calmness and compassion revealed his arrival at the place she was still searching for. She felt that he, too, had suffered the mental turmoil of the eternal seeker of truth and had found at least some of the answers that so far had eluded her. It's as though I've known him all my life!

Nina had never felt this way about anyone before and she was determined not to lose the opportunity of his companionship, and insisted that Nanny should invite him to meet her father when he had recovered sufficiently.

"Do you sometimes feel that you've met someone before?" Nina asked Erik one sunny afternoon while they strolled through Hyde Park, following a few paces behind her father and Claudia. The Serpentine was full of families boating or paddling in its warm waters, children were running around the edges of the lake feeding bread crumbs to the ducks and wild geese, screaming and laughing, while their smiling, indulgent parents looked on. It was a picture of London found in all the guidebooks, unexpectedly charming, an oasis of green, watery pleasure in the middle of a noisy, crowded, polluted capital city, but Nina hardly noticed it.

"What I'm really wondering, I suppose, is what your views are on reincarnation - do you believe it's a possibility?

"Almost anything is a possibility, given that no-one knows for certain. There are many times you feel an instant recognition, but that might only be a chemical reaction, or an instant reading of another's character from the way they move and talk. I think I incline more to a rational, physical explanation. What do you believe?"

He spoke thoughtfully, with long pauses between each different idea, and Nina sensed he was being careful not to hurt her sensibilities.

All the time she looked up at him, her eyes soft and loving, yet not recognizing her own feelings, and not realising that they were so obvious to everyone else. She found it intoxicating that he treated her like a mature woman, expecting her to give him rational answers. Many adults seemed to ignore the views of children as uninteresting or uninformed and therefore of no value. His attitude was refreshing, and so like that of her family.

Claudia had walked on ahead with her father. She was far too impatient to amble and talk, and was keen to arrive at Rotten Row to study the horse riders. Otto was duty bound to accompany her, though being more inclined to saunter slowly and converse with the others.

"I know reincarnation doesn't come in to the Christian religion, but I feel as though I've known you a very long time," Nina admitted shyly. Then she added with more conviction, "If you accept that it's possible to have lived before, then you must advance some reason. There would be little point in coming back to earth again and again for nothing."

"No more than coming only the once, I should think," Erik smiled.

"Yes, yes!" Nina stopped abruptly in mid-step as she grappled with the new thought and Erik paused alongside her, watching her eyes withdraw as if they were looking at something far away in another world, and yet they were animated and alive.

"So, what is your answer?"

"I don't have one yet," Nina admitted. She flashed her winsome smile at him. "I used to think I knew everything, but now I seem to know nothing."

"Ah! That's one of the first signs of growing up - being able to admit to ignorance."

Over their few weeks in London the attachment Nina formed for Erik deepened and strengthened until she thought of almost nothing else.

Nina had always been a thinker. As a small child she had loved the wet, cold days when she would sit in the schoolroom with her nose pressed to the windowpane. While Claudia fretted, running up and down impatiently, willing the rain to stop, Nina would examine the raindrops or the snowflakes as they slid down the glass, questioning where they came from, why they were shaped the way they were. Even then she had been happy on her own, just pondering and wondering.

As she grew older, the pleasure shifted more towards discussion with others of like mind. Now Erik encouraged her to channel her intelligence into more challenging areas. He was like a fresh wind, fanning the immature thoughts within her into provocative existence. Blowing away the cobwebs and immaterial odds and ends; leaving only the worthwhile ideas to ponder over, ideas that she would continue in correspondence with Erik after she had returned home to Germany.

She did not appreciate for a long time that she had found her intellectual equal, even her superior; a mind that could stimulate her even more than Eva had done. She simply knew that she liked him immensely and wanted him in her life always.

When news of the arrival of Anna's first child came, Otto was keen to return home immediately to see his new grandson, Kurt. He had not wanted to admit that he was tired. His lungs had worsened with the extra physical effort of the tour, and he was having some difficulty in breathing in enough oxygen in the poor London atmosphere. Both he and Nanny Watson longed for the clear air of home.

Nanny was tired, too. She was used to the slower pace of rural life in East Prussia and London had changed: the noise and speed of modern life were too much for her. Besides, she felt she was needed once again! There was a smile of anticipation on her shining, well-scrubbed face as she planned the new nursery.

Claudia was secretly delighted to be going home early. Next door to her uncle's home in Pomerania lived a young man, Johannes von Rott, for whom she had recently formed considerable affection. He had just qualified as a lawyer and was beginning a promising career. For her there were no pleasures in London that compared to those back home. To Otto and Nina's great surprise, Claudia suddenly developed a fondness for babies that she had never displayed before.

Nina was devastated. She promised Erik that she would write to him and assured herself that one day she would come back and see him again, just as soon as she was allowed to travel alone. She had not expected the strong emotion that she now felt. As a small child she had lost a puppy, run over by a careless visitor's car. She had refused to have a replacement, because she could not bear the pain of losing a second pet. That feeling of profound emptiness and despair, of never seeing someone she loved again, overwhelmed her now and engulfed her in depression.

For the two days they had to wait while their travel arrangements were altered she cried alone in her room each night before Claudia joined her, unable to bear the parting still to come.

"I wish I was old enough to make my own decisions, and then I would stay here in London," Nina confided to Erik and Claudia after their last lunch together at their hotel. "There's a freedom here we don't seem to have at home."

"Yes," Claudia agreed impatiently, "You constantly have to guard your tongue in case someone reports you to the authorities. I don't care for myself," she added defiantly, "but I wouldn't want anyone in the family to be hurt, because of me."

Eric was becoming increasingly concerned for the safety of these spirited girls. "There are other ways of undermining a bad government. Many who speak out in a dictatorship disappear. It's wise to be cautious."

He watched Nina toying with her coffee cup and hoped they both heeded his words. 'Claudia says things off the top of her head, but Nina always thinks first. I like that about her. I shall miss her,' he mused as they stood up to go.

Otto felt he had been away too long. Germany was in political turmoil and events were being reported in the English newspapers that worried him. He wanted to be home, to see for himself, to be near his family in case they needed protection. Some Germans and Prussians he met in London seemed full of hope and excitement at the changes, but their views did not coincide with those expressed in the better English newspapers. Nor did Erik have any faith in the way things were turning out, and Otto had formed a highly favourable impression of him.

He found himself comparing his son-in-law Peter with Erik and almost wishing that he had married into the family, not Peter. He considered Peter to be naïve and gullible, and his opinions merely a reflection of the views of the last officer with whom he had conferred. He politely listened to Peter's notions and then forgot them, whereas he found himself drawn to Erik's judgements, especially about the new Germany. Erik struck him as a straightforward young man who spoke with candour and judged men impartially, but with tolerance - a liberal like himself. His ideas were based on knowledge, understanding, and he had a sharp analytical mind.

"I've learned more of the German character through Nina than through anyone else I've met," Erik told Otto frankly before their departure.

"She has English, Swedish and Russian ancestry, so perhaps she isn't as Germanic as you think!"

"Ah!" was all that Erik said, but it conveyed the feeling that he generally thought little of the German character.

"So, you do not approve of us Germans as a race?" Otto asked softly and not unsympathetically in the light of current German attitudes towards other countries.

"I didn't mean to convey that thought, but you may have a point. We none of us know our prejudices until we're confronted by them. I suppose it's only the current trend in Germany that I abhor. How can I approve of Hitler's ideas? Germans as individuals are no different from any other, but it seems as though something happens when people join together as a race or nation; they take on the characteristics of the whole. We all have them lying latent within us. I suppose I have the melancholy of the Swedish nation within me, too, but I won't succumb to it. Nina will never acquire the nationalistic pride of the National Socialist Germans... nor you or your family I think."

Otto could not imagine Erik as a stereotypical Swede, he had too much life, too much enthusiasm; and yet there were times when he had been quiet and thoughtful, and there was a look on his face that Otto could only describe as melancholic. "We've always tried to widen their horizons, to give them an understanding of other nations. When you have friends in other countries it's that much harder to go to war with them. Everyone should travel when they're young."

"I should like to agree with you, but humnas fight amongst themselves, families, civil wars. I have a great fear that the world is moving against the values of goodness, because it's seen as weakness. I believe somehow we must show the world that true goodness is a great strength. Think of what it must have taken for Jesus to follow his destiny, and there is no record of anything greater that I know of."

Again the thought crossed Otto's mind that he would like Erik as a son-in-law. He dismissed it quickly, Nina was still too young, but he would not discourage her from writing to him.

"This Hitler of ours is turning out to be a double-edged sword. At first he looked as though he might be able to solve the problem of our warring political parties, you know the idea of 'it takes one to put one down'? He's like them, he thinks like them and there was always the hope that those who put him in power would one day remove him. Now he seems to be causing more trouble than they were, and there's no sign that anyone's about to get rid of him. Quite the contrary."

"It seems to me he's a symbol. Germany has been exhibiting signs of extreme self-pity since Versailles. The Herrenvolk were so amazed that everyone disagreed with them that they've been unable to reconcile themselves to the modern world. Hitler still thinks he's owed something he didn't get after nineteen-eighteen."

81

"You might be right, I don't know. All of us are still affected by the loss of land, especially those of us in East Prussia. He certainly seems to be making noises that sound very warlike to me. We have to fight to get back what we lost in nineteen-nineteen, that's his suggestion and the countries outside of Germany see that as warmongering."

When he took his leave of the family Erik knew it would be hard to live without Nina's constant brightness and happiness. But the impressionable sixteen-year-old needed time to discover her own approach towards the questions he considered important. He had felt the cutting edge of her incisive mind more than once and recognized that in a few short years she would be a force to reckon with. He already felt attached to her as though they had an unspoken agreement.

As they left, he gave Nina a parting gift, wrapped in pretty pink paper, tied with a ribbon. "Promise me you won't open it until you're on the train to Berlin."

Nine

Nina kept her promise. On the train she opened the parcel and found a small framed print of an old master she had seen hanging in the National Gallery in London, and a note: 'I remember you admired the colours and the light. It's only a print, but it will remind you of a visit that I found memorable. I hope you enjoy looking at it and remembering, too. Erik.'

She stared at the painting for a long time, until Claudia playfully grabbed it from her. It was as though Claudia had removed her heart and Nina could barely restrain herself from seizing it back. All the way home she felt gripped by despair: suppose she never saw him again? She mourned the loss as if he were dead, seeking some refuge from her mental torment in bright, aimless chatter with her sister.

Nanny stopped her in the corridor of the train. "Nina! It's one thing to be sad at the loss of a friend, that is acceptable and only to be expected, it's quite another to indulge yourself in it! That amounts to masochism! Pull yourself together, child." She softened her tone as the dejected Nina studied her feet, unable to look the older woman in the eyes. "There, there, child, you're still a great baby," and she proffered Nina her handkerchief.

Immediately repenting her compassion, she reverted to severity, "Your mother would never approve of you showing your feelings so openly. You must control yourself. You're almost an adult. To have reached your age and still to be so emotionally unstable! Tut! Tut! It won't do, Nina, it simply won't do!"

"Does my father know?" Nina faltered, appalled that her grief had been so apparent.

"Your father? Goodness gracious me, no! What do men know of the finer emotions to which young ladies are prey? He will have noticed nothing! I'm sure of that!"

83

"Hilde, I'm worried about Nina," Otto confided. "All the way home she was very quiet and pale. I don't think it was much of a holiday for her. Have a word with her will you? It'll put my mind at rest."

"I'll ask Anna; Nina's been with her every moment since she returned. If there's anything troubling her, I'm sure Anna will have found out."

To fill her mind and dissipate her dejection, Nina spent hours each day playing with baby Kurt, regaling Anna with tales of their curtailed European tour and describing their time with Erik.

Claudia quickly persuaded her parents to allow her to stay with her cousins for the remainder of her long summer holiday, before returning to university. There was much more activity there; galloping horses over open countryside, with friends of her own age, was far more to her taste than looking after invalid sisters or small babies. And there was Johannes.

Claudia thoroughly enjoyed the impression she made on him; she loved seeing his face light up as he caught sight of her, and his bemused expression after she flirted with some of the other young men. Inward looking and pleasure seeking, a hedonist at heart, love was just a game to her.

Anna had already sensed that Nina's intellect had matured beyond hers, and after Nina's impassioned description of Erik she understood that Nina had found someone on her own spiritual level. She had tried in the past to understand what it was that drove her sister to debate the most difficult topics, which she considered insoluble and too time consuming to discuss.

If there was no possibility of finding the answer, how could there be any value in debating it? Clearly someone had made the earth and arranged everything on it, so there must be a God, but it was obvious that no proof of God's existence would ever be found; consequently she would spend no more time worrying about it. But she could not dissuade Nina from the quest.

Now Nina had a soul mate with whom to make the spiritual journey through life, and her correspondence with Erik was used to explore religion and politics. Nina would discuss his letters with her sister, much to Anna's despair. She could barely understand Nina's views on such matters, but now Nina wanted to deliberate over Erik's opinion of Hitler with her as well.

Anna felt the same way as her parents, preferring to leave things alone, but she was caught between Peter's enthusiastic support of the new regime and her family's antipathy towards it. She could not decide whether she should follow the way of her upbringing - the traditional tried and tested values that all her family accepted - or the new, untried path that her husband, and his friends and colleagues, favoured. Although she made no deliberate choice, little by little, by virtue of being mostly in the company of her husband, she began to support his views. But she would not discuss her decisions even with Nina. She quickly found she could not justify them, so she closed her mind to them.

Nina had no one at home with whom to debate. Claudia was at university and even when she was at home she always dispensed with talking in favour of action. Anna was busy with her baby. And their parents forbade any involvement with political groups. So increasingly it was to Pastor Liebermann at her local church that Nina turned for guidance.

His advice was moral rather than practical or political, for he now had to walk a fine line between the new laws of the land and his conscience. Having taught all his life that the peaceful solution was the right approach, the Christian way, now he faced the moral dilemma of whether it could ever work with men like the Nazis: should violence be met by violence or by prayer and forgiveness?

Like most others of his calling, he acquiesced publicly with the new laws, but privately, to Nina and others, he discussed methods of circumventing them.

It was not until the end of the following March that Nina's mind was crystallized, and she was goaded into action against the government. What provoked her was the Nazis' command to its citizens to boycott all Jewish shops.

The Steiners were not friends of her family, nonetheless Nina felt sorry for them. Anneliese had already left her school, and now their three stores all had the word 'Jude' and a big Jewish star daubed in thick paint on the windows. All their shops had Hitler Youth members standing guard to turn customers away, and all were the scenes of fights or scuffles. Even Nina, after a half-hearted attempt to pass the Hitler Youth on the door, allowed herself to be persuaded not to enter.

In her heart she knew that if the shop had belonged to the Rosenthals she would have succeeded not only in getting through, but also in persuading the youth on the door to move aside. Her family still had considerable rank and status, and she would even have used Peter's name in her attempts to save them. It grieved her later to contemplate that, perhaps, had a few more like her made that extra effort the whole boycott might have collapsed then and there. How could she have allowed herself to be so cowardly?

Later, when anger at her ineffectiveness had ruffled her usually calm nature, she appealed to her mother, "We just can't stand by and do nothing!"

"What could you have done, Nina? You said they were aggressive and the crowds were on their side. You might have felt better if you'd braved your way through, but you might have come to some harm. The very least it would have done would be to draw attention to yourself and to your family." Hildegard was soothing, but pragmatic. "And remember what happened to Alice!"

"You did the right thing by not getting involved, Nina," Anna added. "How do you think the army would have reacted to Peter being related to a rebel? They would probably have called you a traitor and him one, too. It would certainly have curtailed any chance of promotion for him."

Nina bit her tongue. She would like to have retorted, 'Is Peter's promotion more important than the livelihood of people like the Steiners?'

Her mother's remark about drawing attention to herself had made an impression and she remembered her father's remark some time before, forbidding Claudia to openly join anti-Hitler organizations. Ideas began to take shape; there were things she might be able to do.

In an unguarded moment, Pastor Liebermann had once remarked to Nina that some of the Nazi laws were shocking and he wished he could somehow aid the Jewish people from the village. At the time he had elicited not only a promise from Nina not to reveal what he had said, but also that she would assist him by any means she could.

Her anger at her own impotence increased when Hildegard read out a letter from Alice saying that she, together with a friend, who was in her eighties, had refused to allow the boycott in their local shop.

"But she's over eighty! They wouldn't dare molest elderly women like that. You would have received quite different treatment."

Nina imagined her aunt's friend, a formidable woman even at her great age, sweeping aside the limp attempts by the Hitler Youth to stop her entering the shop, perhaps even hitting them with her umbrella, and she winced in embarrassment at her own poor, weak struggle.

Rumours were increasing amongst some circles about Hitler's unstable state of mind and what would happen to the Jews, but already they had to be careful what they said and to whom they said it. Pastor Liebermann was certain he was under surveillance, and Otto's brother Franz no longer telephoned so frequently from his home in Pomerania, because he had been warned by a well-placed friend that his telephone was tapped.

Both the Pastor and Franz had moved in circles, which had been quite outspoken against the Hitler regime, and they and their friends were now marked men and reported upon.

The von Ludens in East Prussia were, so far, left outside the surveillance net, perhaps because of Otto's standing and connections with the army, which he still maintained on a social level, or perhaps because of Anna's marriage to Peter, a pillar of support to the new regime.

Nina should have come under suspicion. She was in contact with Pastor Liebermann and she was known, like her sister Claudia, to have made disparaging comments about Hitler's government, but Nina had matured into a young woman of charm and grace, and to Nazi eyes she was fair of face and fair of form. She had the semblance of all the flaxen German girls held up as shining examples of the peak of German womanhood. The ideals, the politics, of someone so Aryan could never be doubted and her good looks ironically became her safeguard. Even hardened Nazis could not suspect her of anything more than misplaced loyalty under her innocent Aryan gaze, so overwhelming had the propaganda on race been.

Nevertheless, the Brauns, who had caused Nina so much consternation at their Christmas party in the last year of the old regime, were keeping a careful eye on the two younger members of the family. Herr Braun was now a respected member of the National Socialist Party, and Franz had warned his brother to take care of what he said when he was in the their presence.

One day when Peter and Anna were visiting, he commented to the family, "Things may seem bad right now, but once Hitler has things really under control, these small isolated disturbances will soon disappear and everything will be back to normal."

"For us perhaps, but not for the Rosenthals or the Steiners," Nina answered more bitterly than she meant to, quickly pleading, "Peter, you don't really believe Hitler is a good man, do you?"

"Of course I do!" Peter was both amazed and amused at her question. "Nina you've been listening to too many rumours. Wait just a few months and you'll see. Everybody will be back at work; hunger and unemployment will be things of the past. Those who won't work or don't support Germany will have emigrated, and then we shall be a country of happy people, all in accord. And we'll know exactly where we're all going. We're in the middle of change, and it's difficult to see how it will turn out, but it will be better for all of us, I promise!"

"What an idyllic picture, Peter!" Claudia intervened, sarcastically. "But I don't quite understand. Mr. Rosenthal worked very hard, so why did you stop him? Will you close down Mr. Steiner's shops and then accuse him of being unemployed?"

Peter was irritated by how little Anna's sisters were prepared to give Hitler a chance. "In the first place we did not stop Mr. Rosenthal from working, he chose to go, and in the second place Mr. Steiner's shops are still open."

"You know what I mean!"

Claudia disliked Peter more each time she saw him and, with the callousness of youth, took every opportunity to try and trip him up. The young woman who normally smiled and laughed, with seeming carelessness of life, became a barbed arrow of sarcasm whenever Peter came within firing range. In his presence she revealed an understanding of the political situation that was generally hidden. Because she was such an active young girl, those who did not know her well were apt to believe she was uninterested in mental pursuits or incapable of understanding politics, but this was no longer a trivial pursuit. Even her own parents underestimated the full extent of her concerns. That was not their fault, for Claudia had only formed her opinions recently.

The group of young intellectuals who lived near Franz, with whom she and Nina would argue whenever they stayed at their uncle's house, was of more than passing interest to Claudia. She was not averse to a little competition between the young men and, with tongue in cheek, she would actively encourage their rivalry; she had decided long ago who would be the eventual winner. Her affections were centred entirely on the young lawyer, Johannes. He was the one she intended to marry.

Her feelings were reciprocated. Johannes was a cool, sophisticated young man, ten years her senior. His calmness neatly complemented her ardent nature. They were two halves of a circle, each providing what the other lacked, yet being similar in outlook, ideas and humour. Subconsciously, Claudia had pinpointed the man whose character would best respond to hers; she had recognized that fervour needs composure, and explosiveness needs stability. It was not what she wanted, but it was what she needed.

For his part, Johannes was very taken by this bright, vivacious, passionate young woman, but could not imagine what she saw in him. He was conventional, rather slow and placid, whereas Claudia craved excitement and change. It flattered him that she clearly favoured him above the other younger men and in return he gave her his unswerving loyalty and affection.

When he asked Otto for her hand in marriage, Otto and Hildegard insisted on a long engagement, because of her young age and impetuous nature. It was to be two years before they were allowed to marry.

With Johannes and his friends, the girls could openly say what they thought on any subject. Here, even within the new totalitarian atmosphere of the nineteen-thirties, they would never be betrayed. When they were with Peter and his friends, Nina had increasingly to lay a cool, restraining hand on Claudia's foolhardy outbursts. Fear of being punished for saying what she thought was unknown to Claudia, but a very real threat to Nina. For all her seeming innocence, she was beginning to understand the current world far better than her elder sister.

Fate dealt the two sisters polarized personalities and thoughts: Claudia seemed to be down-to-earth and practical, but her mind dwelt on intangibles: what might be, what ought to be, what could have been. Whereas Nina, who appeared to have her head in the clouds, was the first one to find a workable solution to problems. Her correspondence with Erik had rounded her political education and she had cleverly learned to use historic events to make comparisons with Hitler's policies, without using his name. Erik had marvelled at her skill and answered her in kind.

At Franz's and Ruth's home there was always a group of young men: a pastor, a priest or one or more of the theology students from the nearby college. Discussions were lively, yet liberal and good-humoured. The large, nineteenth-century house was some distance from other homes, so the excessive number of people spilling out into the grounds did not interfere with the lives of their neighbours.

It was an old, established area, where friendships amongst families were not transient, depending on one generation, but lasting literally centuries. Like feuds, they went back so far that their origins were forgotten, but their loyalty was not. Here were many of the higher echelons of the army, the future caucus of discontent with Hitler.

University had been slowly schooling Claudia into an appreciation of discussion, but once she had said her piece on any subject, it was finished. She still preferred more physical pastimes and was always the first out into the snow to throw snowballs at everyone as they emerged.

Her uncle and aunt were not for a moment fooled by her physical energy, they knew underneath the impatient exterior she was fired with a desire to help people; she simply could not sit still for long periods. Claudia still had that dream of making a grand, noble gesture. Only Nina of the three sisters really revelled in the cut and thrust of debate and would always be right in the thick of it all, from start to finish.

In nineteen thirty-six, Nina and Claudia stayed for the summer holidays with their aunt and uncle before they both returned to university. Claudia was finishing her degree in history and geography, and Nina was just beginning her first year of philosophy and politics. The twins, Susanna and Wilhelm, were old enough now to join in the discussions and held strong views of their own. Like Claudia, they were unable to refrain from openness and honesty, already causing great concern to Franz and Ruth, by saying in public things that should only have been said in private, drawing the attention of the authorities to themselves and the family.

Hans, their eldest son, was in America teaching German in New York.

There he had met up with Eva, after Nina asked him to take her a gift. Together, they had formed an émigré group, dedicated to supporting any Germans wishing to establish themselves in a new life.

His sister Christina had married a half-Jewish writer, Gerhard Roessler. It was during this holiday that Christina and Gerhard had made the difficult decision to finally leave Germany and live in Switzerland. The new government's policy towards Jews was transparent now. New laws had already forced Gerhard out of his job, along with thousands of other professional Jews, and he existed on the charity of his relatives. They were being restricted in many ways and, married to a Jew, Christina herself was also in danger, and increasingly shunned by the local population who feared for their own jobs. It was only a matter of time before Gerhard, and perhaps Christina, would be put into a camp. The tentacles of the Nazi regime had begun to reach into their family.

Christina spoke to family and friends lounging casually half-in and half-out of the living room, some sitting outside on the patio in wicker chairs, bathed in the hot summer sun. "It's all right for us, we can afford to emigrate, but what about poor Jews, the majority, how do they get out? I feel as though I'm running away when I'm needed most. I really ought not to go. Gerhard must, but I shouldn't."

"You must!" Ruth intervened fiercely. "Jews are being taken off the streets, dragged from their homes. It won't be long before Gerhard is arrested; you don't have much time. Go now, as soon as possible!" Ruth had seen others taken while they were still dithering.

"If you leave, will it still be possible for you to keep in touch with one of us?" Nina swung round and asked with apparent innocence. She had been leaning against the open French windows, staring across the low hills towards the nearby sea, less than two miles away, apparently lost in thought. But she had been listening to every word.

"They should be able to," Franz answered for them. "Though letters might be opened and telephones tapped, like ours."

Nina moved a step towards them, the sun framing her shortened golden hair like a halo, her tall, slender body enhanced by figure hugging white silk slacks and a pink short sleeved blouse. "It's just that... I was thinking. Maybe we have the chance to do something really useful and you'll feel that you're not running out."

The young men and her family looked at her with anticipation. "Well? Come on, Nina, what's your idea?" Gerhard asked, eager for anything that would ease his feelings of guilt. "Don't keep us in suspense!"

"Eva and Hans have their émigré group in America. If you set up something similar in Switzerland, would it be possible for us to organize ourselves into a group and move out Jews who can't afford to leave by themselves, and then you send them on to America or somewhere else? Do you see what I'm getting at?"

The group fell silent. No one had wanted to admit that things were so bad that it was necessary to escape, but each had wanted to do something for those being attacked or imprisoned by the regime, and now Nina had suggested a possible way.

Ruth broke their silence. "We'd need to sort it out very quickly. You two must go as soon as possible," she nodded to Christina and Gerhard.

Franz put an arm around Nina and hugged her tightly, "Then we'd best get started on it!"

"Would America take them all? They operate a quota system, don't they?" Gerhard was angered by countries that kept their gates closed to Jews. "All those who have reason to be afraid should be able to get away from here, should be helped by foreign governments. What's America doing, what about Sweden and England? They only take professionals with skills or money, but what about the destitute, what happens to them?"

"They have no choice but to stay and make the best of it," Franz began, but each of the students wanted their say.

"The poor never have a chance..."

"All Jews will be poor soon if they're sacked from their positions. How will they eat, let alone escape to another country?"

"They could become refugees on foot and hope to survive long enough to reach a friendly country."

"Name me a friendly country within walking distance!"

"How many Germans would help a Jew to survive long enough to reach France or Belgium, or Holland? They need money and food and transport before they set off."

Nina had started at the mention of Sweden. Her mind, ever willing to focus its attention on the man she loved, began to dwell on the possibility of contacting him. "We already have two connections, Hans and Eva in America, you in Switzerland, and we'd also have another one in Sweden. I'm sure I can make an excellent link there with…"

Ruth had been listening intently, and now suddenly stood up. "Don't tell us where or with whom. We're playing with fire! You do all realize that, don't you? The less we each know the better."

Everyone went very quiet. They understood the implications only too well. Hitler stayed in power through the use of force exercised through the Gestapo and the SS who had no restraints on what they did. It would be a dangerous game they were about to play.

Franz was grateful to Nina for making the suggestion, which gave both Christina and Gerhard a focus to their emigration plans. "We already have a lot to sort out. I'm sure we have some excellent contacts between us. Perhaps we should all take a little time to think about it, how we can build up some kind of organisation, who is going to do what job…"

Christina asked, "How will we all keep in touch when we're organized? The post from Switzerland will probably be opened, and most of your telephones will be tapped."

"Don't worry about that!" One of the young men half raised a hand, "I've the perfect solution!"

"Don't tell us! Tell only whoever we decide is to lead the group. That way only one or two of us will know and we can't give much away." Ruth shivered, already feeling the remorseless hand of the Gestapo gripping her collar.

Shortly after that first discussion, Gerhard and Christina crossed the border into Switzerland; their hearts in their mouths in case they were stopped at the last minute and turned back, as so many others had been before them. A large bribe to the lax and greedy border guards on a particularly hot, enervating August day ensured their safe passage through to Switzerland.

They settled with friends near Geneva, contacting churches and sympathetic organizations, and quickly gathered around them a small group willing to look after the refugees until their transfer to other countries could be organised. A code had been devised for letter writing and a procedure for changing it and letting people know when it was discovered. Another method of transmitting messages had been arranged between Gerhard and one of the young men for emergencies only.

It did not occur to those in this group of lifelong comrades that any among their number would be other than dedicated to the same worthy ideals. Over a period of months, their friends had been fined down to those who felt the same way; trust between them was implicit. The honour of their country was at stake, and they would be its guardians until Germany could be led back to the path of decency.

Since Peter was a dedicated follower of Hitler, Anna could not be included in their meetings and a pact was made not to discuss anything in either her, or her parents' presence. They would be safe from accidentally revealing anything to Peter; though, as yet, there was nothing to disclose, except a caucus of disagreement and alternative thinking. But many had already been tortured and killed for much less.

Ten

Erik stepped confidently off the boat at Danzig, sure of why he had come, but wondering what he would make of the new German government and its outrageous laws; and how long it would be before he fell foul of them. He was diametrically opposed to almost everything Hitler stood for, and his response to the conspirators' plans had been immediately sympathetic, though cautious. Germany seemed to be heading in a singular direction, broadcasting the next diplomatic or military moves well in advance.

Somewhat to his surprise, he discovered that few were sensitive enough to perceive the meaning behind the diplomatic communications emanating constantly from Berlin. The messages were not in code, they seemed provocatively clear: this new Germany would not rest until it had regained all its territory lost after the Great War, and had an army and an air force equal to or better than any state of its size. Even then, he believed it would continue to grow until it controlled all of Europe. Then it would dominate Russia and overthrow Communism.

He wondered how long Sweden would be safe. What would happen to the people in the lands Hitler ruled? He had made it clear that many would perish and many more would be enslaved in a new and brutally totalitarian empire. The future of Europe looked bleak. The new Germany signalled a return to the worst excesses of the Dark Ages.

He had been dismayed and alarmed that a proud, intelligent, cultured nation, with centuries of civilisation behind it, and scores of men of genius, should entrust its future to a dangerous madman. For Erik could not dismiss *Mein Kampf* out of hand as many others had done.

If it were fiction, it was written by a man who would say anything, and was mentally deranged; if it were not, this was a dangerous man indeed! Either way, Germany was now in the hands of a highly unstable personality, like a train with faulty brakes travelling on the fast track. His plan to follow a religious course in life would have to be changed.

He had been contacted quietly by Johannes who had been visiting London a few weeks before, with some lawyers studying differences between the legal systems within Europe, and had been invited to Johannes's wedding with Claudia. Both Claudia and Nina had been sure that Erik would be a willing addition to their group and would assist them in finding homes in Sweden and England for any refugees. When Johannes had explained their purpose to him, Erik had thrown himself wholeheartedly behind their plans. Even before his visit to Germany he had busied himself making contacts in both England and Sweden.

His mother willingly offered her large ancestral home as the first stopping place for any refugees, and volunteered her services and those of her friends in such a worthy humanitarian cause.

"I might as well be doing something useful with the house; look at the size of it! And there's only me at home! What's the point in having servants if they've nothing to do? Make use of us as much as you like, Erik dear."

"We might fall foul of the German government..."

"So! That's never stopped anyone in our family from following their conscience. Don't let us set a poor precedent for future generations," his mother had warmly responded.

Erik's visit was officially for the wedding, but covertly to discuss the *modi operandi* of their group, the functions of individual members, and codes that would be necessary for writing and telephone calls. The sheer volume of the practical problems of moving people between different countries so far apart were enormous, and might take weeks of planning.

Free to travel all over Europe, Erik was in a unique position to contact each member and transmit new codes, new plans, and even warnings to each of them.

"If there is a war - heaven forbid - Sweden is bound to remain neutral. Then your position will be invaluable," Johannes had suggested persuasively.

"My position might be compromised if there is," Erik had responded, "but I shall do it nevertheless!"

As Erik emerged from the customs hall in Danzig he searched for familiar figures amongst the waiting crowds. He recognized Otto first. Otto had not changed at all since they had last met, he was still the slim, distinguished, upright, grey-haired man who had so charmed him in London, but the young lady by his side had almost outgrown his memory. As tall as her father, and elegantly adult, Nina was as different from the gauche schoolgirl who had slumped so awkwardly against his door as a caterpillar to a freshly emerged butterfly. Yet she was still Nina.

As their eyes met, he realized she had been observing him for some time. Her Mona Lisa smile showed the thoughtfulness and rapt attention of one who had sought and found the object of her affections, of one who had watched his every movement, and whose every move had pleased her.

He solemnly shook Otto's hand, but Otto covered Erik's between his two palms, overcome with pleasure at seeing him again. Erik was greatly surprised by the warmth of his greeting, but he was even more taken aback by Nina. She stepped forward, and reaching out with both her arms, she held him for a while, gently searching his eyes for his feelings. Then she hugged him generously, her cheek pressed to his, as though he were an old friend to whom she always gave such an effusive welcome.

Previously she had produced in him a protective, almost paternal response, with her gentle questioning and modest yet affectionate smile, and her childish plaits; but now he recognized other, more dramatic feelings. From her letters he had appreciated that the child had become a woman of some humanity and spiritual depth. Her face, though not beautiful, revealed a tranquil calm and her demeanour showed the graceful casualness that came from an intimate and long-standing relationship with the best of everything.

"Nina, you look enchanting!" He whispered in her ear before she gently disentangled herself, but her eyes glowed and the smile playing around the edges of her lips invited him to repeat his comment later when they were alone. "Absolutely bewitching! I can't get over how you've matured, Nina! Oh," he added, hesitantly, "forgive me for reminding you of a period you might rather forget."

Nina laughed. "We'd all rather forget those years, wouldn't we? They're so painful."

"I almost forgot you still have some growing up to do. How old are you now? No, don't tell me! You'll only remind me of my age!"

"You'll never be old, Erik, not to me."

Erik was to stay with the von Ludens for a month, travelling with them to Pomerania where Claudia had insisted she wanted to be married. She had made it seem to be a feminine whim, but it had been prearranged with them all. Kösslin was a much safer place to talk than Elbing, and this was likely to be one of the few times all of them would be together in one place, with a genuine excuse.

The long journey around the Polish Corridor was worth the effort for the absolute privacy they would enjoy in Pomerania. Everyone in the escape group understood that in Kösslin their talks could be moved from house to house, from friend to friend, whereas at Otto's home too many of Peter's colleagues lived nearby.

Franz's house between Kösslin and the sea was full to overflowing with excited relatives and friends, many of who had not seen each other for some time. They all had decades of family news to catch up on. The noise of chattering guests resembled a gathering of geese, and the exuberance continued for days. Each new arrival was somehow accommodated in the ample house, where doors opened and unexpected rooms miraculously appeared behind them as and when they were needed; it had a life of its own, expanding or contracting to suit the needs of its occupants.

No one needed to sleep on the floor or in a corridor, and if they had run out of rooms, Johannes lived only a few hundred yards away, though his home, too, was overwhelmed by his relatives and friends.

Both he and Claudia not only came from close, large families, but they were also extremely popular. Weddings were always an occasion for family reunions on a grand scale and there were plenty of goods and food available for those who could afford them.

Staying with Johannes was another pastor, a man who lived in the area and knew its people well; a towering giant of a man over six feet tall, with a proportionately large physique. From his comely face his sagacious blue eyes beamed benevolently around him, and he greeted everyone as though they were old and sadly missed friends.

To Nina's surprise, it appeared that he and Erik were old acquaintances. They had met originally in Stockholm where they had immediately found much in common - not least their antipathy towards the Nazis, then only a distant threat. By chance their paths had crossed again in New York, and they had renewed their friendship a third time in London, only a few weeks before. Erik introduced him as Thomas Dietermann.

This was no ordinary pastor quaking in his shoes at the government's latest edict, wondering if his job was safe for a while longer, or if he would be required to take an oath of loyalty to Hitler rather than to God. This was a man to be feared by the authorities, a man of conviction and conscience.

He and Erik compared the situation priests now found themselves in within Germany with the English Reformation. "I sometimes feel I know what it must have been like for Sir Thomas More when he was required to swear an oath of obedience to his king. How could he in all conscience put a man above God? How can priests now be expected to do the same? *This* man above God?"

He put his head back and roared with laughter at such an absurd thought. "And yet I know most of us will. If you had death by fire facing you as a mediaeval priest it must have made it easier to recant. Today, we have death by another torture facing us. Who is strong enough to face up to it? When the cock crows thrice we all give in to fear. But Hitler? Ha!"

Many in the clergy had already been imprisoned or had their living removed, because they refused to acknowledge Hitler's decrees. There were others, too intimidated to resist, who accepted whatever was issued either from cowardice, or from the faint hope that whilst still within the church they might yet have a voice and be able to curb the worst excesses.

But men like Thomas Dietermann were the rare exceptions. Their very sureness seemed to produce uncertainty on the part of their antagonists. Faced with a will of steel, even the iron fist of dictatorship was stilled for a while. All who remained in the Kösslin house after Claudia's wedding drew strength from his presence, and from his faith in the ultimate success of their mission.

"I am absolutely delighted to make your acquaintance at last." He pumped Nina's small hand furiously between his two capacious palms. "When I met Erik in London he told me so much about you that I half anticipated being asked to perform the same ceremony for you!"

His eyes twinkled with mischievous good humour.

Nina blushed. From the day she had first met Erik, she had known that he, or someone like him, was exactly the kind of man she wanted to marry. The colour rose to her cheeks now at the revelation of how Erik must have spoken of her. Did he love her? Had he intimated as much to Thomas? "From what I hear, it seems possible you won't be able to perform any ceremonies soon," she answered, referring to the new decree banning all churches other than those approved by Hitler.

"We are struggling, it's true, but we fight on. In the end we shall win, but the battle may be long and dangerous. We'll lose many good men on the way. There'll be no dealing with these people once they have complete power. But," he added light-heartedly, "marriages are made in heaven! They don't need my consent."

Neither Johannes nor Claudia felt much like participating in a lavish ceremony such as Anna had gone through; they wanted to get on with the group's activities as quickly as possible. But they had been persuaded to have at least a traditional, if smaller, wedding performed by Pastor Liebermann, who had travelled with them. In deference to Hildegard's insistence on convention, Claudia wore a white dress, but no veil, and she suffered what she saw as an archaic ceremony with good grace. But she absolutely refused to have bridesmaids, and grimaced when her father was asked to give her away. Hildegard still managed to wipe away a tear or two at the loss of a second daughter, despite her high standards being eroded.

After a bountiful meal, the couple departed for their honeymoon, while Nina, Erik and other close friends stayed on at the house, discussing the group's future plans. After other guests and relations had left, the honeymooners returned quietly, in the dark of night within three days, to join in the group's discussions.

While they were away, Nina had set to with a will, and explained to the others that she had plans drawn up, codes organized and undercover names for each member. Thomas would become their spiritual leader and Nina was the undisputed administrator and practical manager. When the honeymooners returned the practical work was almost accomplished and the conversation turned to more philosophical topics.

It was here that Thomas came into his own, dominating the discussion. "We must not; we shall not let the world sink back into another Dark Age. That's what this man means, not just to Germany, but to all nations. He must be stopped, now, before it's too late!"

The group sat quietly, as though at a lecture, digesting his words. They had spent some days in a happy, relaxed frame of mind after Claudia's wedding. Nina had done all the hard work. They had simply listened, examined her plans and either agreed, or made suggestions for changes. Now they were brought back to earth with a jolt.

"If a man has any worth, he must be prepared to give up even his life for his cause. I think there are many such men here today, and women." He looked at Nina and Claudia. "Men here dream of honour and gallantry and the old-fashioned virtues that are disappearing fast under this government. It's endemic in the history of this area I suppose."

"The old Teutonic knights," someone suggested.

"So, Thomas, you're prepared to die. But would you be prepared to kill for your cause?" Erik asked, searchingly. Although he had known Thomas for only a short time he had become aware of more dynamism within him than was good for a priest. Without realizing it, he had stumbled on the main dichotomy in Thomas's thinking.

"That's a difficult question. Would I be prepared to become a martyr to the cause? I'm not a fanatic, but neither do I know yet if I have the makings of one!" He ridiculed the thought of being so important as to go down in history as a martyr. "Quite apart from the moral question of whether one should ever contemplate the idea of killing, one must consider the practicalities: the times, the person - or persons - to be assassinated, the place, the likely result, and the reactions of others. All these things would have to be carefully examined to ascertain whether the results to be achieved would outweigh the moral wound the act would cause to one's soul. You have to live with your soul forever!"

Erik was not to be sidetracked and restated his question, "But would you kill, not some hypothetical person, but you, if you felt that by your action Germany would be safer? Or are you saying you would only do so if you were sure of gaining the title of martyr?"

"If I were attacked, or any of my family or friends, by a madman, let's say, then I don't know what my reaction would be. I can't say I'd be so enraged that I'd kill the man in revenge. My hope is that even under those circumstances my response would not be a violent one. But if you are asking me would I plan deliberately to execute someone in cold blood, however evil a person he - or for that matter she - may be, I don't know what my answer is to that. But..." he lifted his hand up to stop Nina interrupting him, "if you truly believed that the person you were planning to do away with was the Antichrist, only then would it be right."

"But, surely there's no question that it's always wrong to kill?" Nina interrupted fervently. "Even when He was threatened with a horrible

104

death, Jesus didn't falter. It didn't occur to Him to take their lives. How can there even be any discussion?"

"Then the life at stake was His own. But suppose they had threatened His Mother, would He have stood by and let them? Who knows? When your own life is at stake you may act in one way, when it's another's you may act quite differently. And if one person is murdering a whole race or country, what then? How many lives have to be lost to make someone evil enough to be executed?

"There are other ways..." Nina began.

"Indeed! It should be possible to stop someone by laws for example, which seem to be conspicuously lacking from this government. But if it isn't, do I then arm myself and shoot him knowing my soul is irreparably damaged? Or lost? I think each man must answer this when the time comes."

"And can you answer it, Thomas?" Erik pressed.

"No! I have to confess that I don't yet know how I would act."

"If a man deliberately lay down his own soul to save others," Erik theorized, "wouldn't that very act save it? Wouldn't it surely be interpreted on High as martyrdom? It's said the greatest thing a man can do is lay down his life for others, but surely laying down your soul is even greater?"

"Ah! Now you're getting into dangerous waters, opening the way for all criminals to excuse their crimes."

"No, because the criminal has only selfish desires; the truly noble man will have self-abnegation written on his heart. Your motives cannot be hidden from God."

"I always believed all Christians were pacifists!" Nina exclaimed, surprised at their discussion. "Or... are you merely examining ideas?" she added with dawning realization, after seeing the smiles on their faces.

"Of course!" Thomas roared. "All Christians are great theorists! When they're not pontificating that is! But," he added more seriously, "there is great latitude within the Bible for individual interpretation."

"Surely 'Thou shall not kill' means the end of the conversation?" Nina persisted.

"If we have this government for much longer," Ruth pointed out sadly, "I believe we shall all have to account to our consciences, and many of us may have to face, or even to make, that ultimate sacrifice."

"But you're still taking life even if you do it for the best of reasons. If, to overcome wickedness, you have to sin yourself, then you, too, have become evil."

"Each of us has to decide whether he will never at any cost take a life, or at what point another man's life is worth less than his own. What would you do Nina, if a man was about to murder one of your sisters?" Thomas was not just probing Nina's beliefs, he had become very fond of her over the few days they had all been together and now he wanted to test her mettle.

There was no hesitation in Nina's voice, only conviction. "I would try to restrain him, or try to put myself or some object between my sister and her attacker, but I wouldn't attempt to kill him."

"And if he succeeded?"

"I couldn't do any more for her, but I hope I'd try to make her assailant realize what he had done to his soul. My sisters have lived exemplary lives, and they have faith, so they are in no danger, but his..."

"Nina, you know that their salvation is a gift from God," Franz interrupted. "You must come down to earth some time! You live too much in a world that doesn't exist. There will come a time when even you will react instinctively to save either yourself or someone else. You have to recognize that you are human, too. It's one thing to try to live up to ideals, but quite another to avoid realities."

"Yes, indeed," Erik agreed, admiration for Nina's spirit clearly showing in his eyes, "but if she could she would be a saint, and the world is in sore need of them today."

"Saints, nonsense!" Claudia snorted, bored with the discussion and seeing a quick way out of it. "What we're really in need of today is a good marksman!"

"Many a true word is spoken in jest," Franz mused more to himself than out loud. Such thoughts had occurred to him, but on analysis, he had always acknowledged that it would be impossible to shoot one's leader. There was a thin line between killing in wartime and assassination in peacetime, which even the army generals could not cross. In their capacity as soldiers they could butcher any number of the enemy quite unmercifully, but none could stoop to become a cold-blooded assassin. To do that required a whole change in orientation, a giant step across a chasm dividing loyalty from treason.

Franz wished his brother were there. As an ex-army man he might have been able to explain their attitude more, but Otto had gone home along with Anna and Peter and his family. For the moment he was not privy to the group's existence.

Eleven

The following spring Nina married Erik; the ceremony was performed by Pastor Liebermann in his small local church, where Anna and Peter had married. Unlike that occasion, Nina and Erik only invited family and very close friends, and the church accommodated them all comfortably. A few locals hung about outside, waiting for the newlyweds to emerge, but there were no Hitler Youth or armed forces to worry about this time. Even Peter was away, unable to obtain leave. And other members of his family had used his absence to excuse themselves from the event, preferring to distance themselves while they could from the too liberal von Ludens. Anna herself was too heavily pregnant with her second child to attend.

Nina would rather have worn something simple and saved the money for her resistance work, but she had capitulated to both Hildegard and Erik, who insisted that this would be a very special day.

"It won't happen again in your lifetime, I won't allow it," Erik chuckled. "You'll want to remember this day forever. I don't want my wife getting married in dungarees; I want you at your prettiest, just for me. So put up with it and wear the beautiful dress your mother bought you."

"Just for you, then, sweetheart. And Mother."

When she walked down the aisle on her father's arm, beaming at everyone, she knew they had been right. She looked a picture of loveliness in a three-quarter length, white dress, with a layer of Brussels lace over its billowing skirt. A wide-brimmed white hat, short white velvet gloves, and svelte satin shoes added a highly fashionable finish to her outfit. As her bridal bouquet, she carried a few simple daffodils.

She felt nervous and excited in equal measure; nervous, because she wanted everything to be perfect for Erik and her mother, and excited, because she was on the threshold of a new life. She was about to leave home, and, like her sisters before her, she would have to learn to cope alone with a new set of servants, house-keeping, bringing up children and, above all, learn how to live in close proximity to a relative stranger.

Erik was enchanted with his bride-to-be as he took hold of her arm at the altar. They listened to the Pastor, made their vows, exchanged rings, then kissed and hugged each other. Nina had forbidden formality, so at the end of the service the family gathered round them, the men shaking hands and slapping each other on the back, the women kissing each other and wiping tears from their eyes. The Pastor, too, joined in; only a few in the family knew just how important he had become to Nina.

The newlyweds journeyed home round the walls of their estate in their parents' elegant, open carriage with the family crest on the side, unaware of anything or anyone else in the world. The straight-backed coachman drove the horse and his two charges under the entrance arch, down the long avenue lined with poplars, and round to the back terrace where tables had been set outside for the reception. There he opened the half-door and let down the steps, and Erik gently helped his wife down. They quickly went inside to freshen up and greet the rest of the party, who had followed by car to the front steps.

The house was filled with sunlight and spring flowers, which had been specially cultivated in the long greenhouses at the side of the main building. The perfume of a hundred hyacinths wafted through every room, enchanting each of the guests as they entered.

Nina was particularly keen to be at the front door, at the top of the steps, to greet her new mother-in-law, Ursula, whom she had met only a few days before, and Erik's sister Maria.

"Mother," she said, stepping forward with arms outstretched, enthusiastically using the term for the first time.

"Mother, or Ursula, whichever you prefer," Ursula replied, unable to resist the wide, inviting smile on Nina's face. She saw a young woman of charm and conviction, with something of her own campaigning character.

Unlike many a mother who can never admit that any girlfriend is good enough to marry their only son, Ursula thought Nina was Erik's perfect companion. She would fit into the Larsson clan like a glove.

"You must find some time to have a long chat with Maria," Ursula indicated her daughter. "Get to know each other." She looked around her carefully before adding, "She has more energy than I have these days, and has established contact with your cousin in America. She will be your contact in Sweden when you begin sending your refugees to us."

"We've already started. Some have gone to Switzerland and on to the States. We'll discuss everything when we're in Sweden next week," Nina responded, her arm stealing around Maria's shoulder in sisterly affection, "I'm so pleased that you will be one of my helpmates."

Nina and Erik took them through to the terrace, leaving Hildegard and Otto to greet the other guests at the door.

"Ah! How beautiful it is. This reminds me so much of home," Ursula said, "all those portraits of your family inside and your terrace faces out on to a fountain just like ours."

"Houses of this sort have a shared architectural heritage all around the Baltic," Maria said.

Nina flashed her a knowing smile. "We'll have to discuss that later, Maria. Ursula, I'd like you to meet my aunt. I think you two have a great deal in common. She'll be here any minute."

She had seen Alice walking with Anna and Claudia, and quickly pulled her aunt aside. Alice took Ursula and Maria under her wing, found them two seats beside her, and briskly began a conversation about how young people had changed since their day.

Thomas arrived chatting amiably with Johannes. He had been invited to the wedding as a friend, and was to be the main speaker at the reception. Once everyone was seated, he gave a short, unrehearsed speech with his usual gusto, over-praising Erik and Nina, giving Pastor Liebermann, Otto and Hildegard thanks for the ceremony and reception. He was about to launch into a political attack on Hitler when he caught Erik's eye and laughed. "I think that's enough, let's all tuck into Hildegard's wonderful spread and enjoy ourselves. But first, I think a toast to Erik and Nina, my two favourite people. A long life and happiness to you both. Though," he paused looking apologetically at Erik, "I think there may be some rough times ahead." He raised his glass, smiling jovially around him. Only a few understood he was talking about the future Hitler had in store for them and not the normal rocky road of marriage.

Hildegard nodded to the head caterer hired for the occasion and the servants began to bring in the food. Having married two daughters in quick succession, Hildegard had been more malleable to Nina's persuasive pleas to scale down the event, and to make the ritual meal afterwards far less abundant, in fact, no more than a normal Sunday family meal. Nina had noted how hard her mother worked at both Anna's and Claudia's marriages and how drained she had looked afterwards, and vowed she would not let her suffer so much at her own wedding.

"There, you see, Mother, you didn't have to do half the work, yet look how happy everyone is," Nina later said triumphantly, feeling it necessary to justify her cutbacks. They were all seated haphazardly at the long table, having dispensed with name cards and seating plans.

"I must admit, dear, that it does seem to have worked out rather well."

"As the Nazis are breaking with traditions left, right and centre," Nina responded, "I think we may be allowed to do the same."

"I'm disillusioned with both you and Claudia," Alice chipped in. "I quite expected one of you to disappear, get married, and then arrive home with a husband. The old ways may be fading away, but not fast enough for me. If anything, women are going backwards."

"I agree," Claudia said, heartily tucking into her duck a l'orange, a new speciality of the French caterers, "we're now supposed to stay at home and just produce babies."

Nina laughed merrily. "I can't see you doing that, Claudia, nor me, come to that."

Hildegard looked disappointed. "I hope I'm going to have a few more grandchildren. Anna's doing her bit, but it would be nice to have more."

"Eventually," Nina said briefly, with a little smile to her mother, and quickly changed the subject.

"Maria, tell me all about your home in Sweden. I'm really looking forward to our honeymoon there." She grasped Erik's hand and smiled sweetly at him, then bent towards her, listening intently to her answer.

Even whilst taking in what Maria was saying, she was noting how happy everyone was and knew she had been right to have a simple family affair. After the near riot at Anna's wedding and the secret sessions after Claudia's, Nina was only too glad to have an uncomplicated reception.

Two days later the happy couple left for their honeymoon in Sweden, with Ursula and Maria. Ensconced in Erik's top floor suite in the Larsson family home, they were at liberty to do what they liked. For three days they spent most of their time alone, in their rooms, walking together in the woods on the edge of the small family estate, enjoying each other's company, even eating alone. But it wasn't long before the nagging, urgent question of refugees from Germany claimed back their attention, and both of them began discussions with Ursula and Maria.

Maria was both charming and intelligent. Ursula was diplomatic and discreet, leaving them alone or offering advice now and then. Nina had never been so happy, and when they finished their planning they still had several days left for Erik to show her all the sights of Stockholm.

A woman of considerable character, Ursula Larsson had already cajoled and bullied her friends into offering their homes for Nina's refugees when needed.

"Darling," she said to one long-standing acquaintance, "you always wanted to learn another language, didn't you? You tell me which one, and I'll send you a couple of refugees who speak it."

Her friends couldn't refuse her charming way of twisting their arms.

The huge house near Stockholm in Sweden had been Ursula's ancestral home for several generations of lawyers and diplomats, and was full of portraits and mementoes of their past lives. Unable to maintain it on her own, but loath to leave it for a smaller, more manageable place with no history or atmosphere, she was grateful it was to be fully used once again.

It was to become Nina's headquarters in Sweden. When she was there, columns of refugees would trudge through it like weary birds of passage, resting briefly, but thankfully, on their way to America, England or to other homes in Sweden - anywhere they could wait out the insanity in their native countries. Later, as the conspirators swung into action, helping greater numbers of those threatened by their government, to emigrate or escape, the family would find exiles in all of its spacious corners, drawn together by the common bond of fear of the same dictator. It became a mini League of Nations, presided over by Nina, Ursula or Erik, with everyone attempting to live in some kind of domesticity, communicating with each other in half the languages of the Continent. Those who came under Nina's influence became fired by her enthusiasm for the idea of a united world, and left there later fuelled by the same optimism to return to their devastated homelands and make wars aberrations of the past.

Throughout the fortnight they stayed in Sweden, no one voiced the opinion that Nina might remain there while the situation in Germany was so unstable. It did not occur to her to seek sanctuary from the legalized anarchy that was gradually taking over her country. At the appointed time they returned home, Erik accepting that it was also to be his residency for the foreseeable future. But he believed the time would come when he would have to insist that Nina, and perhaps her family, move to Sweden for their own safety, until Hitler was removed.

He sensed that his new kinsfolk, like other Germans, were prepared to face any kind of future Hitler had in store for them and he was frightened for all of them. In some mystical, Wagnerian way Hitler represented their destiny and such was the power of this feeling in most Germans that even the most enlightened subconsciously gave credence to the old myths of Power and Glory or Death and Destruction. If he made them great, then it was their duty to keep him to the path and not allow him to degenerate into another ambitious, imperious dictator. If he dragged them down with him, then that was their destiny; but either way, they would be there to try to avert the carnage, Hitler's threatened Götterdämmerung.

Erik's view of their future was bleak.

After her marriage, Nina took everything in her stride, accepting that no one would expect her to be a capable manager right from the start. She fell pregnant immediately. Theirs was a happy world, with each partner prepared to give more than they took.

Claudia, on the other hand, was never bothered by other people's views; what they thought of her was not relevant. She shaped life to her own way of thinking and made things happen as she wanted. "I shall bring up my children as I see fit. I don't see why I should refer to Johannes, to see if he concurs or not. They will be my domain," she wilfully defended her opinion to Anna one day. "I will have produced them, so I think I have the right to the greatest say in their upbringing, don't you?"

To which Anna responded, "I think women know best how to raise children, but men are better at discipline."

"Not in my house!" Claudia retorted. "I'll discipline even Johan if I have to!"

Claudia's home was on the whole a happy, carefree one. She left all the domestic arrangements to her housekeeper and other servants. Johannes indulged her, knowing that one day she would become a woman rather than the self-centred child she could sometimes be. He took a long-term view, visualising a depressing future for them all under the Third Reich; Claudia would need to keep her spirit strong for the years ahead.

Nina and Claudia and their husbands, now mixing within various official and unofficial circles, listened to the reports about the state of Hitler's mind or about impending war, and stored them up to be transmitted to their group. Claudia's training in history gave her an understanding of how to judge the value of evidence, and this now became an invaluable tool in her dealings with some of the devious, ambitious, secretive people in positions of power.

Domestic duties, parties ... became rarer for Claudia and Nina; they had their eyes, minds and hearts on other matters. Marriages and children assumed less importance when their whole world was in turmoil.

Anna's most urgent tasks were to maintain her image and ensure that her new family's standards did not decline. There were certain traditions to be maintained, and her husband expected her to be as capable a hostess, right from the start of their marriage, as his mother had become after years of experience. His concept of how to bring up the children, and build their characters, slowly became hers.

She also had the additional stress of juggling two opposing ideologies in her daily life, mentally walking a tightrope between them; not accepting Nazi ideas, but not dismissing them entirely either. And she had to learn to conform to the opinions of Peter's family, whether she genuinely believed them or not. Whilst Anna was inward looking, living in her small, enclosed domesticity, she forever had to entertain Peter's friends and colleagues. Rumours to Anna were always just that and she thought no more about them, unless they were connected in some way with the movements of Peter's regiment. If they had no immediate effect on her or her family she would try to ignore them, as did most Germans.

All the family were trying to live normal lives in abnormal times, all hoping each day that whatever Hitler did he would do it in such a way that they could hold up their heads again and be the proud nation they had once been. What did speculation matter in the end if the country achieved stability and avenged their former dishonour? If he could bring that about, then Hitler had his country's approval for any of his deeds; the end would justify all of his means.

Twelve

It was raining hard and Otto was comfortably ensconced in his favourite armchair smoking his pipe, and Hildegard was embroidering her initials on to a small handkerchief. They were sitting in the drawing room waiting to see if the rain would ease so that Anna and the children could take Bismarck out for a run in the grounds. The children were both obediently quiet; four year old Kurt was struggling to read a few words in a book and Helga was tracing round the pictures with her finger, explaining very quietly to anyone who might be listening what the pictures were. Now and then Kurt would look at her and frown, but tolerantly said nothing.

"Hitler's been very fortunate so far," Otto remarked to Anna.

"I said that to Peter, but he didn't think so. He said the British agreed we should get back the land we lost after the war and expand our armed forces again. So he believes they are on our side."

"He was still lucky France didn't attack, especially when we took back the Rhineland. I can't understand why they didn't."

"Peter's sure France has lost the will to fight." She glanced down at Helga, sitting at her feet. "Yes, dear, that's a ball, and that's a B, the first letter of ball," she explained aside to Helga, bending down to point out the correct letter; her mind split between her conversation and Helga's activity on the floor.

"Never underestimate your enemy! That can be fatal," Hildegard suggested.

"That's right!" Otto agreed, "There might be something in what you say. France was devastated after the Great War and certainly didn't want any more fighting after that. What does Peter have to say about Czechoslovakia?"

"He says the Czechs will come to an agreement over the Germans in the Sudetenland."

"For Heavens sake, what are the British doing? Giving in to him? I thought they were a courageous nation, not cowards," Hildegard flung at Otto as though the international situation was his fault. "Mind you, something ought to be done for those poor Germans stuck there, at the mercy of the Czechs."

Kurt looked up at his grandfather, and cheekily tickled the palm of Otto's hand, which was dangling over the side of his armchair.

Otto absent-mindedly caught a strand of Kurt's straight, blond hair, and curled it around his fingers. "If Britain does accept that, then they are beginning to give in to Hitler. If he takes the Sudetenland, it won't stop there. He'll take the whole of Czechoslovakia sometime. Then what? We're still stuck out here, cut off from the rest of Germany. What if he goes for The Corridor and tries to reunite us? What will we do? I know I shouldn't accept it, because it goes against Versailles, but I live here, I've been inconvenienced as much as other Germans who lost their farms and their homes when they were given to the Poles. We'll be cheering in the streets along with the rest if he does take The Corridor back."

Kurt pulled at Otto's fingers in his hair. "Let go, Grandad!" He cried.

Otto smiled down at his grandson, unaware that he had been hurting the boy.

"No you won't, Otto," Hildegard said. "Pass me the red silk, will you, Anna dear? You won't, because you know what it might lead to. There's nothing any of us can do about it, is there? So we should all just try and make the best of it."

"Can't Irmgard do that for you, Mother?" Anna asked as she passed the silk across.

"No, dear, she can't embroider the Hs the way I like them!"

"That's just the trouble," Otto said, a little despairingly, "too many of us making the best of it. All putting up with it. Whatever 'it' is. Perhaps, if we did complain, Hitler would have to stop. But you know what the real trouble is? People want him to continue, they like what he's doing." He heaved himself out of his chair, swung Kurt up off the floor and sat him on his shoulders. "Now this is what we do with young German soldiers," he said, and began a slow jog around the room. Kurt giggled, holding one arm around Otto's neck and the other hand hitting him as though he was whipping his horse.

Helga jumped up, stretching her arms in the air towards her grandfather. "Me, too!" She insisted.

"Grandpa can't manage you both at the same time," Hildegard put her sewing down. "Come and sit on my lap until Kurt's had enough. Then perhaps Grandpa will give you a ride."

"I'm not sure I'll have enough puff for both," Otto said, trotting gamely onwards.

Anna got up and went to the window to check if the rain had stopped. "Children are so easily pleased, aren't they?" she remarked. "If only politicians were the same."

Hildegard bumped Helga up and down on her lap in time with Otto, who was still plodding around the room, his breathing becoming more laboured.

Anna studied her children. "If there is to be war I thank God that my two …" she patted her now heavily distended abdomen, "three, won't be old enough to take any part in it."

"You mustn't even mention it," Hildegard scolded her, motioning towards Kurt. Armed conflict was still a distant worry. For now, her grandchildren took centre stage. "Little ears," she added in a whisper. "We don't want him asking questions at his age. And anyway, you said Peter didn't think there would be one."

"Let's hope he's right."

Anna suddenly screamed and doubled up, clutching at her abdomen. "Mother!"

"She's going into labour, Otto. Call the doctor immediately; it'll be quick this time."

Ullrich was born at his grandparents' home within a few hours, a healthy boy with black eyes like his father.

And not long afterwards Europe was heading for the brink of war.

A year after their marriage, Claudia and Johannes moved to Berlin from Pomerania. A colleague had helped Johannes apply for a position in the Abwehr: the secret intelligence section of the Army. It had meant joining the Nazi Party, which went against the grain, but he thought it worthwhile in order to be right in the thick of it. It had been a difficult decision for him, but the conspirators had needed someone in a position to know when new laws might mean changes in documentation. And Johannes had seen it as an opportunity not to be drafted into the army.

Claudia had been heavily pregnant when they moved into their small, detached house in the suburbs. Her baby boy Klaus was born after a long exhausting labour. Five days later she was still in need of rest.

Johannes put down the phone and turned to his wife who was relaxing on a sofa. "I hate all this … Always having to speak in code, hiding things, because they might be listening in." He carefully tucked a blanket around her legs. "There's a sharp draft in here. It feels like winter, and you need to keep warm."

Claudia was holding little Klaus, studying him intently, wondering how long it would take before she discovered her mothering instinct. 'It isn't so instinctive,' she thought, 'or I'd feel it now.'

"Did you get the gist of my conversation with Erik?" he asked as he fussed around her, making sure she was comfortable, and making clucking noises at Klaus who stared back at him with big blue eyes.

"Yes. When are they coming over to see our new home?" Claudia found his ministrations annoying and wished he would stop.

"Erik's trying to get time off."

"I hope they'll stay a couple of weeks. I'm so glad we're in Berlin now. We'll have lots to show Nina. Places to go. She'll love the lakes."

"There will be a lot to talk about. We have to decide what our response to the new laws is going to be. I'll check if anyone else can come at the same time."

"Well?" Thomas boomed along the hall towards Claudia. He glimpsed her sitting on the settee, holding a bundle in her arms. "How's the new mother?" He strode towards her and bent to kiss her cheek. "He's a feisty little thing, isn't he?" He shook the little finger that baby Klaus had grabbed in a vice-like grip.

"I'm fine, Thomas, thank you," Claudia smiled up at him.

The nurse came in to check on her patient. She extricated Thomas's finger, gave him a sharp look, and took the baby away. As soon as she had gone, Claudia shook off the blanket and got up. "I think it's about time I rejoined the human race."

Both Johannes and Thomas reached down to help her.

"Are you sure you're ready?" Johannes asked dutifully, yet relieved that Claudia seemed to be returning to normal.

"There's too much to discuss for me to play the invalid any longer. I've had five days doing nothing. That's enough for me."

"Is anyone else coming?" Thomas asked.

"Erik and Nina will be here any minute now. They said they'd be in time for lunch," Johannes responded, "and Franz and Ruth will be joining us tomorrow. Between the seven of us we can pass on messages to everyone else."

The doorbell rang and the maid scurried along to answer it.

"Erik!" Thomas shook his hand warmly, and embraced Nina, while Johannes took their coats and bags. "Wonderful to see you both again."

After greeting Johannes, Nina rushed to embrace Claudia and see her new nephew.

"The nurse has just put him to bed," Claudia said.

"Then if I can't coo over him, tell me how *you* are? I've got to go through it in a few months so I need to know all about it." She patted her stomach, which as yet hardly revealed her pregnancy. "Imagine, all three of us giving birth within a few months of each other!" They chattered away for a few minutes, getting all the talk about motherhood out of the way before joining the three men in the dining room.

A cold buffet had been set out on the long table in the dining room.

"It looks as though war has been averted…" Thomas began.

"Which is just as well since none of us would have been prepared for one," Claudia interrupted. "Wine, Thomas?"

"Red, please, Claudia."

"Where are the servants, Claudia?" Nina asked, to be certain no one would overhear their conversation.

"We've told them we'll help ourselves. They'll be in the kitchen, I expect."

Johannes had already discreetly dismissed their two servants, a maid and a cook who between them had to do everything in the house. He did not trust them; they could easily inform the authorities if they heard anything that sounded anti-Hitler, and on the strength of one person's testimony, guilty or innocent, people were being sent to concentration camps. Claudia had wanted to do without servants at all, but Hildegard had insisted that until her daughter had recovered she must have some domestics, and she had sent over one of her own maids.

When they had closed the door securely, Johannes answered Thomas, "It isn't over yet, though. Suppose the British and French get tough with Hitler?"

"They didn't when he walked into Austria, did they?" Claudia snorted. "Why would they now?"

"No, that's true," Thomas said. "They made all the right noises, but did nothing. And Czechoslovakia is a small, little known state. I think they'll do everything they can to avoid war."

"What if it does break out, though?"

"According to Anna, Peter says the army is ready," Claudia said.

"That's the problem, the armed forces," Thomas suggested, between mouthfuls. "You know the resistance group already has an entire government-in-waiting, don't you?"

Johannes double-checked that the door was closed; Thomas had a loud voice and seldom thought it necessary to lower it.

Claudia looked up, her eyes wide with surprise. Johannes had told her nothing. "You mean if Hitler is killed there's an opposition ready to take over?"

"They only mean to have him declared insane or put his henchmen behind bars, and take over all the main administrative posts immediately."

"The trouble is, as I hear it in the Abwehr," Johannes said, "there's a deep split in thinking between those who believe Hitler's every whim should be obeyed and those who want him stopped at all costs."

"So there's no general agreement," Erik suggested.

"Literally," Johannes smiled at Erik's unintended pun. "Amongst the generals there is any number of different views. Some have organized a putsch against him to begin as soon as he moves troops into Czechoslovakia," Johannes said.

Nina had been concentrating on her food, "But what happens if England and France succeed in appeasing Hitler? Where does that leave us?"

"Thwarted!" Thomas sighed. "If he goes in we have a legitimate reason to depose him: he's attacking another nation. The international community will see that as justification for removing him. But, and it's a big but, if there is no blood spilt we have insufficient cause."

"If you get shot of Hitler anyway, whether or not he goes into Czechoslovakia, the German people will think their army has stabbed him in the back just at the point when he was doing so well," Erik countered.

"Exactly as they thought after the Great War," Johannes agreed.

"That's really our problem, isn't it?" Nina said.

"Yes," Thomas threw up his hands in disgust. "They'll call it treason."

"It really is extraordinary how so many have fallen under his spell," Erik said.

"Not really," Claudia said, "Goebbels is a talented propagandist. A horrible little man, but brilliant at what he does. I'll bet his next move will be to make Chamberlain out to be the villain of the talks that have been going on between him and Hitler."

Nina looked at Claudia with renewed respect, "You might be right. From Hitler's point of view Chamberlain has stopped him from taking the whole of Czechoslovakia. Yet all Chamberlain has been after is peace for Europe." After a short pause, she added, "So, what happens now? Are the generals going to continue with their plan?"

A sudden frenzied knock on the door made them all freeze in their tracks. For a moment they had forgotten that they were talking treasonably; now they were reminded of just how dangerous a position they were all in. The maid pushed open the door without waiting for Johannes to give his permission.

"Excuse me, sir, madam," she said, with a slight curtsey to the guests, her eyes afire. "Sir, we thought you should know…" she pointed towards the radio on a side table, unable to explain what had excited her so much.

Johannes asked, "Something being broadcast?" Relieved, he strode quickly across to turn it on, dismissing the maid with a brief wave of his hand, and ensuring she shut the door properly behind her.

They listened in stunned silence as the news bulletin informed them that England and France had finally agreed to allow the Germans to occupy the Sudeten part of Czechoslovakia. The bulletin made it sound as if it was to be done in order to protect the Germans living there.

"They've invited Hitler to walk into Czechoslovakia, even if it is only a small part." Thomas leaned back in his chair, dumfounded, "the British and French have lost their heads."

"Or their courage," Erik said.

"Don't they realize that he won't stop there?" Claudia snapped, as if about to burst into tears. "He wants all of that country, not just the German area."

"They haven't averted war," Nina shook her head sadly, "they've just put it off. Sooner or later he'll turn against Britain, too."

"Well!" Johannes said, "The generals have no justification now for taking action against Hitler. You saw the maid's face, didn't you? I imagine the whole German nation feels the same way she does."

"They like it," Erik agreed. "As far as they're concerned Hitler's getting all the Germans into one great Reich. The people still love him. But do the generals?" He looked at Johannes.

"I'll find out how they've taken it tomorrow." Johannes answered, putting his arm around Claudia, trying to calm her down. Childbirth had left her rather more emotional than usual.

Nina shifted uneasily in her seat, her unborn child suddenly becoming a future burden as she thought out what the news might do to her escape line and how she might have to be fit and healthy soon after the birth to do all the necessary work. "Do you think we will have to help Czech Jews to escape as well?"

Just a few weeks later Nina was aboard an early morning Swedish ferry, escorting a Jewish family to Stockholm and freedom. The boat was in international waters and Nina relaxed. If anything happened they would be nearer to Sweden than Germany. She had a Swedish passport and felt personally safe each time, but the refugees weren't out of danger until they docked. She always tried to book passage on Swedish boats in the middle of the night when the customs officers on the German side were at their least zealous, and the refugees might slip past more easily. They were never safe if it were a German boat.

She smiled at the husband and wife she had escorted all the way from Elbing and put her arms around their two small, bewildered children. Their faces were drawn and they couldn't conceal their fear from Nina, though they were making brave attempts to appear normal to the other passengers: trying to smile and make small talk.

"It's all right," she reassured them, "you really are free now. We've been in Swedish waters for some time. We'll dock in less than an hour."

The man took her hands, kissing them; his wife had tears streaming down her face as she embraced Nina. "Thank you, thank you..." She hugged her children. "We're safe, little ones, safe," she wept, wiped her eyes, wept again, and tried to hide her face from curious passengers.

They vigorously breathed in the cold, early morning air as though it was the beginning of spring, and gazed excitedly as the Swedish islands glided past, and they rapidly approached the port.

Their strain was manifest, and she felt sorry for them, but one tiny part of her harboured the traitorous thought that they exaggerated the threat to themselves. After all, she hadn't seen much violence against Jews lately either in Berlin or East Prussia. Were the Jews really still in such danger or had everything settled down? She was well aware that their newspapers were filled with propaganda and looked forward to reading the free press in Stockholm. But that tiny, niggling doubt continued to exist at the back of her mind.

When they arrived, Maria was waiting in Ursula's car to take them home. "You shouldn't be doing this work in your condition, Nina," she scolded as they settled themselves into the front seats. The husband and wife each had a child on their lap in the back and for the first time in the entire trip the children began to chatter and laugh.

Nina knew Maria was right, but it had to be done.

Maria was quiet during the drive and it was not until they arrived home and Ursula had taken the family to their new temporary quarters that she told Nina the disturbing news about *Kristallnacht*.

"I didn't want to say anything in front of them, it might have upset them and they've had enough to contend with, haven't they?" She excused her silence in the car.

During the night, even as Nina had been taking them to safety on board the ferry, many synagogues were burnt to the ground, thousands of Jews were forced out of their homes, rounded up or killed. Jewish shops were totally demolished or had their windows smashed to smithereens and goods thrown out onto the pavements. In one terrible night of mindless violence, which was to be known as *Kristallnacht*, Jews learned what could happen to them in the future.

Nina groaned in anguish, remembering her doubts. How could she have thought they were exaggerating?

In Sweden, she rapidly regained her equilibrium, and realized just how much she had been deceived by the propaganda. It was bliss to live in a normal land for a while and she put off thinking of the return journey, which was like contemplating a move to another planet. She knew she had to trust her own instincts and not listen to their dishonest newscasts.

She telephoned Thomas and learned that the Steiners had remained physically unmolested only due to Otto's intervention. He explained that Otto had approached Berthold Braun, still the Chief of Police and now a locally important Nazi, to see if something could be done. Otto had always been fair towards him and it flattered Berthold's vanity that his past overlord should now be coming to him seeking a favour. He did not tell Otto that because of the numbers of Jews who had been rounded up, all the local jails were full and there was nowhere else to hold them; they would have been returned home anyway.

Meanwhile, one of the Steiner family's stores had been burnt to the ground, with its hidden cache of money and other valuables, and the others had been broken into and ransacked. But they still had their home.

Peter saw the wider scenario rather than the individual parts, and for him, resettlement of Jews into another area would solve many problems both for the Jewish and gentile races. He favoured the separate existence of different ethnic groups, but he also could see nothing wrong with leaving the Steiners where they were for a while longer; it would not change the overall strategy. He had a lot of respect for his father-in-law, but unknown to Otto, this had created conflict for the young army officer who had been approached by his superior.

"My father-in-law is old fashioned; it's hard to change him now, but he has a lot of influence in this area. That's how Herr Braun became involved. Can we not compromise on this occasion and leave the Steiner family where they are? What does one Jewish family matter?" He reasoned with his superior.

"Is your father-in-law a Jew lover?"

"No!" Peter did not want to be associated with anyone who liked, or even tolerated Jews. "No, of course not; but the Steiner boy helps him on his estate, with the harvests and other vital work. While they are useful to him he will want to leave them alone. If we resettle them amongst the last Jews to go we won't upset one of our most influential families, and the harvest will be safe."

A thought had occurred to Peter as he spoke, "The Steiner family could actually be useful to us..."

"No Jew is useful."

"Not in the long run, no," Peter acquiesced. "But Mr. Steiner knows a lot of local residents."

"So how will that help us?"

"As an informer. If he's told to keep his ears and eyes open for Communist agitators, for example. He's well known to be fanatically anti-Communist."

"A strange Jew, to be against the very people who support him. Very well! See to it. Inform him that unless he gives us names, his wife and..." He paused as he studied the file, "his two children will be taken."

Leon had no choice, with his family's future at stake, but it was not a hard decision for him. Over the years he had decided who was a Communist and who wasn't. Over the next few weeks, whenever the authorities leaned on him hard, he gave them another name and he continued to survive in one shop and a small flat above it.

Although he would never admit it to his own family and especially not to Otto, his attitude towards the Nazis had begun to change. Outwardly he maintained his former opinions, but he had finally seen the extent of the danger they were in, and began to cast around for ways to escape.

The other two shops, and three small farms, which he had bought from property owners leaving East Prussia, were taken from him with no compensation. He had most of his money hidden in his home, and some under the floorboards of the shops he had lost. His position was now uncomfortable, but while he still had sufficient funds to bribe his way out of trouble, it was secure. However, he now kept his valuables closer to himself and Berthe, and was on the point of asking Otto, the only gentile who would even speak to him, whether he could secure some of his assets in an account under another name.

Before Leon had time to act the whole family was rounded up again and simply disappeared.

The Steiners, like others, learned too late that Hitler had meant what he wrote in *Mein Kampf*. Against Jews anything was now possible; no one stood up for them. Money, jewellery, shops, homes, farms, banks, were all simply plundered by the state. The luckier Jews were those who were taken as a whole family: they at least knew what had befallen their loved ones. Others were stolen from off the streets or their work places. Some had gone out to buy a loaf of bread and never came back.

Nina was staying with her mother after returning from Sweden when she heard the Steiners had vanished. "Mother, I feel as though I personally let them down. I don't know what to believe has happened to them."

"I expect they've been sent to one of the new places set aside for them. They'll be with their own kind," Hildegard responded, more concerned about her daughter's distraught feelings than with the Steiners' futures.

"I don't believe that. I'm sure there's something awful occuring."

"Don't be silly, dear. What could be going on? They're safe in some new life by now."

"But you've seen how the Nazis round them up. They're quite brutal. It suggests they don't really care. I don't like it. It makes me feel like a traitor to Anneliese. I should have done something."

"Why would the Nazis allow people to take their luggage with them? What you say doesn't make any sense. I don't like what they're doing, the Steiners should be compensated for their property, but I'm sure the whole family is being well looked after. Don't worry about them any more."

Nina knew her mother meant 'don't worry *me* about them any more,' and felt a little afraid for her. She was joining the other comfortably off women in closing her mind to what was taking place around her.

When Hildegard had left the room, Nina confided her thoughts to her father. "I didn't even like the Steiners very much, did you?"

"No," Otto conceded. "He was a pompous, arrogant little man, but that was no reason to treat him and his family like that."

"Do you believe they are safe and sound in some new life?"

Otto remained tight-lipped. He knew in his heart that Nina was right; something very ugly and alien had entered their land. But he did not want to voice his concerns to the women. "Your mother's right, they'll be somewhere secure."

The world's outraged reaction to the deeds of that November was totally ignored by the Nazis. Apart from a few intelligent, farsighted Germans, there were not many inside the country who understood that from that night an ominous new factor had burst upon their land. Until then the bullying, beatings, burnings and killings had been carried out by small groups, seemingly unconnected to or even disowned by Hitler. But on *Kristallnacht* Hitler himself had ordered the 'disorders' and had not forbidden genocide to take place. The head of state had become the butcher. Those near Hitler watched helplessly as his megalomania took over. The iron grip of totalitarianism now controlled the land.

Thirteen

Erik had abandoned his intention to enter the church long ago when he saw the direction in which Germany was moving. Instead, he remained in the diplomatic sphere where he had access to documents and official stamps. The chaotic state of Europe and the menacing stance of Germany meant that he could no longer pursue any kind of personal life. His first posting was to Lübeck in northern Germany.

Nina knew that he had applied for a new post as soon as they had arrived in Germany from his London branch. She was inured to the atmosphere in Germany, but Erik had been shocked by it. The differences between living in the tightly controlled Lübeck and free London or Stockholm were transparent. He quickly perceived that Hitler was contemplating expanding his country's borders to include the rest of Czechoslovakia. Poland and Hungary were the next two obvious targets. He reasoned that if he were already established in one of them he would be in a better position to support the local population, and they would be more likely to trust him if he were there before the Germans arrived.

"Nina, if I'm eventually transferred to Poland or Hungary, will you come with me?" he asked tentatively.

He had little hope; he was aware that she would stay with the resistance group, even though their son, Dieter, had been born in Sweden on her last journey there.

"Sweetheart, I'll come for a few days at a time if I can. But the work here is important, too. I don't want to be away from you for long, but... Do you really have to go?" She flung her arms around him, "You'll have to come home to East Prussia sometimes, to see your son. And me!"

He held her gently, kissing her hair. She still looked frail after the birth; he wanted to have her with him all the time, and take care of her. They might have so little time together.

"We shall have to learn some Polish. If Hitler goes for the Corridor, I shall have Poles to hide," she said, thoughtfully.

"I think it's when rather than if. Taking back the Rhineland and Anschluss with Austria was just practice. Poland and Russia are to be the main events, don't you think?"

"Yes, I know," Nina responded quietly. "Right now, he's just concentrating all the Germans in Europe into one great country, but when he's finished... Erik, I'm frightened. He won't be content with just a greater Germany, will he?"

Erik and Nina had no secrets. Now he spoke his mind even though it would alarm her even more. "No. I think he's made it very clear he wants the east. He'll go for Russia, and to get that he has to take Poland, Hungary, even Romania and Bulgaria. He can't afford to have any enemies behind his lines. Unless France acts now the whole of Europe is endangered." He paused and his eyes withdrew. "Even Sweden isn't safe."

Early in nineteen thirty-nine Erik was transferred to Warsaw, while Nina went home to East Prussia with Dieter.

Peter, like Erik, could not follow any family life; the Wehrmacht called, with the insistence of the audacious. With reckless speed the German army was growing into a large, well-equipped, bravura organization of dedicated and fearless young men and Peter wanted to be in the forefront.

After a dinner party at his home, the men, separated briefly from the ladies in time honoured tradition, their field grey exchanged for stylish dinner suits, conversed amongst themselves, all of one accord, united by adverse world opinion.

"You see," he explained to a few colleagues, "it is so important for us never to be weaker than our enemies again. If we'd only had more guns and tanks in the last war we would have won."

"If they hadn't sold us out, you mean!" Captain Schulz suggested, sourly.

"Yes! This time we'll have so many tanks and trained men that our enemies will have no chance at all! We must never again be pressured into a position where we can be so humiliated!" Peter raised his glass. "Here's to Germany's strength and independence!"

They raised their drinks and drank in great gulps, and then self-importantly emulating the thousands who had gone before them they threw their glasses into the big stone fireplace.

"We have another *Kristallnacht*, ja?" Captain Schulz laughed as he added his to the hundreds of pieces of shattered crystal covering the hearth.

Peter knew Anna would be infuriated by their actions, and tomorrow he could look forward to a piece of her mind. He rather liked her angry outbursts, he found her more interesting and thoughtful.

Peter was proud of what they had achieved right under the noses of the French and British. Yet, as he looked around him at his friends, and joined in the back-slapping camaraderie, he knew in one small corner of his mind that all was not right. Had he not met and married into the von Luden family perhaps all would have been well, his past and future blending into one long continuous tradition, unchangeable and accepted by everyone as normal. But his new family caused him to question himself. Why was it that he felt slightly ill at ease, he wondered, as he contemplated his friends and participated in their antics?

He brushed the thoughts aside as he always did, but each time they would arise again, quicker than before. Some day he would be forced to examine them, but not now.

Johannes, like Erik, immersed himself into finding out as much as he could about how the Abwehr worked. If the conspirators could say to the SS that their actions were illegal and quote the Nazi law itself, they stood a chance of rescuing more people, or even of saving themselves.

"As a junior officer, I have a chance to get close to the powers that be," Johannes explained to Claudia. "That's where we really need someone, right at the heart of the intelligence system. It's a good place to learn about actions before they happen. And from what I've heard..." he was about to say that he had discovered a small anti-Hitler group within his new unit, but thought better of it. He passed on a great deal of information to Nina, but withheld most of it from Claudia. She was still too outspoken with her opinions, and she might just let something slip.

Claudia found Berlin thrilling, exciting and innovative, with its artistic originality and experimentation, which outsiders called decadence. Now it was at the centre of a new Nazi period of innovation: the streets and parks were full of colourful pageantry, rallies, torchlight parades, and fireworks.

She found herself plunged back into socialising, with or without her husband. But, despite the exhilaration it offered, she always longed to be amongst her honest and down to earth family and friends in the provinces; Berliners were too shallow. It was an exciting place to visit, but not to live in permanently.

"The problem is, Claudia, if we hadn't come to Berlin, and war breaks out, I might be sent to the front instead, wherever that may be!" Johannes said. "I'm a lawyer by training, not a soldier. How can I fight anyone?" He smiled at the thought. "Anyway, you are keen on investigating new places and you enjoy the parties, don't you? The men and women at those events are the ones in the positions of power, after all."

"The women are so superficial. All they want to talk about is babies or their servants! It's such a bore!"

"Some of them actually know Hitler, Claudia, think about that. Your job is to look as though you're enjoying yourself and to find out anything you can, and give the impression that you couldn't care less about knowing it. Going to parties is hardly a sacrifice, is it?"

Johannes was normally patient with her, but sometimes she became too self-centred even for his tolerance. "As for my part, I can't say I shall like being in the Abwehr, but at least I won't be called upon to kill anyone. I haven't the least desire to discover how I would answer Thomas's riddle."

Claudia had a rare ability to seem at home with almost anyone, even those with whom she disagreed. Her temperament was so open that she was unable to disguise her own thoughts, but her directness was tempered by her good nature. She might sometimes voice some opposition to Hitler, but her eyes were always twinkling, her laughter was never far from the surface, and people were disarmed by her. They might not like her viewpoint, but they liked her.

In Berlin, she rapidly became as much a fount of information as Johannes: his came straight from the horse's mouth, Claudia's came from their wives and secretaries. And Claudia found that she gained a different kind of pleasure from these occasions. "I like to test my wits, my cunning if you like. I have to think quickly to outwit the other person."

"Take care, Claudia!" Johannes cautioned. "It isn't a game; we're not in some kind of competition. Some of those in power are very astute. Don't give them any chance to put two and two together."

"Oh, I don't, I won't..."

He reached out and pulled her close, hugging her tightly, afraid of her excessive courage. "You must think before you speak, sweetheart. And, God forbid, if the worst happens and they..." He choked at his thoughts, "If they torture you, then my life, your son's, and all of your family may be at risk. These are dangerous, powerful people. For all our sakes," he appealed, "don't get on their wrong side, Claudia!"

Fourteen

Even before the war began, members of the resistance were beginning to separate into quite distinct groups. The Kreisau Circle were opposed to using any form of violence, and contented themselves with talking, and planning a new government consisting of their own people, to be installed after Hitler was deposed. Thomas was heavily involved with them and Johannes was privy to many of their thoughts and ideas.

A second major resistance group was not satisfied merely to discuss politics. They were prepared to risk their own lives in order to rid the country of 'the little Bohemian Corporal'. They made many attempts on his life, most of them unnoticed by Hitler or his bodyguards. Hitler's genius at changing the plans for his daily routine played havoc with the plotters, who were often left with bombs primed and ready to go off just as Hitler left the scene. Thomas had also become a member, though he had not yet taken any active part. Again, Johannes in the Abwehr, was a trusted listener to some of their discussions. Apart from him, no member of the von Luden family belonged to either faction.

Johannes had established himself in the Abwehr as someone sympathetic to both groups, but who was unwilling to become active himself. They had access to secret information, which emanated directly from Hitler's headquarters, and which Johannes quietly passed on when he could. He had no intention of sabotaging the government or even of disobeying it; he merely wanted to be one step ahead. In order to assist Jews to escape he needed to be prepared for changes in documentation.

Thomas was the only man who wavered between thought and action, with a foot in each camp. The pacifists were later a little perturbed by the Prussian officer corps's constant attempts on Hitler's life, certain that they would end in the eventual discovery of them all. At the very least they were undermining the pacifists' efforts to gain credibility in the eyes of

Britain and America, with whom they were in contact through Switzerland and Stockholm.

For all of them, the decision to join any kind of resistance group was hard, and cut their conscience to the quick; it was paramount to becoming a traitor.

On a beautiful summer morning in late June, nineteen thirty-nine, the family and friends in the escape group came together for one of their regular meetings. They sat on deck chairs in dappled sunlight beneath the fruit trees on the edge of Franz's orchard in Pomerania. Away from the house and the ears of the staff, their voices low and conspiratorial, their eyes constantly surveying the garden around them for intruders. They arrived at different times, and Franz had made spare keys to the large wooden gate in the estate wall so some could go straight to the orchard. That way the servants did not know who were gathered there.

The breeze was light and warm and the place full of insects, buzzing with life. "It's now certain that Hitler will quite deliberately precipitate a war with England!" Johannes dropped his bombshell, ignoring the gasps around him, "He wants a confrontation and he knows that this time they won't turn away. If he goes for Poland, England and France will have no choice but to commit themselves. They've tied themselves up with treaty obligations."

"But why should he be actively seeking a war with England?" Franz asked. "They've shown themselves only too willing to avoid conflict at any cost. Providing we only go for The Corridor and not the rest of Poland, won't they simply accept it?"

"Apparently, Hitler doesn't believe the English can agree to another peaceful settlement, so he wants to take the initiative and force them into a situation he's convinced we must win, because we're ready and they're not. To strike first puts us at an enormous advantage. But they say Hitler doesn't want an actual physical war with Britain, he would like to finish his dispute with Poland quickly and then the English will be so impressed they'll join us in a battle against Communism. I'm not sure they're right. Personally, I think Hitler's too astute to look for a real fight with England."

"Who is this coming from? Can we trust this information?" Franz demanded.

"They have the ear of Hitler, and they're not the types to exaggerate or try to impress. They believe it's true."

"Anna said Peter thought there'd be a war and we would win, because we're much stronger, we have more men and equipment," Nina conceded.

"Some of them don't think it will actually come to that," Johannes said, "but anyway the new blitzkrieg tactics mean we're likely to win before the other side has even mobilized."

"A modern von Schlieffen plan, Johannes?" Franz nodded in agreement.

"Mustn't make the same mistake as we did in the Great War, though," Johannes warned. "We thought the Russians would take sixty days to mobilize and they took much less."

"What about Russia? I know we're strong now, but are we really powerful enough to take on England, Poland, probably France, and Russia?" Claudia asked. "It's almost certain to mean a war on two fronts isn't it?"

"Russia is being taken care of diplomatically. If you knew the negotiations going on behind the scenes between Berlin and Moscow, you'd be amazed. Russia wants to regain her old territory, too. It looks like there'll be some kind of non-alliance pact signed soon, then Hitler will feel free to tackle England."

"What, between Hitler and Stalin?" Franz was astonished.

"Yes."

"Well, what an unlikely pair! I can't believe that will ever happen."

"Yes, but it seems it might." Johannes turned to Claudia. "He's too aware of history to commit himself to two fronts at the same time, he remembers what happened to Napoleon. There's no turning back now."

"It would be ironic if having failed to go to war over Czechoslovakia - a country that we had no right or justification to invade - England does battle with us over the Polish Corridor, which we have every right and justification to retake from the Poles!" Franz mused.

"Are you absolutely sure of all this, Johan?" Claudia asked, voicing the disbelief of them all. He had told her nothing about it before.

"There are many more like us than we're aware of, some in quite important positions. Even information from Hitler's secret meetings filters through to us from some of the Chiefs of Staff who are on our side. There are generals, and one or two even above them, who are most unhappy about Hitler. But they've sworn allegiance to him and can't go against him, unless he issues commands that are clearly suicidal. Even then I wonder if they would disobey the order."

"I have a friend in the army," Hermann, a friend of Johannes said, "and he has never sworn the oath!"

"How in heaven's name did he manage to get away with that?"

"I can't remember where he was stationed, but he was on a charge at the time, and when he came out of the military prison ten days later he'd missed it. Then he was moved to another camp where they'd all already done it."

"So he won't have to worry about his conscience. Lucky man! Can't we recruit him?" Erik said jocularly.

"The less you know the safer it will be." Johannes continued with his news, "But, one last point. I think it may be soon! And probably Poland."

Thomas smiled wryly, "We can't say we weren't warned. Do you remember that speech in the Reichstag? He listed all the countries he promised not to attack or invade, and he left out Poland! But such is his charisma that no-one noticed at the time!"

"He sees himself as having a divine mission," Erik suggested.

Thomas sat silently while Johannes was speaking. He had heard it all before from his contacts. "I'm not so sure that it isn't much worse than that," Thomas mused quietly. Then added dramatically, "I have to say that

I do now believe him to be the promised Antichrist!"

Erik half laughed. "Surely not! He does appear to be helping the workers at least!"

"That's it precisely! *Appears!* In fact he does give assistance to some, but only providing they obey his rules." Thomas counted on his fingers to mark off his points, "They mustn't be Jewish, or any other race but his beloved and mythical Aryan. He prefers them to be German, but some other nationalities will be accepted if they have blue eyes and blond hair. They must be prepared to turn a blind eye to all kinds of iniquities. They mustn't notice anyone being dragged away, families being split up, businesses being taken over and individuals left in penury. Nor must they see any bribery and corruption, even though it's increasing, nor hatred and violence erupting all over Germany, and Europe, or freedom of speech and action forbidden."

He paused to allow the full significance of his words sink in. "If they can ignore all that and much, much more. And if they're racially 'pure' according to his tenets, then they might be acceptable to him."

Thomas made his point as though he was in the pulpit, but his delivery was so powerful, his rhetoric so full of facts and ideas, his listeners were frequently spellbound.

"But heaven help the person who questions. The Antichrist will have all the appearance of being a saviour, but the results of his 'messianic' ministrations will manifest themselves as destruction, brutality and malevolence. Everywhere you look there will be wickedness. It seems to me that Hitler fits the matrix; it's from him, from his inspiration alone, that all these things have sprung. A mind that can produce such ideas is sick. One that not only produces them, but actually sets about putting them into practice is pure evil."

Thomas's sermon had quietened the group, and even Claudia was looking about her, concerned to see that no intruder had overheard.

"Therefore, to my mind, Hitler is an evil man on such a scale that I can only see him as the long promised Antichrist. The propaganda tries to hide

141

it, but the effects are all around us for those who would see and are still capable of rational, unbiased judgements."

"If you are right," Erik conceded gravely, "then the fight will be long and bitter and the future for the German… no, the human race, will be literally hell if he wins, or is allowed to carry on as the leader. Even if he loses, future Germans, our children, will be singled out for vilification by the rest of the world. We owe it to the next generation to finish this fight as soon as possible, so they have a life worth living."

"So, what do we do about him?" Nina asked pragmatically. "If we don't do something, we will be the ones blamed later, not the average person who doesn't understand what's going on. That's not farsightedness. They're already saying in Stockholm, 'Why don't they do something to stop Hitler? Why do they let him get away with it?' So, why do we?"

"It seems we have a choice," Franz began, "we can either assassinate him, engineer some kind of scheme whereby he's arrested and eventually tried or put away in an asylum, or we can go on putting up with him. But the first choice means we have to find someone willing to kill him."

"Or able to. He's surrounded by so many guards," Johannes said.

"Or we have to arrange a putsch, which would involve thousands throughout the whole country. It's no good staging one in Berlin only to find that no other town or state is with us. That would only lead to civil war. We've nearly been torn apart by that already, in Berlin and Munich at any rate."

"Assassination is the easiest, though someone else might step into Hitler's shoes," Claudia suggested, "Although those likely to be contenders for power could fairly easily be put under guard."

"To answer your question, Nina, about why don't we 'do something'?" Franz said. "The real problem, as I see it, is we need to be united. All the resistance groups, civilian and military, need to agree on what to do and how to go about it."

"But we're not, are we?" Johannes picked up the point. "The army generals can't see eye to eye. There's total disunity amongst those in the

Abwehr. So we're left with individuals, or single groups like ours, maybe, who attempt against all the odds, to take the course that the army will not take."

Thomas had listened to their comments quietly, his eyes watching each one in turn. "It seems to me that it's more important to get rid of him, no matter what. Even if he's totally successful and carries the whole country with him, and he succeeds in conquering the whole of Europe without a war, he is pure evil. And if we are to have a future in which people like us can live peaceably, there is only one course of action open to us."

A wry smile crossed Erik's face, and he spoke in the uneasy silence that followed Thomas's statement. "If anyone had told me even as little as three months ago that one day I would be sitting down drinking with friends, discussing in cold blood how to murder a *lunatic*, I would never have believed them. Yet, here I am!"

"He's a dangerous lunatic, Erik," Thomas said. "Each of us will have to commit ourselves, sooner or later, to a course of action, which may lead to our death. Make no mistake about it."

"If anyone wishes to withdraw, or feels they have too many responsibilities – family members who might be at risk – no one will think any the less of you if you decide to get out now," Thomas said quietly and firmly. "Each member of this team must face the fact that we may all get into deeper waters than we expect to now, especially if we go to war at some time in the future, as I believe Europe must. This will be a life and death struggle like none that has gone before, and each of us must be absolutely sure of our reasons for being here."

No one spoke or glanced at anyone else; each gazed only at Thomas, weighing up what he had said. After a full two minutes he looked around the group, neither approvingly nor disapprovingly. "Well then, we begin a new chapter! Let's go to work."

Fifteen

In late July, two months after the army had liberated their countrymen in Czechoslovakia, Peter arrived home in a state of some exhilaration.

"Anna!" He almost blurted out the news all East Prussians so wanted to hear. "Anna, I can't give you any precise details, but this may be my last leave for some time. Things are happening fast now. I wish I could tell you. But, Anna," he caught her hand tightly between his in a rare moment of emotion, "it is so important to Germany, and to us!"

She looked into his face, intensely alive with excitement, his dark eyes sparkling, as though his ambitions were close to fulfilment, and she knew immediately.

"The Corridor? This time it will surely mean war with England?"

"I've told you nothing, Anna," he said, but his face gave his affirmation. "The British won't fight us," was all he would concede.

She found herself at last in agreement with Peter, with no inner conflict between them.

"Anna, do you know how long it took the old Imperial Army to build up just seven new divisions?" Peter asked, hardly pausing for her negative response. "Sixteen long years! The Third Reich has built up not just seven, but forty four, and in only four years!" He announced these facts proudly, expecting Anna to be impressed. "And we did it right under the noses of the English and French, even with their acceptance. And our air force and navy are formidable, and they grew from next to nothing! Imagine it, Anna, no one has ever increased their strength as we have in such a short time! Hitler is right you know, Anna, we are invincible."

"Yes, I suppose you're right, darling." Anna listened with a troubled face. "It is an amazing achievement, but, now we have this truly great army, won't the British and French think we are going to use it?"

"It doesn't matter if they do! We will beat them easily and quickly, if they want to fight us. We're too strong now to lose! We'll push our borders back to where they were before the war."

"Yes. I suppose it would be a waste not to capitalize on it," Anna said, unhappily.

Her comment, full of unexpected irony, was a timely reminder to Peter that she was not just a sponge soaking up all his ideas, like most of his colleagues' wives, and she had not reacted at all the way he expected or hoped. Peter quickly reverted to the formal soldier. Her words had momentarily caused questions to dart across his mind. Why was it necessary to use their new force? Was it really not enough that they were now equal to, or even greater in strength than anyone else? Did they have to prove it by using this force, too? That was something he remembered Otto saying. It was safer to be the unquestioning subordinate and, after all, he knew nothing of the pressures in the diplomatic world.

"Anna, I've told you too much" He took her hand and kissed it gently. "Don't repeat anything, even to your sisters or parents. I was told in secrecy and shouldn't have said anything. But it's such a momentous time for our country and our future that even for a soldier it's difficult to control one's excitement!"

"You mustn't worry Peter, you've told me nothing that I couldn't have guessed. You mustn't reproach yourself. Will there be war with Russia, too, do you think?"

"We must talk no more of it, Anna. Except, if things should not go as well as we would like, I want you to do something for me." Still clutching her hand, he stared at her, his black browed eyes deadly serious. "Promise me that you'll take the children and go to your aunt in Pomerania or Johannes's family?"

He knew war with Russia might leave East Prussia in a vulnerable state.

By late August, 1939, the Third Reich had achieved the impossible - a friendly pact with Russia! The world was utterly astonished that the two polarised nations, who had made no secret of their hatred for each other, suddenly became friends overnight. The conspirators thought they understood the reason behind it: with Russia's self-inflicted isolation, the field would now be clear for a war with England and France. This event made the group even more desperate, but they were not the only people who were concerned. There was now a general air of suppressed tension, of imminent action of some sort.

Then without warning, on the twenty fifth of August, all communication with the outside world was stopped. British and French foreign correspondents who had not already left hurried home, and an English journalist friend of Erik's was advised to leave immediately, without time to pack his suitcase.

Johannes telephoned Nina, who was on resistance business nearby. From his cautiously coded speech she understood that something important was about to happen. She received the detailed message from Claudia, who had been forbidden by Johannes to do anything until Nina arrived.

"They're simulating an attack on Germany!" Claudia announced. "Just as Johannes predicted they would!"

"Claudia!" Nina was aghast at her sister's rashness in speaking before the door was secured and the servants were back in their quarters.

"So, they're going to do it, after all!"

"Oh, Claudia!" Nina's heart was heavy with emotion. "It's even worse than we thought. Thomas was right! Is there no end to what they'll do?"

"No, it seems there isn't. Johannes saw the order for one hundred and fifty Polish uniforms and guns. It will make a perfect reason to enter Danzig and regain The Corridor - if we've been 'atttacked' by a group of 'armed Poles'! And what's worse, with no foreign newspapers any more, we won't be able to judge what's truth and what's propaganda."

"We'll be at war with England before the weekend is over," Nina calculated miserably. "How long can we all go on supporting a government that sinks to these levels? You can almost feel the noose tightening around your neck, can't you?"

"Don't say that, Nina! I'm really not as brave as everyone thinks I am. When I stop and think what might happen to me, to you, to everyone..." Claudia looked tearful and Nina quickly and affectionately threw her comforting arms around her sister.

The gloom that descended over the two siblings was dissipated slightly when Nina began to inform the other group members of the possible consequences. Throughout the long evening they could think of nothing else.

It was not until midnight that Johannes returned home smiling in jubilation, "It's over! Hitler cancelled the operation, because he heard that an English-Polish agreement has been signed. When it came to it he didn't dare risk war with England."

Claudia rushed to Johannes, threw her arms around his neck and kissed him on the cheek. "Thank God!" She breathed a deep sigh of relief.

"He thought he'd bought off England, same as Russia, but when they signed the agreement with Poland he literally had to stop and think again." Johannes took the drink that Claudia proffered and sank down in his solid leather armchair, exhausted. "But even so, I don't subscribe to the views I heard in the Abwehr tonight. Some of them feel it's too big a personal blow for Hitler to survive. They think there's no need to try to overthrow him now, he's already finished."

"Surely he must be!" Claudia hoped Johannes might be wrong.

"He's capable of anything," Nina said. "I agree with you, Johan, I don't believe it's over, not yet."

In the following days rumours and counter rumours flowed back and forth like the ebb and flow of the tides. Fear of war ran through the hot summer streets with each new visit to the Foreign Office by a foreign ambassador. The heavy sultry August weather, pregnant with thunder and black clouds seemed to presage an impending crisis. The newspapers and radio kept up a continuous proclamation that Poland was mobilizing, heading for a full-scale assault on Germany. Homes in The Corridor were reported to be attacked and on fire; people were being killed, *German* people! And Danzig was threatened! Pictures of their own countrymen looking dazed and fearful, carrying crying toddlers, telling stories of how they had lost everything, had their homes burned and were forced to flee were flashed across the country to a stunned and horrified nation.

That they lived in a totalitarian state where the notion of a free press was now unknown escaped the attention of the majority, and they believed everything they read and saw and heard through their newspapers and newsreels.

In Berlin, as each country tried to put its point of view to Hitler or some important member of the government, the Wilhelmstrasse came under constant attack from foreign diplomats and ambassadors or couriers bearing messages from friendly or neutral observers. The clatter of well-shod feet was heard almost continually on the dry and dusty old, grey cobblestones. Much could have been learned from the international ambassadors' gait: the slowly dragging feet of the unwilling Italian; the frantic steps of the Polish, slowing as tiredness and despair at the imminent loss of his country took their toll; the busy, misguided, sometimes purposeful, but ever hopeful strides of the British.

And back and forth between them all ran the peripatetic, but ultimately futile neutral peacemaker, the Swedish courier Dahlerus. Tirelessly he sped between London and Berlin, and back again, in Goering's special planes, trains, and commandeered cars, with messages of hope, proposals, counter-proposals, terms, counter-terms, or rejections. Hope, resistant to all tricks, deceptions, snares and machinations persisted to the very last moment.

"I still think he intends to go ahead with his plan," Johannes maintained. "Personal setbacks have little effect on a rising dictator. Besides, he's quite mad. A fanatic twists the blows of fate to mean whatever he wants them to. He probably doesn't even recognize one when it hits him."

On Sunday, the twenty-seventh of August, out of the blue, the government announced to a totally unprepared nation that rationing of food, coal, shoes and other items was to begin almost immediately! There had been no warning. The country was taken aback by the haste and unexpectedness of it. The populace had gone without for so long. They had believed the promises they had been given, but instead of being fulfilled they were being asked to draw in their belts yet again. Whereas before people had kept quiet about their worries and fears, open grumbles began to be heard everywhere.

"Rationing! Shoes? Why shoes?" Claudia moaned. She loved to have many pairs and foresaw a fashion-less future without them.

"They need the leather for army boots, I should imagine," Johannes suggested.

"Then they must be really serious about war." Claudia looked shocked, as though none of the news had registered before. "And it could happen soon." She stared at her husband and sister who were both sitting silently, lost in their own thoughts. "This time tomorrow we could have bombs dropping on us." Claudia exploded. "Isn't there anything we can do?"

"Don't you think we've tried everything to avoid it?" Johannes gave Claudia an impatient glance.

Nina let out a long sigh. "I'm just so tired of all the toing and froing, one minute there will be war, the next... I wish something would happen."

Nina remained in Berlin, waiting impotently until she had some tangible facts to impart. Rumours could not be acted upon; she had to be sure. Johannes told them what he could, but he was unable to leave his office while so much was happening.

Tangible news came on Monday, the twenty-eighth, while the sisters were out, pacing the open, airless streets like caged animals; Klaus and Dieter left at home with their nannies. Claudia and Nina had tried over the last few days to create some semblance of normal life, yet they were bursting with the suppressed desire to get out of their confines and do something.

They were continually shackled by the invisible bonds of their ignorance.

As they turned a corner, they very nearly stumbled into a strange column of young, exuberant soldiers being transported in hundreds of army trucks and an uncountable assortment of vehicles from pushbikes to commercial vans. The column moved past them non-stop, the eager faced youths, driving or being driven, unable to suppress their excitement. Officers were riding up and down the column, yelling out instructions to keep moving, keep up, but the soldiers needed no encouragement. Small groups of Berliners were standing watching, some like Nina and Claudia looking puzzled, others who seemed to have comprehended some hidden significance were waving, or running alongside, trying to shake the soldiers' hands. "Good luck!" called out a nearby onlooker.

"Nina!" Claudia gasped, watching the slowly moving cavalcade with mixed horror and agitation. "They're going east!"

"Yes," Nina responded slowly, quietly, unconsciously tightening her grip on Claudia's arm. "It's The Corridor!" She had already felt the hairs on her neck stand up. "I must telephone Aunt Alice and father."

If the column had consisted solely of conventional military transport or soldiers on foot in marching order they might have dismissed it as just another army manoeuvre. Seeing their smart young soldiers, laughing and communicating with the public, in all manner of commandeered vehicles, most of them comic and out of place, indicated that this was gravely important. To the uninitiated it bore more resemblance to a retreating army than a conquering one, as though, anxious to be gone, they had grabbed anything on wheels.

It was a heart-stopping moment, stirring yet apprehensive, and, for a while at least, the average Berliner could push into the background all thoughts of a cold, hungry and shoeless future. Those were their soldiers going off towards the east. It was an instant of enormous jubilation, especially for those who had relatives in East Prussia, with whom they would soon be reunited.

Hitler, the iron-fisted twentieth century dictator would at last call the bluff of the old-fashioned, nineteenth-century diplomat Chamberlain who was bound by honour and decency to uphold his treaty with Poland. He had staked his reputation on it. Hitler had walked into the rest of Czechoslovakia and annihilated their fledgling democracy; he was not a man to use the tools of diplomacy as the English used them. At last Chamberlain understood the nature of his opponent. Now he had no option but to take up the gauntlet and commit his country to the fight.

"I must contact everyone, Claudia. How long will those troops take to reach the border? That's all the time we've got." Nina strode home as fast as she could; Claudia struggled to keep up with her. "There must be something we can do to stop this! I feel so useless, so powerless."

"I feel the same way."

"It's already public, here at least. If we informed our newspapers, what good would that do? They're not allowed to print anything adverse. If we could contact the British government they'd say the same as last time, get rid of Hitler first, then we'll talk."

"They might warn Hitler that they will declare war immediately if he attacks Poland."

"But Johan believes that's exactly what he wants. It would look as though Hitler is the innocent party! You see how clever he is; as the saying goes, there is method in his madness!"

Nina waited for the call from Claudia that would inform her the final act had begun. She telephoned Erik's mother in Stockholm and in the course of an ordinary, chatty conversation about the family, she slipped in the prearranged code words that informed her mother-in-law that this was likely to be their last conversation before the outbreak of a war. And so the message was passed to diplomats and foreign governments. But such is human nature that when confronted with the final reality of imminent conflict, no one really believed it and, therefore, did nothing to avert it.

The whole group was ready for the outbreak of hostilities long before the rest of Germany understood the meaning of the troop movements. They were not all clear about who they intended to save. They were already coping with Jewish escapees. Would they have to extend their work to include Poles with whom they might be at war? Foreign soldiers trying to return to their own lines? To do that, would be to make traitors of them all.

With each new dishonourable act that Hitler instigated, with every recognizable lie, the members of the group grew more resolved in their opposition to him, and in the absolute necessity to uphold the values of the old Germany at any cost to themselves.

Franz and Ruth had already passed several refugees to Nina. From her they went to safe houses in or near Lübeck and Danzig before their passage on to Sweden. And Thomas had sent many down the second line to Switzerland, through to Gerhard and Christina. Johannes was busy gleaning information from the Abwehr and forwarding it to Claudia or directly to Nina. Messages came to her from all directions as though everyone was anxious to prove they were capable of doing their job, of preserving their link in the chain. She analysed, sifted, and interpreted it all. Each member was told what he or she needed to know and no more.

On September the first, everyone awoke to startling, jingoistic newspaper headlines and inflammatory radio reports of Polish attacks on German soil and German retaliation. Western correspondents, travelling to cover the big event, found themselves in a crazy land where the news they dispatched back home simply had not occurred. The German papers made no mention of the mobilization of their troops, their constant sniping, or the build up of their army at the frontier. They only screamed accusations at the Poles for mobilizing a million and a half men, for the massing of troops on the frontier with Germany, for German families being forced to flee before the Polish soldiers, and for innocent passenger planes being shot at.

German writers told such different stories, the foreigners wondered if they were reporting on the same country. The newspaper propaganda was so successful that the majority of Germans really believed Poland was about to attack, even though her armed forces were totally inadequate to take on a modern mechanised force, as Germany now had.

Even so, people were generally apathetic, not jubilant and keen as they had been in nineteen-fourteen. There were no cheering crowds in the streets this time, no flowers being thrown to the soldiers, and only a few women to run alongside the troops, blowing kisses of encouragement. Reuniting Germans displaced by the Polish Corridor was one thing; another war was quite a different matter. It was not popular, even against the despised Poles, so the propaganda had been necessary to whip up sufficient support for the government's action.

All day the planes droned across German territory towards the major Polish cities, all day news of the battles screamed from the radio.

"It'll be over by next week-end!" Johannes had reported. "That's what the top brass thinks!"

"They're probably right. Poland hasn't got much of an army." Claudia agreed.

"Except that they're stubborn, like the Russians."

"Mother always says never underestimate your enemy."

"Indeed. They may not have the equipment, but they might surprise us anyway. They're fighting for their homes, and their lives."

Members of the group found no way to salve their consciences; they were overcome with a state of inertia and uselessness, unwilling just to bow to the forces of mindless violence. Johannes reported frantic signals hastening between ambassadors and ministers, but no specific action. The view in the Chancellery seemed to indicate that either England would again take no action or war would be declared within a few hours. The chill touch of a juggernaut, too large and dangerous to control, was now set in motion…

On Sunday, the third of September, Claudia waited outside the Chancellery in Berlin for a 'special announcement'. It was a beautiful day with clear blue skies and a hot sultry sun, a day to spend out at the lakes enjoying life and cooling down. She was nonetheless surprised to find that only a couple of hundred people had thought it worthwhile to wait for what must be important news. Perhaps others were unaware of what was about to happen; perhaps they did not really care, believing in the propaganda of their own invincibility. Or maybe they felt war was imminent and that they could do nothing to stop it. All Berliners loved to retreat to the woods and lakes on a Sunday, to escape the brooding heat and not even war was going to change that habit.

She stood silently waiting, Klaus asleep in his pushchair, shaded from the sun by a frilled canopy. For once, she had taken him out on her own, wanting a reason to be walking the streets at midday. She had on a pretty red and white floral cotton dress, which she considered was far too cheerful for the solemn thoughts racing through her head. Such scorching days were not meant for sober or deep reflections.

It was eerie, so unreal. Standing there alone and uneasy, she felt as though she was the only person in Berlin, in all Germany, aware of what was going on. Then, suddenly, around midday, the loudspeakers set up on the street corners blared forth, informing the small, stunned assembly that Great Britain had declared war on Germany. The little crowd spread out over the large square in small groups of twos, threes and fours, stood silently rooted to the spot, angry and uncomprehending, heedless of the blazing sun. Hadn't Hitler assured them that he personally would make sure there would be no war with England?

On such a day as this! For a while her own anger abated and she wanted to laugh at the absurdity of the scene. The declaration had been made to this little, unrelated collection of individuals: to so few. How ludicrous! Out at the lakes so many others were happily swimming and boating, still unknowing, cooling themselves down, while in the Chancellery things were only just beginning to warm up.

She had never really believed Hitler's promises, but like every other German, a part of her mind kept alive the hope that he could just possibly be the great saviour of the German nation they all dreamed of; he might, somehow, avoid armed conflict. He had evaded it on each previous occasion, so had it been naïve to suppose he could have continued without some country eventually calling his bluff?

She reeled along the road, mechanically pushing Klaus in his pram, dazed from the heat and the long awaited, yet still grim, news. The noise of the loudspeakers, blaring out their accusations of England's deception, receded around the corners, as she made her way home. The only comment she heard from other pedestrians, still stupefied like her, was agreement that England was guilty of causing it.

So Hitler has won after all! He has his battle with England, and his people's affirmation that he is not to blame!

Sixteen

Peter was called away to the west after war began, his regiment forming part of a small, inadequate army waiting apprehensively for the expected French attack on the Ruhr. But despite the threats they had made, the French did nothing. Peter's battalion waited anxiously to see if the English would do the same, hoping that neither nation really wanted this dispute. With Russia diplomatically out of the way in the east, and England and France still dithering in the west, they were left blessedly free to finish off the war in Poland quickly, to crush the fierce yet totally hopeless resistance brutally fast. The Poles had no time to understand what was happening to them, and the world was given a new and terrifying word: *Blitzkrieg* - lightning war.

The western front remained stubbornly inactive and all remained as quiet as Berlin in August. Peter's battalion was recalled and sent to Poland to tidy up the chaos. Once there, after the fighting had finished, Peter was promoted to major and transferred to a desk job in Warsaw. Even though he had become adjutant to a colonel and had very high status, and his family saw his promotion as recognition of his outstanding service to the Third Reich, Peter was not happy.

It could be said that Peter was self-indulgent. He was only being exactly what he wanted to be: a soldier giving and obeying orders, forcing his family to fit in with his wishes, not doing what was necessarily good for them.

He had always been a man of outward composure, "One must never give in to feelings," he had once argued with Erik. "Once you let in one, you open the gate to all kinds of excesses."

"It's a happy man who is not encumbered by his emotions, but it's the human condition to have them," Erik responded. "Suppose you were able to love without expecting any reward or thought of self."

"That isn't possible! All love expects response and what difference is there between that and lust? The one is only an extension of the other, after all, and both are forms of self-indulgence. To invite someone to devote their life to you is merely to be narcissistic, to want them to see you as you see yourself, or as you feel you ought to be seen. I won't pander to the greed of my ego."

"We're not perfect. I see nothing narcissistic or self-indulgent in giving love where it's needed. I think we differ in our use of the word," Erik argued warmly, sadly reflecting that he had never seen any affectionate impulse from Peter towards his children; they were always kept at a distance.

"I see no difference. I do not intend that either I, or my family, will be governed by emotions. My children will learn self-control from the earliest possible age."

Erik restrained his exasperation and tried hard to find a side of Peter that he could like, for Anna's sake, but Peter seemed to be as rigid in his thinking as in his actions. "What about love for one's neighbour, as the commandment says? Or for human kind as a whole? And those who dedicate their lives to the service of others, do you condemn their benevolence also?"

"Philanthropists!" Peter dismissed them. "I have always heartily disliked them. They are like the Freemasons or Jews. Help given to their fellow man is for a reason, cloaked under a screen of 'ministration to the needy'. Those they aid have a price to pay."

"You serve your country as a soldier, because you're proud of it and wish to protect its people," Erik was always willing to show his opponent a way out, even if he totally disagreed with him.

"Love of country is the only kind worth having," Peter accepted. "It is the purest form."

"What is it, but attachment to folk you live amongst? Do you have less pride in the Germany that includes Alsace, Lorraine, Austria and the Sudetenland? If you can include them why not the whole of Europe?"

"I love my country, not Europe! There are many ethnic groups within Europe I would not wish to be associated with."

"But Hitler would ask you to fight for, and protect a Germany which includes many other nations. Can you not accept that there are individuals who have the ability to love everyone - of all lands?"

"And there will always be rebels willing to destroy the order of society," Peter countered, unconvinced. "Why should I be expected to even like them?"

Erik changed his tack. "Would you not agree that control of passions can be used for either good or ill? Is it not the case that Hitler plays on the uncontrolled feelings of the masses for his own ends?"

"I would rather say he guides their emotions into a governable force for good. If you wish to change the world you have to lead your citizens to a position they think they have led you to. That is what Hitler excels at. What may seem like emotional chaos to you is in reality a controlled and deliberate policy founded on Hitler's ideas as he wrote them in *Mein Kampf*."

"I thought you were of the opinion that what he wrote there was not all to be accepted slavishly," Erik studied Peter's face carefully, wondering how he could persuade himself that the policies he had disagreed with before had now become more acceptable.

"I still do not fully accept some points from *Mein Kampf*," Peter admitted, honestly, "and I still do not believe that he will implement them all. In my judgement a lot of what was written down then was a form of expiation, a purging of the soul; and then forgotten by him."

"A man of Hitler's intelligence and political ability wouldn't write down anything to be forgotten. A man who senses his vocation as he clearly does will leave in his writing his view of what that destiny is to be. Every word will be framed for future generations to heed and applaud. A man like him wants an audience for everything he does. What Hitler said in *Mein Kampf* was what he intended to happen, not an exercise in polemics."

When the order came through for his transfer to an administrative position in Warsaw, Peter knew it must be necessary and he accepted it dutifully; but his heart was out on the battlefield, not behind a pile of papers. He could not reconcile pride in his country with paperwork, however indispensable it might be.

His readiness to give his life for his country did not include the willingness to expire from boredom. He would die heroically, stoically, on the field of battle, but not in bed, or at a desk! His high ideals, the tradition of honourable death in his family were instilled from birth; that was all he had been born for, anything else was unacceptable. To Peter, an office job meant demotion. Promotion to major was no recompense.

Sitting at his desk all day, dealing with reams of paper in duplicate or triplicate, month after month, gradually alienated him from the reality of the army's role in Warsaw. Human beings became cyphers; papers were stamped and signed with no real thought for their content. Whole groups were consigned to eternity with little comprehension on Peter's part of his connection with the operation. So great were the demands of the efficient administrative system that he seldom had the time to read through what he was signing, and he relied on his staff officers to keep him informed of their contents.

When Anna saw him after a few months in Warsaw, she worried at the change in him, but after eighteen months she became thoroughly alarmed. He had become withdrawn, distant, absent-minded, no longer the man of action, but a man of constant reflection, for whom thought itself had become a torturer.

To him the children did not exist: he talked through them as though they were not there. Helga would sit quietly examining his face as Anna spoke to him, and Anna's as he absently replied. Even before she was four years old she understood that reactions were as important as their causes.

Anna was unable to get through to him at all, or to discover what it was that had driven his orderly mind over the edge into such confusion that when he was with her he was unable to construct the simplest, coherent sentence. She became so distressed she asked for Nina's support.

Nina pitied Anna. Not because Peter was ill, but because her life pivoted on him and her children, she had nothing else. For Nina, love was not so all consuming; she loved Erik with what she described as quiet passion, yet neither he nor Dieter was the centre of her world. They were the two dearest people in her life, yet she could stand back and see that others were worthy, and to devote herself exclusively to these two was to diminish her life and the lives of those around her, and she would have no existence as a separate person. Nina needed to accomplish greater things than the rearing of children and keeping house.

Anna was paying the price that such an enclosed life demanded: she was sick with worry, and her concentrated love allowed no way to diminish or eliminate her pain. She had foolishly made a rod for her own back.

Nina understood suffering far more than her older sister. It had to be shared or the sufferer would become bowed and crushed under its weight. She had no wish to burden Erik with extra problems, especially those of someone with whom he was out of sympathy, but Peter's depression was affecting Anna, and in turn Nina and all their children. Nina's responsibilities were such that she needed to remain alert at all times if she was not to commit a terrible, and possibly fatal, breach of their security.

She contacted Erik in Warsaw where he had been since the end of the Polish campaign, and asked him if he could bring himself to do what Anna wanted, to see Peter.

When Germany attacked Poland in nineteen thirty-nine, the Swedish Embassy in Warsaw closed down and diplomacy was conducted from Berlin, and Erik was forced to re-examine his role as a diplomat. He believed passionately that he could have some influence on events in Warsaw and was reluctant to work from Berlin, where he would be too distant from those who would need him most.

161

He chose to change direction yet again, and became a neutral Swedish businessman, expanding his hobby of buying and selling art works and paintings. He opened an office in the centre of Warsaw from where he would conduct his affairs and immediately employed several people, including a receptionist, a secretary, a clerk and two painting restorers.

Many soldiers found their way to his door, wanting paintings they had looted to be restored and sent home to Germany. Despite his immediate distaste, he realized that he could do nothing to stop it, but he could keep records: he meticulously detailed the names and addresses of the Germans, as well as those from whom they had looted their paintings, sculptures or other art works, hoping that one day these treasures might find their way back to their rightful owners.

Later, he opened a studio on the outskirts of Warsaw, mainly for restoring paintings, and used this business to give work to dozens of Jews, some of them with special skills. Gradually, with the assistance of one of his old contacts from the consulate in Lübeck, he was able to spirit one after the other away down Nina's escape line.

He was prepared to violate Swedish neutrality and break his own country's laws in order to save as many lives as he could; he recruited many of his like-minded friends to provide Swedish passports and new identities, some of the escapees being given his own, or his wife's relatives' names. They would return to Sweden, and someone else would take over their identity.

"I can't stand by and see people disappearing, Nina," he explained one day, justifying his career change. "It's the only way I can be of real use. I won't be able to live with my conscience if I don't do something."

Nina had been sceptical at first, not really understanding how his new profession could help. When she saw the possibilities, she offered to find the escapees sanctuary and get them to the boats at Danzig. "Be careful, my darling, won't you? Warsaw must be a dangerous place to be at the moment."

"It's the same all over the Continent, sweetheart. None of us are safe."

Erik's character was such that within five minutes acquaintances knew they would like this young man, within ten they had forgotten that he was a newcomer in their lives, and within fifteen they had told him their life's history, family details, ambitions and hopes. He made people feel as secure as in the confessional. In diplomatic circles and at social gatherings he was seen as engaging and trustworthy, willing to put his hand to anything; a practical man as well as a philosopher. He could walk tightropes of discretion where colleagues literally feared to tread, and their trepidation was real, even if not for themselves. The wrong word in the wrong ear could lead to incarceration, torture or death. Tact was not so much needed as coercion and he had his mother's ability to twist arms quite disarmingly.

While some of the Germans responded to reason, most reacted only to threats or blackmail. There was a feeling abroad amongst some, especially the SS, that they could get away with anything, and had the power of life or death over everyone - especially in Poland. There the victors were too sure of themselves, too indifferent to their victims, and totally unconcerned about any future in which they might have to account for their sins. The possibility of losing the war never entered their heads. Erik had the ability to make some of them stop and think that such a future was a possibility, but even his political strategy and finesse had its limitations on deliberately closed or indifferent minds.

Erik agreed to meet Peter in Warsaw, though he was certain that his brother-in-law was perfectly capable of sorting out his own problems. And he was unsure of his role as a neutral in occupied Poland.

Erik was not unaware of the rumours circulating amongst the local Poles, and some local Jewish leaders, about the function of certain German officers, Peter amongst them. The routine rounding up of the intelligentsia amongst both the Jewish and gentile Poles was increasing both in number and violence.

Perhaps he could combine his visit on Anna's behalf with questions of his own, and find out what truth there was to these tales - especially Peter's part in the programme. They were, after all, related, posted by chance, or perhaps by some divine design he believed, to the same war-torn town and should have met before now in the ordinary course of social life.

That they had not was partly due to Peter's extended home leave and to some extent to Erik's discreet avoidance of social intercourse with the Nazi representatives. But it could not continue without the Nazis becoming suspicious that members from the Swedish community were biased against them when they ought to have remained neutral.

"So, how do you enjoy being a man of leisure, Peter?" Erik asked pleasantly.

He meant it ironically, but Peter was not amused.

"I don't," he snapped back, briefly coming to life, only to sink back into apathy. "If you mean doing paperwork as opposed to being a soldier, it is neither exciting nor rewarding. My work consists almost entirely of administration, which any efficient company clerk could do. In fact, I now leave my staff to do most of it."

"But there must be some special talent that only you can bring to it? A reason why they chose you for this particular job?" Erik had an inkling that the qualification most needed in Warsaw was a long, unbroken record of submission to authority, which Peter admirably fulfilled. No one could do the job Peter had to do without being able to ignore the destruction around him. Obedience to orders blinkered the soldier like the poor donkey winding up water from the well; he only saw what he was allowed to see, and no more.

"I have no qualification for administration, unless you include estate accountancy. I want to get back to doing what I'm well trained for."

Peter saw such understanding in Eric's face.

"This I find so frustrating!"

Erik looked at him with some sympathy, recognizing the deep well of normally suppressed emotion behind the words. Peter was no longer the self-assured, overbearing young officer; he looked his age, with lines across his forehead that gave him a perpetual puzzled appearance, and the thick black hair was thinner and greying fast. The questions were coming all too frequently, but the answers were not to be found.

Having always given Peter credit for analysing Hitler's ideas and finding them to be what the country most needed, Erik's quarrel with Peter had been over his unwillingness to see the dark side of the dictator's policies. Erik understood that a mind that wished something to be so could cut out all other arguments, and see only what it wanted to see; yet he could not believe that his brother-in-law was capable of so blinding himself. Peter had never been as arrogant as many of his colleagues.

Erik was not a soldier and he did not allow for the decades of army discipline, or the centuries of loyalty to their monarchy. Hitler was their new king, and for better or worse, he was to be accorded the same allegiance.

"We are now protecting Belgium, Denmark, Holland and Norway from England. The English have been pushed back into the sea. France has collapsed before our army. We are currently involved in Yugoslavia and Greece. All this has happened while I've been here. Think what history I have missed sitting in this... this backwater! I could have been a part of it all; pushing the British out of Greece. But this! This isn't soldiers' work!"

So it's the making of history that's important to him! He wants to be able to tell his grandchildren of the heroic deeds and wars that were won, and in which he had taken part!

"But it is the result of soldier's work, isn't it?" Erik tried to make Peter acknowledge that his paperwork was in reality enforcing movement or imprisonment of entire populations conquered by his army. "And if you had been in the west you would probably be doing the same thing over there. It seems sensible to post a man to an area he knows."

Erik had been in Warsaw long enough to learn through the diplomatic and social grapevines what Peter's general function was and that there was probably something more troubling him: the invisible burden now shaming and crushing his bowed shoulders.

165

"As a soldier you understand the necessity of administration." He took a deep breath, "Isn't it rather the nature of your responsibilities that you don't like?"

Peter stared at Erik absently. "Of course it is! I've already explained how much I dislike it."

He was distantly annoyed at Erik's apparent misinterpretation of his disclosures and regretted having made them.

"I meant that as an upright Christian gentleman, you must find your conscience in constant conflict with what you have to do here. It is, after all, somewhat removed from the usual activity of soldiers." Erik was still guessing.

Peter's face glazed icily. "How is it that you are acquainted with my duties?"

"All Warsaw knows it!" There was an element of truth in his statement. The Polish and Jewish communities seemed sure of his involvement.

Peter suddenly grew angry, and stood up, knocking his chair back. "Are you telling me that my task is common knowledge?"

"Common enough."

"Then I think it's your duty to tell me exactly who knows, and how you came by it. This is secret information apparently being tossed around like gossip!"

Erik ignored the slight and studied him, with profound pity, for some time before replying. "Every Jew in Warsaw knows what you do here," he replied quietly, though this was not the case; only a handful of Jewish community leaders knew. "And so does each one of the Poles now being sent to Treblinka or Auschwitz, and all those being uprooted and sent to unspecified places for so-called resettlement. We all know these are concentration camps, and few emerge from them alive."

He was restraining his anger for being asked to befriend someone involved in the monstrous things the German nation was allowing without a murmur! He was furious with Peter, a decent, law-abiding man, for being so blinded by duty he was unable to see what was going on around him, or his own part in it, or worse, not caring.

Peter was hampered by an emotion of which he was unaware – pride in what they had achieved. The fact that all their conquests had been achieved unlawfully escaped him. The terms of the Versailles Treaty had been cast aside with the willing connivance of his compatriots who could not entertain the idea that they were now guilty of binding not one, but many countries under their power. As long as he kept strictly to the legal guidelines received from Berlin, Peter believed he was staying within acceptable limits.

Erik could not explain to him that his Embassy in Berlin, and his own art shop in Warsaw, had become focal points for dissident Germans from the lowest privates to majors, and occasionally even higher ranks, who were so disillusioned they were ready to risk being seen with neutral observers; but not yet ready to risk death by refusing orders. Somehow they felt that by talking to Erik they were allaying their own guilt; perhaps the Swedes would be able to do something to get the atrocities stopped.

The Germans organized or attended many functions where diplomats and other nationals working in the occupied countries would be expected to socialize with their officials. At first Erik's natural reaction had been to avoid them, but gradually, as one by one soldiers sought friendly neutrals to whom they could pour out their stories, he realized his presence would encourage others to come forward. The intelligence he gained in this fashion was passed on to London.

It also reached Moscow through underground radio operators either in Poland or through Nina, who had one known Communist in her line with links to Moscow - though neither Erik nor his wife knew of the Moscow link at that time. She and all the members of her group had code names, which the Russians came to know. And now Nina gave Erik one, too: Firefly.

It was a perilous game he was playing, but personal danger had never stopped Erik from following his conscience. Most of the risk was from not knowing whether any of the soldiers had been planted; to give phoney

167

information, to test his neutrality, and that of others, which, if confirmed from other sources, would be passed through Nina. Thus Erik was directly putting her life in jeopardy as well.

Both agreed to continue. What they were learning from these dissident veterans was probably true and too valuable to ignore. Logically, false intelligence would have been about the front lines - the fighting units, not about Jews, Poles, and other nationals being rounded up and herded into cattle trucks and driven to concentration camps. This operation was being kept hidden; even the SS did not want it revealed.

With difficulty Erik had suppressed his conscience over Peter's role in Warsaw, but now it caused an explosion of honesty, which would have had the gravest consequences had he allowed it full rein with any other German officer.

"Anna is extremely concerned about your health and asked me to find out how you were. How can I possibly tell her that your condition has been caused by your scruples fighting against your orders! And what's going on here in Poland and what you are doing? How could she possibly accept your part in it?"

Peter began to redden with rage at Erik's impertinence. "How dare ..."

"Are you totally ignorant? Do you really not know where all the Jews are going and what's happening to them? That's criminal incompetence! Or does their suffering not bother you? You sign their transfer papers for God's sake! Don't you look at them? Have you ever visited any of the places you've assigned these people to? The ghetto in Warsaw itself... have you been there? The conditions are inhuman, totally degrading. It's overcrowded; there's little or nothing for anyone to eat; they're starving. And they're shot if they try to leave to buy food outside or smuggle it in. *You* shoot them! How can you justify this treatment? How?" Erik could not contain himself; he had an overwhelming urge to throttle Peter.

Weariness and distress afflicted Peter's features, as he finally had to come face to face with reality. His innate honesty forced him to admit there was some truth in Erik's tirade, but he was not yet ready to give in.

168

"Why should I have to justify my role to you? You are only here at the invitation of the Third Reich. However... Hitler informed us all personally that things would happen in Poland, which would be distasteful to us, but we were not to interfere. We must restrict ourselves to our military duty. I am therefore only carrying out his direct orders."

Unable to look at him, Peter paused, turned his back on Erik and stared out of the window. "It's only because you are my brother-in-law that I've allowed you to speak to me in this manner, but I must warn you that you are very close to the limit of your immunity as a neutral. Don't push my patience too far!"

Erik was too incensed to take any notice of the threat. "You excuse the wholesale deportation and possible murder of Jews and Poles - some of even higher rank than yourself – and most of the intellectuals of Poland, on the grounds of *military duty*? What is *military* about killing civilians? What became of your moral duty - to treat people in conquered lands humanely and honourably? Where is your honour now? Duty! Pah! To whom? To a madman? A psychopath, with a group of lunatic followers? What has happened to you - *all* of you?" He threw up his arms in exasperation.

He could see the muscles working in Peter's neck as he struggled to control himself. In a quieter, more guarded voice, Erik asked searchingly, "Have you not yet realized that fate has placed you here in order to open your eyes? These wars are not about fighting armies, your kind of warfare, or the clean, quick kill and revenge for past humiliations. They're about subjugating the whole of Europe under the heel of a dictatorship. You have the opportunity to see it before others, perhaps so that you can do something to stop it. What's taking place in Warsaw, in Poland, is what the whole of Europe - France, Norway, Denmark - can expect in due course. England will be next, then Russia, and one by one countries will be ground down to suit the whim of a mad dictator who thinks he's Napoleon and Ghenghis Khan reincarnated!"

Furious, Peter had listened in silence, but from the second he admitted, briefly but honestly, that he had not in fact visited the ghetto, he allowed in doubt. He needed time to think, to reassess. "Soldiers are not given to know the overall strategy, but to carry out orders - and to expect total and immediate submission from those we command. How could an army function, if every time an instruction is given someone questions it? We would grind to a halt within five minutes. But I would not expect you to understand warfare."

He moved to the door, indicating that Erik's presence was no longer acceptable.

As Erik left, he paused, "At what point do you ask, 'Is this an honourable order even if it is part of a grand strategy?' When does the end justify the kind of means that are being employed here?"

Peter's moral dilemmas were to be of no further interest to anyone, other than Anna, for a while, for the eyes, ears, hearts and minds of all Germany were suddenly deflected towards the east, as Operation Barbarossa began. When Germany invaded Russia it opened up the possibility of that most frightening of all military circumstances, a war on two fronts. Yet the conflict in the west was active only in the air and at sea, their land troops were not engaged. And they were winning everywhere; everything they did worked in their favour. They were like gamblers who had struck a winning streak and could not lose.

Seventeen

In the conference room in the Abwehr, Johannes was still setting out the papers on the huge oblong table ready for a meeting, when the generals entered. He was not to be in attendance when they had their discussion, but he had become a known and accepted member of the resistance group, and after a brief acknowledgement of his presence the generals continued their conversations within his earshot.

"We tried to enlist Hitler's adjutant," one began, "he was generally sympathetic, but balked at the idea of murdering someone who had entrusted himself into his care."

"That's a chap you'd feel safe with, a man to trust. Pity!"

"Is there no way to prevent this war from spreading?"

"Yes, if you can find a reliable person with a pistol, and willing to use it."

"Why not you then, Ernst?"

"I? I regret that I am not fitted to shoot an unarmed man."

"Then we are lost indeed. Is there anyone within the reach of Hitler who would do the deed? I fear not."

"I might be prepared to pull the trigger if I could be sure that the full weight of the Nazis' fury would not then fall on my blameless staff."

"If someone could be hired as an assassin it would end the likelihood of civil war, for once he has gone the masses would not be mesmerised, they would see the rest for what they are. I suggest an accident... his train might be 'destroyed' by enemy aircraft?"

"If he survived, we would all be lost and Germany would be even more tightly held in this dictator's grip, with no-one, not even us, to restrain him. Pity Germany then, indeed!"

Each felt they had a good reason why they could not be the one to end the dictator's reign. Whilst divorcing themselves from 'the Nazis' - these were loyal, principled soldiers, not butchers - they could not detach themselves from their old lives, their old thinking. Their reliance on solid nineteenth-century values would have to be transformed if they were to fully understand and stop Hitler who cared nothing for their honour, except to use it against them.

There had only been one instant when they might have broken away and obtained a reasonable peace. But now they were at war, and as their Chancellor in waiting Goerdeler put it: "One does not rebel when standing with one's nose before the enemy."

Caught in a circle of their own making, they could do nothing except plot, scheme, talk, and hope. Without the army's support, the resistance groups throughout the country were like poodles yapping at an intruder's heels, when the ferocious bite of Alsatian guard dogs was needed.

Operation Barbarossa presented them with more problems. On the one hand they hated the Russians and feared Communism as a creeping cancer, on the other, to go to war with their huge eastern neighbour whilst they were still uncertain of the reaction of the British was to commit possible suicide.

Johannes heard enough to leave with a heavy heart. There was nothing to be gained from these men; they were thinkers when Germany needed activists. Yet, he understood them, for he, too, found himself unable to take up a gun. He passed the conversation on to Thomas who found it all too familiar.

"You won't get anywhere with men like that. They have the moral certainty of the Middle Ages. Knights in shining armour and chivalry are dead under this dictator. They will get us nowhere." Thomas had deliberated long and hard about who could rescue his beloved Germany.

"I've made my decision," he told Johannes, "from now on I shall do everything in my power to get rid of him. I've joined the active resistors. I can no longer stand aside. I don't have the luxury of their thinking. My conscience wants action, not words."

After his confrontation with Peter, Erik was unusually angry. So much so, when he rang Nina later from Warsaw he was uncharacteristically blunt. Having little experience of losing his temper he was under its unbridled domination, and the renegade incursion of Germany into Russia kept his rage at boiling point for several days.

Although Johannes had assured him Otto's telephone was still safe, he was well aware that his own in Warsaw might be tapped.

"Well, I saw him," he began, without naming Peter, "but he wasn't at all interested in anything I had to say. And when I mentioned what you'd told me, he was furious - as I expected him to be. I would have been in his shoes. But when I broached the subject of what was happening over there, he practically threw me out!"

Nina was conciliatory. "But at least you tried!"

Anna picked up the phone to hear Nina talking to Erik on another extension. She held on, with the intention of speaking to Erik herself, but she was so deeply upset by what she had overheard she retired to her room, where Nina later found her. The room was filled with the stirring sound of Schumann's piano concerto; Anna was leaning back in her armchair, a perfumed handkerchief pressed to her eyes. In times of stress Anna had always turned to music, letting the violins and pianos permeate her being, until she and the orchestra were in such accord there was no room for any other emotions, and she calmed down again. Schumann had replaced Rachmaninov, to whom Anna would normally have turned for solace; in these unusual times Rachmaninov was designated a non-person by the German state, which Anna accepted without a great deal of thought. She had simply not thrown away her records as she ought, but continued blithely to play them, and no-one had the heart to remind her that she should at least have them packed away in the attic.

When Anna explained how she inadvertently overheard part of the conversation, Nina smiled wryly. "Anna, you know Erik doesn't really understand soldiers. He comes from a diplomatic family and that's like chalk and cheese." Nina's arm stole round her sister's shoulders in strong, sympathetic support, despite her inner certainty that Erik knew a great deal about military men, especially those in Warsaw.

"But what exactly did he mean when he talked about 'the things going on in Warsaw'? He said it as though something dreadful is happening there, and that Peter's involved!" Anna dabbed at her still damp eyes and pushed back a strand of hair from her forehead, heedless that Nina knew she had eavesdropped. She would have allowed no one other than her sister to know that she had shed any tears.

Until now, everyone had agreed to keep Anna in the dark. Nina had to make a quick decision: should she pretend that nothing was happening, which she felt would be patronising, or tell Anna some of it at least?

"You've heard some of the rumours..." she began.

"But that's all they are, aren't they?" Anna interrupted her, stating rather than entreating.

Nina paused, suddenly jolted. Erik's reports had made her aware of forthcoming events. The family had been affected by the propaganda machine. They, like many others, had allowed themselves to be persuaded that once Hitler had reached the pre-nineteen eighteen boundaries again they could all live in peace under the German flag. Only slowly did it dawn on Nina's family that the army was not going to stop until Hitler had achieved some burning personal ambition.

Now they were also having to come to terms with the stories from the east, "No, Anna. They're not just rumours." Nina kept her arm firmly around Anna's shoulders to let her know that she was loved, however little she understood. "All the Jews in Warsaw are now enclosed within a high wall, barbed wire, and soldiers patrolling it - in an area only two miles by half a mile. That's nearly half a million people squashed into a space no bigger than from here to the village! And they cannot leave. There is nowhere they can grow food, they are in the middle of a city of concrete and tarmac. Anna, they're being systematically and quite deliberately starved to death!" Anna looked at Nina uncomprehendingly as she knelt in front of her and took her hand in an effort to expunge her own feelings of guilt. "Anna, it is our troops who are keeping them inside, and shoot them if they escape. *Ours!*"

"But it can't be. Peter would have told me if anything like that was happening. I'm sure you're wrong, Nina. Erik must have meant something else; he can't possibly have more information than our army. How can you know, if Peter doesn't?"

Anna gazed out of the window at the familiar childhood view over the courtyard and the lawns beyond, stretching down towards the meadow and Frieda's tree. As a child it had stood for gallantry, honour and sacrifice in the course of duty. She had seen Frieda as a sad heroine, a victim of circumstance, yet somehow unbowed and resolute in her final, tragic act. How could it be that a race that produced her could also produce monsters capable of such inhuman cruelty? It was just not possible.

"Nina, I know you mean well, but Peter would never be involved in anything morally wrong. And if our soldiers were shooting them as you say, he would have spoken out against it. You don't know him like I do. He is a good man!" She said it defensively, knowing that her family did not see him as she did.

Nina had impetuously been on the point of telling her sister about the escape line, to convince her that she was in touch with those who knew the truth, but she bit her lip. She would have to tell Anna some day about her resistance work, and how she had been hiding refugees in the wooden hut in the copse down in the meadow, before moving them on to safe houses. This was not the time. Anna had reminded her all too vividly that her husband was, above all, a Nazi.

After the children had been taken to the nursery for their afternoon lessons, or for well-earned sleep in the case of the active and energetic young Ullrich and Dieter, the sisters meandered together through the garden and down to the meadow, catching up on each other's news. Nina tried not to mention Erik or Peter, and remind Anna of the morning's trauma. They seldom saw each other, relying mostly on correspondence or telephone calls, so time together was rare and the more enjoyable for that.

Nina became agitated as she noted the direction in which they were ambling, and tried to head Anna away from the small grove beyond Frieda's tree. Nina was free of refugees, but Anna would see that the gamekeeper's hut had been cleaned up and rearranged as temporary accommodation; and she might mention it to Peter sometime.

"You know Peter's mother is such a dreadful snob!" Anna stopped under a tree for a moment, resisting Nina's attempt to turn back towards home. "When I take the children to see her she always buys them each a whole new outfit, not because she thinks they need one, but because she insists they have the latest fashions! Can you imagine it, little Ulli wearing the latest designs! Not that they're anything to write home about, what with rationing and so on."

"I don't suppose Ulli notices one way or the other. Did Claudia tell you she's training to become a nurse?"

"No, I didn't know that. How like her!"

"It's a long way from history and geography, but I think she needs to do something. She told me that the moment of her choosing was quite by chance. Johan had been away and she'd gone to meet him on his return, at the station in Berlin, and a train pulled in filled with injured soldiers. She said she was surprised at first, it wasn't the kind of sight she was used to seeing in the middle of Berlin; and then she was frustrated, because she had to stand back and simply observe all the stretcher cases and walking wounded, unable to do anything. And the army kept moving them away as though they didn't want her to be see them."

"I suppose all countries try and keep the results of war away from civilians, they only want us to see the glory, not those who've been blinded or paralysed, or lost a limb." Anna resolutely pushed away the thought of Peter without arms or legs.

"Anyway, Claudia determined then and there that until the war is over she's going to nurse them. So there she is, already half way to becoming a sister, I shouldn't wonder. You know what Claudia's like, she'll have qualified before the rest have got their uniforms on!"

Nina had stopped at the quiet grove in the dip whilst hoping to walk back across the meadow. While she was still talking, she saw Otto's head appear over the hill, hurrying after them. "Look here's Father," she exclaimed thankfully, waving to him.

But Anna had already crossed the small stream and moved closer to the bushes and the little hut, hidden by unkempt trees and their straggling branches.

"Oh, it's locked up now, and hasn't been occupied since the staff went. Most of the workers are off fighting at the front," Nina shouted.

Otto's voice called out to them, "There you are!" Nina turned back towards him while Anna only paused, waiting for her father, panting and out of breath, to catch up.

"Hello, Father. We were just about to look at the old gamekeeper's hut." Anna was used to Otto being winded and thought nothing of it. He never ventured this far from the house normally: Hildegard had forbidden him to go out of sight in case he collapsed. Nina sensed something was wrong; she took his arm, studying his features carefully.

Otto was strangely defensive and answered vaguely, "Oh, yes, it's still there, but falling down now. It's not worth getting dusty and dirty for. And it's unsafe!" he added quickly, as though pleased at the thought that here was something that would really put his daughters off going inside.

"I should like to see it again, though. I once left a doll in there and told her to look after it for me," Anna smiled. "I never went back. I wonder if it's still there."

In her childhood Anna had gained warmth and comfort from the little hut and she was in need of that once again, now her memories had been stirred up. She ducked under the branches before either Otto or Nina could stop her. Neither one knew that the other had good reason to stop Anna from going inside.

"I wouldn't go in if I were you, Anna," Otto called. And with surprising speed he caught up with her, placing a restraining hand on her arm, a tense, pleading look in his eyes. He positioned himself between the door and his daughters. "It really is too dangerous."

"There's someone in there, I saw something move," Anna said accusingly.

Nina looked quickly from the window to her father's distracted face, "We'd better go home, Anna, it's probably the roof falling in! And Father needs to be indoors."

"No, Nina! Wait."

Otto wrestled with his conscience. Had Nina been alone he would have had no hesitation in telling her his secret, but Anna was married to a soldier who had shown no sign of changing his views. Nevertheless, she was his daughter and sooner or later she would find out. As he cautiously opened the door and ushered the girls into the small dark room, the thick, musty smell of damp, dust and decay hit them unexpectedly, sending them reeling backwards.

"It's all right," he called out, "we're friends."

In the far corner, rising timidly from their hiding place, were two figures. As they moved nearer, the two sisters could just make out the features of a bent, elderly lady and a second, whose age they could not determine. As their eyes adjusted to the light they could also see that the older woman was gaunt and emaciated, her hair grey and dirty, and her eyes deeply sunken. The younger one was also painfully thin and angular, her eyes, too, were deep-set and fearful.

Nina instantly recognised the face. She let out a gasp of undisguised horror, "My God! Anneliese?" The girl half nodded. "And Mrs. Steiner?"

Anna stood behind Nina, confused.

"Mr. Steiner and Klaus aren't with them," Otto whispered quietly, unaccustomed tears in his eyes.

"But... what are you doing here?" Anna asked innocently, "I thought you went to a new area?" She was mystified by their unkempt, unhealthy appearance. "Your old neighbour told us there was even a postcard from you."

Mrs. Steiner gave Anna a malevolent glare: Anna's marriage into the Wehrmacht made her the enemy now. "Resettlement camps! There are no such things, only in propaganda films," she answered hoarsely. "Concentration camps they're called, not resettlement camps. We were either worked to death or starved or just killed outright. We were lucky, they could see we were young and healthy, and we were female, they'd get a lot out of us. But now we hear there are new places being built, especially to kill off as many of us as they can. My husband and son were sent to one of these new extermination camps."

Berthe told her story in short bursts, with little feeling; they had been through too many horrors to have any emotions left. All they had was a primitive survival instinct. "Then it was our turn. But at the station there was an attack by some Poles, from the underground, I suppose. Fools! How many more of them will die, because of it? The SS will line up hundreds of Poles for each German who died."

"Go on," Nina urged impatiently.

"Several of us ran away in the confusion."

"How many?" Nina interrupted, eager to find out how many might yet turn up through the escape line and she might have to hide.

Berthe looked at her, bewildered by the unfeeling remark. "Who knows? We had just been about to board the cattle truck. We ran. I don't understand why the soldiers didn't catch us. There were plenty of them, and we were too weak to move very fast."

"Perhaps there were a lot more of you and not enough soldiers to catch you all." Otto suggested.

"I don't know what became of the others. Liese and I walked for endless nights and days through the marshes and over the hills. Through the forests. Hiding where we could. Until we came to the village." She nodded at Nina, "I saw the pastor near the church, and I remembered what you'd said about him being a friend, if we ever needed one. He immediately came to Otto and you came in the car."

Nina looked at her father in admiration. "How long have you both been here? Oh Father, if only you'd told me straight away." Nina's grip on her frightened, starving friend tightened. "It's all right now, Anneliese, you're safe!"

"What if they're found here?" Anna's plaintive plea tailed off as the faces of her father and sister registered displeasure and pity, whilst Berthe and Anneliese did not try to hide their anger and hatred.

Her family knew her limitations; she was clever, but not intellectual, and like her mother she could not bear political complications. Having kept her out of their discussions, they could not accuse her of ignorance. "It isn't Anna's fault, how could she know?" Nina responded, warmly defending her sister. "Everything they say is true, Anna."

Nina felt awkward. How could she explain anything so appalling, in front of the Steiners? They had experienced it firsthand, while she had only heard through stories. "You must ask Peter about a place called Auschwitz."

To save Anna's embarrassment and stop her from asking further questions Otto intervened, "Right now our problem is where to hide Frau Steiner and Anneliese. They can't remain here, there are no proper facilities."

"Where we've been there were none, either. This is paradise!"

"You'll need clean clothes, baths, some good food, and proper beds to sleep in. This is only temporary." Nina turned to Otto, "We'll have to let Mother know."

"She'll greet them with open arms," he averred. "I was never concerned for Hilde. I just didn't want to entangle you two girls and the children in what might yet prove to be a dangerous game. It's even more hazardous for Berthe and Anneliese, of course, so we must hide them in the house somewhere."

180

Nina was still unsure whether to let either Anna or her father know that she was involved in looking after many Berthes and Annelieses. She decided for the time being to remain silent and treat the Steiners as separate from the escape route.

"Very well then," she began with the assurance of many months' practice. "You and Mother can arrange accommodation in the East Wing where no one else goes. Thank God that most of our servants have either been conscripted or are working in the munitions factories! When it's dark I'll bring them both to the house. Keep the servants away from the library windows; we'll come in that way. Put the light on in my room when you're ready, then when you see us coming up the meadow turn it off. If there's any problem before we come in, turn the light on again. Have you got that, Anna?"

Nina repeated her instructions, and Otto and Anna were relieved that Nina seemed happy to take over.

"The less people that know, the better. That includes the children. Later we can talk. Go on you two, and don't forget - light on in my room till you see us coming."

"The police are searching for them. They were here and then the army. They're hunting everywhere in the village, and in the town. Others must have escaped, as well. Too many escaped." Otto said before he went.

"Then we must be very, very careful."

As soon as she saw the light go on, Nina brought the Steiners from beyond Frieda's tree. At the pace of the two emaciated women, they slowly trudged over the quarter mile of meadow to reach the walled garden. Then singly through the gate into the dark garden, Nina in the middle with one arm supporting each of the women. Inwardly, she praised Anna as she saw the light go out.

Painfully, they crossed the lawn and crunched onto the gravel in the courtyard. Suddenly, a light went on above them. The two Jewesses gasped, and Nina looked up. It came from her bedroom. And they were caught in its bright beam, clearly visible to anyone in the house, approaching behind them or from the side of the house.

"Quick!" Nina whispered. She ran to the French windows in the library, opened them, ushered the two women in and pushed them under the huge oak desk. Frantically closing the glass doors behind her and pulling the curtains across, she turned on the light, sat down and pretended to be writing, her heart pounding like a sledgehammer.

The door opened and Otto peered in. "Ah! Nina!" His voice sounded strained, but not panicked. "We have a visitor."

"Oh! Thank God! Thank God!" Nina gasped, and pushing back her chair she helped Berthe and Anneliese out.

"It's all right, it's Pastor Liebermann!" she cried and rushed across the room to grasp his hand. The look that passed between them spoke of fear and a heightened awareness of the traumatic life they had chosen.

"We had to bring them in; it's much too cold down there and..."

The pastor cut her short, "It's all right, Nina, don't feel that you must justify your actions to me!" He took the two women's hands. "I know you will receive the best possible care. I shall pray for you both."

Saying nothing, the Steiners looked at him, alert with suspicion and gratefulness, but their thoughts remained their own.

The fright they all received served to warn them how perilous it was to harbour their friends. It still took Nina four days to arrange papers. While Otto drove them to Danzig, Nina continued to coach the two women in their new identities, and how to behave if they were stopped at a roadblock or in the dockyard. She handed them over to another courier near the dockyard, where they would board a Swedish boat. Once they were on the ship and outside German waters they should be protected.

After they had parted Nina prayed as she had never prayed before that the Steiners would not be stopped, and asked any questions. Their faces were still gaunt despite a fattening diet for four days, and their speech and demeanour were too Jewish; they wouldn't be able to disguise their voices.

Within the week Nina received two important communications. The first was a telephone call from the Swedish Consulate in Lübeck, where she still had many contacts, informing her that the Steiners had arrived safely in Stockholm. The second was from Claudia and alarmed Nina considerably: Johannes had reported two women had been observed boarding a Swedish boat at Danzig. Nothing had been found to be wrong with their papers, but an observant and over-zealous clerk, with his eye on promotion, had thought there was something incongruous about their appearance. By the time he had mentioned what his conscience nagged at him to reveal, and his lazy superior had carried out enquiries, they had sailed.

"I cannot be expected to investigate every time one of my clerical staff thinks he sees something suspicious. I should be checking every passenger if that were the case!" He had justified his tardiness to his superiors. Subsequently, an order had gone through to tighten security arrangements at the docks – which was what had alerted Johannes.

Nina decided that she must review her escape plans more carefully, and, in particular, keep her refugees longer so they had time to regain some of their lost weight. Their thin, sallow faces would have contrasted bizarrely with their crisp new clothes, and the well-fed Swedish businessmen and their wives.

Otto and Hildegard, especially, had been terribly upset by the whole incident. Hildegard had known nothing about the camps, believing like Anna, that the Jews were being taken to other areas in the conquered lands, segregated from the Germans, but allowed to live out their lives. To hear the story from Jews themselves was irrefutable proof in her eyes. To see how their health had changed for the worse compounded it. That former guests in her own home had been treated in so harsh and evil a way was unbearable. She felt tainted by the whole affair, as though she had been responsible, when she had known nothing about it. Hildegard was aghast and humiliated. Both she and Otto were angry and began to question Peter's role, and that of the army in the occupied territories.

"Pastor Liebermann's a good man," Otto remarked over an evening meal, after the news had reached them that the Steiners were safe. He lit his last Havana cigar wondering if he would be able to obtain more: there were bound to be some available on the black market.

"They came to us like hungry, hunted animals," Hildegard could not settle her mind to anything. "How can anyone behave like that? Nina, how many..." she began.

"No Hilde! It's better you don't ask the girl."

Hildegard quizzically looked at Nina, and gave a resigned shrug. "I suppose you're right. The less said the better. But I won't be able to sleep at night any more."

After the incident, Nina told them of her involvement with the Pastor. Previously she had tried to do as little as possible from their home, so that no suspicion should fall on it. Her natural caution and the respect with which Otto was still held locally had so far prevented trouble.

From then onwards, both Otto and Hildegard insisted on Nina using the house when she needed it. The little hut in the copse became the temporary refuge for many refugees, Jewish or otherwise, as they passed from one link in the chain to another. A handful of the escaping Jews had been found by the pastor, who knew his small flock well, including those not of his religion. Singly, or in small groups, they spent their time waiting there or in the cellar, until they were well enough to travel on to Sweden or Switzerland. Sometimes he would leave them in the hut, before he informed Nina or Otto; if he were under surveillance the family could claim ignorance of how the escapees got there; and if the family were caught, he would not be implicated. But involvement in a clandestine movement of any sort in a totalitarian state was sooner, or later, likely to be discovered and the participants were always in danger.

Eighteen

For some months the attention of all Germany was glued to the Eastern Campaign. By October their advance into Russia was halted only by that country's vicious winter, which came early, with grim and devastating effect. The conscripted soldiers and their equipment froze up, and morale began to plummet for the first time. Winter was normally icy cold in North Germany and East Prussia, but they had experienced nothing like this in their young lives.

At home they lived comparatively sheltered, pampered lives. Here, if they were lucky, they lived in farms and outhouses; out on the streets, in the fields, in trenches, if they were not. The buildings were usually destroyed by their own war machine, roofless or door-less, always open to the treacherous, bitingly cold Arctic winds.

Then in December, the Russians launched a counter-offensive so unexpected that it all but shattered the troops. The Germans had been led to believe that the Russians were *untermensch* - sub-humans - as easily crushed as the Poles. Their new method of war had, so far, been irresistible. What had seemed certain to be over by Christmas was approaching a Napoleonic disaster, and only by Hitler's fanatical insistence that the soldiers should hold fast and stop their retreat did the situation in Russia stabilise.

As the wounded came back from the Russian front and army friends called in on Peter, it became clear to him that their simplistic view of the enemy had been hopelessly naïve. The Russians not only had more equipment than the Germans had dreamed of, but the men were well trained, well fed and above all, used to fighting in the atrocious weather conditions.

And they possessed a tank. "Our shells just bounce off it!" one of Peter's stunned colleagues reported, "And on they come. It's incredible!

How is it we were told nothing about it?"

"We'll never be able to fight with the same supremacy against them as we did. They've beaten us now, however temporarily," another admitted to him in private.

So that his letters were never read by a censor, Peter's correspondence home was always sent through colleagues returning on leave to Berlin or to East Prussia. Anna always breathed a sigh of relief when she received a message, but each month they were becoming increasingly reckless and she worried that one would fall into the wrong hands.

In a letter, sent via a personal friend and delivered by hand, Peter revealed the first hint of a change in his thinking: he could no longer automatically accept everything that was done in the name of the regime as justified. "They will see themselves now as we saw ourselves at the beginning: unbeatable. Psychologically we have turned a blind corner. What is worse, they have right on their side; we attacked them, we violated the treaty."

On top of the humiliating reversal of their fortunes, came another catastrophic blow: the Japanese attacked Pearl Harbor and brought the Americans into the war. When some of the top brass in the Abwehr saw newsreels of the massed ranks of fresh, clean Americans, unacquainted with failure - swinging along in step, singing and whistling as though on parade at home rather than going off to war - they were completely demoralised. This was going to be a long, hard fight after all.

"It was a dreadful error to force the Americans in," Johannes told Claudia. "The amount of equipment they'll bring in to the war will be enormous, given the number of factories they've got. And they're out of range. We can't bomb them into submission, or even damage their war effort as we have the British. Our only hope now is to win quickly. The longer it goes on, the worse it will be for us."

It was at this time that the army plotters were actively seeking to persuade several Field-Marshals to join them; to replace Hitler with an anti-Nazi government and sue for peace, and end the slaughter. But the high-ranking officers held back, unwilling to forswear their pledges.

"If Hitler were dead, your oath would no longer be binding," the conspirators coaxed, but to no avail.

The generals remembered the last war and thought how easy it would be for the rest of Germany to suggest that the army had stabbed Hitler in the back. It was not until some of them had been on active duty in Poland or Russia, and seen to what Hitler's directives led, that they became sickened and one by one joined the intrigue. Their numbers were growing, but their willingness to openly disagree with Hitler had still to be secured. This was perilously close to high treason and these were not men willing to have history accuse them of such a heinous crime.

To the great consternation of Nina and Thomas especially, security amongst the various resistors could at times be stunningly lax. Some played the game with fatalistic unconcern: when two Russian agents who parachuted into Germany were caught, they revealed a hitherto unknown organisation called the Rote Kapelle, the Red Orchestra.

When they were alone at one of their regular meetings in the East Wing, Nina asked, "Thomas, had you heard of them?"

"Yes, but I'd no idea just how many were fighting against this government. It's encouraging, though, don't you think?"

"I'm astonished at the number of old, prominent Prussian families who are Communists. Did you know that von Tirpitz was amongst them?"

"No, I didn't. This means that every Ministry in Berlin has an agent who's infiltrated it. I found out they had radio transmitters all over Germany."

"How many of our secrets have been given away to Moscow, I wonder?" Nina said, "The other day we had some information that could only have come from the Russians. So, one of us must be in touch with them. That puts us all at risk, doesn't it?"

"They'll certainly torture them. Watch your back, Nina, and tell the others to do the same."

They later learned that, of seventy-five captured leaders who were charged with treason, fifty were hanged. Although horrified by the numbers killed, they were encouraged that so many were actively opposed to Hitler's regime.

Otto and Hildegard were both stunned by the deaths of several friends who had been to their Christmas parties.

"Who next?" Hildegard asked.

"Men must be prepared to die for their convictions," Otto suggested.

"And women," Nina added thoughtfully.

But the dilemma for the conspirators had been very real and compellingly urgent: if they used the facts and advice the Russians gave them, the group would have been upholding the Communist regime. They would surely be asked for German intelligence in return and could not refuse to reciprocate. This would be to the detriment of Germany and they would have become traitors. Saving Jews was simply their Christian duty, and they had never seen acts against Hitler as anti-German, but they couldn't take that next step. When they had thought it through they cut all connections with Russian agents.

Wilhelm and Susanna, now at University in München, had no such qualms. Steeped in the conspiratorial, hothouse atmosphere for most of their young lives, they had both become recklessly outspoken. They joined with many of their friends in taking every opportunity to oppose the regime. Away from the sensible, restraining hands of Ruth, Franz and Nina, they had become foolishly brave; talking openly against new laws; distributing leaflets on the university campus - and off it. Such imprudent conduct would have horrified the family, and inevitably have brought them to the attention of the authorities.

"It's our duty to get rid of this dictator and his henchmen in whatever way we can," they had declared defiantly to Franz and Ruth, "And if we have to use the Russians to do it, then we must!"

It had caused a family row of gigantic proportions. Franz and Ruth, like the rest of the family, saw using the Russians as fraternising with the enemy.

"This war is the politicians', not ours. There's only one fight that matters: to get rid of Hitler! That's our battle and we have to win it," they had both agreed vehemently.

"You can't stand against your own government!" Ruth had been aghast at their behaviour, and at the strength of their convictions. Where had they got such ideas?

"It's treasonable to go to war with your own leader!" Franz protested.

"That's exactly what the Russians did in nineteen-seventeen and that's what we're trying to do!" Susanna cried.

"Maybe it won't work for us as it did for them, but we have to try!" Wilhelm agreed.

The majority of Germans were horrified for a different reason: how could so many of their best families, supposedly upholding the fine traditions of German and Prussian life, have become traitors and given away secrets to, of all people, the Russian Communists? They deserved to die!

The opinions of their compatriots served as a warning to the von Ludens of what they might expect if they were discovered.

Yet disillusion was spreading fast through the ranks of the armed forces, as well as within the civil service. Although the break up of the Rote Kapelle, and the brutal hangings that followed, may have temporarily decimated the conspirators' ranks, perversely it served to breed the idea of dissension amongst others. There were a number who were anti-Hitler, but not anti-German. They wanted an end to the regime that Hitler had set in motion, but not to see Germany defeated again. Their cry was, 'To whom do you turn if you are anti-Hitler?' The Americans or the British? But they were further away and difficult to contact. The Russians were now partly under

German domination and easier to contact. And they were, after all, allies of the Americans and the British. If Russians could help rid them of this barbarous dictator, then so be it.

But the Russians, like the Americans and British, had difficulty in believing that there were any Germans disenchanted with Hitler, or that they were willing to do deals with them in order to ensure his downfall. The conspirators were therefore damned by their own people, and held in the highest suspicion by the Allies.

All too soon the Allies were to announce that any end to the war would be unconditional and therefore the plotters could make no deals, no terms for surrender; even Hitler's death would not be enough on its own.

Nineteen

The following spring Peter came home on enforced medical leave. For hours at a time he sat in his plush leather armchair, now and again jerking forward as though about to expound a theory to an invisible friend, then slumping back in embarrassment as he realised what he had done. Sometimes he would sit motionless, his mind a hundred miles away, filled with the despair of a dozen lifetimes. His sightless eyes would gaze at a spot a few feet in front of him, never flickering or blinking, like someone in a trance. Every now and then a frown would rack his brow, as though an event from the past, which had tortured him, was being painfully re-enacted over and over again.

When he had first returned home he had told Anna of a recurring nightmare. "I'm walking up to the Seat of Judgement in Heaven. There is a woman there. And she keeps shaking her head at me, from side to side. And she looks so disappointed in me. She resembles my mother, but it isn't her. Then suddenly there are two paths, one to Heaven and one to Hell, and no signposts. I keep running from one to the other, backwards and forwards. I don't know which one leads to Paradise. Which should I choose? I don't know... I don't know..." he repeated, tormented by indecision and uncertainty.

Anna could scarcely bear to be with him on such days, and would leave him alone. She tried to avoid asking him about Warsaw, and to this end she kept family and friends about her as often as possible. She did not want to hear that Nina's suspicions - for she still believed them to be just that - were true, yet, like her mother, she found the evidence of the Steiners damning.

Then, one day, she was alone in the drawing room staring at an unobtrusive painting above the fireplace. It was a small, modest, Dutch portrait of a woman at her domestic chores in a sunlit kitchen; with no cares, at peace with herself, in a happy world. Anna was studying it lovingly, coveting the artist's ability to capture light, and the contours of the peasant's face, suggesting a woman concentrating so fully on pouring wine from a jug that she was unaware of anything else around her. Anna wished that she could have returned to so simple a life.

Deep in thought, she reflected on how complex and unhappy her life had become. She had hardly been with Peter more than a few days at a time, and thought how little she really knew him.

She recalled a conversation with Nina, when Anna had said how all three of them had been unlucky in love: with Erik in a foreign, unhealthy and dangerous land; Johannes working all the hours God made; and Claudia now hundreds of miles away from him. And she herself had only had a few months of happiness with Peter. "No," Nina had answered, "it's the times we've lived through. Everyone has a tale of thwarted love, benighted love, interrupted love. It's the war."

How Peter's eyes would twinkle under his thick brows, whereas now, when she caught sight of them reflected in the glass covering the painting they were deep and brooding, with who knew what hidden depths.

"Do you remember where that came from?" Peter asked her as she swung around. He was standing in the doorway, his face, like hers, thoughtful, but not tortured any more.

"No," she lied. She did not want to talk about it or about the Steiners, but they were on Peter's conscience.

"I bought it from Leon. When they were leaving you said they had a few paintings they might not be able to take with them, and I bought that one, and one or two others. Quite cheaply, too."

They stared at it in silence, Anna uneasily recollecting both the occasion of the purchase and the more recent hauntingly gaunt face of Berthe Steiner. She ought to have returned it then. Oh! I wish I had remembered it then, she could have taken it, and the others, she moaned inwardly to herself. I'll give them to Nina to send on to them in Sweden, and then they'll have something of their past, or some money from their sale.

"I saw them several months ago," Peter remarked quietly. Anna drew her breath in with fear and stood stock still, apparently still studying the painting. The colour drained from her face. Did he know?

"I had occasion to visit another town and when I arrived at the station there was a convoy of Jews from this area leaving for..." He could not bring himself to tell Anna where they were going, what their final destination was.

"I thought I recognised the daughter, but not her mother; I would never have known her, she looked so old..." his voice tailed off and he was silent for a moment. "It was only later when I thought about it that I realised who they were. There was another face I thought was familiar, too, from the village. There was a raid by a group of terrorists while I was there, a bullet only just missed me. It hit a woman standing right beside me. I suppose it was meant for me."

Anna recoiled at the knowledge of how near Peter had come to death, but he seemed to be taking it fatalistically, standing almost casually, scrutinising the painting. "In the confusion I saw the two Steiners and some others duck between the carriages and run away on the other side of the train."

He paused and Anna could not restrain herself from blurting out, "They didn't say anything about you being there..."

She stopped in absolute horror as Peter swung her round to face him, alive for the first time in months, and she felt his eyes boring into her face, as though he was trying to ensnare her in her deception. The intensity of his stare frightened her.

"You have seen them?" He demanded, grabbing her arms and gripping them in a vice.

Anna was too afraid to answer. Suddenly she understood what it meant to be a Nazi, to have their terrifying power over ordinary people. She had been safe from that feeling, that fear, while she was married to one, but now she had crossed them, she had deceived her husband. Yet she still had a duty to obey him.

"Anna!" he shook her, "I must know. Have you seen them? Where are they?" The command that he once had returned to his voice and Anna was compelled to submit to his authority.

She answered slowly and apprehensively, not for them, they were safe now, but for herself, and her family. "They're... they're in Sweden," she whispered timorously. Like her father, she judged others by instinct and she knew Peter's heart would never allow him to contemplate a dishonourable thought or deed, once he recognised it as such. If she had to, she would persuade him that the Nazis had been wicked in their treatment of the Jews, but for now she had to trust her intuition. "I can't tell you how I know," she began with frightened determination, but to her surprise and huge relief he shook his head.

"No! Don't say any more. You've said too much already. Anna you have no idea what this means to me, to know that there are others who feel as I do now. When I realised... When I allowed myself to realise what really is going on in Warsaw, I couldn't decide which course of action to take."

Peter's shoulders relaxed and for the first time in months he understood which of the two roads was the right one for him. "Other officers just shrugged their shoulders and suggested I do the same," he continued, "some said we had to obey orders. One man told his superior officer quite openly that he was sickened by it. He was imprisoned and demoted. Others have been arrested, some have even been sent to..." He could not end the sentence with "concentration camps"; this was his innocent wife, who knew nothing of his world.

Anna's eyes widened; unaware of what the pressures on him had been, she now began to understand his illness.

"They'd have trumped up some charge or other, dereliction of duty or cowardice, anything. It doesn't matter what it is when you're already dead. You'd have been told I was killed by terrorists in the course of my duties, or something like that. I wouldn't have minded losing my life for speaking out, but I couldn't bring myself to do it when no good would have come of it. I thought, what's the point in saying to my superior, 'I will not carry out these orders,' and then being shot? You would never have heard the truth. I had to be able to bring it to people's attention, my finale had to be a worthy one, a heroic one!" He scoffed, shaking his head in disbelief at his own former arrogance. "Why couldn't I have been content just to have made the gesture with a clear conscience?"

"Oh, Peter. I didn't know."

Anna had waited patiently while he uncharacteristically spilled out his innermost emotions, with passionate excitement, still fearful that he might revert to the strict Nazi and report what she had told him. The passion of his former belief in Hitler's plans for the destiny of Germany was now replaced by an equal intensity in his conviction that he had been misled by him. His experiences in Poland had undermined his faith in the honour of Hitler, and set him firmly on the same road as Anna's family: a road that led diametrically away from Hitler and Nazism, back to real respect where he could hold his head up high again.

"You were brought up that way, Peter. You can't help your background any more than I can. We do what we feel is right." Anna tried to understand, despite her misgivings about his reaction to anything she might say. "We make decisions with whatever information we have to go on at the time."

"You can't imagine how difficult it is to contravene orders. From the moment you become a soldier it's drilled into you to obey your superiors without question. It's in total conflict with all our training and inclinations. But when you discover the instructions are against every moral and ethical code, how do you then balance your duty to higher-ranking officers, to your country, and to God?" He looked Anna squarely in the eyes and she became aware that for the first time in many months he was seeing her and not looking through her to some past experience. "It's good to know I'm not alone anymore. To get to Sweden needs a small army of collaborators, so there must be many who feel as I do."

Anna, always naïve and truthful, said, "You never were alone Peter. I didn't know it either, but Nina and the others have saved..."

"No, no! Don't tell me! And you must tell no one else either, no one! You don't understand the dangers of saying too much. You're still too innocent, Anna." He touched her face gently with his hand for the first time in months. "They have the power to drag your name out of me. I don't want to hear any more."

He held her gently as though discovering her for the first time, and kissed her forehead. He did not feel he had the right to kiss her on the lips.

"What will you do now?"

"What I should have done before. Refuse the orders when my conscience tells me they are wrong. They won't shoot a major!" He added, more to reassure Anna than in the belief that it was true; and he did not tell her that he would ask for a transfer to a fighting regiment. From then on he was a changed man. Hitler no longer had power over him.

The situation of the Jews in Warsaw had become so appalling that, after his return to duty, Peter was no longer able to remain silent. He had increasingly spoken out and refused to sign documents when he knew where the Jews were being sent. "It is dishonourable for a soldier to issue such orders," he insisted belatedly to his superiors. The commands were issued through the SS and Peter was followed.

On one occasion he allowed merchants into the Ghetto to sell food, but this too was a failure. The traders and the Jews were suspicious that it was some kind of a trap. The pattern of behaviour had been set by too many officers. Peter's change of course caused only mistrust amongst the population he was now determined to help, and his colleagues and superiors. It seemed to him that no one on either side was willing any longer to accept his authority.

The Jews were more afraid of him than they were of his colleagues. Their experience of Germans had given them no training to accept a 'good' one, so they saw his intervention as a ruse to get more of them into the transports. His brother officers thought he had gone mad and his superiors could not tolerate his growing resistance to their orders for much longer. He became more and more isolated in his defiance, and it was only a matter of time before the High Command was forced to act.

He was belatedly discovering what each of the conspirators already knew: that though their numbers were increasing throughout the country, and together as a concerted group they raised their morale, when they were each doing their own job, they were totally alone. Each moral decision they made was made in isolation. They could expect neither support, nor rescue, nor any relief from the relentless terror they lived with every minute of their lives. Peter also suffered from the increasing sadness that his resolve to do good was met with resentment and opposition from those he was willing now to assist.

Then came the last incident, which ended in new orders for him. A cattle-truck train full of Jews from the Ghetto was due to leave the station for Auschwitz under the auspices of the SS. Peter headed directly for the station when he learned it was leaving and tried to have the train delayed. His mutinous confrontation with the SS Major in charge was witnessed by many of his own startled men who were not used to officers disputing in public. Peter was out-manoeuvred and out-shouted.

As he was leaving the station, simmering with anger and humiliation - his head down, deep in ideas for stopping the transport - he almost marched blindly into a small gathering of the Jews on the platform, arguing with SS guards who were forcibly dragging them on to the train. In the middle of the group he recognised the tall, blond headed figure of Erik, towering over the wretched refugees. He, too, was rowing volubly and angrily with the SS guards. Peter stepped in, demanding to know what was happening. Erik explained that they were all working for him and held Swedish papers. He showed his perfectly genuine documents to Peter who immediately understood what Erik was doing.

Peter angrily turned on the SS Major in charge and said fiercely, "This train may be in your charge, but these people are neutral civilians and as such they come under my jurisdiction." He signalled his men forward. "Escort them back to their workplace immediately," he barked, slapping their papers into Erik's hand. With a smart military salute to Erik and to the SS officer, he strode out of the station without a backward glance, sure for the last time that his order would be obeyed.

Erik watched him go with sorrowful certainty that the change he had so longed to see in Peter had at last occurred, and sure that it would in all probability become Peter's personal nemesis. His superiors would not condone that kind of action, and the SS would never leave him alone. Peter was now a marked man.

Peter left the station inwardly seething at his humiliating public castration; an officer who could not get his orders carried out was not fit to for the job! His minor victory in gaining a dozen or so their freedom was too small an accomplishment to diminish his melancholy.

Retribution came swiftly. It took only a few days before the order came through transferring him to the Russian front. He received it with very mixed feelings. Freed at last from the onerous duties of an office job and having constantly to carry out orders that had contradicted his conscience, the prospect of facing an enemy he could see and hear, and was trained to deal with, ought to have relieved him. It was what he had longed for; paradoxically he no longer had any heart for front line duty.

Killing the enemy was not the simple task it had once been. You aimed a rifle and fired on the signal and your conscience was clear - you had been ordered to shoot, and you must obey. Now he had seen some of the Poles closely, their homes, their children, and he understood their problems; he had lived with them for many months and it was not so easy to view them as foes.

What, who, was an enemy? They had always been 'the Poles' or 'the Russians'. Now they had become individuals, each with hopes, ambitions, and skills. An occupying army had no option, but to break the cardinal rule, 'never fraternise with your enemy'. However hard they may have tried to keep separate, something of the habits, traditions, and philosophy of each side would be infused by the other. The longer you were there, the more chance there was to absorb part of their culture.

Before he left, his last words to Anna were enigmatic and full of sadness. He wrote, 'I return to the front with no real wish to fight. There was a time when I could barely contain my frustration at not being allowed to do the job I was trained for, and I would have given anything to be able to get to where I am now going. How ironic! When you want something so much that you would be prepared to give your life to have it, the moment you cease to want it, it comes easily within your grasp!

'Tell Erik, or Nina, that I understand now what it was he was trying to tell me in Warsaw. It wasn't just about my work, it was about life itself. Being a soldier implies you have accepted that we can slaughter each other when the state allows, but I believe Erik to have meant that no one should kill anyone, on any pretext. I think he is wrong; there are times when it is necessary to execute someone to save one's country. But I understand his belief now and I respect him for it. He continuously risks his own life to protect others, and when you look at those he shields you wonder if they are worth the risks. But they are human nevertheless, and I have seen doctors, surgeons, teachers, all kinds of educated, intelligent, highborn people looking like scarecrows and half-starved tramps. Who is to say that amongst those he is saving there is not another Goethe or Bach? I know what you will say, Anna: even if they are all unimportant, ordinary people, they are still worthy; even if none of them turns out to be a Bach!

'And you are right. But it is to my everlasting shame that only now do I begin to recognise that fact, or to admit it, at least.

'Where have I been living Anna, with my high ideals that mean nothing! Nothing! And honour - of what value is that when it is used in so prejudicial a fashion? How could the honour of the regiment be

199

maintained by killing defenceless children and their mothers? Even if they are the enemy's wives and offspring. If you knew what horrors I have seen. You cannot have pride in a regiment, only in abstracts, and honour cannot be paid to people, only to ideals.

'Everything I was taught to believe in has to be re-examined now. Each order I receive has to be inspected for defects before I act on it. It is an intolerable situation, which can only get worse. I no longer know if I am able to shoot 'the enemy'! I shall make a very poor serving officer from now on.'

Peter put his last letter before he returned to the Eastern front on his dressing table at home for Anna to read after he had gone. He left instructions for her to burn it immediately after reading it.

Shortly after Peter left for Russia, Anna revealed to her family that she was pregnant again.

Twenty

In October, Otto was informed that a Russian prisoner was being forced on him, and being made to work on his farm. The first thing he noticed about the man was the uneasy watchfulness in his eyes. He spoke no German and reacted to every remark directed at him with a sullen stare; and there was venom in his glare, which kept everyone at a distance. He was undernourished and his clothes were offensive rags. Otto was ordered to keep him in an outhouse with a strong lock, and to underfeed him in order to maintain his servility. The idea of deliberately starving and enslaving someone was distasteful to Otto, but he had learned long ago not to reveal any disinclination to conform.

Once the prisoner's escort had departed, with other prisoners to be delivered to nearby farms, Otto immediately released the piteous man and took him to the servants' quarters. There he asked the maid to run a bath. The horrified girl refused. And eventually Otto had to direct the task, ensuring that there was someone else with him the whole time the Russian was there. Despite a long refreshing bath, clean clothes, and a huge meal, his face remained impassively guarded.

Anna and Nina watched him reflectively from a first floor window as he was shown around the outhouses surrounding the courtyard at the back of the house.

"I wonder if he has a wife or children at home," Nina pondered.

"Do you think it's safe to leave him alone with Father?" Anna asked.

"Jürgen's there, too," Nina said, then added, grinning, "Come to think of it, he wouldn't be of any great assistance, would he? He's all of sixty!"

Jürgen had been in the family so long that he was like an old uncle to the girls.

"Anyway, where could he go? He wouldn't get very far without speaking any German."

Nina was less concerned with her father than with the prisoner. "I wonder how he came to be here. We don't know if he was captured fighting or taken in an occupied town." She paused for a while, and then unexpectedly said, "Anna, I shall learn some Russian; someone has to be able to communicate with him!"

The thought that Erik might be taken prisoner by the SS, by the Polish underground or by Russians if their army pushed them back, was never far from her thoughts. What would happen to Erik if he should find himself in a similar situation? Who would come to his aid? By helping the Russian, she felt that perhaps she was only doing what women in other countries might do for her loved ones.

Concerned only abstractly with the Russian's welfare, Anna felt secure in leaving communication with him to Nina, and she withdrew to her room to read again a letter from Peter at the front. It was sent soon after his arrival and was largely uninformative, giving Anna no real hint of where he was, though it was clear he was somewhere in Russia. 'We are told that the snows will not be long in coming and the temperature will drop below zero suddenly,' he wrote. 'Our winter clothing will arrive soon and we all await it expectantly - it would be hard to fight if your fingers were frozen.' He went on, 'the army would never let that happen.'

As it continued, Anna realised that this letter may have come through the normal army post or had been carried by someone Peter did not know, and he had to be very careful what he said. She was disappointed, she had hoped for something more substantial and revealing, but she was given hope for something yet to come by a small note at the end. 'I am writing a longer letter to you, which I hope to send out with the next plane.' She waited impatiently for the next message to arrive.

After she had consulted Erik's library of language books, hidden in the attic with other forbidden fruits of their previous life, it took Nina only a few days to converse with the Russian in a few simple words. Copious use of her hands, and laughter when she was hopelessly lost, gradually forged a bond between them. His name was Alexei. Nina's delight in being able to speak some Russian communicated itself to him, and occasionally he gave a grudging reply to her halting questions.

One day he surprised her by using the only German word he ever admitted to having learned, "Kamerad Nina." He had been a farmer in a small village west of Stalingrad, she discovered, and had been rounded up by soldiers and sent to East Prussia with many others. His wife had been taken at the same time, but he had no idea what had happened to her.

At the same time, a wounded friend of Peter's called on them briefly to tell Anna that Peter was alive and well, and was somewhere near Stalingrad.

"Just think, Anna," Nina said, "Alexei and Peter may have met or seen each other."

Otto voiced the opinion of himself and Hildegard, "I think it would be wise to remove any photographs of Peter while he is here. We don't want to tempt fate."

"But, surely, he won't be coming into the house?" Anna was aghast at the thought.

"These days anything seems possible."

The children began by being a little afraid of this dark, stooped stranger. He would fix them with a black stare, but then one eyelid would slowly close down in a wink and Dieter would giggle; Ullrich would copy Dieter, and gradually the children all came to enjoy his company. Alexei might be a strange and frightening figure, but he was there; their fathers were not. And the children in their turn brought some semblance of normal family life to the brutally exiled and lonely Russian.

Christmas came and went in tense anticipation as bad news from the Russian front slowly filtered back home, enlivened or watered down as the censors thought fit. The Christmas day message by soldiers, over the radio through a direct link-up from Stalingrad, gave them some hope of a change in their fortunes.

"If they're on the radio it can't be as bad as Johan suggested," Otto surmised. "He gave the impression that they were cut off. They can't be, there must be a gap in the Russian lines large enough to come and go."

Johannes was right. He had heard that the radio broadcast was a fake; a propaganda coup organised from a studio in Berlin, but had not had the heart to tell the family so near Christmas. It would be more humane to leave it until the New Year when the situation might be clearer. Only he within the family knew that the entire Sixth Army was surrounded, and no one could possibly get through to Stalingrad to interview the soldiers.

Christmas was a bleak, Spartan affair compared to the huge lavish parties of pre-war days. None of the family had much heart for celebrating, especially not Anna, and she and the family went through the motions for the children's benefit.

Then towards the end of January, a colleague of Peter's, Captain Schulz, arrived at Otto's house. He explained to the family that he had been injured in the battle for Stalingrad and had been flown out of the city just before the airstrip was captured by the advancing Russians. He had been in hospital at Königsberg for over two weeks and had only now been able to deliver a letter from Peter.

"It was fortunate that you received your wounds when you did," Anna commiserated, even though the only hope now for Peter was in him having been captured. His unopened letter bored into her hand, but her duty to her guest must come before her own selfish relief.

"There is no fortune in being removed from the battle," Captain Schulz answered sharply. "We should still be there, fighting it out, doing what we were sent there to do. And what good is being made a Major if you are not at the front anymore?" He paused, clearly angry not to have been left at Stalingrad. "Did you know Peter was made up to Colonel?"

"No! Good gracious! No, I was not notified," Anna answered, astonished, but his new position did not seem important at that moment, she wanted Captain Schulz to go so that she could read Peter's letter.

"Yes, I am to be a Major, but it is not official yet," Captain Schulz's pride was undiminished, despite the severe blows the army had suffered for over a year.

Otto wondered why, after Peter's transfer to the Russian front under strained circumstances, he should have been elevated to Colonel. And Captain Schulz a Major? He could see no reason why an upstart like him should be promoted at all. Otto did not know that Hitler, in a vain attempt to keep the soldiers fighting, had up-graded huge numbers of them, including von Paulus, who had become a Field Marshall. No Field Marshall had ever surrendered before, and this was Hitler's way of trying to ensure that they should fight on to the death.

Anna had learned much more about the Stalingrad campaign from Captain Schulz than she or anyone else had from the heavily censored newsreels and radio broadcasts. But what she now read was to shatter the confidence of all of the von Luden family in an ultimate German victory.

'I am writing this in the hope that it will reach you via Heinrich who has been wounded and will probably be flown home. You may have already surmised that we are at Stalingrad. You cannot imagine the cold! Overnight the temperature plummeted. Even in East Prussia we suffer nothing like this; or perhaps it is because we have to live out in it at all times that it seems far worse. The men freeze at night, and through the day. There seems to be no difference. There is no possibility of getting warm. If we have any hot rations, which are quite rare, the icy winds cool them before they reach our mouths.

The guns are frozen. The fuel in the tanks turns to ice, as does the oil, so the engines seize up. The war itself freezes to a halt, but we must drag ourselves out of our pitiful little shelters and pretend that we can continue to wage war! It is a dreadful place to be. Morale is at its lowest. If the Russians were to offer us boxes of matches I think we would give up the fight just for the warmth of a single match. I do not imagine you hear anything of this from our news broadcasts - it is 'not good' to let the families back home know what the troops are really suffering.

'The responsibility of keeping morale high is crushing. They have little extra in the way of winter clothes. Half the men are wounded. And everyone is half-starved. The situation is really desperate. Whatever you are being told at home, there is almost no hope here.

'A few days ago, on the eighth, three Russians came through our lines under a white flag and presented an ultimatum. It seemed honourable, at least the wounded would receive treatment and we would have had more food. But Hitler apparently dismissed it and we must fight on. It is obvious to most of us now that he would rather lose two hundred thousand men than allow us to pull back or surrender, and General Paulus seems only too glad to agree.'

Anna recoiled almost physically as she deciphered the number and her imagination transposed it into real, flesh and blood soldiers. "Two hundred thousand!" She gasped out loud, clutching at her throat.

'Madness, madness! How was it that we couldn't see before that he is insane? A human with inhuman tendencies. He has condemned his nation to death, for when this battle is over, so few will remain. Most will be either dead or prisoners. The German people will lose their resolve to fight and morale will sink too low for us ever to win again. The Russians will be so bolstered up they in their turn will become invincible. They already have warm clothing for these sub-zero temperatures and they have full stomachs. And warm homes to go to. That in itself will lose us the battle.

'The three who came through our lines seemed courteous and civil, not at all the wild animals we had been led to expect. But nevertheless, Anna, when you hear of the collapse at Stalingrad, for you will hear of it, there is now absolutely no hope of any reversal, it is too far gone, then the Russian onslaught will not be long behind it. And after what I have seen and heard of our behaviour to them, they may not give us any quarter in return. They will not stop to ask how you treated others, they will only want to exact revenge on any German in their path.'

Anna suddenly felt her hair stand up in electric fear. With increasing dismay, she sensed what the full extent of the tragedy was likely to be; and that Peter expected to die. She understood that he foresaw the imminent collapse of the army and the unthinkable consequences of it: the Russians invading Germany, just as the Germans had invaded Russia. Her sense of hopelessness and foreboding mushroomed.

She stood up, transfixed by what she was reading, wanting to share it with her family, but unable to drag her eyes away from his words. She walked slowly, a little unsteadily, towards her bedroom door.

'What I have seen of our treatment of the Poles and the Jews of Warsaw pales into insignificance when I see what we have done to the Russians. If we thought of the Poles as sub-human then we see the Russians as little more than animals. One soldier in my company came to me last night to unburden his soul, I imagine. He was in a place in the Ukraine called Dubno, in October. The picture he described to me was so horrific that I cannot begin to tell you about it. Suffice it to say that there are probably no Jews left in Dubno, they were all killed just as he told me. I have heard enough of these improbable stories now to start believing them, and on our way here we passed such scenes. I no longer have any heart to fight on our side in this war. How can I fight for such murderers? Oh, God, Anna! What has Germany done to deserve such a monster? How did we ever let it happen? What blindness we must have suffered from. The havoc we have wrought here in Russia, the murders I have seen amongst the civilian population are unimaginable to you.

"When they win this battle and push us out of Russia, they will not stop until they are on German soil. And then heaven help us all for they will seek a terrible revenge. And in all honesty I could not blame them.'

She had reached the last page and slowly descended the stairs to where her parents were. Hildegard heard her footsteps and turned, then cast a shocked, expressive look at Otto. Anna paused in the doorway, still reading through the tears coursing down her cheeks.

'For obvious reasons you will not see this until Heinrich is allowed out of hospital and can bring it to you in person. I only hope I am not the cause of his death by firing squad for carrying defeatist literature, or yours for sending it to you. But what is to come from the Russians is far worse than what you might suffer from the Nazis! Heinrich does not know what is in this letter, and he does not feel as I do now, so do not tell him what I have written. He is an honourable man; I know he will not read it. He thinks it is simply the last letter from a man to his family.

'I cannot write much more Anna, my hand is in considerable pain from the cold. I thank God that pencils do not freeze as quickly as pens so that I have at least had the opportunity of giving you all warning of probable events to come. If I were ambidextrous I could have warmed one hand in my pocket for a while!

'**Anna, you must all leave for the West just as soon as you are able**.

'If I come through this I will find you through Nina's home in Sweden. Show this to Nina, she of all your family will know how best to act. Nemesis is all too near for all of us. Go **NOW,** Anna, while you have a chance. Pray for me? All my love to you and the children.'

Despite the grave and frightening news, Anna could not help noting the irony of how Peter had enlisted the services of the unsuspecting Captain Schulz to bring back news that the Captain would have shot Peter for revealing.

The over protective Otto tried to explain away Peter's fears to the tearful Anna "He's probably battle weary and demoralised."

"Whether he is or not, he's got a point," Hildegard said. "If we do lose... What would you do, Otto if you were a Russian commander?"

"Probably push back towards Germany, and just as soon as I could. Don't give them time to recover. Hit them hard, immediately." Otto answered as an army man, momentarily unaware of the effect his words might have on civilians.

They sat thoughtfully, each digesting the tragic reports of their army's collapse and the probable death of Peter and many of his colleagues. Anna feared for the children's future, and about what her husband might be suffering at that very moment.

Hildegard, pondering Otto's words, mused, "Perhaps that was just the way Peter was thinking, Otto, and he was trying to warn us."

"I expect he was looking at the worst possible eventuality. It won't happen like that, these things never do." Otto realised his attempts to comfort Anna sounded more like platitudes and stopped. "Peter was probably right, the Russians never seem to do the predictable thing."

The official news from Stalingrad became increasingly grave and though Anna received constant support from her family, there was little anyone could do except mouth empty reassurances that neither they nor Anna believed. On the third of February, their hollowness became transparent when a sombre roll of drums preceded a special communiqué on the radio, informing the German public that the battle of Stalingrad was over.

What alarmed the family most was the statement that they had fought to the last breath. The country as a whole may have taken it as the normal colourful, if exaggerated, form of praise for their fighting skill, but after Peter's letter, it may have meant precisely what it said.

There was no word for weeks, and Anna kept going on the expectation that he would be recorded amongst the prisoners when their names came through. But he was not on any of the lists.

Finally, one day, a telegram arrived.

On that day Nina came home completely shattered from a long, arduous mission to Danzig. There were still Jews and other nationalities to save, and life had to go on as usual. Her line had become increasingly disrupted and she had to do much of the escorting between safe houses herself, a nerve-wracking and mentally exhausting task that put her increasingly in the front line, all the more in danger of being followed and caught. She was always careful not to park the car near her destination, but to leave it in the suburbs and take a bus or tram in to the centre; that way she had time to check the people around her. Her survival might depend on her memory and she had spent some time cultivating the art of Kim's game from a Rudyard Kipling's book - which Nanny bought for her a long time ago in another life.

He trained his memory to become a spy for the British in India, and as children she and Claudia had amused themselves with it. She had revived it as an essential skill needed for her new role. Now she found it was of great assistance in remembering who had got on the train at her stop. She could check if any of them alighted when she did and walked in the same direction. Her ride home had been punctuated by frequent checks in the rear mirror and short stops to see if any car was with her for any length of time.

As she approached the house down the tree lined drive, as far away as the ancient stone archway with the family's crest chiselled into the brickwork, above the car's engine, she could hear the sound of music coming from the house. She swung the car round the fountain to a halt. The noise had increased and she saw Irmgard hurriedly closing up all the shutters. Nina passed Alexei, standing on the grass, a spade slung idly over one bowed shoulder, his hand on his hip, listening and watching, with a half-amused, puzzled expression. Hildegard and Dieter met Nina in the hall.

"Mother, it's Rachmaninov! What's wrong?" she demanded, briefly hugging Dieter and tousling his hair, but never taking her attention off of her mother's face. In Hitler's Reich, Rachmaninov did not exist; to play his music was forbidden and highly dangerous; to Nina it was a warning of something disastrous.

Tears formed in Hildegard's eyes as she took Nina's hands. "Anna had a telegram," she stated, struggling to keep her voice from breaking.

Nina understood instantly. She sprang from Hildegard's embrace and with unaccustomed agility, raced up the stairs to Anna's room. The volume was lowered and then stopped. And, with relief, the house breathed again.

Later, Anna apologised to everyone, including the few servants they had left, for putting the whole house in jeopardy.

"I'm sure if anyone had heard it, under the circumstances, they wouldn't have done anything, dear," Hildegard soothed.

"Alexei was right outside the door," Nina said.

"He's only a farmhand. I doubt that he'd be aware that Rachmaninov was one of his compatriots. And if he did," she added, "he wouldn't know he was banned here!"

"Nevertheless, he's an enemy of Germany. You never know what he might do!" Nina could have added, 'Whole families have been sent to concentration camps for far less innocuous acts.'

The telegram said starkly, 'Missing, presumed dead.'

After the initial shock, Anna took Peter's apparent death stoically and grieved only in private. She had already had many weeks to imagine all the worst possible events that could have occurred. 'Missing, presumed dead' gave an almost clean, clinical approach.

Many problems sprang from the indecisive telegram. Not officially declared a widow, she could neither claim any benefits nor dispose of any of Peter's property. She had to live on her own capital and rely on money from her relatives if that ran out. But she had a home and fortunately the children were barely affected, they had seen so little of their father.

Despite its inconclusiveness, she felt as though some decision had been made. She knew now in which direction to go. If Peter, the one time fanatical follower of Hitler, had come round to accepting Nina was right in what she was doing - the Jews were really being murdered and desperately needed rescuing - that was enough for her. From then onwards she became of greater assistance to Nina, doing whatever she could to help with the escape line.

Nevertheless, Nina never quite took her fully into her confidence.

Twenty One

"Nina, I wanted to talk to you about something special," Thomas paused, trying to find the right words before continuing. "I find that I have some other bad news." Never usually at a loss for words, he looked hard at Nina as though probing her mind for any weak spots. Could she take what he had to tell her? "*Very* bad news."

They were alone in the East Wing of the house, where the servants could not overhear.

"Is it... Erik?" Nina faltered, anxiously bracing herself for the worst. They both knew the risks he took in Warsaw every day, and the passport of a strictly neutral country might not always save him. Each day she found the time to thank God that Erik had survived. His work was so essential she did not feel guilty about asking God to watch over him above others.

"No! God willing, he is still safe. No, this is closer to home. Had you heard that there was trouble in February at the University in München?"

Nina shook her head, her brain running off in all directions trying to tie up events in München with her family.

"Several young people were arrested a few days ago after a meeting. I don't know the exact details, but some of Hitler's henchmen seem to have made lewd suggestions to the female students. There was a near riot and they were thrown out. It was bold, brave, but in the circumstances, very stupid. Many protestors were detained later when they tried to distribute anti-Nazi leaflets."

He saw that she had not yet made the connection. Her tiredness and her relief that it was not about Erik had clouded her usually quick mind. "Wilhelm and Susanna were both arrested," he said, as gently as he could.

Nina's hands flew to her mouth as she suppressed a gasp of disbelief. "My aunt and uncle! I must go..."

Thomas stopped her. "They are already under surveillance. You mustn't go near them. I'm so sorry, Nina." He silently studied her brave attempt to hide her own fear. "I don't think any of us are being shadowed, yet," he added.

"They're being watched?"

"Yes. When Susanna and Wilhelm were held, a tail was put on their parents. Franz managed to slip a message to a mutual friend, but we must not go near them, nor 'phone. I'll keep you informed when I can. They know they're being watched, they'll be careful. But we'll have to take them out of the line, for now at any rate," he added gently.

"They'll be all right then, won't they? The authorities can't have any proof, can they?"

"Nina, there's more," he took her arm, led her to a chair and made her sit down. "I heard of it only this morning. That's really why I came straight here today. I had hoped not to burden you with it." Thomas was trying to find ways to give Nina the dread news that he carried, without hurting her too much, but he knew there was no possible way that she could remain undamaged.

"Please, what is it, Thomas?" She asked, grasping his hand.

"Some of the students have already been taken before the People's Court and found guilty of treason."

He paused for some time, trying mentally to prepare her. "They have already been hanged." There were no easy words to soften the blow and he looked on powerlessly as Nina's miserable eyes filled with tears. "I don't know if Wilhelm or Susanna were amongst them."

He lied badly, and Nina let out a moan of intense misery and pain, as she understood what he could not bring himself to say. The tears coursed uncontrolled down her face as she sat mutely looking up at Thomas for signs that she had mistaken his message.

Although they had lived at some distance from her cousins, she had always been fond of the twins. Being only four years older, she had observed their

214

progress with interest; seeing them make the same mistakes that she had just made herself, aim for the same high values to which she, too, had aspired. It had been like studying herself, or seeing her own children grow up at times. She had drawn closer to them as they reached their eighteenth birthday. Bright and quick-witted, they had both streaked ahead and passed their final examinations with ease. She had missed them when they went off to university together. They seemed to find strength in each other's company and had both willingly joined the anti-Nazi group, throwing themselves into writing, printing and distributing leaflets both on and off the campus.

She and their parents had worried, with good reason, that the twins would do something rash and get themselves into deep water. And they had all spent hours counselling them to be more circumspect.

"Have Franz and Ruth been told?" she asked, gaining some control over her wayward throat muscles.

"I don't think so." This time she was confident that he was telling the truth and it relieved her a little to know that they were ignorant of their youngest children's fate.

Thomas could not bear to see her so unhappy. When she rose, and with a cry clung to him for support, he held her in a bear-like embrace until she wrested herself free, regaining some of her composure.

"The news won't kill me, but you will!" she said wryly, belatedly remembering that both Susanna and Wilhelm had been quite as prepared as she was to face death for what they believed in.

She disappeared to tidy her face up and when she returned she looked subdued and calm, but very pale. Every now and then her features creased into pained lines and twists as she fought against breaking down again.

"What was the other reason you asked to see me?" she asked, trying to recapture a semblance of normality. It seemed to be the only thing to do.

Otto, Hildegard and Anna would have to be told, but Thomas would be with her.

"Other reason? Oh, yes!" This, too, would only add to her unhappiness.

215

"I've made the decision," he said finally.

"Oh Thomas! All the time I have this fear of losing Erik. I couldn't bear to lose you, too." The tears came unbidden.

"I have to do it." He stared at her saddened face; aware of the amount of pain he had brought her. It lay like a huge physical burden on his shoulders, bending them and bowing his back.

"I know, I know, but..."

"I'll take care. Don't worry; you won't lose either of us!" He hugged her again briefly and affectionately. "After the war is over we will both come back and fight a duel over you!"

Nina smiled at him thankfully, knowing he was trying to dissipate her unhappiness. "I wouldn't have either of you if you fought over me. You know my views on fighting. Come back to us safely, won't you? Will you be able to live with your conscience afterwards?"

"God willing I shall. My religion can't be divorced from ethics; I can't turn my back on the world, I must act! I'll be all right. If I'm caught I shall give no one away. Even if I should, each and every one of us has made this commitment carefully, with full understanding of all the possible consequences. You have Nina, as I have, and both Erik and I worry about you, but we can't change your decision, and you cannot change mine!"

"Well then," she blew her nose noisily to hide the sound of the sobs she could not control, "if you need me I'll be here. Neither Switzerland nor Sweden are far away."

They were silent for a few moments, each gripping the other's arms.

"There will be a lot less decent people when this is all over, Thomas. All the selfless ones will be gone," Nina lamented softly.

"Not all. It often takes the death of a good man to bring out the best in others, have you noticed that? It is such a massive loss, it inspires others to try and take his place. The death of a bad person is seldom mourned."

"I hope you're right. When I stop and think of everyone I love, the danger we're all in, it makes me tremble. Do you have no fear, Thomas?"

"Yes! But I fear ideas! Hitler's fill me with terror for what they can do to mankind. I can't live with that any longer. Physical fear! Now that's different. Someone hits me, I bleed! They pull out my fingernails, it hurts and I scream. They hang me, I die! Pain and death is the lot for us all, so why should I be afraid of it?"

Life was that simple for Thomas. He never dwelt on thoughts that might bring suffering, when it might never come. He was neither a coward nor consciously brave, but took life as it came. If it brought trouble and torture, he would deal with it as it happened.

"Johan said that he's already had to lose or misplace some incriminating papers, which pinpoint some of the members of our group. We're all marked. You especially, Thomas. And Johan can only cover us to a certain point. It's possible that he can lose your details, too, but please be careful who you talk to, Thomas, be sure of them before you say too much."

"Never! There comes a point where you must just trust people."

"But you're too open and trusting! These are not times for placing confidence in anyone without testing him or her first."

"No, Nina! You're falling into their trap. You've become wary of your neighbours. I take people the way they are. If one wants to betray me to the authorities, then that is how he is. That's what they feed on - our trepidation. I won't let them do that to me."

"But we have other lives in our hands, we must be sure..."

"No, Nina, I will not become suspicious or cautious of people just in case one of them wishes to report me. They will if they want to. If I give in, the Nazis triumph and humanity loses. So I won't change! They are not going to win. But, can you do something for me? Pray for me next Sunday?"

"That soon?" Nina thought quietly. "Thomas, suppose I arrange an alibi for you. Would that help? Let me know quickly."

Before they left the East Wing, Thomas helped Nina to her feet, holding on to her hand longer than he should. And Nina, vulnerable and miserable, hugged him to her as a good friend. He kissed her on the cheek briefly.

217

"Thomas, don't go. Don't do it, please?"

As he sat with her hand in his, watching her struggle to regain control of her emotions, he felt pangs of love for Nina stirring. While Erik was alive it could never go further; Nina's heart was Erik's, not his, but he knew that he loved her.

"We must go and find the rest of the family," he opened the door, deliberately ending the opportunity to be alone with her.

"Yes," she answered, dreading telling her parents. "Stay near me, Thomas."

On the following Sunday, Nina arranged for Pastor Liebermann and his children's choir to come to the house and spend all day practising for their Easter service. This was to be an alibi for Thomas who had already been involved with a group working out the details of a plot to kill Hitler. The resistors had fashioned a bomb out of a brandy bottle, to be carried by an unsuspecting General accompanying Hitler on one of his plane trips. At the time the device was due to detonate Thomas would be helping the Pastor with his choir practice in front of dozens of witnesses.

Nina spent the day smiling brightly at the hard working children and their parents whilst trying to hide her inward anxiety. The children brought with them an air of respectability. No one looking in on this family could imagine them being involved in any plots when they clearly had their hands full. It was a useful cover and Pastor Liebermann found himself called upon more than once to lend his choir to the von Ludens.

Thomas attacked the piano with great élan, ignoring every piercing telephone call or authoritative knock on the door. Nothing was normal that day, every interruption had hidden meanings. The atmosphere was strained, or bright and cheerful, depending on whether you were a conspirator or one of the innocent visitors.

The redoubtable Frau Braun dropped by to see her grandson singing in the choir and found it all rather strange, as she later said to her husband, who was now working for the Nazis in the town hall, "There's something funny there. I can't quite put my finger on it. There were some strange looks between Nina and the Pastor when the phone rang, as though they were expecting some bad news. I think you should keep an eye on them, Berthold."

Nina had been wary of this woman since the Christmas party in nineteen thirty-two when she had discovered Frau Braun was a staunch Hitler supporter. Now, Nina chose her words carefully when they were close to each other. She passed round the refreshments with a charming smile, and no hint of the panic rising inside her, as the expected call had not come. Had something gone badly wrong? Had the bomb been uncovered? Were the SS on their way to arrest them all even now?

She inwardly smiled grimly to herself, picturing a fictitious scene as the Gestapo burst in and Frau Braun found herself having to give both Nina and Thomas an alibi! So Frau Braun might be useful to the cause. She found the thought captivating.

Eventually the strain became too much, and Nina dispatched Thomas to the village to find out what was happening, preferring not to let him make the calls from the house.

He was gone for nearly an hour and the children and parents began to notice his absence. The children were all waiting for his return to start their rehearsal again.

"Nina," Pastor Liebermann cornered her, "where has our pianist got to? We need to begin again soon."

"I think he's just having a quiet rest," she suggested, hating herself for lying to the good pastor. "I'll go and find him."

She rushed off to the back of the house and impatiently drummed her fingers on the windowsill until she saw Thomas pushing his bicycle across the meadow.

Letting him in through the French windows, she asked impatiently, "Well?"

"I had to ring several people, and this machine kept letting me down." He brushed off some mud from his trousers, evidence of the occasional spill he had suffered en route. "It didn't go off! The whole group was alerted and waiting for the signal that Hitler's plane had been blown up, but it apparently landed when and where it was supposed to. It's unbelievable! That man has more lives than a cat! The problem now is that there's a bomb disguised as a present of brandy on its way to someone and we don't know if it will detonate or not! It has to be retrieved before it's opened!"

"So!" Nina breathed a heavy sigh, "We have to go through all this again tomorrow, or the next day? There is a hand in all this, isn't there? If he had been anyone else, all these attempts on his life would have produced a result by now."

"Precisely!"

"Do you suppose we're being made to suffer this tyranny until it reaches such awful proportions we'll all be so sick of killing that no-one will ever again be able to stomach it, and mankind will at last outlaw war itself?"

"That presupposes that everything is written and unalterable. If we can manage it, his reign of terror will be over quite soon."

"Why was it so necessary to try to get good terms from the British or Americans before trying to get rid of him? Surely if he is so evil, wouldn't it be better to kill him quickly and save as many lives as possible, and worry about the terms of any surrender afterwards?"

"Beware, Nina! You're coming round to the idea that killing in some circumstances is acceptable!"

Her shoulders sagged. "Sometimes I think you're right. But I'd rather he was put away in a mental asylum than assassinated. I just want this all to be over one way or another. But I haven't really changed my view on taking life."

"Unfortunately there are too many generals and colonels involved. It never ceases to amaze me how an indomitable general, a king of courage on the battlefield, can become a timorous mouse when he's involved in politics. It's as though they're terrified their careers as soldiers will be finished the moment they sign the surrender unless they choose the right person to hand over to. I suppose to some extent they are entitled to be apprehensive; any conqueror would disband the armed forces immediately, much as we did to our occupied countries. No wonder they try to bargain the terms first, to keep their jobs and their heads! I don't believe the British or Americans will accept that we're in earnest, however many contacts we make with them and however much we plead and try to bargain with them, until they see some action on our part. We're losing our opportunities."

Nina belatedly remembered the Pastor and his choir. "They're waiting for you, Thomas. Tell them I found you asleep in one of the bedrooms." She quickly ushered him back along the hall and switched on her bright smile again.

The bomb was later ingeniously and successfully exchanged by the conspirators for real brandy bottles, the General and Hitler both being none the wiser. The conspirators, wet with perspiration, and heavy eyed from lack of sleep, heaved sighs of relief. But unlike Hitler they were running out of lives.

Twenty Two

Johannes stared at the open report in front of him in total disbelief. He picked up the loose sheets of paper, his eyes fixed on the typed names, addresses and telephone numbers. Franz von Luden. For a moment he could not understand what Franz's name was doing in a file on his desk at the Abwehr. Ruth von Luden, Thomas Dietermann, then in quick succession almost every name he knew, and many others he did not recognize. This was in connection with their group.

He searched through quickly for his own name, but did not find it, nor those of Claudia or Nina, but the rest were all there. Incredulity rapidly turned to terror. It could only be a matter of time for all of them. He skimmed through the pages scooping up the evidence as fast as he could; it was damning and there was too much for him to take in. There had to be a traitor in their group, but try as he would, he could think of no one who would sink to such a level.

Franz and Ruth were being watched after the twins' execution, but he thought they had all been very vigilant. He, Claudia and Nina especially, were conscious of being followed when they went out. And while making sure they knew where their shadow was, they pretended not to, by wearing an air of innocence. But, if they were all being spied on why were their names not on the list?

The Pastor was not on the list either; it was through him that Nina still had safe access to her escape line. There were many ways out of their estate; the wall stretched for miles around twisting roads and the Gestapo could not keep an eye on every section all of the time. She was always able to spirit her charges away from their home and into the Pastor's safe hands. But she had to be cautious when she returned, so that her pursuer did not know she had been away. Using a bicycle and disguised in old clothes had kept her safe so far.

Johannes was suspicious of this find. Why was his name not amongst them? After all, he was related to some of them, and he saw them all quite frequently. It did not add up. Was it some kind of test to see what his response would be? What would he have done under normal circumstances? There were too many references on too many pages for him to quietly tear up a page here or there. He would have to lose the whole file. He agonised for several vital minutes, wasting time when someone could have arrived to retrieve the lost papers. Normally, he would never have been intended to see the information. It must have been slipped amongst his other documents deliberately. But who had put it there? Who was waiting to catch him?

He could not decide what to do. He would ask the Colonel. He had been involved in the group for longer than Johannes. Taking the papers, discreetly hidden amongst other records, he strode quickly down the corridor. And with a trembling hand, he knocked on the Colonel's door.

There had been no traitor. Himmler himself had become suspicious of the entire Abwehr and had all of them watched, and their telephones tapped. And those they contacted were also investigated. The whole group was under suspicion, though Johannes was carefully not mentioned. It was believed that he might be a minor cog in a spy chain. Should this information fall into his hands, he would have to take it to his superiors, and they would then have to make some move. Whatever they did would reveal their real intentions. It was an elaborate game to trap Johannes, which had already reached check without one side being aware he was playing.

Unknowingly Johannes had performed his part, and the web had accomplished what it had been spun to achieve: he had pinpointed the top traitor, the brains behind the anti-Hitler plots within the army itself.

Less than two days later the house of Franz and Ruth, near to Kösslin, was suddenly invaded by the Gestapo. At the same time Thomas was arrested.

Their houses were ransacked, documents were seized, names and addresses noted and their farm workers and domestics whisked away. No one else in the family was informed.

The labourers and maids managed to persuade the Gestapo that they were completely innocent, and several weeks later, when they were released, they were able to give Otto information that led to him tracing his brother's whereabouts. Franz and Ruth were both in the same prison in Berlin where they had been taken immediately after their arrest.

At the same time, many of the top men in the Abwehr disappeared, including the Colonel, and Johannes was unable to discover their fate. Johannes for the moment was still free, though he was transferred shortly afterwards and lost his information-gathering position.

Nina was inconsolable after the loss of so many to whom she was devoted. She would willingly have risked her own life to save theirs. She pleaded with Johannes to do his utmost while he still could.

Johannes had already found and then lost the file on Franz and could throw no light at all on why they had been locked up, unless they had all been under observation from a different source.

Johannes revealed his own personal fear that he, too, would be arrested soon and was planning to disappear. He advised Nina to leave as quickly as she could. "Its time to go to Sweden yourself, Nina. Save yourself before they catch you, and take Claudia and the children."

But Nina would not go. She traipsed disconsolately from office to office, from police stations to army posts, posing as Thomas's sister, his cousin, any relative, but to no avail; she could find no hint of where he had been taken. He had been spirited away and had disappeared without trace.

The family was devastated by the series of arrests, as they had been by the deaths of Wilhelm and Susanna. Otto rallied his high-ranking friends, and tried to find Thomas and obtain the release of his brother and sister-in-law, with no success. The Gestapo was in control and both Franz and Ruth were irrevocably imprisoned to await trial at the People's Court.

Thomas had simply vanished.

Johannes suggested the reason he was free was that he was unimportant in the Abwehr. And neither Nina nor Claudia was connected to that group, except through him. Franz and Ruth had been followed, because of the twins. Claudia was no longer anywhere near the rest of the group, and Nina was living with Otto. They all knew Thomas as a friend, but so did many others who were not in detention.

Claudia was in Königsberg where she had been sent to nurse the wounded from the front line. Nina now insisted that she stay where she was. There was nothing she could do and if Johannes was arrested, then she, too, would be in danger. If she remained in Königsberg she had a cast-iron alibi and could not be connected with the others.

Very soon after she had married Johannes, Claudia realized that she had made a mistake. She was a free spirit, needing to roam, but she had become restricted and shackled. When the call had come for more nurses, she had taken her chance to escape from entertaining highly placed Nazis, a task that increasingly filled her with dread. She had shed the responsibilities of running a home and the restrictions of motherhood, happily leaving little Klaus in her mother-in-law's hands. She frequently made the journey home by train to Pomerania to see him, but was quite happy to leave him in his nanny's care for the rest of the time.

There was more than a little hypocrisy in the speed with which she had made her decision; Johannes was perfectly aware of her reason; he understood her character and her needs better than she did herself. He hoped that one day she would grow out of her restlessness.

In Königsberg she could live freely as though she were single again. But she was shrewd enough to see the need to retain the friendship of those in high places, those she had cultivated in Berlin.

Nina, too, was safe for the moment, married to a neutral official and living near Elbing. She was further removed from suspicion than those near Berlin or Kösslin, where many of the conspirators, especially those in the army, had their family estates.

"Father, Thomas is such a good man," she grieved to Otto, after failing to find him, "if they kill him it will be as though a light has been put out. It all looks so black and hopeless, doesn't it? All over Europe men like Thomas are being imprisoned and killed. So many of the best will be gone before this is over."

"You'll still be here, Nina, bringing up the next generation of Eriks and Thomases. You must be, for their sakes."

He meant it as a compliment, but the anger and stress caused Nina to explode impatiently, "Is that all we're here for? To produce and inculcate the next generation ready to be killed? When, when, when will the human race stop this madness! I can get on with people, why can't others? Why do they find it so difficult to talk that they have to resort to attacking each other?"

She stopped abruptly. Such a tirade was rare for Nina and she could not sustain such a negative mood. "You hardly ever see women striking each other," she added, once again pensive rather than judgmental, "Perhaps women should become more involved in politics. Under men, we're still governed by the law of the jungle. He who hits hardest, wins. What kind of a world is that for our children to live in?"

"That's how it is," Otto answered her rhetorical question sadly. "We try, we do our best, but we can't be in control of everything. When folk learn to compromise and give a little more and take less, perhaps we'll find it easier to live together. But we're selfish animals. We're too worried about saving face and not enough about preserving life. Two thousand years on, and we're still a long way off the Christian kind of peace."

Nina spent fruitless hours each week searching for Thomas. She never consciously gave up, but could make no headway against officialdom.

Johannes had briefly reported that there was a rumour that all those arrested from the Abwehr, and other important prisoners such as Thomas suspected of being implicated in plots on Hitler's life, were being held together in a concentration camp, though he did not know which one. He thought that they were in no immediate danger.

After another abortive attempt to see Franz and Ruth, Nina called in to see Johannes in Berlin.

"They have suspicions, but nothing in writing. Those they have watertight information against have already been dealt with," he told her. "To convince outsiders they are being fair and just, they must have proof. But in the end if the prisoners don't break, the authorities will trump up some charge, and manufacture some evidence."

His information had been truncated by the wave of arrests, and he had little to go on but hearsay and rumour.

"There'll be more taken soon. I've discovered how those arrests happened. It seems some businessman was being used as a courier by the Abwehr to smuggle money into Switzerland for a Jewish émigré group. He was stopped at the frontier, but his employers did little to cover him, which was foolhardy in the extreme. To save his own skin he revealed all.

"He gave Himmler's men the details of everyone in the Abwehr connected with plots on Hitler's life, and apparently he knew many. How on earth such a man was chosen as a courier is unimaginable, or how he was in possession of so many names! Some, even at the top, think we're just playing games! They've no idea of the dangers. Not to have gone to his aid immediately was naïve and reckless. And we're all paying the price of their stupid mishandling of the situation!"

"All those brave people imprisoned, because of one man!" Nina was stunned. "Thank God, we've been more vigilant. Thomas didn't know that many conspirators." She paused, as the full implication hit her. "But I do! Since we lost the others I've had to find more recruits to fill the gaps and now I'm the only one running it. I know too many, Johan!" The dread of physical torture suddenly overwhelmed the normally courageous Nina and she broke down.

"Be very carefully, Nina, they must have you under surveillance, all of you."

"I didn't have a tail."

228

"Nevertheless, don't do anything to bring attention to yourself. You must turn refugees away rather than hide them if it becomes necessary."

"But then I will have become a murderer. If I do that they'll be caught."

"What if they torture you?"

"Don't!" Nina winced with pain at the thought.

"God! What a mess, all this from... It was short sighted and clumsy planning. He was clearly not checked out thoroughly before he was chosen for the task. He might even have been a plant, one of Himmler's men. Fortunately he didn't know me and I was always very careful, but I feel the net closing in." He put his arm around Nina's shoulder. "It's time for me to disappear, too, Nina."

They arranged to return quickly to East Prussia where they had many more contacts and places to hide, and Nina would find a way to get Johannes and the rest of her family out of the country. If he were caught, he was to say he was going to visit his family before asking for a transfer to a fighting regiment. She was to make immediate arrangements for his transportation to either Sweden or Switzerland, whichever could be organised the fastest.

The last thing Johannes said to Nina before she left, was, "Keep alert, Nina. Swedish papers may not save you. You were born a German, remember."

He hugged her to him, not knowing when they might meet again and watched her go with tears in his eyes.

He remained in the shadows, looking to see if anyone was following her, but he saw nothing untoward. She slowly walked down the street, pausing to look in a shop window, using it's reflections to verify her safety, Her trained eye took in those around her, noting their size, their clothes, even their walk: any characteristics that might give them away at the station where she would check again.

"Good girl," Johannes whispered to himself as she disappeared from his sight.

While he packed a small suitcase and destroyed any incriminating letters and notes, he thought about her courage, her tenacity, and about her gentleness, and how unlike Claudia she was. He wished he had been married to Nina instead of Claudia. He felt secure with Nina. She would never let him down, and she would never go her own way without consulting her husband.

And yet it was her recklessness that had attracted him to Claudia in the first place: that vigour, that independence of spirit. He loved her dearly still, but sadly felt that she no longer loved him.

He shook off his nostalgia, picked up his belongings and closed the front door behind him. He turned, to confront two SS men pointing Lugers straight at his chest.

Twenty Three

Nina's last link with safety was cut. She no longer had eyes and ears inside the system to inform her if she, too, were being followed or when papers and official stamps were changed - which they were increasingly in order to catch groups such as hers. When Erik heard of all the arrests, he left his business in Warsaw, and immediately returned to East Prussia to be of some solace to the rest of the family, and to help make arrangements for the line somehow to be renewed.

Nina greeted him unexpectedly, whispering, "Hello, Firefly!" in his ear as she threw her arms around him, hugging him until he had to disentangle himself. Her face was wet with tears, but she said nothing else. With so many of those she loved now gone or living at a distance, Erik was the only one left. Seeing him again was bittersweet; he would go back soon.

The news he brought with him had no comfort in it. "I was glad to come home. I needed to put some distance between myself and Warsaw for a time. What's happening there is a crime against all humanity; truly appalling. The world must learn of it and never, ever forget."

He spoke as if he would not come home again after his return.

He sank back into the deep, comfortable armchair and closed his eyes. This was the first time he had been able to relax in months, but he could not switch off. The softness of the furniture, the sweet smells of flowers and perfume that linked their home to the civilising influence of women, reminded him of a way of life that had ceased to exist for him. He had no time for any pleasures or social life.

He looked at the von Luden's mansion and their possessions with new eyes. What Erik had once seen as elegant and simple good taste now seemed to be a display of ostentation. Reality was back there in the cold, grey, despairing back streets.

His first acquaintance with the occupying powers in Warsaw had almost made him laugh out loud. The strutting German officers ordering people about peremptorily had seemed farcical, and he envisaged a shout of, "OK, now let's go back and do that again, and this time let's get it right!" from a hidden film director. They were all overacting. He simply could not believe that this was supposed to be taken seriously. Surely they had all to be playing some mad game with the public? As a kind of warning.

But slowly over the days, he, too, became caught up in the systematic and sudden checks on papers. He saw law-abiding men, intent only on reaching their place of work on time, restrained and hauled unceremoniously aboard lorries. Women with, or without their children, were bundled into trucks, their shopping baskets carelessly knocked from their hands.

Erik became horrifyingly aware that not only were these individuals unlikely to see their homes again, but their families would be forever ignorant of their whereabouts. They simply disappeared. In many cases the breadwinner was taken and the family left to fend for themselves or starve.

The drama in Warsaw had become a brutally grim existence and his visit home had begun to take on the aspect of a rehearsal for the local theatrical group's current production. They had got the period right, but this opulence, cleanliness, security and simplicity were all imaginary. This luxury of having time to think, have a drink, sit down and pat Bismarck on the head, read a newspaper, all seemed like parts of a carefully timed and perfectly staged play. Reality was back there in Warsaw: chaos, dirt, hunger, and gnawing fear as constant companions.

This was like straying into heaven. Three worlds collided in the fading elegance of this outdated home. War: fighting, wounds, death and destruction. The plotters: fear and conspiratorial silences. And normality: home, relative safety, routine and servants. Each world only partially understood the others, and each believed they had the worst of it.

It dawned on Erik that this must have been how Peter saw it. Only in his case he also had to face the fact that he was largely responsible for those grim and hopeless conditions; for the lives so easily squandered; and the terror that flickered briefly in those tortured faces before being unceremoniously extinguished. Once that realisation came to him there would have been only one course of action left: to make amends and die with some dignity and honour.

"If you prefer to leave it for another time when you feel more like talking," Otto suggested, seeing the exhaustion on Erik's drawn face. He looked grey, lined, ten years older, and his eyes had a haunted quality.

"No. I shall only dwell on it."

He did not really want to speak about it at all, but it was necessary that they should be made aware of exactly what was taking place, and therefore understand what might be in store for them if and, in his opinion, when the Russians overran East Prussia.

"You remember, I explained to you about the ghetto, how they were deliberately starving the population? Apparently they were not dying quickly enough."

He paused to make sure they understood the gravity of what he was about to say.

Hildegard and Otto exchanged alarmed glances and Anna looked puzzled.

"Once they opened the new extermination camps, they speeded up the process and moved the Jews out in their hundreds and then in their thousands. Only, at last they decided to resist. Somehow they equipped themselves with guns, and fought back with tremendous courage. It has been a long, slow and very bloody battle and, I imagine, it's continuing. We weren't supposed to find out, but how could we not do so? They're systematically blowing up the buildings in the ghetto, or burning them, with or without the Jews inside; house by house, street by street, until there's nothing left, absolutely nothing!"

Hildegard gave a stifled cry and clutched her handkerchief, staring at Erik all the while. Anna held her hand over her face, her startled eyes almost afraid to peer out over the top.

233

"You can hear the noise all over the city and see the smoke - all the time. It's unbelievable! Hitler's Götterdämerung! How they must be suffering!"

Erik could not continue for a moment and they could see the muscles in his neck working to prevent himself breaking down. "And there's nothing I can do to stop it. I've complained to everyone and anyone. Soon they'll all be dead, or in camps, which means they must die soon after."

Erik had peppered his story with pauses when he wiped tears from his eyes, but now he was unable to carry on. He got up and poured himself a drink. They all saw the tears streaming down his cheeks and looked at each other in shocked silence.

"I'm sorry. It isn't easy to tell, but you must know. I've tried to save as many as I can, but there has to be a limit to what one man can do. I feel I've done so little of any real use to relieve their agony."

They sat, stunned at the harrowing story, each one in their own way assimilating the intolerable implication that they, the German people, were responsible for this barbarous act perpetrated on the perfectly innocent Poles.

"And now I come back to this - Thomas, Franz and Ruth arrested, Wilhelm and Susanna... and now Johannes, and the others... "

He gripped his head in his hands trying to relieve the weight of all he had endured.

They waited in the awkward quietness, each with their own thoughts, none wanting to speak.

Erik looked up directly at Nina, her arm inadequately around his shoulder; he was too tired and defeated to care if they saw the tears and read his true feelings. "Nina," he entreated, unabashed, "don't you think it's time that you all went home to Sweden?"

"Oh, Erik!" Nina looked pleadingly across at Otto, now her only real helper, hoping to have some support in what would hurt Erik even more. "How can I abandon the search for Thomas and Johannes, and just leave Ruth and Franz in prison? We can't just give up at the first major setback."

She knew it would cut him to the quick. He had been wounded enough, they all had, but there were still too many relying on them.

"I'm sorry, Erik," she said as gently as she could, "but I must go on as long as I know I'm safe. If they had any suspicions, surely I would have been arrested by now, or I'd have a shadow whenever I go out. I don't. And Claudia has linked up from Königsberg and we have a line again, of sorts. We've got a link with someone via Moscow so we'll get advance warning of any Russian offensive. We'll have time to leave later, Erik."

Erik had not expected Nina to agree. Anna would, but Nina was completely sure of her motives. She allowed no emotional problems to intervene. She had no divided loyalties as Anna would have had.

"I'm thinking of the future, too, Erik. What will the world say about Germany, and the German people, when this is all over? That we wanted Hitler? That we liked him? It may have been true at the beginning when he seemed to be doing things for our country that we all wanted, but not now. If you could take a vote on it, I'd say the huge majority would choose to be rid of him. Thomas tried. Others have, too. We've failed so far. If Hitler's still there when it's over, or even if he isn't, the world will find it hard to say a good word about us, won't they? How can we run like cowards just because we have papers and money? I won't desert my country, even if it is in the wrong. Just because I have a Swedish passport, I can't leave my family and friends when the going gets a little rough. When I've found everyone we'll all leave."

"I know, Nina. That's the fine side of the German people that I always loved in you, your personal integrity, but I just wish … I remember Thomas once saying that his duty was first, last and always to God and to no man. He would have been proud of you, too." He added a last thought in the hope that Nina might think again, if not for her sake, then for their son's. "You can't blame me for wanting to see my wife and son safely out of the holocaust to come. After what I've seen, I know there will be one."

The family looked at each other as they felt the first signs of nemesis about to fall on the German nation, about to fall on them!

235

Twenty Four

From her hospital base in the suburbs of Königsberg Claudia had been pestering the authorities for news of Johannes, until she herself was warned that unless she stopped she, too, would be arrested. In Berlin, this resourceful woman had made the acquaintance of Rommel's wife and had maintained their friendship. Rommel was powerful, having the ear of Hitler; even the SS kept their distance from him, and Claudia made sure that she retained his protection.

The news of Johannes's arrest had not been totally unexpected. She feared it might happen after the others were imprisoned, but he had refused to abandon his country while he could still obtain vital intelligence. He could not desert Nina who needed to be aware of changes in passes and papers. His sense of responsibility was as strong as Claudia's desire to shed it.

She was fond of Johannes, but she valued her freedom above her feelings for him. She was dismayed when he was taken, but not crushed, and felt sure he would be released. Claudia was a complex person having both a wayward and a finer, more prudent side. She did not stop either her clandestine work with Nina, which provided information from some of the unguarded wounded officers, or her social life that added a little fun to her life. And she also made use of her friendship with Frau Rommel to try and trace Johannes's and Thomas's whereabouts.

Although she went home at least once a fortnight, she saw her younger sister infrequently; Nina was often away escorting refugees to safe houses. Their paths crossed shortly after Johannes's disappearance and they spent a weekend commiserating and reminiscing together.

"Erik went back to Warsaw," Nina said despondently, after repeating his heartrending tale.

"Couldn't you stop him?" Claudia asked, reading disconsolation in

Nina's drooping shoulders.

"He said he couldn't live with his conscience if he didn't return to rescue more poor souls left in the ghetto."

"Don't blame yourself, Nina. I did my best to get Johannes to leave. I even told him to ask you to spirit him away to Sweden. But he wouldn't hear of it. Our husbands are two of a kind, aren't they? All heart and no sense! Both tilting at windmills."

"Do you remember, when we were young, how we used to talk of a vision for the future? We used to dream of what we would do to make the world a better place?"

"Don't remind me, Nina! We were very young then. Perhaps it was all part of growing up. All my friends at school felt the same way."

Nina was thoughtful for a while. "Yes and the awful thing is that they still do; only their visions are poles apart from ours now."

"How we've changed since those days."

"I don't think we have, Claudia. They're the one's who've changed. They used to believe in honour, but look how they've twisted it. How can they attach a sentiment so full of ideals to a man like Hitler? Have you had any luck with Frau Rommel?"

"She said she'd ask her husband, but she didn't think he'd do anything. He's too tied up. We can't expect any help from him."

"It was worth a try. How's Aunt Alice? Give her my love when you next see her."

"She's the same Alice, gruff and unbending, but she's a little more circumspect with the Nazis. Did I tell you she's been hiding Jewish children?"

"No"

"I won't tell you where, just in case."

"No, the less I know the better. Almost the last thing I said to Johan was that I knew too many people. If they catch me I won't be able to hold out. I scream if a needle sticks in my skin."

"Me, too. I've been helping Aunt Alice with the children when I have

238

time off. I might have to ask you to send them down the line."

"That would be almost impossible without someone to act as a parent. Adults are one thing, but children would do something to draw attention to themselves. Our line is barely working again. I'm sorry, Claudia, but I honestly don't think I can do anything now. Can they stay where they are for a while longer?"

"I think so. But we must get them away before the Russians come."

Since she had persuaded Claudia that it would be safer for her to remain where she was in Königsberg Nina had to undertake the task of searching for Johannes as well as Thomas.

It was all too much for her; she had to give up looking for them. Coping alone with the refugees who were still somehow brought to her through Pastor Liebermann or the few remaining members of the lifelines was taking its toll

It was no easy task to work with a disintegrating line, or to fill the gaps created by arrests. And one by one contacts who had until now slipped through the net were being caught by the authorities.

Who was now a friend and who an enemy, even a Nazi plant, was impossible for Nina to know. Earlier she had been acquainted with virtually everyone, understood their views, how far she could trust them, and knew to what responsibilities and pressures they were all subject. Some had been lifelong friends of hers or Claudia's. Now they had either disappeared or were too frightened to continue. Any one of the new recruits recommended to her or introduced by other members could be an agent of the Gestapo.

With only two sisters, a few reliable old friends, and her parents, how was she to judge who could be trusted? The three men on whom she had placed total reliance - Erik, Thomas and Johannes - were either far away or in prison, and she knew no one from Thomas's line. In spite of all that, gradually, over the next few weeks, she began to forge workable new links in the chain. The task simply had to go on, whatever the risk.

By the spring of nineteen-forty-four she was able to report to Erik that her patched up line was now capable of taking refugees from him again, but she was unable to go through either Switzerland or Pomerania. She could only go directly to Danzig, so Claudia and Alice were increasingly drawn in. Alice became the oldest, and in some ways the most active link. A lifelong member of the local church, she in turn used those of her congregation who were still alive and able to help.

One of her greatest friends was a volunteer in the convent a few streets away from the hospital where Claudia worked. Together they set up a line of aides stretching from the convent to Danzig, and Nina. Above the cellars where the children were housed, German soldiers were being nursed back to health by the nuns. They worked constantly in fear that the children would accidentally give them away.

Alice managed to swear Claudia to secrecy. "You remember that grand gesture, dear? Well, here's your chance. Keep it to yourself, and then if either of us is discovered, your sisters will not be involved!" But now Nina had to be included.

Since her mother had died, Alice had little else to do, and she revelled in her new identity. She loathed the Nazis and constantly chuckled to herself at how 'a bunch of women' could outwit them.

"You know, Aunt, when Nina and I were children we decided we wanted to be like you - when you were younger and campaigned to get women more rights."

"Goodness, no you don't, dear! Those were hard, difficult days for women; you certainly don't want to be like I was then! Nowadays, you don't know you're born! You've got everything! Look at the three of you driving around in cars."

"We've got everything, except freedom!"

"No such thing! You'll never have that, whatever that is! But what are you moaning about? Don't you think you're doing your bit? You're working as a nurse, and you're a mother, then there's your work here with the children and your escape line…"

"I just feel I'm still not doing enough."

"You're talking nonsense, dangerous nonsense, too, in times like these. Be grateful you're able to make the contribution you are. There are plenty who could wish for so much. Wild ideas will get you killed. Stick to what you're doing and do that as well as you're able, that's my advice. And keep it to yourself! That's the grandest gesture you can make, my girl!"

In February, nineteen forty four, Hitler disbanded the Abwehr and arrested many of its people. Responsibility for solving the attempted plots on Hitler's life had more often than not been given to the Abwehr, and they had, therefore, been perfectly placed to divert evidence and suspicion away from themselves. But Himmler's men had been getting closer all the time. Now, intelligence was placed into his hands and the SS. The army no longer had a centre for gathering information, and no easy meeting place; the heart of a major conspiracy had been broken.

While the Abwehr had still been in existence, Nina believed there was a chance for Johannes to be released and to rejoin his colleagues. Then he would somehow be able to effect the release of her family and friends from prison. When it was dissolved, she felt even more isolated.

Anna was with her, but she was incapable of making important decisions, she simply did not appreciate the risks. If Nina were unsure of the trustworthiness of some members of the line, Anna would certainly have no idea. She had been friendly with some of the Nazi officers Peter brought home; it was even more difficult for her to see how dangerous they might really be. She still trusted them as Peter had done and could not conceive that they could act in anything but an honourable way. Nina was too aware that Anna might let some important information slip.

The army had never recovered since Stalingrad. After that, there had been no real advances. The previous summer offensive had rapidly been turned into a Russian strike, which had been almost as fast and overwhelming as their blitzkrieg two years before. Now they were unbelievably retreating on all their Russian fronts. For the military men, the net was closing in fast.

The diffident army men who had irresolutely toyed with the idea of what to do about Hitler in previous years, and had put it aside while they were winning, returned to the question in nineteen forty four. The Russian war machine was clearly superior to their original conception of it. Perhaps Hitler should go now, before Germany was overrun.

While Nina struggled on, believing she and her tiny band were alone, the generals were recruiting more and more disillusioned, embittered top men to their cause, amongst whom was Hitler's favourite, Rommel.

The war itself seemed to be against the conspirators. Rome was abandoned to the Allies; D-Day caught both Hitler and the Germans napping; and the Russian offensive was of a toughness and thoroughness for which the Germans were unprepared. Troops who should have been fighting on the newly opened Western front, pushing the Normandy invaders back into the sea, were rushed to the East where the Russians were already at the borders of East Prussia.

Whereas before D-Day the Americans had been mainly confined to the Pacific theatre of war, now they were pouring men and munitions into Normandy. Each day their foothold in Northern France grew stronger and safer, and the Allied footsteps moved further and further away from the beaches into the pretty apple orchards of Calvados and towards Caen. As the weeks went by they neared Paris and central France.

To the Germans the Russians seemed as unstoppable as they had been themselves four years before, and the generals knew they would find the war increasingly difficult to win.

"They'll be in Brussels by the end of August, and Berlin by October," Otto remarked to Nina one day.

"I don't know what I'm supposed to feel any longer," she was confused, but vaguely heartened by the news. "Five years ago, I would have said, let them come, and I hope they topple Hitler. Last year I might have thought that we had to back him for the sake of Germany. We're surrounded by enemies. Our standing in the world must be low or there wouldn't be so many against us. Whether we like it or not, we're stuck with him and we have to play this out to the end."

She threw up her arms in a helpless shrug. "Now? What can I say? Come and save us from him? Everyone will hate us and we'll be as divided amongst ourselves as we were after the First War. People will say we helped the enemy, we're traitors ..." she tailed off and was quiet for a moment, weighing up the pros and cons.

"But please, God, let it happen," she suddenly added in a rush, "let them get to Berlin before the Russians."

"It's the beginning of the end for us, isn't it?" Hildegard said. "Time for us to really think about what we're going to do. Stay here? The Russians will almost certainly overrun us. Or do we uproot ourselves and move to Pomerania, where the Americans and British might reach us? At least we can move further west more easily from there if we need to."

Otto picked up Nina's thoughts, "If they do reach Berlin before the Russians at least the world will be a better place to live in."

"The German world at least," Nina interrupted.

Otto nodded to his daughter, "I suspect Comrade Stalin is as bad a dictator to live under as our own."

"Then we've got to move further west," Hildegard interrupted sharply. "If we remain here, we'll still be living under some form of dictatorship in fifty years. It's time we made arrangements! For goodness sake, who would you rather live under? Hitler? Stalin? Or Roosevelt and Churchill?"

The propaganda still told the German nation they were only losing a few minor battles and they would soon regain their lost territory, but the generals knew the real, dire circumstances they were in, and their dilemma was even greater. The plotters had finally steeled themselves to the ultimate act, the final betrayal, to kill Hitler, but now they faced a new and unsuspected decision. By killing Hitler when the war was all but lost, would they not plunge their country back into the same psychological error they had made after the first war? Would the German people again blame the army for stabbing Germany in the back and losing them the war, this time with justification? Should they not leave Hitler alive to be defeated in his own time, since defeated he would certainly be? The blame would then be his alone.

Otto passed the information he had heard from a friend amongst the generals on to Nina.

"How can I condone even the murder of Hitler when I don't agree with killing? On the other hand, if they don't kill him and we lose the war, Hitler may get the blame, but the rest of the world will think that we all supported him. That would be unbearable!"

"That was what General von Tresckow thought. He said they must prove to the world that the German resistance movement dared to hazard their lives on it." Otto added sadly, "As if they have not already tried and failed. They will have to keep trying until they succeed."

And so the army did, at Rastenburg, in East Prussia, in July.

They made their final attempt to kill their leader, but the bomb, housed inside someone's briefcase, was inadvertently moved away from Hitler at the last moment by an unsuspecting aide. It blew up the room, but failed to kill the distanced dictator. Instead, it roused his terrible anger and he wreaked appalling revenge on anyone he thought had been involved.

After Hitler's miraculous survival there was another wave of arrests and the brutal, retributive killings reached prodigious proportions. The bomb killed or maimed many of those standing around him, but did little apparent physical damage to Hitler himself. Yet the barbaric torture he unleashed on both those responsible for the attempt, and on some innocents, showed that his mind was now deranged. From that time onwards, anyone was likely to be pulled off the streets, questioned, and then killed or left to rot inside a prison.

Even ordinary Germans were alarmed by the numbers taken in the army. It was not just the plotters who disappeared; it was anyone who was so much as acquainted with them. Hitler's vengeful fingers reached into many homes and at long last the eyes of the people began to open, and they realised what kind of a man they had made their master.

Otto was arrested at the end of July. He was amongst hundreds imprisoned simply because they were friends of a general. He remained stubbornly silent, only admitting that he knew various army personnel, but not acknowledging that he knew anything of their movements or intentions. He knew nothing of the July plot, but the von Luden family feared that he might reveal what they were all involved in to the SS.

The three sisters were frantic. Anna stayed permanently with Hildegard, trying to persuade her that they should leave immediately. Nina, at great risk to herself, tried to discover where Otto had been taken. And Claudia immediately telephoned all of her high-placed friends, insisting on her father's innocence. But Rommel himself was implicated in this attempt and Claudia's friends now put her in gravest danger. Nina warned her to stay put and keep quiet, on no account was she either to telephone or see anyone.

One of the very few to be released, Otto came out of prison two months later. He had lost so much weight, all his clothes had to be taken in, and he looked a decade older than his sixty four years. Many of his friends or former colleagues remained inside. He would say nothing to Hildegard or his daughters of what had befallen him in the prison.

What he said separately to Nina, slowly and with difficulty, left an indelible imprint of both despair and hope on her. "They made a film ... of the trials of the conspirators ... and of their hangings. It was so barbaric ... when they showed it to the soldiers as part of their training ... they walked out, young men... Hitler youth ... just walked out... refused to watch it."

To Nina it was confirmation of Thomas's often expressed view about Hitler's brutality, but the young soldiers' reaction gave her optimism that soon more would rebel and refuse to continue to fight for such a man. She did not know if Thomas was amongst those filmed and she set her mind unswervingly against such horrendous thoughts.

The conspiracy that Thomas had once supported was in ruins, few were left alive and thousands imprisoned as a result. The arrests went on. As the weeks passed, 'justice' and show trials were speedily devised and the barbaric executions meted out peremptorily.

Whilst Otto was in prison, the Allied forces reached Paris. On the Eastern front the Russians pushed south into Rumania and captured the Ploesti oil fields, which the German war machine relied on. The military men were convinced they could no longer win. They had a full-scale war on two fronts, something they had warned Hitler about for so long. Reports were passed to the family through Otto's old comrades. It was not 'if' but 'when', and that knowledge steeled Nina and her escape line to keep going just a little while longer. They themselves would need it soon.

Twenty Five

Once their escape lines regained some semblance of normality in late autumn, Nina received a letter from Claudia.

'Dear Nina,

'You must have often wondered what made me choose to take up nursing when I've fought against looking after children for so long. You know how I've felt about them and the endless years of coping with their odious bodily functions. Thank goodness, I'm not caring for infants!

'I needed to be useful in some way and there's such satisfaction in seeing a patient return slowly to life again - rather like watching someone give birth, I suppose. And right now I am immensely grateful to have something so exhausting to do; it keeps my mind occupied every waking moment, and I have no time to think of ... anything else.

'Incidentally, the post here is dreadful. Do you remember the two recent parcels that went astray?' Nina understood that Claudia referred to Johannes and Thomas. 'I write to everyone I know and generally create a stir. What else can I do? I am sure you are doing the same, and if it's humanly possible one of us should succeed in tracing them. I do sometimes despair and wonder if perhaps they are no longer there to be found. In these times any loss, however small, assumes a greater significance.

'I need you here Nina, you are so strong, so rational, whereas I imagine too much. You sensibly stick to reality; not imagining what might be as I do. But I must not dwell on this; we are all doing as much as we can in the circumstances.' Nina shuddered at the all too revealing words. 'Nina, I heard about something the other day that would astound you and I know that Anna, with her artistic inclinations, would love to have been here to have seen it. I've written to her separately - would you deliver it for me?

'Do you remember King Frederick's Amber Room? It is here, Nina, in

247

Königsberg! I haven't seen it, but I met someone who did last year. He said it appeared to be in excellent condition; but now it's been dismantled and stored away in the castle cellars. How marvellous that it's still safe! It would be such a great pity if so fine a work of art was damaged. It's always been of great interest in East Prussia, because of its swap for sixty of the biggest and best of the Czar's guard. Now that it's back in German hands do you suppose we shall have to nominate sixty East Prussians in return?'

As Nina read her sister's seemingly inconsequential chatter, she became full of admiration at how well Claudia was adapting to the disappearance of Johannes, though she knew her sister would have been deeply affected. If it were Erik, would she have been able to cope as well?

'Nina, I must get to the point before I fall asleep at the desk. I'm on night duty and tonight it is my first opportunity to write for some time.'

Reading between the lines, Nina realised it was the first night for some time without war casualties coming in continually, or bombing raids.

'On my few trips to the shops I came across some of your favourite cheeses. They are so rare and difficult to find just now that I knew you would want some. They've obviously come in from the country farms. I'm sending two of them to you via Uncle Ernst, so they don't go astray! I hope they're still in good condition when you receive them!"

Uncle Ernst was the code name of a courier and the 'cheeses' were refugees. Nina deduced from 'rare' that these refugees were neither Jews nor Poles, but a different nationality.

They were Russian. She hid them in the old woodman's hut, and how she was ever going to get them to Sweden or Switzerland without their true identity becoming known she could not imagine. They were obviously, and remained stubbornly, Russian. Their faces and mannerisms revealed their nationality, without any word being spoken. For the first time in all his months with the von Ludens, Alexei came to life. From the sullen, unhelpful farmhand, with his compatriots he became a laughing, dancing Cossack. And both Otto and Nina smiled for the first time in months, too, despite the noise coming from the hut.

The two refugees were different again to Alexei, grinning all the time, grateful for the smallest gifts. Soap and towels had clearly not been seen for months. Their pleasure in them was almost childlike, and their thanks profuse. To the two Russians it mattered not one bit that they were given by their 'enemy'. They were being fed, clothed, looked after, and they responded without rancour.

Perhaps the main difference, Nina thought, lay in the fact that they had volunteered to be soldiers; their families were safe and well, behind the front lines. Alexei was an unwilling victim, torn apart from his wife and children, not knowing if they were still alive. His brooding depression was not natural to his character, but the result of his tragic life.

Nina never discovered whether the two Russians were on their side or had simply strayed into the German lines and been picked up by one of their couriers. She presumed that they had done something to help Claudia, so she gave them her protection without further questions. But there were times when she was aghast at what she was doing. Here she was, hiding their bitterest enemy! What if they should be found? She and Otto had decided to keep Hildegard and the servants ignorant of their presence, just in case.

Their caution was well rewarded. One day, just as Hildegard arrived home from shopping in the town, a truck of soldiers arrived at the front of the house. The officer saluted her smartly. "We're searching for some escapees who were seen in this area. Do you have any Russians here?"

Hildegard was scandalised, "Don't be so impertinent, young man!" She retorted, and the officer inwardly recoiled, memories of his old nanny and her fearsomely sharp tongue flashed before his eyes. "Do I look like the kind of woman who would harbour our enemies?" Hildegard turned her back and stalked towards her front door. Then she stopped and turned quickly. "Yes! We do have a Russian here!" she said sarcastically. "There!" She pointed to the end of the drive where Alexei was walking their old horse back to the stables. "He's Russian! You foisted him on to us. We don't want any Russians. I'll admit he's useful on the farm, but we still don't want him!" Hildegard left him to decide what he was going to do and closed her door against him.

The dilemma of what to do with the two refugees was pushed aside forever when news of the Russian advances began to filter through to the ordinary German people. As the German Reich began to contract on all sides, pessimism turned to despair and dread spread across the countryside, faster than any enemy could advance.

Fear was an ever-present lodger of the remaining conspirators as they, too, felt the iron grip of war closing in on them all. On October the fourteenth, Hildegard received a telephone call from Claudia informing her that the 'nation's hero' was dead. Even Hildegard realised that Claudia was referring to Rommel. She had learned that he had died by his own hand and not from his war wounds.

Over the next few days, they pieced together the whole story from various sources. Himmler's men had learned from a tortured general that Hitler's favourite had been involved in the July plot to kill him, and rather than have the story made public, they allowed him to commit suicide.

Without her protector Claudia began to fear for Johannes's and her own future safety.

"At least they allowed him to take an honourable way out," Hildegard remarked to Claudia when she came home for a weekend.

Claudia was amazed. "I don't see what's so great about being allowed to kill yourself. It would have been better to have come out and said he was anti-Hitler and taken the consequences."

"Had he done that, we would never have heard about it. It would have been a wasted gesture," Otto reminded them.

"Well, anyway, dying in the course of battle may be considered dignified, if you're a soldier, but when you constantly see the results, the dreadful physical wounds and the mental anguish, you begin to question its validity. The more I see of this war, the more I wonder whether all the old values we held were so worthwhile. It's only right to do what damages others least, regardless of whether it hurts oneself, surely?"

The death of Rommel, by fair means or by foul, was irrevocably forgotten in October. The news that all East Prussia dreaded had been filtering back to them since August, when the Russians forced their way through to the Vistula River opposite Warsaw. Nina now shouldered the added burden of worrying about Erik's safety.

Fright turned to anger and spilled out onto the streets, and for the first time in years civilians spoke out against the troops. Where were they? What were they doing? Fear of the Russians was far greater than fear of the Nazis. Stalingrad was already forgotten, and the hundreds of thousands killed or captured, and the fact that the Red Army had fifty German divisions bottled up around the Baltic area. Their army was not doing its job of protecting the German nation.

Then, came October the twenty-second, a day that brought a rumour, which spread like a pine forest fire in a tinder-dry summer. A rumour so unbelievable that each person hardly dared disclose it to their neighbour. Adults cried out in fear, and old soldiers mercifully despatched their entire families, with tears of despair in their eyes. *The Russians were on East Prussian soil.* True or not, news of barbaric events flashed throughout the country. Panic ensued. No one stopped to think why these cruel deeds were inflicted. The whole of East Prussia rose up and prepared to flee the enemy.

Otto and Hildegard were concerned with how quickly they could leave, and Anna was worried about the children.

Nina remembered the words Peter had written to Anna at Stalingrad: 'They will seek a terrible revenge on us.' And the haunting words spoken by Erik: 'There will be a holocaust.'

251

In her opinion, they lived far enough into East Prussia to hold on. She had to wait for them all: Erik, Thomas, Johannes, Claudia and Alice; she could not go without any of them. Her love for her family bound her to the soil, the home, towards which she was certain they would all head. She stayed and the family waited behind her; she was their leader now, more than Otto, whose spell in the Nazi jail had left him frail and old.

By January nineteen forty-five the Russians were advancing in some places at a steady rate and in others with lightning speed, despite the atrocious weather conditions; it was the worst winter anyone could remember. Yet on they came, spreading death and destruction as they conquered, just as the Germans had done to them in previous years: pushing before them a huge tidal wave of hysterical, frantic, panic-stricken refugees.

By the middle of January, Warsaw was suffering from the most horrific bombardment and was on the point of collapse.

Nina was torn. She was on the point of collapse from worry over Erik, and at the same time she was resigned, they had to go immediately. Contact with Erik had been cut, but she prayed every night that he would somehow get through to them, or Danzig and home to Sweden. Home! What a sweet thought! His mother's house, safe in a land untroubled by war. It was all too much for her to bear. There was so much pain to live with, she had to give herself things to do - anything to keep her mind from wandering into the past; that hurt too much. 'I must think of the children's future. If I don't act they won't have one.'

"Father, should we go into Elbing and find out about transport? See if anything's still running? And the quickest way to Danzig?"

She did not want to admit that Russians on German soil paled beside the idea of the enemy already at the gates of Warsaw. Would Erik live through the bombardment? And if he did, would he survive the Russians? Would they take time to check out his code name?

Could they use her escape line? It was already in chaos. She would have to contact members quickly, many new recruits had already disappeared, joining the column of refugees while they could. The countryside was filling with tides of people of all shades. Perhaps their three Russians might be safely set on the road to join hundreds of others already trekking west.

"What about Claudia and Alice?" Hildegard asked, more worried than the others. "They're much further east. The Russians could be in Königsberg already."

Hildegard looked at Otto and Nina appealingly, "They wouldn't leave an old woman like Alice to fend for herself, would they?"

"Claudia will be evacuated with the rest of the hospital, don't worry," Otto reassured her. "She'll be better looked after than any of us. She'll find a way to get Alice into the hospital so they can go together."

They listened to the German news. It was no longer rumour, it was now official. They listened eagerly to the forbidden BBC, their ears pressed closely to the set through habit rather than any fear that anyone cared anymore. It gave them a wider perspective, and a different viewpoint, but that made them even more pessimistic. It was much worse than they had feared. The pincers were closing in on them rapidly.

Until that moment, the civilians had continued to run their businesses - farms, shops, offices - as usual. They had given no heed for their future, except to believe that they would be able to sort everything out when things got back to normal. Now they were brutally brought down to earth. The British and Americans were pushing them from one side, the Russians from the other, squeezing them tight. One minute they were the victors, or had been told that they were, triumphant and excited, and the next everything had changed and they were fleeing for their lives.

The main thought for countless became, 'Which enemy to be captured by?' Few chose the east, most decided on moving west. Perhaps the wily old man in the Kremlin had deliberately unleashed his most barbarous troops in order to spread panic and confusion, but whether the policy was pre-planned or not, the effect was achieved.

Every day hundreds, then thousands of people flocked along the roads going west. Most were on foot, some in cars or tractors - until their fuel ran out. Vehicles lay abandoned on the sides of the roads, their only use as a place to sleep out of the cold and snow for the foot weary refugees far behind, or as shelter from the Stormoviks. Businesses were abandoned with no thoughts for lost profits or stock; 'Leave everything; just run!'

When Nina and Otto risked their car being commandeered and drove into Elbing they were both shocked and frightened by the sight before them. As they reached the town, not a single highway from the east was passable. Roads that had once felt the steady, ordered tramping of their soldiers' boots, now felt the ragged westward shuffling of millions of feet, running, walking, stumbling, dragging. Some refugees had overcoats on, but many escaped in what they stood up in. These were the first to be overrun: the farmers from the border areas. The desperate German army was even then fighting for its life; to give its people a long enough reprieve to reach the west.

They carried suitcases, bundles, bags, infants … Some pulled carts piled high. Work worn horses pulled wagons loaded down with possessions on top of which sat children and old people, dazed and blank, too weak to walk. Others brought their animals: sheep and horses.

As they passed, some called out for food, but were too frightened to linger for any. They had been through many pogroms, wars, and campaigns. They knew what being captured by the Russians would mean. They were well acquainted with both enemies, and they were all more willing to take their chances with the one in the west.

Many had makeshift, reddened and dirty bandages wrapped around wounds inflicted by the Stormoviks strafing this easy target of moving, black humanity below. Yet still they came on like columns of ants. And however many got crushed underfoot, countless more appeared in their place. High drifts of snow each side of the road effectively trapped them in narrow target areas, with nowhere to run. Seeped in the blood of hundreds of refugees, pure whiteness of winter gave way to crimson.

Blizzards raged and fingers of ice gripped the insides of windows, but nothing, neither weather nor Stormoviks stopped the oncoming flow of humanity. The Russians were behind them! The Russians were already in the North! The Russians were all around them! The tanks were coming! They were surrounded and they could not get out! Tanks had mown down any stragglers who got in their way. Some had been caught in the crossfire as their own troops counter-attacked. Wild, frightening tales came with them, stirring up each town or village through which they passed; increasing their number as each place emptied behind them, adding yet more miles of desperate figures to the end of the column.

On they tumbled in a winter nightmare, blown hither and thither, caught here and there, pieces of them left behind, but inexorably they were blown westwards. Dread swept the whole area. The SS guards could not stem the tide of panic; fear of death at the hands of the Russians was greater by far than any other. Their only hope was that safety lay in the west. Like animals, they pushed and screamed, frantic to get away. Gone were the upright, proud and forceful nation of yesteryear, instead, rich and poor alike, they were all praying to be captured by the Americans or the British.

The irony, lost on them all, was that for most it was already too late! Ahead of them there were queues of refugees miles long. The Russians were indeed in the north, the south and the east, and they were at that very moment racing to cut them off in the west. To get through would take a miracle.

Otto and Nina learned with mounting horror that the Russians had nearly reached Königsberg, where thousands of the refugees had already flocked. Instead of finding safety, they now fled before the fire of an avenging foe to Danzig. Such was their angst that they faced thick snow, ice, and blizzards, froze and starved all in the hope that somehow, somewhere there might still be a way through.

Except for a small stretch of Pomeranian coast, there was no way of escape through Russian lines. The Russians were trawling their captives; pushing them in ever increasing numbers and panic to one outlet - the great Bay of Danzig. At Elbing, the westward flow diverted to the north, to the ports around Danzig, to Hela, and Gotenhafen, where there must surely be boats to take them west.

The Russians had nearly reached the Gulf of Danzig, at Königsberg and Pillau. What vessels were left were controlled by the military and no civilians were being allowed onto them, only soldiers, or the wounded from hospitals. Once they had all been evacuated, then, but only then, would civilians be allowed onto the boats.

Inside the circle, the massive army was told by Hitler to prepare themselves for a fight to the death. Soldiers were to be shot or hanged publicly if they moved out of their ranks, whether or not they were deserters. Old scores were settled as the SS men cleaned up. Defeatism was punishable by immediate execution. Posters all over the towns proclaimed that civilians would be shot or hanged if they were heard to utter a word against the state. There was to be no mercy, even in flight.

"We must go home," Nina stated, almost apathetically. "There's no point in finding out train times now. If there are any, they'll be full up and we'll be lucky if we can get on one."

She felt terrible pangs of guilt; she had left it too late. Erik had been right they should have gone long ago. They drove home quickly in stunned silence, until Nina said, "I must contact Claudia and see if she's all right. And try once again to get through to Erik." Then she prayed, "Please, God let them both be safe."

They were greeted, with desperate relief by a breathless Hildegard and Anna. "Claudia telephoned, it was a terrible line. I know something awful has happened. She couldn't say what it was. She only had one minute, and then she was cut off. They must be queuing to use the only phone."

Nina calmed her mother and sister by kissing each on the cheek and hugging them. "What did she say?"

"I don't understand what she meant. She said she had a lot of small parcels and she couldn't carry them all. And could you go and help her. She insisted you go to her immediately, but that's all we know! It can't have just been about her luggage. Something's happened to her, Nina." Hildegard's face contorted as she tried to hold back her tears. "What can we do?"

Nina raised her eyebrows in astonishment. Claudia would not have asked her to go unless the situation was urgent. But how was she supposed to get to Königsberg when the Russian army might be there already and the roads were jammed with refugees? She said mechanically, "Then I'll have to try and get through. It doesn't usually take long."

"'Small parcels', that can only mean she has some very young refugees. I can't let her down."

"For goodness sake, Nina, you have children of your own here to look after! You can't go running off when your own need you!"

"She wouldn't have asked if it wasn't important, Mother, would she? They would have simply gone with the hospital staff and be safe now. I must try."

An hour later, she was ready with a pack of food, spare winter clothing, a car with enough petrol to get there, and two smiling Russians who did not know what was happening, but had some primitive trust in Nina. One of the Russians was to be left with Otto, as security in case they were overrun before Nina could return home. "If I have Alexei and Sergei with me they can say I'm their prisoner."

"My God!" Hildegard broke her calm stoical surface, "This is a ridiculous scheme. No, no, no! I cannot allow you to go, Nina. Otto, you said Claudia and Alice would be moved with the hospital!"

"Yes, yes! Of course! She'll be all right, Nina, your mother is right. You must not go. We, and the children, need you."

"You said yourself she sounded dreadful. She'll stay with the children instead of being evacuated. We can't let her or Alice be taken by the Russians! The children have all of you. Take the horse and carriage and go now. You'll get to Danzig. Make for Hamburg from there. Father, you have connections in both cities. Anna and Nanny can look after the children." She scribbled details of safe houses on a scrap of paper, "Here are some addresses, just in case."

"And after Hamburg, we'll make for Claudia's in-laws over in Bocholt, you remember? Over by the Dutch border. We'll go there."

"You must turn back if the roads are impassable, Nina, or there's any sign of trouble ahead?" Hildegard entreated.

Twenty Six

The distance in miles from their home to Königsberg was short, but the journey took her several hours. Some of the main highways were packed with refugees who were too cold, tired, and hungry to move out of her way, and she was forced to stop and wait for them to go by. The one thing she feared was a roadblock, but it was as though the soldiers had retreated in the face of these vast numbers. Not one held her up, only the miserable lines of numbed humanity. The nearer she got to Königsberg, the fewer the stragglers, as though everyone had already left town. She had not seen one of the Stormoviks that the refugees in Elbing feared.

At the hospital, in the south-eastern suburbs, all was in chaos. Patients were being evacuated into ambulances and all manner of vehicles, and transported to the railway station. Trains were still getting through, but were strictly for the military. The building was a warren of rooms on several floors. Firstly, it had been the home of one of the minor aristocracy of the old imperial family, then a private rest home for the rich, and lastly a hospital. Nina took the spare clothing and food, and left the two Russians near the car, where they could dodge behind some bushes if anyone came their way.

"I can't help you! You can see how things are. Go up and have a look for yourself," a young doctor told Nina impatiently.

At any other time he would have been aghast at sending in a civilian unescorted, but what did it matter any more; in any case most of the patients had gone. The world was falling about their ears, the town was already crawling with Russians, and he just wanted to get out like everyone else.

Nina searched each room and ward as she came to it. There was no one there. She was too late. Claudia had gone – or been taken. Then she saw another nurse, no more than twenty years old, wandering around in a daze, her mouth hanging open and her eyes protruding in terror. "Have you seen my sister Claudia?"

She got no reply. Gently she took the young woman by the arms and persisted, "I must find my sister. Where is she?"

The petrified face looked into Nina's eyes, took her hand and pulled her along the corridor to one of the wards. Nina grasped the door handle nervously, and turned to say, "Thank you …" but the girl was already halfway down the corridor, running as if for her life.

Inside the beds were draped with sheets, partially covering lifeless, swollen bodies, indecently dressed and sprawled in all directions. SMaxet stains and slits in the linen told their own horrible stories. Not even in the agonies of their confinement had these women been spared the excesses of man's basest brutal nature.

Retching, Nina forced herself to look, "Dear God, it's the labour ward!"

As she moved along the ward, Nina heard hiccoughs coming from under one of the beds. "Claudia, is it you?"

Tears running down her face, Nina pleaded, "Please come out. It's me. There's no one else here except us."

"Hic … hic …" Claudia's chest jerked persistently with involuntary hiccoughs. Deeply traumatised, she was incapable of speech.

Nina got down on her knees and reached under the bed. To her horror, her hands felt sticky and warm; instinctively, she snatched them away to find them covered in blood.

"You're wounded …" Nina took hold of her demented sister and gently pulled her out. Her shoulders were covered in blood, and yet there was no injury. As Nina slid her sister, stiff with terror, along the shiny tiles blood dripped onto the floor from the bed above. She hugged her beloved sibling to her breast for a few precious seconds.

The sound of distant gunshots galvanised Nina into action, and she adopted a stronger tone. "Come on. We have to get out of here, *now*."

Putting her arms around Claudia's waist she hauled her to her feet. "Don't try and talk. Just walk, and do hurry."

She tried again to pull Claudia out of the ward, but it was as if she had to relive the whole terrifying experience in her mind before she could leave. Even the rattle of guns close by failed to persuade her.

Then suddenly, Claudia ran to the sink in the corner of the ward and was violently sick. Her hiccoughing stopped.

Nina splashed her sister's face with cold water and dried her. "Claudia, we must go right now." She put aside her sympathy for later; there were more urgent things to be done. "I have the car downstairs," she whispered as she helped her sister on with her warm clothing. "Here, I bought this extra jumper and scarf, and your thick boots, you'll need them."

As they reached the outside, a blast of the cold air wrenched Claudia back into life. "The children!" she gasped.

She steered Nina around the corner.

"My car's this way," Nina began.

Claudia ignored her and led the way down a maze of small back streets, and stopped outside a large, high stone wall. After peering around corners to satisfy herself that all was clear, she took Nina through an inner courtyard and knocked at a black wooden door, with a small square iron grille at face height. The grille opened and they were surveyed by a wary eye. The nun who answered the bell looked worried and fearful, with none of the serenity expected from years of dedicated service to God.

"Quickly," she beckoned them in. "They'll be coming for us in the trucks in less than five minutes. There's not a second to waste." As if in agreement, a huge explosion rocked the building. "God help us!" The nun crossed herself, "They've brought the big guns up now!"

While they waited impatiently in the hallway, Claudia finished explaining to Nina how the SS made regular forays into the convent and only suffered the nuns, because they nursed the SS wounded. They never discovered the children hidden in their warren of cavernous cellars. "They

261

can't join the ordinary refugees. They're Jewish. And even now they're being hunted down and shot. Imagine! The Russians are here, the Americans, British, French are pounding us from the other side and still the SS looks for scapegoats amongst the children!"

The nun quickly returned holding a small child, and pulling and cajoling three small boys, while a teenage girl ran behind her holding two little girls' hands. Most of them looked no older than seven or eight. As they saw Claudia, they broke away from the nun and ran to her, "Aunty Claudia!" Nina was momentarily astonished, but whoever they were, they had to get away as soon as possible.

"How old is this little one?" Nina smiled, taking the child from the nun, swinging her up into her arms, and for a moment remembering Dieter.

"Regina is two and a half. The parents of all these children were taken." She pushed an envelope into Nina's pocket. "That will explain who they are, their histories. You must hurry." The nuns pressed food into the children's hands and pockets as they hurried towards a side door. "Don't wait or stop, just go." She waved away Nina's outstretched hand and thanks. "Don't waste time. Sister Angelika is seeing that the road is clear. They're evacuating us any minute."

"God go with you!" One whispered and crossed herself, as they hurried out through the small side entrance. The others joined her, and their retreating figures were lost in the shadows.

They passed quickly down the narrow road and into the labyrinth of back streets, as a truck with several motorbike outriders swung into the convent compound to evacuate the nuns and wounded soldiers. A shell exploded south of the convent and the children screamed. Nina immediately tightened her grip on Regina, and stopped and spoke to all of them quietly.

"Listen children," she said urgently, "You'll hear lots of those noises, but you must ignore them. Above all, you must not make a sound. If you do, the bad soldiers will hear you and they'll know where you are. We have to reach the car."

They continued their terrifying journey in darkness, punctuated by guns, shells, flashes and occasional groups of soldiers running down major roads towards the south.

While Nina went alone to find the car, Claudia waited with the seven children, hiding in blackened doorways along a side road. Nina came back within seconds, scrambling and slipping on the icy pavements. "It's gone! Claudia, it isn't there!"

"Did you leave the keys in it?"

"No! How could the Russians have taken it? I can't believe they would."

"What the hell do we do now?" Claudia asked in unexpectedly strong language; fear, shock and worry over the children all undermining her finer instincts.

For the first time Nina's shoulders sagged and she looked as though she was going to cry.

"There's only one thing we can do, we have to join the rest of the refugees. There was never any certainty that the petrol would have got us all the way back, anyway."

In any troubled times, if she couldn't pray, she would give herself time to think and work out her problem by plunging herself into action. Now she tried to remember their names while making sure they all had their clothes done up properly, with their hats, scarves and gloves on.

Leah tugged at Claudia's arm, with all the might a five year old could muster, and pointed to a group of fir trees at the side of the hospital, which was making strange movements and a curious whistling noise. Nina saw that Claudia was standing transfixed, her eyes wide with remembered terror, and she, too, froze, fearful that the Russian soldiers had returned.

"Kamerad Nina," came a persistent whisper.

"It's Alexei!" Nina gasped, her momentary fear broken. She scrambled down the snowy bank towards the trees, sliding the last few feet. The children broke into giggles at the spectacle of a sliding, uncontrolled adult, regardless of Nina's rule of quietness. They were not old enough to have learned the value of silence nor had they suffered enough to have lost the art of laughing. Alexei and Sergei stood there grinning. Nina's few words of Russian helped her piece together the story of how they had hidden behind the firs and watched, unable to do anything as the car was commandeered by soldiers, to be used to evacuate more patients.

The children slid down the bank after Nina while Claudia attempted a more gracious descent. "How did they get it started?"

"I don't know how to ask that! Perhaps they joined two wires together, or towed it behind an ambulance. It doesn't really matter. What we do now is more to the point. At least they can help to carry the children."

Alexei pulled persistently at Nina's sleeve, pointing to something hidden behind the trees. There stood a cart with a thin, but docile looking horse.

"Where on earth did they get that?" Claudia asked, her terror alleviated a little by Nina's obvious acquaintance with these Russians, and at their somehow familiar faces. She remembered Alexei after a while, but she had forgotten the two Russians who she had helped to send on to Nina. All that was so far in the past.

Nina asked Alexei and her face broke into a grim smile. "He said soldiers brought wounded comrades in to the hospital and he took it while they were inside. Well, it's ours now. Providence has provided for the children. Who are we to argue? Even if it is the mangiest old horse I ever saw!" They piled the children into the cart and Claudia who knew the area well sat up front with Alexei. "We must head for Pillau. That's where the patients were going."

Nina walked alongside, carrying Regina. They were half a mile out of Königsberg when she suddenly stood transfixed. "Claudia!" she half whispered, half gasped.

Claudia stopped the horse, her blood running cold with mounting terror. What new horror had Nina to tell her?

"We've forgotten Alice!"

For an instant Claudia could not focus properly. "Who?"

264

Nina stared at her sister who was still in a state of shock. "Aunt Alice! We didn't look for her."

"She's gone! I got her into the hospital a few days ago, with suspected pneumonia. She was to be put on a boat yesterday. I would have told you, but so much has happened."

"Where was she heading?" Nina walked on, relief that they had not failed her elderly aunt gave impetus to her rapidly tiring feet, shod as they were in her leather boots with a high instep and heel; she had not set out from home equipped to walk for miles.

"I don't know. But she has addresses in Pomerania and Bocholt."

While they were making their way through the back streets on their own, Nina tried to get to know the children.

Shells were exploding further to the south and, at least safe from the bombardment for the time being, they encouraged the old carthorse to keep up the walking pace of the column, taking it in turns to walk or ride. Nina had a renewed sense of danger, not from the Russians who seemed to have been contained for a while, but from their own army. If just one soldier, or one civilian, were to realize that these children were Jews they were all lost.

She was disturbed to hear that three of their names were noticeably Jewish and might pinpoint their background. Peter, Joe, Ilse, and Regina, could pass as German names with little trouble.

"I think we should call Leah, Hannah and Jacob by more German names, don't you? At least until we're safe." So Leah became Martina, Hannah became Heide, and Jacob became Paul.

When the children's feet were so frozen that they cried in pain, they were allowed into the cart, and the other children rubbed and pummelled some life back into the numbed limbs. Slowly, laboriously, they persuaded the old horse to plod onwards through the snow and ice towards Pillau, and the promised ships.

Twenty Seven

Nothing was heard of Claudia or Nina that night, or the following day. Otto grew increasingly unsettled. With each news broadcast the stories became more alarming, and hysterical rumours continued to spread like a modern plague, leaving behind the virulent infection of panic. All the roads were filled with a terror-stricken stampede escaping the outlying districts towards the relative safety of the west and north, to the towns, with their warrens of hiding places.

Some of the appalling tension was relieved by recounting events they had seen or heard. Telling their tales seemed to give them validity, essential for their tellers' sanity. They needed constant reassurance that they had not dreamed up the nightmares. The adrenalin transfusing their petrified bodies had made them alert; physically stronger and tougher than many of them had been before. Their minds able to cut off the cold, the distance, the agony, concentrated only on flight. Yet that made their eventual collapse all the more disastrous. Hundreds, thousands, died when they thought they were safe, because they let go the tension that had driven them on and sustained them. When they relaxed, their bodies, until then primed to flee, gave in to quaking, their teeth chattering from the intense cold, their bodies shaking with fear. Exhaustion, starvation and demoralisation all took their toll. Many simply died. Others dropped, defeated, into snowdrifts and fell asleep instantly, freezing as they slept. A hundred and one deadly traps lay in wait for the unsuspecting refugees who thought they had nothing more to fear.

In view of the vast numbers and the urgings of friends and family, Otto decided it was now imperative they leave immediately; they could wait no longer for the girls to return. All the servants who had not already left were given food and clothes, and told to go home to their families, and then to go on to Danzig. The partings were made with indecent haste. When Hildegard had a moment to reflect, she was grieved that Jürgen and Irmgard who had been with them since before the children were born were dismissed, perhaps never to be seen again, without any kind of reward for all the years of devoted, uncomplaining service to the family.

"Otto, we must call in at their homes on our way, to give them something. Perhaps the gold-plated clock or some jewels. Anything they can use to buy their way onto a ship..." Hildegard insisted. "It isn't far out of our way to Jürgen's house and we pass Irmgard's. We owe it to them."

Their solid workhorse and a carriage were made ready. Small suitcases were hastily packed with essentials and everyone wore at least two sets of clothes. Both Hildegard and Anna took their jewels as insurance against hunger and destitution. They had no idea what would happen when they reached Danzig.

Hildegard justified wearing her jewels, feeling somewhat overdressed, "We might have to buy tickets when we get there, or stay in a hotel, before we can get on a ship. And you might not be able to get to the bank."

Virtually all the food in the house was packed and taken by the children who thought it was all a great adventure. They had never been allowed to ride in the horse and carriage in January before; they had always been told that it was far too cold. When they were finally ready Hildegard, concerned about all of her children, left a letter on the kitchen table, "In case Nina and Claudia should come by. Although I know it would be out of their way. They must be making for Danzig by now." She left some packed food on the kitchen table, just in case.

The unusually stern Otto sat on the coachman's seat with Ilya, the Russian POW. Anna, with little Peter on her lap, and Hildegard sat behind, with Kurt and Helga between them. Ullrich, Klaus and Dieter were opposite them, with Nanny.

Not wanting to leave his cousins and return to the quiet home in Kösslin, Klaus had remained with them after a visit to Johannes's parents.

How they all bitterly regretted they had not insisted he accept Johannes's parents' invitation for the others to stay for a while as well. How much safer they would all have been there, and how much easier it would be from there to Lübeck or Hamburg.

The fierce Arctic wind drove the snow directly at them. Their only protection would have to come from the thick bedding they took with them to wrap around their legs and feet and to cover their heads. Anna and Otto enveloped the younger children and arranged straps over the covers to keep them tightly swaddled. But Kurt and Helga disdained the ties. Each had two blankets with which they made igloos, tents, cloaks, and other exciting disguises to entertain the family on the journey.

Helga, who was quite old enough to know better, felt rebellious and angry and kept removing her glove to scratch her nose.

"Helga! If your nose itches, rub it with the glove, but don't take it off until we're inside in the warm, and keep your scarf around your hood or the wind will blow it off." Anna and Nanny nagged constantly.

Helga ignored them.

Their slow, painful journey had been made lighter by the children's laughter at Kurt's and Helga's antics and by Bismarck's tail, which wagged constantly. Even when he became entangled in the material, the children could see its regular movement.

But by the time they reached Elbing they had all tired. The biting wind's icy tentacles had reached through a fourth blanket. Misery had taken hold. And frozen limbs were not conducive to hilarity. The horse slowly pulled them along the snow-lined street towards the centre of the town.

Too late, Hildegard remembered she had forgotten to take one last look at her house - home of Otto's ancestors for centuries, and her home since their marriage - to fix it in her mind, in case they should never return.

Before her sentimental tears had time to freeze on her half covered face, Otto put up his hand to keep the others from speaking. The strange quiet in the town had kindled an instinctive fear in him, and his training as a soldier slowly took over. It was silent. There were no more refugees -

none at all. To Otto, it was far more ominous than the last time he had been there with Nina, when the town was jammed with fleeing people. Questions flooded into his brain, alert as the adrenalin flowed through his body. Had everyone gone except them? Were they the last? Were the Russians right behind them? In the town already?

Suddenly, a door opened, making them leap out of their skins. The single sound echoed eerily against the banks of iced snow. An old man scurried out, hastily pulled a shutter over a window, and hurried back into his house, slamming the door quickly behind him. They heard the bolts rammed across. Was this a signal for something to begin?

As they made their way in total silence through the town, the children picked up the adults' fear They looked cautiously from the faces of Anna, Nanny or Hildegard to where they directed their attention: to the shuttered windows, down the side roads, ahead, or behind. The little bell on the reigns, which up until then had been a pleasant reminder of normality, proclaimed their approach. Otto reached forward and unhooked it, and Kurt leaned over and took it from his grandfather, placing it carefully in his pocket.

All the way along the main street Otto expected to hear the crack of a rifle pointed at their heads. What if snipers were strategically placed in the bell towers or on the roofs? Every window, every roof, and every corner posed a potential threat. Hildegard and Anna sensed his tension as he warily checked the roads ahead and sometimes those behind, and they, too, looked around nervously and listened with mounting apprehension through their heavily muffled ears for ... for what? What did an avenging army sound like?

The snow, which had held off for a while began again; the flakes, whipped up around them by the angry wind, made it increasingly difficult for the horse and passengers to see the way ahead. Irmgard's house was down a narrow country lane to the east of the town. Lined with trees, in summer, the sun seldom managed to penetrate the leaves to touch the tarmac. Now the lane was covered in a white blanket of snow; flakes billowed and blew in and around the naked, defenceless trees; freezing together wherever they landed. Tree trunks had all but vanished under the drifts into which refugees had fallen, fresh snow blotting out all trace of their existence - to fall into the ten-foot mounds was to disappear until the spring thaw.

The children knelt up behind Otto to look for Irmgard's house. With the defiance that came from her anger at the situation, and not caring if her mother could see her, Helga removed her glove again and scratched her nose.

The horse, tired out by the constant effort of pulling its immense load, made heavier by the extra snow, now dragged its legs in and out of the deepening banks, with mounting exhaustion.

All around East Prussia the Russians were closing in with frenetic speed. Otto knew the conflicts would be ferocious, last ditch battles to the death for every inch of their territory. The troops around Danzig were some of the most fanatical Nazis, prepared to fight to the last man, to obey Hitler's every command, even if it meant taking the civilian population down with them.

The thick blizzard not only obscured their view of the lane ahead, but also concealed the crack German troops, dressed from head to toe in white camouflage, lining up behind the trees on the left of the lane.

Kurt saw them first. He jumped up out of his seat and cried, "Look! There's a soldier!" His high childish voice rang out clearly, echoing over the apparently empty, white lane. Helga stood up, her glove falling to the floor. She clung to Kurt for balance and peered in the direction he was pointing.

Kurt had given away their own soldiers' position to the enemy hidden in the field on the other side of the lane, and the Germans had no option but to start firing. It was as if the trees themselves erupted in gunfire.

The tired old horse, gathering her last strength, reared up in the shafts, her hooves flailing at the snowy air. Panic-stricken, her eyes rolling in terror, she dragged her load a few yards further along the lane before being cut down by bullets, and she fell, dragging the carriage over on its side. Kurt and Helga, still clinging to each other, were hurled out into a deep snowdrift at the roadside. As the children hurtled past, Anna heard Kurt scream in pain. Otto and Ilya were also thrown out.

Bullets whined past, through and over them in a cacophony of carnage. Anna, still cradling little Peter, feverishly untied the makeshift straps, that held her and the other children. They were all badly bruised and shaken, but miraculously none of them had been hit. They crawled out, too terrified even to cry, keeping the carriage between them and the Russian guns.

Bismarck, yelping and whining in terror, shot away into the fields and disappeared.

Holding her head, blood seeping between her hands, and groaning in pain, Nanny collapsed in the snow.

Anna, crawling on all fours and dragging little Peter in a blanket, slowed as she saw both Hildegard's body behind the carriage where she had tried to find shelter, and Otto's sprawled gracelessly next to the dead horse. She gazed numbly at lifeless limbs flung in ungainly postures. She had never seen death before. These were her parents, her Nanny, her children's Nanny! And she had felt their deaths as if it had been her own body receiving the wounds.

Aware that Kurt and Helga were nowhere in sight, her agony increased, she cried out in shock and pain, "Oh, Father!"

Suddenly, roughly, unceremoniously, white hands grabbed her and half threw, half pushed her into the snow behind a tree. The children came tumbling through the gap one by one as two sharp-shooters roughly bundled them out of their way.

"The other two ..." Anna cried to the soldiers, "my children ..." She pleaded with them, still not losing control, still too dazed by the speed of events. Crouching behind a tree she drew the rest of the children around her protectively. Klaus, Dieter and Ullrich were not sure yet whether to cry at their harsh treatment or take it in their stride. They were all on the edge of hysteria.

A volley of bullets from distant rifles whined past and thudded harmlessly into a deep drift. One ricocheted off a branch and embedded itself into the trunk of the tree behind which Anna and the children were hiding. She had to find the other two, and proper safety for them all. She resolutely refrained from thinking of those she loved lying dead out there in the cold wilderness.

'Oh, Nina!' She entreated her distant sister's heart and mind to hear her. 'Where are you now? God preserve us all, and keep you safe, too. I need you so much!'

"Stay here!" She commanded the children and turned to crawl back to the place where Kurt and Helga had fallen.

Soldiers, who had no time for good manners, fiercely dispatched her into the low field behind the lane. One shouted as he pushed her down the steep bank, "Get out of the line of fire, and stay out! Don't you realise they're using your dark clothes to fire at? You're making us all targets. Get down!"

"The children ..." she cried, but they, too, came rolling after her, propelled by the unconsciously rough hands of the men. Even little Peter somersaulted down the bank like a huge snowball, protected by his clothes and the blanket. He giggled as he came to a halt and called out the one word he could say: "More!"

The company commander ordered two of his men to move her further back from the trees. "Get them into that house down the lane and lock the door behind them. The lads will follow if you take the woman."

"I must find the other two," she shouted desperately and started to run, crouching down at the bottom of the bank towards the trees. She was caught, turned round, and frog-marched across the small field to a house, hidden under drifts of snow. The youngsters were carried or pulled along behind and roughly pushed inside and told to remain there.

"My children!" Anna screamed, the beginnings of desperation in her voice.

"Look, lady, there's a war on over there. They'll have to wait!" He didn't tell her they were probably already dead.

"Where's Nanny?" Ullrich asked, his blue lips quivering with fright and cold.

"Where's Granny and Granddad, Aunty?" Dieter began to cry.

Klaus remained silent, his big dark eyes alert to all the sights and noises around him, wide with silent inner terror.

"We'll find them soon," Anna promised, more to herself. She knew these East Prussian soldiers would not let East Prussian children come to harm. Yet something in their voices frightened her, and she did not dare disobey them any more. She waited with the young ones inside the house and tried to make them comfortable and warm.

Anna looked around. This was the house they had come out of their way to reach, because Hildegard had wanted to reward Irmgard and Jürgen. This wooden dacha-like cabin was Irmgard's home, small, but big enough for her and her mother. Now it was empty, and Irmgard had already gone. There were things left scattered around, suggesting she had left in a great hurry. A photograph of herself and her parents when she was younger had been left lying on the table. Anna picked it up and put it in her pocket. Perhaps they would meet up at the boats in Danzig, if they ever got there.

Now that Otto, Hildegard and Nanny had all gone, and the horse was dead, Anna had neither help nor transport, and she alone had to cope with the four children left - and find Helga and Kurt. Panic rose inside her. She sank heavily into the one armchair and prayed.

And then she cried. All her misery, all her pain, her grief and distress were poured into her tears. Her heart was broken by so much anguish and she sobbed unashamedly until she had no more tears to shed, and her body ached from so much unendurable exertion.

The boys watched wild eyed and terrified, too young to know what to do and not understanding what was happening outside. Dieter's tremulous voice announced, "I'm hungry!" Anna was brought back to the present. There was little food in the house, most of it had been taken, and their own had been left in the carriage; it was out there, scattered and buried in the snow. The children had a few scraps in their pockets: a small bar of chocolate and a half-eaten sandwich, which they devoured between them.

The gunfire sounded much closer than before. Soldiers outside shouted something she did not understand. Strange, sinister, tinny, mechanical noises echoed in the distance, and further away there were loud thuds and bangs that made the very floor vibrate. Galvanised back to life, she made everyone huddle down together on the floor, and then she pulled blankets and mattresses from Irmgard's beds and quickly covered them. She tried to make a game of it, but their teeth were chattering from fear and cold. Dieter looked up at his aunt, his little face twisted in misery. "Where's Mummy?" he whimpered.

"She's all right, dear," Anna lied, her own voice quaking, "I expect she'll be at the boats waiting for us."

If they ever reached them! They were still a long way from Danzig.

Somewhere out there were two small children; perhaps sheltering behind a tree, terrified, alone, frozen; perhaps buried under the snow unable to free themselves; perhaps on the wrong side of the road running across the fields right into the arms of the enemy! Her imagination tortured her for hours on end, but she could not leave her nephews to search, especially since the soldiers were so adamant. Anna was not an imaginative woman, she was practical like her mother and would always do the right thing by all of the children, not just her own.

Now that very practicality, that necessity to do the best for everyone, constrained her from rushing out and digging through the snow to find her son and daughter, fighting off the warriors, whichever side they were on. She knew, too, the soldiers would not let her near the lane until the battle was over. And those strange noises and distant thuds she could not explain to the children, suggested the battle might take a long time. There was no telling how it would end.

The sinister noises came from the tanks and the big guns the Russians were bringing up to completely surround Danzig. They had been caught in the final defence of the area and the Russian pincers were closing in on them: Götterdämerung was imminent.

As evening approached, Anna's self-control began to weaken appreciably. The intense fighting in the lane and the fields on the far side of the dacha grew worse. Occasionally bullets hit the walls and they would all throw themselves onto the floor; even though the windows were protected by wooden shutters both outside and inside. Thick drifts of snow in the lane became deeper, with layers of bullets, spent cartridges, and bodies.

The children were cold and tired, hungry and fretful. Anna was little help to them, her mind overwhelmed with thoughts of Kurt and Helga somewhere outside in the snow, maybe Nanny as well, perhaps alive and screaming to her to come and rescue them. Night was falling fast and the temperature was plummeting. She tried to find work, to distract herself from dwelling on their plight.

In the kitchen she found some wood and a box, with a dozen matches inside. The three children settled down to tearing up old newspapers to start a fire. There were two or three tins of meat in the cupboard, but Anna could not find a tin opener and fretted around looking for something to open them with, to no avail. They had to go without.

Trapped inside the house, with the battle raging outside, she did not sleep that night or the next day. Strange, sinister sounds were coming slowly nearer, and shells from the big guns were landing perilously close. 'Maybe in Elbing itself,' Anna thought. In front of the children she remained deceptively calm, but her head was in turmoil. The emotional trauma of the previous day had become the misery and pain of the morning, constant unwelcome companions.

Anna accepted her parents' deaths and grieved for them openly, helping the boys to understand what had happened, coaxing them to cry and get their unhappiness out of their systems. She could not manage later with what might still be to come if she had children crying all around her. She gave each of them a job to do, to keep them occupied, while she looked after little Peter. She had no nappies, and little idea of how to cope with a baby. That had still been Nanny's province, though it had proved too backaching for her at times, and Anna had been forced to take over after the other servants had left. To have sole responsibility for Peter was now a double-edged sword: a task she was unfitted for and unable to do well, but one which kept her mind occupied most of the time that Peter was awake; because try as she would, she could not accept that Kurt and Helga were both dead.

Soldiers who occasionally stamped into the house in two's or three's, to warm up or to eat during a lull in the battle, insisted in their casual, almost callous way, "Impossible. No one could have survived outside in that temperature last night. Not a chance!"

In her despair, Anna shouted hysterically that they had not even tried to find Kurt and Helga, her words cascading out, disordered and incoherent. Tiredness, pain, misery and heartache, all choking back her finer instincts; all demanding their turn to be felt.

Once the men had opened the tins and fetched some of their own rations there was enough food for them all. They bought in another box of wood from a small outhouse where it had been stored, and they had a constant fire and hot drinks. The taps dried up, but the men brought in saucepans of snow for boiling. They dare not open the shutters to let light in, but they had enough food and water to sustain life in the forcibly darkened rooms. The children even began to play together, inventing new ways to occupy themselves in their imprisonment.

"That's not new!" She heard Klaus say scathingly to his younger cousins. "That's the summerhouse game! I've played that for years and years!" They continued for as long as they could and as far as their young minds could manage it. Anna joined in willingly, helping them to remember rivers, towns, countries, colours, trees, birds or whatever category they chose beginning with the letter each one decided on.

"I choose... B!" Dieter said when it was his turn.

"Give me a country," Klaus demanded.

After a little thought, Dieter said "Berlin!"

"That's not a country!" The knowledgeable Klaus responded, looking at Anna, "is it Aunty?"

"No, dear, it's a city," she answered absently, her mind elsewhere. "It's the capital city of Germany."

They went through all the letters of the alphabet, and once again, before the day was out. It stretched their young minds and kept Anna from dwelling on their situation.

Between the pastimes she spent the next day urging anyone who came into the house to try and find her lost children.

They would wearily repeat, "There is a war going on. We'll search for them when we've won the battle."

'What's the point,' they implied.

She wanted to scream at them, shake them, hurt them in some way: make them wake up and realise that the children must be alive and frightened. But she had to hold onto her self-control for the other children's sake. After the pain and heartache had taken their toll, the tiredness blessedly, belatedly intervened, and Anna slept.

She slept through the remainder of the second evening and on through the height of the battle, which flared up savagely through that night. Reinforcements were rushed to the front from Danzig to hold the beleaguered line at all costs.

It was, as Otto had foreseen, a fight to the death, and it raged all around Irmgard's cottage.

Twenty Eight

Anna woke after two freezing nights to silence. Not a sound leaked into the isolated cabin. She leapt from the bed to find the three boys already awake and outside, throwing snowballs at each other as though they were back at home, and she heard their laughter for the first time in days. For a few seconds she wondered fearfully who had won. Then she realised they would not have been left alone if the Russians had.

She ventured outside into the fields. The snow had stopped some time during the night and the air had cleared. She could see the lane ahead with figures moving about. Not the white clad soldiers who had been in the early fighting, but regular troops, rushed down from Danzig. Yelling at the children to stay where they were, she ran across the field as fast as she could through the thick, crisp pristine snow and into the pathway.

A ghastly sight met her horrified eyes.

In the weak morning sunlight, filtering falteringly through the leafless branches, she saw the bodies of dead fighters of both sides, in grotesque positions, just as they had fallen. Patches of snow were stained with their blood. Casually smoking and joking with each other as they worked, the regular soldiers were digging through the snow and dragging the stiff corpses into the field. Anna passed through the lane as quickly and silently as she could, stopping only to stare at the body of a Russian. She stared at him, not because he was the enemy, nor because in death he was a frozen and grisly sight, but because he had almost reached them!

Then she saw her Russian, his frozen body lying at the side of the roadway. Near him she found the horse and carriage, and the half-covered bodies of her parents, both dead before they froze, and she screamed involuntarily. She had accepted their deaths, but to see them left alone and sprawled out, was more than she could bear. She pulled her woollen scarf across her face and sobbed into it uncontrollably.

The working party had not reached the members of her family and they were still as she had last seen them two days before. Nanny Watson had stumbled through the snow several yards, blood blinding her eyes, until she had hit the tree and sank in front of it, dying, cold and alone, in her adopted land. Through her grief stricken, swollen eyes Anna saw her, leaning against the trunk, her hand still clutching the side of her head, frozen to her skin as she died.

Anna could see their outlines, but not their faces, which were covered by a thin layer of ice. She did not want to see their faces. The trauma of both the event, and seeing them all now, began to numb part of Anna's brain. She could not mourn for any of them. Not yet.

Logic told her that her children must also be dead. After two nights in freezing weather there was no possibility that they could be still alive, and she must accept it. She knew she should now spare time to grieve and pray over her parents and Nanny properly, and perhaps persuade the men to dig them a grave. Another part of her brain urged her on to find her children's bodies.

A loud tearing sound suddenly came from behind her. She stared with anguished fascination as two soldiers pulled the stiffened body of a comrade from a tree trunk against which he had casually rested. They looked at Anna's face and laughed unfeelingly. It meant nothing to them any more, they had grown hardbitten with war; this was just another grisly part of their job. If they had stopped to think about the meaning of it all, they would not have been able to continue. The need to survive had drained their emotion.

Where they had removed the body the deep snowdrift had been disturbed and Anna, already half-turning away from the sight, was transfixed. Two little boots were poking through the white coverlet, pointing up towards the sky like two early black crocuses. She was totally unaware of the cry that issued from her mouth as she dropped to her knees and frantically scratched at the snow with her gloved hands. The soldiers, who had before watched her curiously, but unemotionally, now gaped in astonishment.

"What on earth is she doing?"

"Who is she?"

Another pointed to the bodies lying out in the open. "Didn't you hear? That's her family!"

They had wives and families at home, and some sense of caring returned. "Poor woman!"

Pushing her aside gently, but firmly, one said. "Here, we'll do it."

They started digging vigorously with their shovels, but Anna screamed at them, "No! No! You'll hurt them!"

They stood back, one leaning on his spade in astonishment, and looked at each other, "They can't feel a bloody thing!"

"They are alive!" She screamed, "They've got to be!"

They stared at her as though she was deranged.

When they had finished, Anna gently wiped the top layer of snow away from their uncovered bodies, away from their white hooded faces.

The men gazed at the children: their two faces pressed to each other, Kurt's arm protectively lying across Helga's body, consoling her in death.

Anna knew they must be dead, but she could not cry. Her mind still refused to accept the inevitable.

Then she saw Helga's hand and she screamed and moaned uncontrollably. Helga's ungloved hand had been uncovered for two nights of extreme cold and it was dreadfully frostbitten. It looked horrible on her little daughter.

One of the soldiers took hold of her and shook her hard. She would not stop screaming. He slapped her face and shouted at her as though she were deaf. "Look at it! Don't you understand? Don't you see? She's alive!"

Shocked that he had dared to slap her face, Anna looked to where he was pointing. But she could not believe what he was saying.

"Look at her hand. Her face! If she were dead, she'd look like him over there," he pointed to their comrade, the one she had watched them tearing from the tree. "She'd be frozen solid."

Anna tearfully scrutinized the two lifeless forms: their frozen comrade and her daughter. She understood, but could not bring herself to touch her child. It was not possible! She wanted to believe it with all her heart, but she could not.

The soldier shouted to his colleagues and in seconds men came slipping and sliding from all directions. Anna heard their comments, but she did not dare to even glance at her child again. She just willed them to be alive. Helga must be alive, she must be! If she was, it was a miracle! One of Hitler's soldiers looked then crossed himself. It was such a quick involuntary action, and he tried hard to make it seem as though he was buttoning up his greatcoat, but Anna had seen. It was indeed a miracle! She stood still, her hands covering her mouth, not daring to breathe.

The cold, but unconscious Helga was picked up and rushed to a waiting ambulance. When Anna turned back to Kurt another man was carrying him to the ambulance. The hard-headed soldier had tears in his eyes, and Anna knew that Kurt was alive, too! Both alive! It was unbelievable, but it was true.

The insulating snow had acted like an eiderdown, keeping the two bodies warm so they survived in the subzero temperatures.

Helga had been clinging on to Kurt and her hand still clutched his coat underneath the snow quilt. They had fallen together and their warm breath had kept the frost away from their all but uncovered faces. Their scarves had been wound tightly around their hoods and they were still firmly in place. Only Helga's hand was uncovered. The scream of pain that Anna had heard as Kurt was thrown from the carriage had been caused by a bullet hitting his leg. The blood had congealed quickly in the low temperature, stopping him from bleeding to death.

They were rushed to the local hospital, where they were quickly and temporarily patched up. Then they joined the staff and other invalids being transported to the railway station.

Anna quickly found out that the two wounds, which at first sight had seemed likely to end their flight to freedom and keep them in hospital long enough for the Russians to reach them, had become their salvation. They were no longer alone, but had joined the official withdrawal of wounded soldiers and civilians. They now had the bureaucracy of the armed forces working out their safest routes, speeding them to the only safe area left in all of East Prussia. Their injuries had become their tickets to a place on one of the great hospital ships at Danzig, part of the biggest evacuation ever seen.

A fleet of ambulances, trucks, cars, even motorcycles, anything that could take more than one person and move fast, was used to ferry the wounded from the hospital to the station. There they were transferred to the one train left.

It was no ordinary train that Anna and the children found themselves inside. It was a cattle truck. They were wedged amongst dozens of others, with no heating, just bare boards and slatted wooden sides, with gaps that allowed in the freezing winds.

After the war, Anna was able to see something of the wretched irony of their journey to Danzig in the cattle truck. That same train which, heading in the opposite direction might have taken thousands of Jews to their deaths at Auschwitz, was now headed north, to safety and was filled this time with terrified Germans.

At the station, panic had settled in and whilst some care was being taken with the badly injured, Anna and the children were pushed in alongside the stretchers and walking wounded. There was no longer any time to be careful, their hours of freedom were slipping away, ticking into the past as the soldiers tried to obey the orders of their fanatical leaders. The Russians were at their very heels, reminding them of their presence with salvos that were landing increasingly close to the station.

Each truck had a guard on the door and, once inside, no one was allowed out again for any reason, nor was anyone else allowed in. Anna and the children were in the middle of the carriage with Kurt and Helga on one stretcher. Ullrich, Dieter and Klaus all had to crouch, kneel or sit down on the stretcher or floor where they could, and Peter lay asleep on Anna's lap. There was no room to move, even to stretch out their legs. The middle of the truck had the advantage of being a little warmer than leaning against the freezing outer walls. As soon as it was full, the guard pulled the door across, leaving only enough room for him to stand and listen to orders before the train started.

As another salvo exploded in the vicinity of the road, right outside the station, Anna prayed, 'Please, God, let's go soon!' She heard screams and shouts from that direction, but the guard pulled the door nearly shut so they would not see what was going on. Outside, the noise, which had flared up with each burst of fire from hundreds of voices screaming and pleading for help, gradually diminished as more and more passengers were moved into trucks further up the train. Beyond the station entrance, kept back by the metal and wooden fences and armed soldiers, hundreds of refugees were being denied access to the train. They were not wounded, nor were they soldiers, nurses or otherwise vital for the protection of the Third Reich. They were expendable.

As the train rattled to a jerky start and began its awful journey to the docks, the troops guarding the perimeter ran one by one in orderly fashion and jumped into the nearest wagon, helped by the guard. They closed the door against the shouting, horrified civilians. The noise of the train easily covered their retreating cries, but the booming thud of the Russian weapons and their own German guns responding was a never-ending cacophony accompanying them all the way into Danzig.

At last on their way, Anna began to wake up to what was happening around her. It was a journey of fear, of appalling cold, of defeat. None of the wounded soldiers spoke, each was too far-gone in misery, wanting the war to be ended, and above all wanting to escape from the Russians. They were afraid to speak to their neighbours, afraid that their words even now might be deemed to be defeatist by their guards, and they might yet be shot by their own soldiers.

The one nurse kept her own fears to herself and devoted all her time to looking after her patients as well as she could, though there was little she could do except to dispense love and kind words. All the medicines had been packaged up and placed in one truck at the head of the train. There had been no time for even the super-efficient administrative team at the hospital to organize properly. Their contingency plans had not accounted for the blitzkrieg tactics of a Russian onslaught.

The three healthy children seemed to feel the anxiety and said nothing to each other or to Anna. They simply looked at her nervously whenever something happened, seeking Anna's reactions so they knew how they should respond. When she smiled at them it made them feel better.

To keep her mind occupied, Anna watched the nurse, unsteadily trying to move from stretcher to stretcher without stepping on any patients, and wondered if Claudia was doing the same thing somewhere else. The thought of her sisters overwhelmed her. 'Let them still be alive', she prayed silently.

She glanced at Dieter, and saw that he was watching her, with his big eyes wide with fear. She tried to smile in encouragement, but her face creased into tears that coursed soundlessly down her cheeks. 'Poor little Dieter, he's looking to me for help, for peace of mind, and all I can offer him is tears!'

The train stopped and started, sometimes crawling, sometimes achieving normal speed. All the time each person's unspoken thoughts were on the guns and the whistle and whine of shells, each person trying to judge the distance they had landed from the train, each one praying that the tracks ahead would not be hit. They had little idea of their exact whereabouts unless the guard opened up the door a crack, and let in the crisp, fresh air.

Despite the intense cold, short bursts of cold air were welcome; the stench of gangrenous flesh, or urine and faeces from the stretcher cases unable to control themselves, grew unbearably strong. There were no doctors in their truck and the nurse was neither qualified nor equipped to diagnose and treat the worst cases; they could only continue to suffer.

Helga was crying all the way and neither Anna nor the nurse could do anything to help her or stop her tears. Her hand had been bound up, but she had not been given anything to kill the increasing pain. Kurt lay quietly sleeping. 'When will this nightmare end?' Anna asked, 'When will I wake up and it will be all over?

Twenty Nine

As evening approached and the cargo of human misery drew near to the city, the train slowed down to crawling pace, and a distant unfathomed yet human noise turned into a single loudspeaker voice repeating the order for the doors to be opened. Each guard pulled his wooden door right back so that all the cowering occupants could see the SS troops lining the side of the track at regular intervals.

The children saw the figures hanging from the telegraph poles before Anna could turn their faces away. Soldiers and civilians alike were swinging from the poles; line after line of them, swaying in the icy wind; all with notices pinned to their clothing - 'Deserter', 'Thief', 'Traitor', 'Defeatist'.

Even at this late stage, with East Prussia almost crushed, the SS were ensuring that everyone saw the bodies and understood the message. To the SS these were the enemy within. The order had gone out not to allow anyone to leave Danzig, but to defend it to the last man. Anyone trying to leave was classed as a deserter. The dead were a powerful reminder of what would still happen to anyone who disobeyed the SS and an even more shocking reminder of the power they still held.

'We deserve to lose this war,' Anna thought, 'while we have such people in charge.' And with a sudden jolt of realisation she understood why the British had not joined with Germany to fight the Russians. While they had the SS in control, the British could never be their allies. It was these people they were against, not them, not all of Germany. She felt sick as she saw how near Peter had come to being a Nazi instead of a soldier.

The doors were rammed shut again as they crawled onwards through the suburbs of the city towards the docks. A journey, which might have taken Anna half an hour in her car, seemed to have taken half a day.

The train stopped, and they heard the order to open up again. The scene that met their eyes was both frightening and a tremendous relief.

Thousands of people were moving in slow streams in the same direction, and, as Anna was helped down amongst the throng, she could see they were heading towards two huge ships - liners conscripted and transformed into hospital ships.

Hundreds of soldiers, some hobbling on makeshift crutches, sometimes being helped by comrades, sometimes alone; others with arms in splints, or with heads bandaged, were stumbling forward. They had finally reached safety. Stretchers were being rushed up the gangplanks, stopped only momentarily at the bottom to be checked by two uniformed officers and a medical orderly. With administrative efficiency, no one was being allowed onto the ships, even when wounded, unless they were on the official hospital lists.

On the quayside doctors and nurses were issuing orders, supervising or evaluating the patients in what seemed to the untutored eye to be total chaos. Yet each medic knew exactly who was to be expected at their gangplank; and into which cabin, deck or ship they should be put. A miracle of paperwork had gone into the planning of this evacuation.

No account was taken by anyone there that these were all deserters. There were too many of them, with guns, for even the SS to intervene. The evacuation by the armed forces and wounded civilians, would take place despite the express orders of Adolf Hitler - that Danzig, like Stalingrad, would fight to the last man and no-one would leave the area alive.

The army hitherto too frightened of Hitler to disobey orders had at last found the courage to do so. The fear of death from one direction outweighed the fear of death from another. The Russians were nearer than Hitler, and the High Command ruled that if there were to be another battle, they would need all the soldiers that they could save. They had already lost too many at Stalingrad, they would not allow that to happen again. All around the Bay of Danzig they were in command of the ships and the evacuation of as many people as they could save - their soldiers first, then the civilians.

Despite the movement of such huge numbers, it was surprisingly quiet in the docks. People were concerned to get to the ships. They were on the lists so they were confident it was simply a matter of time.

Over and above everything there issued another sound, the pandemonium of thousands of voices, which Anna at first assumed came from those around her. When she had gathered her children to her and followed the orderlies with the stretcher carrying Helga and Kurt, she became aware of the strange silence of those around her. Everyone was too relieved to have arrived at their destination to need speech. The noise was not coming from those now making their purposeful way to the foot of the gangplanks. She saw how tired, ill and in pain they were, and how thankful they felt, like herself, for their safe arrival. She looked around her as they half walked, half ran. Pulling the tired, hungry, frightened children with her, she tried at the same time to seek the source of the threatening racket, which pervaded everywhere and made her nervous.

From her position in amongst the throng of wounded she could not see the dock gates. Outside those gates, un-numbered ragged hordes were being pressed back by one inadequate row of soldiers, their guns raised and ready, pointing towards the thick mass. Refugees were trying to break into the dockyard to reach the safety of the many big ships they knew were there. For a while, their clamour covered the din from the big Russian guns.

These freezing, starving people were exhausted and terrified, and above all, angry. They had been misled by Hitler. He had vowed they would never be invaded, but the Russian onslaught of East Prussia had shown how empty that promise was. They had fled from their homes near the Russian borders, leaving every precious possession behind, trekking westwards across the white blizzard-swept land, away from the massing enemy armies, towards safety. Everything that had gone into making up their normal lives had disappeared forever. They had staked everything on reaching Danzig and a ship to the west.

But the Russian advance had been swift. There were too many of them, and too few places. When they reached the docks, they found they needed the right papers, a proper ticket! Even to flee, you needed the appropriate authority! That was the last straw. Even if they had possessed the money, they could not buy one, there were none available. All places were reserved for the armed forces, nursing staff and wounded civilians, especially those with children. As less and less soldiers arrived, more non military personnel were being allowed onto the boats, but there was a strict order of priority: those who were wounded first, and then parents.

The elderly, anyone with grown children or those with none were always the last to board. They did not know if they might eventually be allowed on or not. They would have to wait their turn. They only knew that the Russians were just behind, bombing them, killing them! And now, they were being beaten, kicked and attacked by their own army! Some had taken weeks in harrowing conditions to arrive at the docks and there in front of their eyes were several huge ships - cruise liners as well as battleships and merchant vessels. They were not going to be left behind after all they had gone through.

The noise of the big Russian guns seemed muted. Few shells were hitting their immediate area. The artillery was being brought up for the final assault, but the Stormoviks were nowhere to be seen. Out in the Bay of Danzig, along the Frisches Haff, there were easier targets. Their army was concentrating on the Hela Peninsular, around which all the ships had eventually to go.

Anna and her little family joined the queue at the bottom of the gangplank and rapidly found themselves on board, in a proper cabin with real beds: four bunk beds, two on each side of the room, with a chest of drawers and a porthole in-between. The two wounded children each had one bunk, while Anna and Ullrich had another, and Klaus and Dieter shared the fourth bed. Little Peter slept in one of the drawers, lined with sheets and blankets. The ship had been one of the cruise liners for special holidays, and lacked nothing. The heating worked and they were comfortable. To Anna it was heaven.

Outside the snow was being whipped up by a fierce wind, but inside their little cabin it was warm, snug and cosy. For a little while Anna and the children could forget their ghastly journey and the horrors they had witnessed and suffered in the last few days. They lay under the bed covers, warming up their frozen limbs and waiting patiently for the ship to move.

Helga and Kurt were whimpering with the pain of their wounds. While the other children slept, Anna went in search of a doctor. She accosted the first nurse she saw. "When will the children be seen by a doctor?"

The busy nurse stopped, and consulted her papers. "The doctor will be seeing them quite soon. He has more urgent cases first. Please go back to your cabin and wait there."

The nurse was tired. She had had the same exhausting journey that Anna and the children had suffered.

"When will we be moving?" Anna asked.

"I don't know," the nurse answered quickly; she was overworked and tired of questions she could not answer. "When we've taken on as many as we can, I imagine. Please go back to your cabin and wait there," she repeated. "You are on the list, you will be seen soon."

"Where are we heading? Kiel?" Anna persisted, finding something of her old imperious voice.

The nurse looked at her sharply, "I don't know," and entered another cabin.

As the children's limbs began to thaw out, the pain became stronger. Outside the greater pain - fear - had swamped the minor. The extraordinary events of the last few hours had eclipsed their ordeal. But now in the warmth the two children began to cry out, and Kurt's bandages were becoming soaked as he threshed around on the bed, trying to find some way of relieving the agony. Helga gave a piercing scream now and then, and moaned constantly. Anna despaired; she could stand their torment no longer.

Outside in the corridors all was quiet, and she could not find a doctor, but nor could she leave the children for too long. Through the porthole she could see the dock below, still crowded with people streaming past, but not near to her ship, they were being shepherded on towards the next one, docked alongside. She picked up Klaus and sat him on the chest of drawers. "While I go and find the doctor, you tell Helga and Kurt what you can see, but don't move from here and don't touch the window or your fingers might freeze to it."

Klaus, suitably admonished, stared at the windows, wondering what it would feel like if his fingers froze to it. Then Helga screamed again and he knew.

Anna found a doctor emerging from a cabin in the next corridor, and in her most self-important, 'I will not be ignored' fashion that she had learned to use with tradespeople, she commanded him to see to her children. For a moment the surprised doctor was thrown off balance, but as he found himself involuntarily following her, his tiredness and his own hostility and fears found some outlet in angry words. "Madam, there are countless soldiers on this ship dying from wounds, which I hope you never have to see." He conferred quickly and quietly with the nurse. "And I understand your children have ... er ... frostbite? And one's been shot in the leg? Cleanly?" He barely paused for Anna to agree. "They have to wait."

Anna had opened her cabin door from where the doctor could already see Kurt. Still thrashing backwards and forwards, and crying openly, his partly unwrapped bandage was sodden with blood and contaminating the bedding. Helga was screaming, her bandaged hand held away from the bed.

"What pain killers have they had?" he asked the nurse who began to consult her notes.

Before she had time to reply, Anna, realizing that at last she had her moment, quickly intervened. "None! Kurt was shot two days ago and both he and Helga were buried in the snow for two nights. They were only found this morning and rushed to the nearest hospital, but all they had time to do there was to bandage them both up. On the train the nurse had nothing to give them. Then we were rushed onto the ship and put in here. No one has seen them and nobody seems to care. You can see they're both in agony. Do something!"

All the while she was speaking the doctor was unwrapping their bandages and looking firstly at Kurt's leg, then at Helga's hand. Helga screamed as he pulled it off too roughly: tiredness and the need to see many more making him less than careful.

"Good God!" Was all he said while she was telling her story. "Two nights?" He looked at them again. "I've never heard of anyone surviving in the snow two nights before." Then he spoke quickly to the nurse, "Get them both down to the operating theatre. The leg's still got the bullet in it, but it'll be all right. But the little girl's hand will have to come off."

He said it with the bluntness that came from exhaustion and days, weeks, months of life or death decisions. He did not see that for Anna, her very existence had come to a halt. Nothing in her life had prepared her for this! She was stunned into silence. Then, while the nurse went to summon orderlies and the doctor was finishing his notes, Anna flew into a rage such as she had never experienced before. The same tiredness that made the doctor tactless made her incensed and wild in her movements and speech. The children cowered before her wrath: this was a mother, an aunt, they had never seen before.

It mattered not one bit to Anna that the doctor had been working for seventy-two hours without a break and had not eaten a proper meal for days. It mattered even less that he had seen things that had driven him to the edge of madness. He had been forced to make decisions of life and death with patients: this one could be saved, that one would have to wait and therefore die. Neither did it concern her that he had to operate on one soldier after another without anaesthetic after it had run out, amputating limbs on men wide awake and screaming - all the while under fire in the front line.

To Anna, Helga's hand meant her life and she forcibly gave him a telling off such as he had not received since he was eight years old. "How could you!" she ended, exhausted and tearful. "How could you cut off any little girl's hand? What can a girl do? How can she cook, or sew, or iron, or become a good wife with only one hand?" she railed at him. "What kind of a monster are you? If this was peacetime you would have done everything you could to save it, wouldn't you? Why are you not doing so now? Why?"

While she had called him all the names she could think of, the doctor had remained quiet; his own anger at her words had given way to apathy. What did it matter what one overwrought woman thought of him? He had saved hundreds of lives, patched up thousands of bodies, he had become a stitching machine, repairing the senseless slaughter, mending bodies to be sent back to the carnage. But she was right of course, he had become a monster, he had looked upon the children as just two more bodies in the endless queue.

Yet, here was this deranged woman screaming at him about normal values, about washing and ironing and lives lived in ordinary homes. He had forgotten all that long ago; what was a normal life now? This had become his normality. He looked at Anna as though she were a species from a distant past. "We'll see," he said and left her, exhausted and crying. 'How on earth can people still think in those terms?' he thought.

When the children were brought back from the operating room, Kurt's leg was bandaged loosely and Anna was given lessons in how to change his sterile dressings. Helga still had her hand and she was told that they would have to 'wait and see' if it healed up; it would probably never heal properly, at best she would have malformed fingers; at worst, she could still lose it. Meanwhile both were given pain-relieving drugs to make them sleep.

The ship was quiet and all the lights were extinguished in the evening dusk, as they waited for other ships to make ready to sail with them. The two big hospital ships, converted from the new classless, but still luxurious liners of Hitler's Reich, were to sail with several other merchant ships in a large convoy, with a destroyer escort accompanying them to defend them from both Stormovik and submarine attacks.

The wait seemed endless, but for those on the dock waiting with their precious permits it was even worse. To them it seemed that the passengers on the ship were saved and the ones left on the dock were lost. But other ships were still to come. An endless chain of vessels of all sorts were to ferry nearly three million people from the east to relative safety in the west.

They were lucky, the bad weather worsened. Outside the harbour a snowstorm obscured the visibility not only for the ships' captains, but also, mercifully, for the Russian submarines. The worst they suffered on their voyage was seasickness. Anna's ship conveyed them to Hamburg where they were taken to hospital.

On other nights, other boats caught out in the bright moonlight were torpedoed and sunk, and thousands of refugees died a horrible death in the freezing waters of the Baltic Sea. The bloated water-filled bodies of thousands of others, less fortunate, washed up slowly on to the beaches of the Pomeranian coastline for months, even after the war had ended.

Thirty

In the further regions of East Prussia, where the German nation's fight for survival was grimmest, hope was fading fast for any end other than a Russian onslaught. They might be able to hold the enemy off for a while, but they had no hope of beating them. As Hitler's army had bottled up the British and French into Dunkirk, so the Russians were now squeezing them into the Bay of Danzig: confining their victims in a huge circular net, gradually pulling it tight until their prey did not know which way to go or whether the exit had been finally sealed.

Claudia and Nina, with their little band of frozen, Jewish children, and the two Russians who did not know why they were on this journey, trudged on in silent misery towards Pillau. When Nina had made her mad, courageous drive to rescue Claudia - from what she did not know - the roads around Königsberg had seemed curiously empty. Now she discovered the reason. Whereas only a few days before all roads westwards had been jammed and impassable, with what seemed like the whole of East Prussia fleeing westwards, now all refugees were being directed north - to the ports, villages and towns around the Bay of Danzig.

The journey from Königsberg to Pillau was the longest of their lives. They moved at the pace dictated by the tens of thousands of refugees in front of them. Only one thought kept them all going: refuge lay in the ports in the shape of ships. They had no way of knowing whether there would be any vessels waiting when they arrived, but they had no other option. At least, they reasoned, the soldiers who now directed them constantly along a predestined route knew of their existence, there must be some designated end to this journey; somewhere they were expected. The Bay of Danzig was now the only protected place.

At Pillau the harbour was in total chaos. Thousands of refugees were jammed into the town and more arrived every moment. Soup kitchens had been organised at frequent intervals. They joined the queue for one and felt at least some semblance of normality in this homely little piece of organisation. It indicated that there was still a state, which cared sufficiently to make sure they were fed. On the road, law and order had all but broken down; it had lain with the strongest. Here they were almost relieved to see soldiers, even the hated SS, in charge of helping the refugees. It meant some kind of order was in force.

At the back of their minds, both sisters registered the disturbing idea that it was a necessary part of social existence to have a strongly organised framework within society or anarchy would break out very quickly. 'Was a man like Hitler necessary to keep them in order?' Nina wondered, yet she knew that in other countries there were no Hitlers and order was still maintained. Their own history left her pondering whether their character demanded a dictator.

For Claudia, the events of the last few hours had painfully taught her that her own life had an element of personal anarchy running through it. As she had trudged towards Pillau, she remembered her own insistence on her freedom to do as she wished, even though she had pledged her life to Johannes in the marriage ceremony. Now she recognised that lack of structure within herself and vowed if she and Johannes ever came through this, she would be a different person.

The highly formalised life they had lived prior to the war had been the product of centuries of experience. She now understood what Anna had accepted without question, that she had been required to follow rules, because they kept her society stable. That stability had broken down all around her. Every person was selfishly fighting for their own existence.

She saw her own egocentricity clearly and longed to atone to Johannes; but would they ever see each other again? Was she condemned to live alone, without him? Tears coursed down her cheeks unbidden, but unstoppable, hidden inside her scarf. She understood that her repentance came easily, but to live her life without receiving his pardon would be unbearable. Claudia desperately needed Johannes's forgiveness, but he was no longer there to give it.

Amongst the ranks of the refugees rumours abounded, flying through the crowds quicker than the dysentery, which threatened them all in their physically weakened and dirty state: There were no ships! The navy had taken them and fled! There were boats at Danzig and Gotenhafen, but not at Pillau! Everyone had to go on to Danzig!

No one knew what to believe or do. Claudia and Nina were too exhausted to think straight and the children demanded constant attention.

"It's every man for himself!" Nina said. "The armed forces will be taken on whatever ships there are before us."

They stared wretchedly at the turmoil around the port, jammed with thousands who had been there for days and were far more determined and anxious than the newcomers. They had seen ships arriving and departing full to overflowing with the people ahead of them. They believed they would be next.

"Claudia, I know it may be the wrong thing to do, especially as it's late in the day. But we can see there are only smaller boats, and they're not going to be of much help. Look at all these people. Look at it! We won't stand a chance here. There are thousands of us ..."

They stood quietly within the jostling throng, the children temporarily all within the cart waiting for them to decide what to do next. Both sisters dispiritedly weighed up the situation: how far back they stood in the line waiting for food, accommodation and help to find a place on the boats. Yet the distance to Danzig was enormous on foot even in good weather.

"Claudia, I know the Danzig and Gotenhafen docks and it's just possible my contact might still be there. I'm sure they'll be better organised. We've still got the horse and cart."

"But it's more than fifty miles!"

"It's a chance."

"The Russians can't be far behind us."

"That's what's driving me on to Danzig. They could be here very soon and then we'll be totally cut off. What do we do? Do we go on, or do we stay here and take our chances? At least we know that from Danzig we can make our way overland along the coast, we know that area like the backs of our hands now. But I don't know what's best any more."

No one had been in this situation before, and time was running out.

"And, there is another thing that worries me," Nina whispered to Claudia, "the children. The longer we wait here the more chance that someone might discover who they are. They're all right now with scarves tightly across their faces, but sooner or later..."

"Yes, you're right," Claudia acquiesced, "we should go on. There's no telling how long we might have to wait here. We might as well freeze to death on the move as die here."

"And we might be able to contact Mother and the family."

"And," Claudia added after an emotional pause, "Danzig is nearer to Pomerania." She meant nearer to everything that was dear to both of them, though neither of them dared to voice that thought.

They both fell silent at the thought of Kösslin. So many memories of people once loved so dearly and now gone suddenly flooded back. Both the sisters were momentarily overwhelmed with grief. Nina was devastated by so many losses. Above all by the pain and worry of not knowing if Erik had survived in Warsaw, or whether Dieter was still safe with their parents and Anna. And gnawing self-recrimination at having kept them all from leaving for so long. They could have gone weeks ago! Now, they might not even make it to the last boat from Danzig or Gotenhafen. And it was all her fault.

Claudia grieved at her loss of Johannes. She had been too casual in her love for him. He had never wanted anything more than to look after her, and to support her and their child, but Claudia, with the casualness that came from her certainty of his love, her sureness that he would always be there, had taken his affection for granted. She had gone her own way, visiting her friends when she wanted to for weekends, certain that he would accept her freedom as her right, as she did herself.

She smarted at the memory. Why could she not have been kinder to him; stayed near him more often? Why had she not cherished him for the work he was doing inside the Abwehr? She had never recognised his bravery. She had simply expected him, and all the others, to behave in an honourable way without need of praise or acknowledgement. Now he had disappeared, taken by the SS no one knew where, leaving her consumed with guilt.

As they moved on through the streets, both sisters tightened their grip on the children, both thinking of their own child, both praying that somehow they were safely on their way to the west. Again they joined the stream of refugees moving out of Pillau, now flowing westwards across the frozen Bay of Danzig itself.

The route to Danzig lay almost directly west from Pillau, but the land route was too vulnerably close to where the Russians might break through, and all roads were now closed to them. They were kept open only for the tanks and columns of foot soldiers of the Wehrmacht, desperately trying to stem the Russian tide. Everyone else was directed to the northernmost route, across the frozen ice.

Around the Bay lay a narrow spit of land, and between the refugees and that land lay the Frisches Haff, a sea lagoon, frozen with ice sufficiently strong to walk upon; thick enough to take horses and carts, but thin enough to crack under a lifetime of possessions. Pegs had been driven into the ice to direct them to the safest places to cross, but these were only temporary and had to be changed when that route gave way.

The ice edges became scenes of harrowing despair as people were directed to empty their carts of the heaviest goods. The sensible complied, with tears in their eyes they left precious items behind.

"I'm glad neither of us was at home, Nina. I couldn't bear to have to decide what to take or leave." Claudia broke their silence as they watched a couple in front of them unloading by the side of the trek, an old woman hysterically begging the man to leave her grandfather clock, the only memento of her mother's life.

"Do you think your mother would want to see you fall through the ice, because of her heavy old clock? It never kept the right time anyway. Good riddance to it," her husband reasoned.

The stubborn refused to unload anything. Sometimes the ice gave way under such heavy loads. Families watched their memories and hard work disappear into the sea. Some disappearing with the very treasures they tried to save. The ice became dotted with pieces of people's lives, abandoned as the owners saw what happened to other loaded carts and prams. The holes soon glazed over, sealing the property below in the freezing, dark water, and leaving the top even more treacherous for the next wave of unwary refugees walking over the new, thin surface.

Floods of migrants pouring across the Frisches Haff had weakened the surface, and by the time Nina and Claudia began to cross there was a thin layer of seawater in places, which coated their boots and rotted the soles. Their feet became wet and frozen inside their boots, with the ever-present danger of frostbitten toes. Neither they nor the horse could get a proper grip on the thin ice. The children had to walk as much as possible so the horse would have less to pull. Alexei got down more than once where the top covering was visibly moving and cracking under the weight. Sergei walked all the way without a murmur.

Nina's mind had cut off from the trek, until a sudden gush of freezing water into her boot forced a sharp intake of breath, and she shot back to reality. Back to the terrifying present, where the mercilessly bitter, winds lashed her half-closed, benumbed eyes. Back to the fighter planes, which sought to destroy her. The frightening present competed with warm, comforting memories for possession of her mind and her body.

A desperate struggle was being waged over her: by her memories, by the elements, and by the Russian Stormoviks. The Black Death rained down bombs from the hostile heavens and machine-gunned both her and the line of defeated and hapless human beings, reduced to being refugees in their own land.

The temperature was a dangerous minus twenty-five below zero. The need to check the children's clothing frequently for gaps where the wind could freeze their delicate skin was ever in her mind, until she blotted out the unbelievable horror of the present with sweet nostalgia. Then, for a while, even their safety was forgotten.

Her urgent, therapeutic nostalgia was for all the worthwhile things and people from her past that she believed had vanished: the values of her nation, the lost honour of her countrymen, and her way of life. Even worse was the loss of members of her immediate family, her own dear son amongst them!

Where were they all? Was it possible that they could be safe? Or had they been captured? Or...

Above all, the memory that kept her sane, kept her moving westwards, ever westwards, was of Erik. Was he even now lying in the ruins of Warsaw? Was he a prisoner of the Russians?

The pain of all her losses overwhelmed her. Involuntarily she moaned, but the sound was taken up by the wind as its own, and no one around her heard anything amiss. Nostalgia and the present mixed together in a never-ending circle, and desire for the recent, wonderful times created perfection in all things past. But the perfect past was dead; the flawed and dangerous present was ever with her.

She trudged on, one amongst many thousands; trying to keep herself going for everyone's sake. Somewhere up ahead, a long, long time ago, someone had set the slow, stumbling pace at which they all now plodded. Sometimes they paddled through wet ice, where the bomb holes had not yet refrozen; like a sore where the skin had yet to heal and which still wept a little, so the ice wept here and there. Often they slid and skated onto their backs or fronts as their feet ignominiously lost their grip. The steely, glinting, grey ice sheet stretched away before her for mile after mile into

303

the distance, to the edge of the world.

Only dimly aware of the people in front and behind her, of the heavy child she carried asleep on her shoulder, of her sister Claudia, at her side or sometimes dropping back with the others - her perception moved in and out of the physical present. Within her mind she had built a new existence, a phantom world populated by all those she had loved, whom she longed to see again.

The real world had become a nightmare from which the grown, twenty-six year old woman longed to run screaming back to Mother and Father for comfort and security; it was a place she was trying, step by laborious step, to bury deep within her. Reality was lodged in her memories.

The dark, negative, despondent side of her brain told her to give up, to sit down and to go to sleep, as she had seen other refugees do along the way.

'I must go on! I must!' she fiercely reminded herself.

She was exhausted, cowed by tiredness beyond anything she had ever experienced. A mental decay ate away at her motivation and determination to save herself, her sister, and the little tribe of Jewish children in her charge. It undermined her will, that indomitable will - which she had inherited from her mother - that had kept her family and her friends alive and fired with hope when there was none.

'Erik will understand, he'll forgive me for giving up, for letting go. Oh, Erik! How I would love to stop, and sleep, but I want to see you once more. I need you so much. Where are you?'

The memory of Erik and the hope of seeing him again drove her legs inexorably west to where she knew he would go if he could. 'I need your strength,' her heart cried out, but her lips, tightly wrapped inside a thick woollen scarf, did not move. A teardrop, escaping from its warm liquid sea, froze to death before it reached the wool.

The fierce Arctic winds howling across the Baltic Sea, drove on across the Frische Nehrung to the frozen Frisches Haff lagoon, a constant cutting reminder of her duty. So many were relying on her. So many had already been saved. At times she imagined this long, dark column of humanity - stretching away as far ahead and behind as her eye could see - were all relying on her to get them to the boats.

The boats!

Would they be there? Would there be any left?

Had she left it so late that the last one would have sailed? Would they all be saved, or would their own army capitulate yet again to Hitler and not lift a finger to help these innocent civilian refugees?

There were Russian submarines out in the Bay of Danzig waiting for them as well as the Stormoviks. The journey through the Baltic would be a risk. So many vessels had already been sunk; so many lives already lost. Nina was rapidly coming to the end of her personal tether.

The column trekked on, each of the hundreds of thousands of refugees engrossed in their individual, private misery, their own singular thoughts.

Moving in and out of sanity, her passion for life spent after her frightening brush with brutality at the hospital in Königsberg, Claudia nervously faltered along in Nina's wake. Then, suddenly, she stopped. She thought she heard voices.

Tens of thousands of people were trudging onwards from Pillau towards Danzig, yet the silence was audible. A voice was seldom heard, only the sound of human or animal feet stumbling and sliding on the ice, the scraping of wheels, or the terrifying whine of the Black Death aiming for those who had escaped their last attack minutes before. Yet Claudia heard voices. She looked around her, feverishly pulling her scarf up around her nose and cheeks with one hand, her other hand gripping one of the children. The words sounded Russian to her expectant ears, and her fear and anguish returned. She screamed in terror as a dark, sinister figure took hold of her and vigorously shook her arm.

"Claudia," Nina was crying into her ear. "Whatever is the matter? What's happened?"

She asked Joe, to whom Claudia was clinging, but he was half-asleep and did not understand what was happening. Nina fell in alongside her, saddened at her sister's terrible recent ordeal, miserable that she could do nothing to change the unspoken events that had brought Claudia to the brink of madness. But intensely grateful that at least one member of her family was alive, and that Claudia might yet recover. Momentarily, she had feared that Claudia was losing her mind. She had not found the courage to remind them how far it was to Danzig, nor how long it would take them to get there.

Before the water had seeped treacherously into her boot, she had been engrossed in a party at home. Home! If only they could reach it now! She glanced up and involuntarily stared towards the south-west where her home lay, as though even at this great distance she might see it. She saw nothing, but ice and greyness all around her. Home! What happiness it represented.

Her eyes fell on to the scrawny horse and the beaten up cart; and the boy pulling it along; and the children huddled inside it. She remembered how they had managed to hide Alexei and Sergei against all the odds. Little Martina was crying. Frightened, cold and unhappy, she was completely bewildered by the events that had brought her here. A voice calling to Nina, tried to break into her reverie. She tried to draw her hood and scarf even tighter around her head and the still sleeping Lisa until the sound became part of the howling wind. Her brain would not recognize it; it was clamouring to return to the haven of the past.

Somewhere behind her a bell was ringing. The merry, tinkling sound of a troika bell. And instantly, wondrously, her eyes transformed the emaciated old nag and the plain wooden cart into their own frisky little gelding, pulling the elegant black carriage, with their family crest on its side. Her thickly hooded head slipped slowly sideways, unconsciously aping the pose she had adopted that Christmas thirteen years ago, and her thoughts willingly returned to the staircase leading up to the ballroom and the little group of people standing there, waiting for her. She was excitedly looking out of the window at the top of the stairs, watching the guests arriving for the Christmas party, and her mother was calling to her, "Nina! Nina, where are you?" Her mother's voice! How she longed to hear it again.

The misery of this exodus was insufferable, and yet, after the first shock of seeing what lay ahead, they endured it in silence. There was no shelter from the bitter wind sweeping snow and hail before it, nor could they ever escape the ice under their feet. Every so often one or more of the children were allowed into the cart to rest their frozen feet. They trudged on, mile after mile, in glacial shock, their hearts heavy with individual grief and their minds numbed with weariness. On they straggled, a never-ending column of desolate, afflicted souls, many doomed to suffer further nightmares of heartache or physical distress, and all with a sense of impending doom.

Each of them had borne the hardship, the suffering, as well as they were able, but now the noise that rent the air brought back the Black Death to taunt them. From out of the clouds Stormoviks swooped down along the eternal file, at first playing with their victims. They flew so low the pilots' faces could be seen staring down at them, trying to alarm and stampede them like a pack of animals, before unleashing destruction. Just outside of Pillau, when the refugees had been fresh onto the route, the noise of the Stormoviks spitting fire and reigning bombs at them had the power to break the line into screaming sections, with panic stricken figures running and diving in all directions.

But now the psychology of this crocodile had changed. This line would not be stampeded. These people were so exhausted and dispirited they had become too mentally disoriented to respond. Not even when the Stormoviks let loose their bombs and machine guns on their easy targets did they move or cry out, unless involuntarily.

Groups of refugees were strafed, and still they trudged on. The wounded were helped onto carts by those who still had human instincts, others walked on by, unable to help or unwilling to stop; some so numbed they were simply uncomprehending: reduced to zombies, the walking dead; so traumatic had the past few days been for them all.

Planes would launch a bomb at the column and in a watery explosion a crater would appear. A cart, a horse, a family would disappear forever and those following hardly gave them a backward glance. There was nothing they could do. It was death to themselves to lean down and try to pull out a survivor, only to be toppled into the hole with no more strength to get themselves out.

Nina and Claudia were within sight of the place where they would first be able to put their feet on dry land when the Stormoviks returned. A long high-pitched scream followed by a dull thud behind their backs shook them temporarily back to life. Hannah, who was now Heide, Jakob, who was Paul, and Elsa, screamed and jumped from the cart, and running, slipping and sliding to the safety of the adults they clutched their coats, arms, any part of them that they could reach. Alexei and the boy ducked under the horse, which had no strength left to even whinny. His eyes rolled in terror, but he comforted himself with a few tiny jumps. One hoof broke the ice and Alexei pulled hard on the reigns to control the horse's movements.

Their cart contained a woman wounded from the previous attack, the smallest of their three boys, and one of the girls, with Alexei driving. Sergei, stumbling alongside, had his hand between the leather bridle and the horse's neck: helping him to stay awake and keeping his hand warm. His other hand held another boy. Oblivious to anything outside their own emotions, they were unaware of the plane coming at them fast along the Frisches Haff. They heard the explosion, but it barely registered in their paralysed, hallucinating heads.

The horse faltered and fell down dead, and the ice yawned and opened up in front of it to receive its carcass. Alexei collapsed sideways, dead before he, too, fell into the gaping black hole. Unable to extricate his hand from the bridle Sergei was mercilessly yanked forward; he slipped and fell under the horse, to be sucked under. The cart inevitably followed …

It all happened within a few seconds. Nina, some way behind, and carrying Regina again, had been engrossed in the Christmas party. She saw the explosion some yards ahead, and watched in disbelief as the sea opened up to become a watery grave. Just like a film being played in slow motion... The full impact of it did not hit her until many days later.

The immediate shock reminded her that she was not walking on solid ground, but water, and the recognition of her vulnerability coaxed some life back into her.

She had not registered that the two Russians and three of the children had gone forever.

Claudia, painfully remembering the scenes in the hospital, had been hallucinating a nightmare about Russian soldiers chasing her, and screamed. With Heide, Paul and Elsa traipsing along behind, clinging to her coat or hands, she had seen nothing of what happened. They all simply came - heads down against the wind and snow - one foot in front of the other relentlessly, sluggishly, onwards. When they caught up with the stationary Nina, they looked up.

"Where are the others?" Claudia asked dully.

"Gone!" Nina answered, staring into the cold black gaping hole in front of her, and then she began walking again.

She looked again at the gaping hole as they went round it. There was nothing to see except black water, and bits of ice and floating slush. She felt nothing, she understood nothing; she was emotionally dead. Less than a quarter of a mile further on their feet touched firm land and snow-covered banks indicated that they had reached the sand spit, with its welcoming forests of pine trees and homes in which to find shelter. Behind them the refugees stretched back for miles, the Stormoviks still swooping and diving over them.

A distant thud, and a huge boom echoed across the land behind them, and made them turn and look. They could see virtually nothing, only a red glow on the distant horizon. It was too dark; night had closed in without them being aware of it. They had crept their way along with the great trek, foot by foot, mile by mile, tuned in solely to the faith that they would arrive at Danzig eventually; there would be ships for all of them; they would escape from the Russians; and this would all end soon.

Ordinary events like day turning into night escaped their attention. Night had fallen and with it the Stormoviks had gone home, but the bombers came in greater numbers to Pillau.

The town they nearly waited in, where they might have stayed in some comfort in the emptied houses, with meat and hot food in plenty, was crowded with thousands more refugees. That night it was heavily bombed even as they trekked away from it, and an ammunition dump exploded killing hundreds of the refugees just as they had thought they were within sight of safety.

Thirty One

They slept briefly in a small village, which had been evacuated some days before. When they finally reached Danzig they were in a state of total exhaustion; the children were too tired, hungry and frozen to cry. They mutely joined the food queue and then for a place to stay until there was room on a boat; tomorrow they would queue for passes. They slept fitfully in the one room they were allocated in a house not too far from the docks. The nightly bombers and the anti-aircraft guns ensured they were woken frequently.

In the morning, with her stomach full of food, Nina began slowly to revive. She remembered the piece of paper in her pocket and studied it for a full five minutes. When she spoke there were tears in her eyes, and in her broken voice. "I'd forgotten their names - Leah, Jacob and Manfred," the tears coursed down her cheeks. "I didn't even remember their names!"

The remembrance of who the children were, and the danger they were still in brought both sisters back to some realisation of the urgency of their situation.

"If we need papers to get on the ships, we're in trouble. We can't get papers for the children. What are we going to do, Claudia? Can you look after them all while I go to the office? I know a back way through."

Nina found the dock office besieged with people arguing over who had priority on the ships. It was clear that the officials could not cope with them all. To her utter dismay, Nina discovered her contact had gone, and she returned to Claudia with the bad news as quickly as her numbed legs would let her. There were ships. But they would have to wait their turn, and they might not get on. And there were armed guards on each of the gangplanks.

Claudia suggested that she might try her luck at obtaining boarding cards. "After all," she reasoned, "I was about to be evacuated with the wounded, and as a nurse perhaps I could argue that I'm in charge of a small group of women and children. I might just be able to obtain them for all of us."

They did not know what else to do. "If you can get passes, then it might not be too long before we reach Hamburg and Max's home near the Dutch border," Nina said hopefully, feeling grateful that someone else was doing the thinking for her.

"And if we can't get to Hamburg, at least we might be able to reach Kösslin," Claudia said in parting.

Nina and the four children waited anxiously for Claudia's return, but as the hours went by, they began to fret. They were fed, sheltered in an empty house near the station with many other refugees, and they were warm and comfortable, but Nina was becoming distinctly worried. What would she do if Claudia failed to come back? One or two of the other refugees had given the children an odd look. What if they told the authorities there were Jews there? They had to move out quickly.

The Russian guns had opened up on the town and harbour area, again, and the earth shook under the bombardment. They were near enough to the port to be frightened, but Nina's fear was more for Claudia. Was she still inside the dock?

She left Heide, the eldest, in charge while she quickly went to places she thought Claudia might be. She knew the system and some of the names of the officials at the dock and after trying in one or two offices, against all the odds, she found one who remembered Claudia.

"I haven't had a cheerful soul in here for months. But she was. Like everyone else who comes in, she enquired about getting passes for the boats, and I explained that I'd need to see her papers. That's when she burst out laughing."

"We lost the papers. In the bombing," Nina hastily said.

"That's just what she said. Then she laughed and said she couldn't believe that with the Russians down the road, hundreds of refugees already waiting in the Bay Of Danzig, and thousands more joining them every day, most of them without papers, we could still be so bureaucratic!"

Nina smiled inwardly, yes, that must have been Claudia and how right she had been. Germans had always prided themselves on their excellent administration, on their care and attention to detail. All that really mattered was to get every one of those on the dock into the waiting ships. If they were still writing out boarding passes by hand, in triplicate, no wonder Claudia had seen the funny side. At least in Pillau they were not so officious. But this was Danzig, home of some of the fiercest Nazis; she had forgotten the nature of the town.

"Do you know where she went?" she asked him urgently.

"Yes! I had just begun to take down her details when a captain who had been talking to the officer on duty in the next office, behind me here, came out. He heard that she was a nurse. I was writing that down on the form you see..."

"Yes, yes," interrupted Nina impatiently, "but where did she go?"

"He took her with him. Just like that! Ordered her to go with him in fact. He said she should have stayed with her hospital and not gone wandering off. That took the smile off her face I can tell you. She looked quite scared."

Nina pressed him, "Where was he taking her? Where can I find them?"

"Gotenhafen. He was off to one of the big liners going in a convoy. Tomorrow, I think... or the next day. They've any number of wounded up there. They need all the nursing staff they can find," he added, believing her also to be a nurse, but Nina had already left.

As she disconsolately retraced her footsteps back to the house, she pondered heavily. Thinking about the children's future had stopped her worrying about her own family and friends. On the way back from the dock she tried telephoning her home, in the vain hope she could find out if her parents and Anna had got away with all their offspring. Unexpectedly the telephone rang twice, and then went dead. 'I hope we meet them in Hamburg,' she thought and then quietly prayed, "Please God, let Anna remember where Johannes's family lives, so we all meet up there."

As she walked back to their room, the sight of loose horses, sheep and goats roaming the streets puzzled her. And then she realised. The refugees who had reached the docks and gained their precious boarding cards no longer needed their animals and carts, and had simply abandoned them.

'I can't get boarding passes for the children, and we can't stay in Danzig any longer. I know where Claudia is heading, but what do we do now?' When she reached their temporary home they were alone. The other refugees had either gone to claim their places on board ship or to join the queue. The children were tearful, thinking that she, too, had disappeared and they had been deserted.

"Don't worry, you're all right now," she told them unconvincingly. "We'll find a way through. But we can't go on the boats; we need papers and we don't have any. We might manage on a train, but there are hardly any now, they're all being used for troops."

Nina was talking to herself; the children did not understand her. She had racked her brains to find a way other than walking along the coast towards Pomerania. They all had problems with their feet after the long trek, either blisters or pains from minor frostbite, and walking again was the last thing they wanted to do. Her boots were in ruins and she could hardly bear to keep them on. She knew the area well; there would be few places to find food, and there were long, lonely stretches where there might be dangers. It would take them too long on foot in this freezing weather; there was ice in the wind today.

For the first time in her life she found thinking difficult, her brain was woolly and dull. There was no choice, they had to start on foot, but the memory of their last trek dredged up grim pictures of what might still be in store. As she buttoned Regina up and made her scarf tight around her hood, she reminded them all of the rules, "No talking, leave that to me. Whisper when we are out in the country, but no loud shouting. We don't want to attract any attention to you."

"Are we going to walk again?" Elsa asked pathetically, "My feet hurt."

All of them joined her cries, none of them had any enthusiasm for another adventure; all they wanted was warmth, food, beds, and above all, stability.

Two streets from their room, they came upon one of the abandoned horses, wandering around aimlessly looking for food. It still had a harness on, but no saddle. Heide looked at it enviously. "Can't we ride on it instead of walking?"

Nina gave her a startled look, about to scold her for talking.

"Why of course, that's the answer! It's been staring me in the face. I must be stupid not to have thought of it," she whispered. "We'll have to learn to ride without saddles. We'll find some more horses, then work out where we're going from there."

"Are we going west?"

"West and north. If we can get to my aunt's home in Pomerania we might be able to get through to Stettin or Lübeck. There might be trains, too. I have lots of friends there and we'll be able to find somewhere safe for you all to stay."

Any number of animals had been abandoned in the streets. The sheep and even the dogs provided good food for the thousands flocking into the city every day. The stock roamed the streets as the refugees did, in search of food and shelter. Nina had no difficulty in finding three horses in good enough condition to ride. She set the children to finding pieces of old sandbags blown apart by explosions. Gathering as many strips as they could, Nina wound them around the horses' hooves to enable them to keep their footing on the icy roads and muffle the sound. She placed larger pieces over the backs of the horses and tied them together underneath -so the children would be able to keep their seats more easily - and led them through the streets northwards to Gotenhafen. The children walked alongside her for a while so the horses could get used to them all.

They would not go near the port, but would try to cut across the country to Pomerania and from there further to the west, where capture might be by the Americans or the British. She chose quiet, suburban back streets, trying to avoid any contact with soldiers.

In the background there was the continual, terrifying thunder of Russian guns and deafening explosions flattening the ports; the ear splitting screams of the Stormoviks, strafing and bombing the refugees; and their own booming guns responding in a last ditch battle. Even the horses had become inured to it and only reacted when there was an explosion nearby. The further north through the back streets they travelled, the fainter the noise became; but it never left them. Wherever they went in East Prussia or Pomerania they could never escape the unremitting din of approaching retribution.

At the north-western edge of the town, where the snow lay deeper, she stopped. "All right. Now the horses have got used to you and their new shoes, you have to get used to them. The same rules apply, even though we might not see many people. No noise, no shouts, no cries. Do you understand? If you speak, you whisper! If we meet anyone, you call me Mummy. Understand, Regina? We're still in great danger from the bad soldiers so you must call me Mummy and leave me to do all the talking. Understand? If we're to survive, we have to be a whole family. We've lost all our papers and possessions. They'll have to accept our word that I'm your mother. That makes you all brothers and sisters."

The children looked at each other, grinning. "Hello, Sis," Joe, the remaining boy, whispered to Heide.

"All right, now let's see if we can't get you up on these poor old horses and go and find them some grass or hay out in the country."

Joe pulled Nina's coat and whispered, "Can I have the little one?"

"What are you talking about, Joe?" Nina whispered back.

316

Joe pointed. Behind the three horses was a little pony. He followed, lonely like the children, and perhaps just as frightened. "Is he their baby?" he whispered.

"I expect so," she answered. It was quite comforting to have children around her, they were so simple and uncomplicated, like the horses, just wanting love and security and food. But Nina was always aware that one wrong word and they were all in trouble.

Joe proudly rode on the pony. Nina and Regina were on one of the horses and Heide took Elsa on another. They kept the third as a 'spare' so when one grew weary, they could change. As Elsa became more confident, she eventually rode alone. The children began by lying almost full-length along the horses' backs, afraid to sit upright. By midday their leg muscles were weary and they dismounted for a while.

Nina was in familiar territory and headed quickly along the coast behind Gotenhafen and across towards Leba and Stolpemunde. By nightfall they had got just beyond Leba, seeing very few people on the way: most of the refugees had headed for the ports or gone west, and the farms were empty. Their soldiers were still a few miles further south holding off the Russians.

It was snowing and freezing fast when they found a farm outhouse where they and the horses could rest a while, out of the bitterly cold night air. They had nothing to eat, but at least the horses had hay and bedding. Sleeping amongst the animals and straw brought them shelter and warmth.

Next day, Nina begged for milk from a nearby farm; she did not dare let the children speak to anyone. They left early in the morning, the distant thunder of battle just a little louder, Nina thought, or was it just her fear making her imagine things? The children and Nina grew more used to sitting astride the saddle-less horses, and their pace increased. Stiff muscles were simply one more pain to be endured.

On the night of January the thirtieth, they reached Kösslin. Ice was again being blown into their faces, and visibility was down to a few yards. Nina knew each and every house in the road down to the nearby port. She was anxious to get past this stretch, she felt too exposed on this vulnerable, open coastline. On horseback, especially, they were easy targets. The planes were concentrating on the ports, but they might turn their attention towards this area at any moment.

Franz's house had been lived in by others and ransacked. The rooms were stripped of much of the furniture and all of the paintings and books. It was too painful for Nina to stay there.

She took them on the few hundred yards to Johannes's old home. It was locked up and shuttered. She broke a small window at the back of the house and they crept in. Here the furniture was still intact. By the good condition of things she judged that Johannes's family had remained there until quite recently. Nina found precious tins of food in the kitchen, wood for the fire, and even more clothing. And the horses lacked for nothing in the barn. They enjoyed more comfort than they had experienced for days.

In the kitchen, under the tins of food, Nina found an envelope with money inside and a short note in hastily scribbled pen:

'Dear Claudia, If you or anyone in Otto's family should come this way, we have gone to my house in Bocholt. It's the furthest west we can go. Take what you need. If we ever come back, you will have returned, too, and if we don't, then all of it is lost. So take it without shame. Good luck to you all. The trains were running to Lübeck and even to Hamburg mid-January. We'll be waiting and hoping at ..."

There followed an address in Bocholt. Even in haste, the legal mind of Max, Johannes's father, had thought of all eventualities: refugees may have lost everything, including their address books, pens, paper and money.

Nina copied the address and left the letter on the kitchen table with a few additions, in case her parents, Claudia, Anna or, maybe, Peter's family came through this way. She took some money for train fares.

Afraid to light candles and reveal their presence in the boarded up house, they went to bed early that evening. They were restless and slept fitfully. Fear of the planes, the bombs and the Russians, and memories of their friends and families, left them no peace.

Out in the Baltic, not thirty miles from where they were trying to sleep, Claudia was cruising by them in a huge ocean liner, the pride of the German 'Strength through Joy' movement. The liner all German workers had wanted to cruise on for a well earned holiday: the Wilhelm Gustloff.

Thirty Two

As Claudia was explaining to the clerk in the dock office that she was a nurse, she was overheard by one of the officers from the Wilhelm Gustloff, which was waiting at Gotenhafen to be joined by a convoy and an escort. Immediately he conscripted her to go with him.

She was unsure if she should plead on behalf of Nina and the children, but his whole attitude and vocabulary suggested that he was a good Nazi and she bit her tongue. If it was humanly possibly Nina would get them away to safety and Claudia simply had no more energy to argue. He was in charge; all she needed to do was to return to being an obedient nurse. In her exhausted and overwrought state it was appealingly easy. No more children to worry about, and no more decisions to make on others' behalf!

The doctor was in charge of a contingent of wounded soldiers and submariners to be evacuated from East Prussia to Kiel, Stettin or anywhere still under German rule. The Wilhelm Gustloff had been commandeered to rescue the U-boat crews operating from the Bay of Danzig. Hundreds of small craft plied back and forth for weeks, transferring everyone to the big liners and merchant ships waiting in the docks or out in the Bay.

In Gotenhafen, Claudia slept in a hotel commandeered specifically for nurses; she was under a strict regime and quite unable to slip back to Danzig and Nina. The following day she and other nurses were taken directly to the ship where they were to nurse the wounded soldiers.

At the harbour she witnessed scenes of chaos and panic, which were to stay with her for the rest of her life. At first she could not comprehend what was going on. Gradually, as she waited in the orderly queue - guarded by many soldiers - the horror of what she was observing began to dawn. On the quayside a baby in a bright red shawl attracted her attention. It was being carried by a frantic woman, screaming and shouting at those around her. Hands were reaching out towards the baby as though it belonged to someone else and they wanted to pass it to its parent. The movement up the gangplank increased, and the woman clutching the baby moved onto the ship. She was given a piece of paper by a steward and moved with the crowd along to the open deck.

Claudia watched, petrified, as the woman suddenly hurled the baby down to the crowd waiting below. Competitive hands clutched and tore at the infant for possession of this valuable commodity. Before Claudia reached the top of her own gangplank she had watched the baby being thrown down a second time.

Too stunned to say anything, her terror-struck mind visualized her own child being thrown about as a passport to freedom. Suppose the child hit the ground? Suppose it fell into the icy water? The refugees, fighting for their own survival, were using the baby as a means to obtain a place on the boat and no longer saw it as human.

The ship had been ready and waiting to go for some days. The refugees, who would have to wait for another boat, were becoming restless, even mutinous on the dockside. They had endured great hardship to get this far, and here was this huge liner, waiting provocatively. Why couldn't they get on it? They could see spaces on the promenade decks - surely they could be allowed onto those? If not, why didn't she go and make way for another vessel?

The situation was becoming explosive, but the boat was still waiting for a convoy of wounded soldiers and their escort. The captain had to decide if the situation on the dockside was worse than the dangers out at sea where the Russian submarines were sitting waiting. If they went without a sufficiently strong escort they would be in mortal danger; if they waited much longer at the quayside, they would be in danger of being swamped with refugees. The ship was not capable of great speed. The only way to outrun the submarines was to zigzag through the danger zone, which would not be easy in a liner of this size.

Claudia and other nurses were temporarily housed in the empty music room where passengers were to be placed when all the cabins were full. They were allocated a particular area of the ship and given lifejackets. Claudia was ordered to the Arbour on the Sun Deck where wounded soldiers had been taken.

"We have a special maternity ward set up further along the Sun Deck. You can divide your time between there and here, as and when we need you. You'll be on night duty. Report back here at eight o'clock tonight."

She could not settle to anything, knowing what was going on outside in the harbour. She slept fitfully and was unaware that the ship had been pulled away from the dockside to avoid a panic-rush by the thousands upon thousands of waiting refugees. Crew and late passengers were ferried across to the Wilhelm Gustloff from the far side of the harbour.

Left alone with nothing to occupy her mind, she could not rid herself of the tormenting images from Königsberg that had been rekindled by the doctor's words. Allowing herself to think about the scenes in the hospital opened up a Pandora's Box of all the other memories she had tried to suppress.

No one could carry the burden of so many tragic losses, so much suffering and terror, and be expected to continue to live normally. Each tried to come to terms with their past. Some, in the warmth and comparative safety of the ship, had already 'let go' and could not cope with even the simplest things. Mothers could be seen slumped in a corner, crying quietly, or with a glazed expression totally ignoring their own children's entreaties. Soldiers on their stretchers or beds simply turned their heads away and remained resolutely silent.

In the face of such suffering, Claudia, like all her family, turned towards others. She suffered as others did, but she buried her own thoughts once again and became a tower of strength, bringing comfort and relief to those worse off than herself. At noon, she observed deckhands moving about the ship more than usual, checking hatches, and she leaned over the side momentarily to watch the tugs coming alongside.

'Oh, Nina!' She prayed silently. 'It looks like we're on our way. I hope you're not still waiting for me. I hope you get on a ship or find a way through! But please, God, come through safely!'

She embraced the work of looking after those around her wholeheartedly, and lost herself completely in helping the sick, the wounded, and the most unenvied of all women, those about to give birth at such a dramatic and terrifying moment in their country's history.

She did not notice the liner stop before it really got underway. Thousands more refugees had been patiently waiting in small boats along the route to the sea, and the moment the liner began to move they rowed right into its path to block it, and sat there pleading with the sailors to allow them on board. Who could refuse them? Hundreds scrambled up the nets thrown down by the sailors. No one counted how many came on board and had to be found room; someone estimated that a further two thousand clambered up to safety.

Her duty stretched out before her through the night. She, like the other passengers, was unaware that up on the bridge the captain lived in fear of a Russian attack. By the time she had started work they had reached the danger zone, where the mines no longer impeded submarines and their own support ships were furthest away. The decision had been made to leave as soon as the rest of the wounded soldiers had been taken on board, despite the fact that their escort had not arrived and they would only have two small vessels, with little firepower, to accompany them. In two or three hours they would be past the worst stretch and almost sure of survival.

It was almost ten past eight when Claudia felt the ship shudder, and heard a dull thud, quickly followed by two more. She looked up in alarm at the orderlies. Almost immediately bells began to toll throughout the ship.

Someone yelled, "Mine!"

"Torpedoes!" screamed another.

The ship began very quickly to list to port.

"Get your life jacket on," the doctor ordered quietly as he went through his 'wards'. Claudia surveyed the women in the maternity beds, some with small newborn babies, some heavily pregnant, one in labour, and she was sick with fear once again, for herself as well as for them.

The loudspeakers broadcast instructions and she helped the maternity cases out to the Boat Deck, expecting them to be helped into the boats by the sailors, and went back to see what she could do for the wounded soldiers.

Neither she nor anyone else knew that the sailors who ought to have been there assisting them had almost to a man been trapped in their quarters down in the ship's hold - the wrong side of a watertight bulkhead door. Without them, lowered unevenly by inexperienced men, most of the boats would spill into the water. And on the Boat Decks it would become a free for all - every man for himself. The women could expect little assistance as they stood there, thinly clad, in the freezing night air.

After she had aided two wounded soldiers she was overcome by exhaustion. The traumatic events in the hospital, her long trek, days on end with hardly any food had all sapped her physical and mental strength. And without Nina who had helped her focus her mind on one thing at a time she could no longer think clearly. Everything was falling apart and she was too weak to pull herself together.

The doomed ship was beginning to list badly and the doctor ordered her to the Boat Deck to save herself. There was no one left to help him carry out the wounded; he would continue alone as long as he could. Men supposed to remain and help him had already run for their lives. Order broke down quickly and swarms of passengers were fighting for a place in the insufficient boats. She rapidly put on her coat and boots, and went on deck.

The ship had sailed without enough lifeboats for all the extra passengers it carried, and the boats that there were had frozen into their davits and no amount of frantic pushing or pulling did anything to free them. The only personnel trained in the emergency procedures, were at that very moment screaming for help; beating their hands uselessly against the watertight doors; drowning in the freezing water pouring in below decks. With no trained crew and frozen winches the eight or nine thousand wounded and ill passengers faced disaster alone and unaided.

As Claudia slipped her way along the rapidly listing deck in search of a lifeboat she skidded past one just being launched. Like an upturned fly, her arms and legs were unable to gain a purchase on anything to stop her progress. She hit a door into a corridor and slid to a halt. As she scrambled unsteadily to her feet she watched helplessly as the men launching the lifeboat let one side down further than the other. The passengers slid down to one end, tipped the boat over, and fell screaming into the sea. Suspended from one frozen line, which snapped under the vessel's weight, it fell heavily upside down into the sea on top of the hapless people who had just been thrown from it. Claudia stood with her hands over her mouth, her eyes wide with horror, shuddering from sheer terror.

Like most of the other passengers, she was half out of her wits. Some, literally out of their minds with fear, jumped over the side as the ship slipped inexorably lower into the water; those without their warm clothing or life jackets, died instantly from the bitter cold and shock.

Others trapped on board shot their children one by one, their wives, and then themselves rather than let their families face a cold, horrible death.

Claudia, her coat buttoned up and her lifejacket tied on, stood insecurely on the angled deck not knowing what to do. One of the few ship's officers still alive was trying to unblock the workings on another small lifeboat. There were some women already sitting in it, one covered in a blanket cradling a tiny baby. She was one of the women Claudia had helped from the maternity room. She saw Claudia standing alone along the deck and called out to her, "Nurse! Nurse! Over here! Quickly, this way!"

Claudia slipped as quickly as she could over to the lifeboat and scrambled into the small craft. Finally he freed the lines and electrical works from ice and snow. As he slid down the rope into the boat, the electric winches carried the boat safely down to the sea, past hundreds of hysterical people lining the decks below. Trapped with no boats they had been unable to find their way up to the Boat Deck. They cried out, "Stop! Let us in!" but there was nothing anyone could do. The electric winches were automatic, and they sailed on by the terrified passengers.

As they hit the sea, the lines freed themselves and the officer ordered them to get out the oars and row away from the ship now towering and listing above them, black and sinister in the darkness of the cold winter's night.

Looking upwards, Claudia saw the size of the dark ship looming above, ready, in its death throes, to fall on top of them. Seized by utter panic she snatched up one of the oars and with frenetic energy pulled on it, over and over again, in a desperate attempt to outrun the liner. She fixed her eyes on it, watching it slowly listing and sinking towards her, magnifying its descent dramatically.

"Stop! Stop!" The officer cried at her, "We're far enough away now. If she rolls over, we'll only be washed further away!"

Claudia's numb brain took in his words slowly.

"You're making us go round in circles!"

The bitter wind on her face, the motion of the rough seas shaking her up and down aroused her, and she sat mutely trying to comprehend her fate. As they ceased rowing and looked around them at the heads bobbing in the water amongst the boats, a hand stole up the side of the boat out of the water next to Claudia. She screamed and hit out at the hand. The officer leaned over and grabbed it and hauled aboard a young woman. She sank to the bottom of the boat, her body shaking with shock and cold, her clothes quickly covered by a layer of ice as the water froze. There were not enough blankets to put over her.

Claudia turned away from her, frightened by her own instinctive reactions and desire for self-preservation. A vision of a former life flashed before her eyes: she and Nina had talked about how heroic they would be. To what depths she had sunk! There was no heroism now, only terror and self-interest. It took a monumental effort to bring her thoughts back to the present: to the knowledge that she was safe for the moment provided she kept moving and warm. The liner was a quarter of a mile away and on its side as it slid towards its grave. They were near enough to see a small loose raft on the deck ride out over the side into the sea on a huge wave, which rolled up and over the deck. They watched in horror as another was swung against the funnel and was smashed to pieces, its occupants flung in all directions. Then, briefly, unimaginably, the forbidden lights on the liner flashed on and the sirens howled, shrieking out their alarm over the water as the sea poured in through the now horizontal funnel. The screams of thousands still trapped on board were silenced forever.

Passengers in the lifeboats dotted all around sat frozen and still, too shocked and mesmerised by the sight of the liner plunging under the waves, taking thousands with her to the sea bed. It was as if the ship bewailing its own untimely demise let out its own death rattle. Claudia would never forget that ghastly, ghostly sound.

For a moment the sea seemed intensely quiet and each boat might have been the only survivor in the cold, black night. Then gradually they heard voices from the water, clamouring to be helped into the lifeboats. Some of the swimmers, with their last strength, hauled themselves over the side; some were helped, and others were thwarted by the callous indifference of the occupants.

"Keep them out, we're too full already," was heard less often as those in the water drifted away in a frozen death.

"Wait for the escort boats, they'll be here soon," voices promised those desperate to get out of the water.

There were rafts and lifeboats quite empty and others over full with people prepared to kill those in the water in order to keep them out.

Within a very short time hardly any sound was heard. The officer in

Claudia's boat kept urging them on, "Keep rowing, and keep moving. Move your legs backwards and forwards, too. If you don't you'll go numb and frostbite will set in quickly. Keep going towards the shore." They rowed on, their strength and their will ebbing away, picking up survivors as they came across them: blue and shivering with cold, dying quickly in the icy water. The longer they had been in the sea, the quicker they died. No one could last more than a few minutes in a sea with ice floating in it.

They were all too emotionally shattered to be alert to what was going on around them. They all but pulled straight into the side of their escort ship before they realised it was there.

The dark side of the Löwe loomed up at them and willing hands began to haul the survivors out of the little lifeboat. Inside the old torpedo boat, thankful to be in the warm again, they slumped where they were put, accepting blankets and hot drinks gratefully. Claudia fainted into a shocked sleep, her first deep sleep for a week. She did not see the sailors push her boat away with its cargo of dead bodies lying in the icy water at the bottom; she had been unaware of them while she had been rowing. Her only thought had been row to survive!

She awoke when she was shaken by a sailor, "Come on nurse. Wake up! You've arrived!"

"Arrived?" She repeated the word uncomprehendingly, her mouth stiff and unresponsive.

"Yes, we're at Kolberg. Off you get. We have to go back for more survivors."

Kolberg! What a blessed word! What pictures it conjured up in her tired, weakened mind! Kolberg - why that was in Pomerania, almost next door to Kösslin! Home! Home! How near it was. She would be able to see Johannes again! How she longed to see him!

'Forgive me, Johannes, please, please, can you ever forgive me?'

The miserable cargo of shipwrecked refugees limped and staggered down the gangplank into the town in search of somewhere to stay. It was the middle of the night and bitterly cold. Some of the survivors had no shoes; some had blankets around them from the Löwe; others had needed to have their own clothes cut away from them on the rescue boat and now had literally nothing, only what had been available on the support ship.

Once each had been a real person, with a home, possessions, a past and a future, hopes, dreams … Twice they had lost everything; now all they had were their memories; and far too many of those were too painful to dwell upon. Like sleepwalking tramps with their eyes wide open and their clothes in tatters, they tottered down the main street one after the other; following sheep-like the one in front, not knowing where they were or what they were supposed to do next. Most of them, like Claudia, would be unable to talk to anyone about what had happened that night: the memory of it would be buried.

Claudia, her mind shattered and frozen like her body, had no idea where she would find immediate shelter, but some primitive instinct made her turn towards Kösslin, to the east - not to the west and safety. In her thin nurse's uniform, her winter coat, lifejacket and two ship's blankets to cover her head and body, she limped towards her past - not remembering that she might yet have a future. The present, the war, the Russians… forgotten. Everything she loved, everything she wanted was in Kösslin, and she gathered her last strength together for the few short miles home.

Thirty Three

Very early the next morning, something disturbed Nina's sleep. She awoke and sat bolt upright in bed, her ears alert to every sound. It was dark. Still with her thick winter coat on, she waited for a few seconds. She got up and prowled about, anxiously checking inside the house, but she could see nothing.

"Come on children, it's time to get up," she shook them one by one until they woke up. "Listen! I thought I heard something, so be very quiet."

"Can't we stay here a bit longer?" Elsa pleaded. "My legs ache so much."

"Ssssh!" Joe whispered, putting a finger to his mouth, a frown darkening his small face. Then he grinned at Elsa.

"I'm sorry, sweetheart," Nina whispered, "but we must go. We don't know when the bad soldiers will get here. You don't want to be caught just because your legs ached do you?"

They had put their trust in Nina completely, she was their mother now, and Nina felt her responsibility towards them keenly.

Each of them took two blankets, one to go over their horse's back and one to wear around themselves. They were all warm with extra clothes from the house, and well fed. Heide opened the back door to take the blankets out to the horses, and she dropped them and cried out, "Nina, quickly, come quickly!"

"You must call me Mother, Heide," Nina began. Just then a moan reached her ears. Had it been that which had woken her? She saw a moving bundle of clothes on the ground outside the back door and recognised a stockinged female leg.

"It's just another refugee, like us," she explained softly to relieve the frightened children. "Help me get her inside."

'Oh Lord, now we're going to be delayed even longer,' she thought, 'and I shall have someone else leaning on me.'

They pulled the motionless woman into a sitting position and removed the blanket cowling from her face. Nina urgently slapped her to try to bring life back. Her eyelashes and cheeks had ice on them and a glass beard sparkled in the moonlight streaming in through the broken window pane. The tears, which she had shed at the door, had run down her chin and frozen. In the darkness, they could not see her clearly, to see if her eyes were open. Nina slapped the face again.

"Come on! Wake up, wake up," she urged. "You must wake up!" She slapped both cheeks again. "Come on, come on! Heide, go and put the kettle on and make a hot drink for her. Joe, rub her hands, she's frozen. She has no gloves. Elsa, run upstairs and get two more blankets, no three! Rub harder, Joe. Come on, wake up!" She yelled in the woman's ear. The grey figure began to stir and groan incoherently, and the iced up eyelashes tried to open a little. "Wake up! Come on!" Nina repeated over and over.

The woman's eyes flickered open a crack, slowly and with difficulty, as she began to piece together where she was. She was half lying down on a floor and she was so stiff with cold she could barely move. Someone was holding her up.

"Is that you, Nina?" she whispered awkwardly, her jaw stiff. It was an appeal, a prayer that it might be Nina, rather than any real understanding that it was her own sister in front of her.

The voice constantly in her ear, urging her to wake up, had found echoes somewhere in her subconscious; the pitch, the timbre, the emotion, all reminded her of Nina.

As Nina looked shakily at the face, startled by her words, the intonation revealed Claudia in the same instant as a brief shaft of moonlight lit up her face. This half-frozen woman whom Nina had thought was simply another refugee was her own dear sister, searching for a safe haven as they had.

332

Seeking the past in Johannes's house as a way out of the present.

Too choked to answer, Nina's arms tightened around the frail body, and she hugged her, rocking back and forth as her tears dripped into the blanket around Claudia's head.

"Claudia, thank God, thank God," she kept whispering. The children obedient to Nina's finger on her lips, quietly whispered to Claudia and put their arms around her, too. She had been their mother long before Nina.

"Heide, help me to get her up to bed. She must rest, and get warm again, and have some food and a hot drink. We'll have to stay until Aunty Claudia is a bit better."

The children took it in turns to lie in bed with Claudia, warming her up and comforting her. Nina spent the best part of the day by her side, using her expressive hands to make all kinds of gentle, caring movements - pushing back strands of hair out of Claudia's eyes, moving the blanket around her to just the right place - in order to show the depth of her feelings as words could not.

She did not know how Claudia came to be there, she only knew how glad she was to have her sister back. She guessed what might have happened whilst putting her into new, warm clothes, and discovered the lifejacket, with the name Wilhelm Gustloff on it, still tied around her chest, but she patiently waited until Claudia felt well enough to tell them herself.

They had to go on just as soon as they could. Every minute, each hour that passed led them deeper into mortal danger. For all she knew the coastal strip had been closed off and their way through to the west cut.

After a day and a night of rest she hoped that Claudia would be able to ride without any further delay. "Do you think you can get on a horse?" She asked Claudia very early the following morning.

Claudia gave Nina a weak smile. "I was born on a horse, remember?"

Those were the last coherent words she spoke for many days. Nina was coping again, leading them all to safety; she could let go now that she knew she was in her sister's capable hands.

They continued riding as before, the children obeying the order to keep quiet, but vying with each other to ride with Claudia. The little cavalcade wound its way over the low hills down to the coast and along to the little town of Swinemunde; swollen with thousands of refugees, flocking in mainly from the boats.

Liners and merchant ships were using Swinemunde as one of the first safe havens for the refugees, nearer than Lübeck or Kiel. From there it was quicker for the boats to return to the Bay of Danzig to rescue more East Prussians still arriving all around the bay, flooding in week after week. Swinemunde was also the first place along the Pomeranian coast where they could catch a train through to Lübeck or Hamburg.

The cold air had quickly demoralised them again and by the time they reached the town, their heads were lolling forward sleepily. They arrived in the centre before they realised they had reached civilisation. They had cut across dangerously open territory, choosing it deliberately to avoid any chance of the children being discovered, and now they found themselves right in the middle of the road with an SS soldier barring their way. He saluted.

"Go straight ahead," he pointed to the street full of refugees. Nina stared at him and shivered. She had barely heard what he said, except for the last three stark words.

"Helmut," he called to his fellow officer. Nina was crying inside, and tears began rolling down her cheeks again. To have come so far, to have suffered so much and now, almost at the end of their journey, to be caught by the SS. She could no longer bear it. She broke down and sobbed like a child. She watched mortified as the two SS officers whispered together, looking at each of the children and the two women in turn. She had failed them. Even as the Russians and the Americans and British were tightening their grip, the SS were still exacting revenge and they would be taken away and shot. They would shoot the children, too. She had never felt so useless. The poor things had relied on her to deliver them to safety and she had lost them all through a few moments' inattention. 'Why hadn't she been awake enough to avoid the centre of the town? Why?'

These thoughts were all milling around in Nina's befuddled head as Helmut took hold of her horse's reins and began to walk it briskly down the main street. He motioned the others to follow. The other horses automatically fell in step behind Nina's; it was a ritual to which they were well used. The SS soldier had seen many refugees in this weakened state before. He had orders to clear the area as soon as possible, there were many more still coming through and these were not moving fast enough.

"Is that you Nina? Claudia?" A male voice called out to them as they passed through the crowds. "It's Johannes!" The voice insisted on repeating.

The two women both jumped out of their skins. They flashed quick looks at the owner of the voice, but it was not their Johannes. "You remember? I lived near your aunt and uncle? When you get through, if you see my wife, tell her I'll get there soon." He disappeared into the background as the SS officer led them all away.

At the station Helmut cleared the way through the throng, mostly now male refugees from the ships, or husbands and wives who would not be split up. He opened up a carriage at the end of the train. "Would you please hurry up! The train is waiting to leave." He spoke curtly, but politely.

Nina let Regina down as gently as she could, then slid from the old horse, and helped the others down. She was not going to hurry to be shot! The children obediently climbed into the carriage and sat waiting mutely for Helmut to join them as their guard. He stood at the door and held out their blankets for Nina to take, and then he closed the door, saluted smartly, turned and disappeared back to his post further up the street. He had no orders to do anything other than direct the refugees to the trains.

"We didn't say goodbye to the horses," Joe blurted out in defiance of Nina's orders.

"No. So we didn't." She sat quietly.

What new trick was this? She looked at the crowds outside, shouting messages to those in the train, their behaviour wasn't right; there were even some with smiles on their faces. They sat silently, waiting, not knowing if they were under arrest or if they were free. The train slowly moved out of the station towards the west, with its cargo of thousands of shattered lives. A woman in the corner of the carriage smiled at the newcomers. "We'll be in Hamburg quite soon," she said reassuringly.

Hamburg! Then they were to reach safety after all. But Nina did not relax; she could not do so yet. She had let go for only a few moments before they reached the town and they might all have been captured. The children and Claudia were still not free from danger.

It was not until the train reached Hamburg that they realised they were really free, safe from the Russians! But Nina knew they were still all living in Hitler's Third Reich.

Thirty Four

Claudia collapsed soon after the refugee train reached Hamburg. Unable to talk about her ordeals, she bottled it all up, and tried to act as if nothing untoward had happened to her. But her slight frame was unable to withstand the battering of the events: in the hospital, the great trek and then the shipwreck all following so quickly one upon the other. Unable to think about the horrors she had witnessed one after the other, she dwelt constantly on Johannes and how badly she felt she had treated him.

During the train journey she compared her own offhand behaviour to Nina's, and weighed up their differences. She could see Nina was putting the children first in everything, yet these were not her own. Claudia knew she must have been feeling her separation from both Dieter and Erik keenly, as she felt her own loss of little Klaus. Where were they all now? Would their parents and Anna have arrived in Hamburg ahead of them or were they all, including Klaus and Dieter, still desperately trying to gain boarding passes for one of the boats? Had they been on her own boat, were they even now at the bottom of the East Sea? A groan of despair issued from her mouth as that ghastly vision haunted her yet again.

Sometimes she caught Nina gazing deeply at her, wondering, wanting to ask her questions, but she could not bring herself to talk. It was not that she knew she would break down and cry or otherwise demonstrate deep emotions or weaknesses in her character; it was because she could not bear to even think about it. The sunken ship with its seven or eight thousand dead, now down on the ocean floor, had also been buried deeply within her subconscious, gone for ever, never to be spoken of.

Nevertheless, she felt shabby for Nina's sake. Nina, who was like the rock on which they all leaned for support, who reached out with both arms to give them all the comfort that she was capable of giving, deserved an explanation of why she must look after yet another fugitive. One who was too weak in both body and mind to be able to make decisions for herself, or care for the children. Claudia simply could not explain.

This same Claudia, who had once been so energetic and full of fun, teeming with the excitement of just being alive, now sat in her hospital bed, an alien in an alien world. Stricken with remorse and self-pity, she sat day after day apathetically, eyes closed or staring at nothing, not even responding to the weak hugs that Nina gave her. The children were forbidden to see her; they were confined to two small rooms in the flat of one of Nina's allies.

When she had lived in nearby Lübeck she had made many useful contacts, and now she had to impose unwillingly on their friendship. She did not dare leave their four Jewish children anywhere else. Refugees were being helped to move on or to find accommodation in the city, but Nina feared their identity would become known if they stayed too long in one place. They all had to keep up the pretence that she was their mother, even in their temporary new home. From the friends in the city she managed to cadge enough food to keep them all going, and as refugees they had been given coupons when they arrived at the main station; and these she passed on to her hosts each week.

A city such as Hamburg, suffering routinely from heavy RAF bombing raids, was unsafe and unhealthy. There were too many derelict buildings and too many dead bodies for what was left of the authorities to deal with, diseases spread quickly.

Nina waited impatiently to be able to move on, either to Sweden, if that were possible, or south-westward to Claudia's family. Erik would go to Sweden if he got out alive, but how could any of them get there now?

She managed to get a message through to her mother-in-law to say she was alive and in Hamburg, without Dieter, but she was unable to get to Sweden herself. She could prove that she and Dieter were Swedish, but with four Jewish children and Claudia, the wife of a prisoner of the Third Reich, to worry about, she did not want to push the SS too far. They had almost forgotten that they were still in Hitler's Reich. They all needed papers, they needed help, but they could not ask for any from the authorities. Anyway, Nina reasoned, there would be no boats going across; the Russians would see to that. They had to go south.

Trying to plan for their future had made Nina think of her own family. Where was Dieter now? Where were Anna, and the rest? A sickening yearning to be with them threatened to overpower her.

How could she continue looking after other people's children when she should be searching for her own? Suppose that Dieter was still in East Prussia and the Russians had got him? She stifled the awful thoughts with increasing difficulty.

While Claudia was in hospital, Nina went to the safe address she had given Anna, but no-one had reached there. When Claudia was discharged due to the desperate shortage of beds and the huge influx of wounded or ill refugees, Nina set about moving them further west and south without waiting any longer. She prayed that Anna or her father would remember where she and Claudia were heading.

Her main concern, like the hundreds of thousands of other refugees from the east, was not to be caught by the Russians. The British and Americans were poised along the Rhine, already bombarding towns inside Germany, ready for their final push straight to the heart of the country. In the east, the Russians seemed to be closer to Pomerania.

They had to go further west to be really safe, and Bocholt, where Claudia's family had a second home, was as far west as they could go. Johannes's parents had left the letter to say they would welcome them all and were waiting for anyone who could get through. Nina was unable to raise them on the telephone, but decided that as soon as they could they would go there.

As soon as Claudia arrived back from the hospital, Nina went to the main railway station to see if there were any trains going south, and if she could get passes for them all. The station was packed with people who had the same idea, all wanting to go further west, or south into the countryside, or into the Ruhr area to where the French were bound to head. Suddenly their traditional enemy looked distinctly favourable.

For three days Nina repeatedly queued at the station, constantly interrupted by air-raid warnings, returning home after a few hours when she felt she could no longer leave Claudia alone with the children. On the fourth day, while she again waited, she joined in the idle chatter of the people in front and behind her without enthusiasm, but sometimes there was vital information to be learned from such conversations. All the time she was worrying about Claudia. There was still the fear of the visit from the Gestapo. Anyone might still give them away.

"I was here yesterday," the woman in front of her was saying, "by the time I got anywhere near the front, there was an air raid and we had to leave. If there's one today, I'm staying put!"

"It's the same for me. I've been here every day for three days. This time I've come prepared to stay all night if I have to," the woman behind her said.

Nina's head turned backwards and forwards as she half followed the inconsequential gossip, and agreed or disagreed, whichever seemed more suitable.

She was deep in thought, trying to work out where they were going, how they would ever find her relatives, how she was going to get them all to Sweden eventually, when, unnoticed at first, a gloved hand took hold of hers, a female hand, tentative and a little limp. Nina slowly became aware of the foreign presence and turned as if in a dream.

The woman's face was questioning, as if unsure that Nina was really the person she was seeking. For a moment she peered straight at Nina's eyes, then her own roved over Nina's face and clothes, as though double-checking that this was still the Nina she remembered. The clothes were shabby and she was wearing a woollen scarf instead of her usual fashionable hat, but the face was Nina's. The probing eyes filled with tears of elation, and she struggled to speak, but so great was her joy that no words would come. Her two hands clasped Nina's, now with warmth and certainty, and relief.

Nina turned towards the pale, thin face, which scrutinized her and returned her steady gaze. The cold wind had frozen new lines into the forehead. It was sunken under the cheekbones where the wind had brought a rush of blood to the surface. Her skin gave an erroneous sense of good health; in the same way the purple tinge of heart trouble gives a false idea of ruddy health. It was unmistakably Anna.

Still clasping their hands in silent embrace, Anna gently pulled Nina aside from the queue and silently the two sisters embraced each other fully, tears of gladness falling down both their cheeks. For Nina it meant she would see Dieter and her family again soon.

They were brought back to earth by someone in the queue asking if she should save her place. Nina turned and smiled gratefully at the person with whom she had passed pleasantries for over two hours.

"No! But thank you," she responded warmly, "my sister and I have too much to catch up on. We haven't seen each other since we were in East Prussia, you see."

They went directly, through the rubble of the war torn streets, to Anna's flat - a temporary one allocated to her when she first arrived. On the way each filled in some of the missing details, and Anna was overjoyed that she had remembered where Nina and Claudia were going.

She, like Nina and hundreds of others, had gone each day, patiently queueing for hours for the precious tickets to the southwest. Their walk home was punctuated with pauses, when Nina learned with the greatest happiness imaginable that Dieter was safe and well, and Klaus, too. For her part, Anna kept back the news, which she knew would bring great sorrow and anguish to both her sisters and instead explained that two of her children had been hurt, but were now out of hospital and would be able to travel.

"So, Nina," Anna entreated as they approached her flat, "we must not split up again. Wherever we go, let it be together."

"That's going to be difficult, Anna. You have six children with you and we have another four that we've brought from Königsberg!" Even now Nina did not explain that they were Jewish. Not that she doubted her sister's charity any longer, but she felt the fewer who knew, the better. "I've tried to keep them all together, but we ... we lost some of them on the way. They all call me Mummy by the way, and Claudia is Aunty Claudia! It's better for them to go on calling us that." She did not explain why and Anna did not ask; she had by now learned to be cautious and not to ask unnecessary questions.

Anna opened the door of her flat and five faces were at once fearful and then relieved when they saw who it was. Helga, with her arm in a sling, was sitting on a sofa next to Kurt who had his legs lying flat along the cushions. The brother and sister had been close before, but their accident in the horse and carriage had drawn them even nearer to each other and neither wanted to be parted from the other. It was as though those two nights under the snow had welded them together as one, like Siamese twins: protecting and needing each other. Kurt was miles away, staring at a little silver bell he was holding, ringing it every now and then.

Ullrich, Klaus and Dieter were playing on the floor with a dice they had found and Peter was asleep where Anna had left him on an armchair.

Nina involuntarily let out a cry as she saw Dieter, looking just as she had left him, healthy and happy, apparently untouched by any of the events he had been through. Whereas she saw the fear on the others' faces relax as they recognised Anna, on Dieter's face she saw no sign of fear, nor any of recognition.

"Dieter!" she cried and in an instant of hearing her voice, Dieter was in her arms.

"Mummy! Where were you? We waited so long... you didn't come.

Then we had to go." Nina hugged him so hard he could no longer speak. Over his shoulder she saw Klaus look down at the floor and knew he was wishing she had been Claudia.

"Wait a moment, Dieter, you can tell me everything soon!" She smiled happily at her son, ruffling his hair and hugging him again.

"Klaus," she called to the unhappy boy. "I have a lovely surprise for you, too!"

The huge smile on her face revealed the answer to the quick-witted little boy before her words were out. "Is my Mummy here, too?"

"Yes! She's at my flat, it isn't far from here. You can come back with me. Oh! Anna! I wish they could all come here. You have three large rooms! We only have two poky little ones, which we share with an old friend, and we all sleep on the floor together. Do you think... can you spare us some room here?"

"Yes! Yes!" the children all cried out. "Let's have Aunty Nina and Aunty Claudia here, too. Can we? Please?"

"Anna? Is it possible?"

Anna agreed. They had been apart so long and so unnecessarily she thought. Nina hugged her sister impulsively. After the children and Nina had all asked their questions and the children had got used to her presence, she took Anna aside quietly.

"Anna, I have to tell you a couple of things and there are questions, which I haven't dared to ask you yet," she looked searchingly into her sister's face.

Anna knew there was only one question, Nina wanted answered and she sadly described in general details what had happened on their ill fated journey to the docks.

"Were they buried properly?" Nina asked after a long pause, during which her tears flowed quietly. She did not want to upset the children any further. She had half expected this news since they were not with Anna, and she had not mentioned them. The manner of their deaths was an unhappy one even though it had been mercifully quick, but it distressed

343

her deeply that she had left them so quickly with no proper goodbye. It was as if she had abandoned them to their fate.

"No! I don't know," Anna admitted heavily, revealing that this was a task she had been unable to perform and which had weighed heavily on her heart. "We were taken away so quickly, the children were in great pain, and the Russians might have come back at any moment," she tried to justify both to Nina and to her own conscience her neglect of this important act. "There was no time to make sure."

"God knows their hearts, but just as soon as we can we must find a priest and have it done properly."

As Nina spoke, the memory of Thomas came back to her, 'After the war is over,' he had said jokingly, 'we'll both come back and fight a duel over you!' And she choked on the memory, trying not to cry again. She had lost them both, Thomas imprisoned somewhere, probably already dead. And Erik, where was he now? Dead in the ruins of Warsaw? Or a prisoner of the Russians? Would he be able to persuade them that he was Swedish? He looked so German - tall, blond and handsome. She could not stop the tears. "I'm sorry... I seem to do nothing but cry all the time now."

"We all have a lot to cry about," Anna put her arm around her sister to console her. "And it helps to get it out of your system. God knows I've cried enough; I don't think I have any more tears to shed."

"I'll go soon and bring the others round here," Nina wiped her tears away. "Then whatever happens, we all sink or swim together! We'll have a proper party when we get back! Oh!"

She stopped as she remembered what she had not told Anna, and she took her arm again and quietly whispered, "I must tell you something about the children. They are..." she still hesitated, but it was unfair not to tell Anna who could still be shot for looking after them. "they're Jewish."

Anna looked at her distantly, remembering Nina's hasty flight in search of Claudia, then gave a big sigh. "So that was it! We wondered why you had to rush off to Königsberg at such a dangerous moment." She held Nina's arm gently. "Bring them anyway. I know I wasn't the easiest person

344

to talk to about such things, but you understood about Peter; I'm wiser now than I was then. And I have a lot to make up for."

"And Claudia," Nina's voice faltered. "Anna, I think she's almost lost her mind!" Nina wept quietly, unable this time to stop. "She's seen things … and I think her mind is unhinged. I'll take Klaus with me if you think that's all right, and God willing, the sight of his happy little face will bring her round."

Claudia stared at the little boy standing in front of her. Dieter had been coached by his mother to smile and say nothing. Nina, careful of her sister's health, had decided to let her see Dieter first before she saw Klaus; it might have been too much for her all at once. Claudia looked at him for a long time before she raised one arm, and reached out to him. Then she rested it back on its elbow and let her head drop sideways on to its fingers. The puzzled frown on her forehead showed frustration at her inability to remember people easily.

Dieter gave up the effort to remain silent and yelling in his quiet voice, "Aunty Claudia," he impetuously threw his arms around his beloved aunt.

Claudia's eyes filled with tears as she shared her sister's happiness. There was joy mixed with such sadness in her expression that Nina felt the pain her sister was suffering and knew the cause of it. She moved from the doorway to allow her nephew to come out from behind her.

As Klaus came into her view, Claudia let out a moan of such ineffable emotion Klaus was taken aback and would have hidden behind Nina if she had not propelled him gently towards his mother. He had not been sure who this gaunt white-faced lady really was until Nina reassured him. When Claudia's arms reached out towards him and she called his name, he knew that it was she, and he entwined his arms around her neck. Clambering onto her lap he hugged her and gave a swift kiss on her white cheek. Klaus's name was the first word Claudia had spoken for some days and Nina was thrilled that he had produced such a powerful effect on her.

"Mummy? We've been with Aunty Anna on a great big liner!" He did not notice her face muscles twitch in anguish and her eyes withdraw inwards from his face. "Then we had a train journey and we had to get out of the train, because there were bombs. But we were all right," his excited voice retailed their whole journey from the time that they had boarded the liner to their eventual arrival in Hamburg. But he, like most of the others, did not talk about what had happened to them before that time. It was too painful to remember the death of his grandparents and Nanny.

"Anna? Is Anna here, too? Oh, that's wonderful! Wonderful!" At last there was something to be happy about. She had spent so many long miserable hours dwelling on Johannes and Klaus, and on her own deficiencies as a wife and a mother, something she would never have allowed herself to do before. But the journey had taken its toll on her body and weakened her mind. There had been nothing to keep her going except for Nina's indomitable spirit.

"Nina," Claudia's eyes appealed eloquently to her sister, "We owe you so much. I don't know how we are ever going to be able to thank you."

Nina took her hands. "You can get better in double quick time! We have to leave Hamburg as soon as possible. It's very dangerous here. We must get even further west. The Russians are still closing in and there's dysentery. In our weak condition we could catch something nasty."

Hamburg was overcrowded, bombed to destruction in some areas, with streets full of debris and people living in their cellars. In other places, some of the best hotels survived relatively unscathed and were doing wonderful business. There was fear of epidemics from the enormous numbers of rotting corpses underneath the rubble, ready to infect what remained of the water supply. Trains ran regularly to cities in the south and even in the west. Only a direct hit on the lines or the need for extra troop trains to the western front interrupted the service.

One day, Nina came back from another long wait at the station, this time triumphant. "I've got them! Twelve tickets! I don't know how far we can get, but we can at least get to Bremen. But we must go immediately.

The next train is leaving in just under four hours." To her sisters she said quietly. "Don't forget, the children are all ours, they must call us Mother or Aunty, or keep quiet!"

The chaos in the centre of town had upset the normal routine at the station and trains seemed easier to get aboard. Nina wondered if the Hamburg natives, who had seemed to the sisters in the past to look down on anyone from anywhere else, were only too glad to rid themselves of hundreds of thousands of unwanted guests, and rules were beginning to be broken. This was not Nazi-torn Danzig; this was sophisticated Hamburg. No one asked to see their papers.

The station was packed from end to end, with people wandering everywhere in search of the right train. They stood on the edge of their platform so when the train arrived they could pass the small children and what little luggage they possessed through the windows.

Heide, Kurt and Helga slipped under and through the throng and held them off long enough for Nina and Claudia to pass the smaller children through the glassless windows. Meanwhile, Anna, using her firmest, old-fashioned imperious tone, kept others out of their carriage until they were all inside and had obtained proper seats. The windows had long since been blown out and it was freezing on the side facing the engine, where the wind blew fiercely in their faces. Anna organised a rota: everyone moved round one seat every fifteen minutes, "So no-one freezes for long!" It kept the children amused and occupied, and helped the adults to ignore the ever present fear of inspection. Luckily, the SS were more concerned with searching for deserters and gave their carriage, filled with women and small children, no more than a perfunctory look, closing the door quickly - much to everyone's relief.

They were out of Hamburg and half way to Bremen before the train stopped and everyone was ordered out. They heard the drone of heavy planes on their way to the town they had just left and kept their heads down in the ditch at the side of the track, praying that the planes were not targeting railways between towns that night.

It was pitch dark as the train passed through the suburbs of Bremen and headed southwest. Klaus and Dieter were lying in the luggage rack above Anna's head and the other children had all fallen asleep, Heide sitting up, had fallen against Nina, while Regina was asleep in Nina's arms. Joe and Elsa were lying against Claudia who had an arm around each one.

Clouds had covered the moon and it was inky black, not a hand could be seen in front of their faces. The train crawled southwards through the night, stopping at invisible stations. Only the name called out informed those awake of where they were.

Their meagre ration of sandwiches ran out and just as their close proximity to each other began to get on each other's nerves, and had ceased being another adventure, the train pulled into yet another invisible station. "Dulmen!" sang out the porter's voice as he walked the length of the train.

"Are we anywhere near to Bocholt?" Anna asked him as he went by. "No, you're not, but on the other hand, if you stay on the train, you'll be even further away. Get off here, Miss and I'll show you which way to go." He was a friendly, unhurried, country porter, unconcerned by the immediacy of war; that was a town problem, not for him to worry about. The war would find him in good time, he felt no point in going looking for it.

"Could you please help... there's rather a lot of us," Anna asked and they bundled the children out to him through the empty window frame one by one.

"Good Lord!" he exclaimed, good-naturedly. "Have you brought the whole choir with you?"

How lovely, each of the sisters thought, to have someone who still had a sense of humour and who had an interest in things other than hiding or simply existing. He had a culture that had existed in the past and was even now intact, whereas they had lost theirs long ago.

After the train pulled away and disappeared into the darkness, they stood on the empty platform listening to the silence.

"You want to go over there," the porter pointed into the blackness where he knew a road soon became a cart track, but it was totally invisible to them. "That'll take you to Merfeld. You want to call in at the village inn. That's my sister's place," he explained proudly. "Frau Wessel. She'll take you in. If she can't put you all up for the night there'll be a barn where you can all sleep. It's dark, but just follow the cart track and you'll be there in about an hour."

They followed the friendly porter's instructions, twisting their ankles in the rutted tracks, arriving in a little under three hours at the tiny village. It was almost ten o'clock at night. They found Frau Wessel where her brother had said she would be, waiting up for them with hot drinks.

"My brother managed to telephone me and I had to see what you all looked like!" She babbled on like a brook that would never dry up. "He said a choir was coming through! We don't see many of those these days, do we? Is that what you do? What kinds of songs do you sing? Do the little ones sing? Well, of course they do or you wouldn't be a choir."

The sisters looked at each other and smiled wanly. "We're not a choir," Nina interrupted Frau Wessel in full flow. "I think your brother was making a joke. We're just a family. We're all sisters and these are our children."

"Bless you all! You could start up a choir with all of these couldn't you... if you wanted to, that is?"

The three sisters were anxious not to be too friendly, they had no wish for an over questioning person to start finding out about the children. They were still in Hitler's Reich and the increasingly fanatical SS were still in charge of it.

"Frau Wessel, it was very kind of you to wait up for us and to give us hot drinks. They've warmed us all up. Do you have anywhere we could all sleep tonight? We're trying to reach our family at Bocholt."

"Bless you, yes. I've one really big room left. It has a big double bed and a single, and a settee and an armchair. I can give you some extra blankets, too. We're full up most of the time now with refugees, moving north, or south, or west. No one wants to go east, except the army, and as far as I'm concerned they can go as far east as they like. I wish they would, go and stop the Russians, I mean! Then we can get it all over and done with this side. We're all fed up with the constant bombing raids, not that we've had any bombing here, but the planes go over all the time. Every night it seems they're going somewhere..."

Frau Wessel seemed unconcerned that her words would have caused her instant death in Danzig. It occurred to the still vigilant Nina that she might be deliberately saying things to provoke a response from them and she trod on Anna's foot to stop her from innocently responding.

In the morning, they had a breakfast that included, magically, three eggs, which they cut up between the children. Regina had never tasted eggs before and quickly passed hers to Heide, with a look of disgust, "Can't I have real egg?" She wanted the powder that the nuns had scrambled into something approaching an egg mix.

After breakfast Frau Wessel pointed them in the right direction for Bocholt. "Keep the sun on your left till after midday, then it'll swing round till it's in your face. Where it sets, that's where Bocholt is. Don't go on the main roads, well, we don't have any around here, but even the track you came down is a main road as far as the troops go. They'll push you off it as soon as look at you, they force anything that moves that isn't a tank out of their way. Watch out for them! They'll be coming through Bocholt, and Borken and Wesel and they'll not care about you!"

"Why not?" Kurt asked before anyone could stop him.

"They're being pushed back by the other side, that's why not! They'll need a clear route. So you watch out for them, dearie. Didn't you hear the noises in the night?" They all shook their heads. Blessed sleep had intervened for all of them. The exercise late at night, the warm drinks, and the sense of tranquillity had made them all drop their guard. They had thought they were almost home and they slept well for the first time in weeks.

"That was the fighting near the Rhine. It's been going on for weeks now. Sooner or later they'll come across, then we'll be in for it."

"What will we be in for?" Kurt asked.

"We'll be in for trouble, that's what! So just you listen to your mothers, and do as you're told. Mind you," she added, "I wouldn't live over in the east whatever you paid me, they'll really be for it over there."

All the sisters still had someone over in the east to worry about, to mourn, someone they hoped had come through as they had done, and each one was now reminded of that part of their memories, a part each one of them would rather have kept buried. They were silent as they started on their last long walk.

They kept the sun on their left and walked across the hills and through the woods. They ate Frau Wessel's sandwiches and began to look for shelter early. It was clear that they could only go at a snail's pace; they had reckoned without Kurt's injured leg. He could only walk slowly, dragging it behind him. He made no complaint, but they could all see the pain he was suffering at each step. When they stopped in the wood, Joe came running through the trees brandishing a long branch with a 'Y' shaped end and after pulling off all the small growths and smoothing it down, Kurt was able to use it as a crutch. The others soon scoured the woods and found another. Nina and Anna each took off one of their two jumpers and wound them around the tops of the two supports to make it softer for Kurt to lean on.

It was half way through the third day, they had been running through a well-trodden footpath in the woods when they came out into the fields and sunshine. The ever-observant Joe stopped short and held up his arm to prevent those behind him from running out into the open. "Look!" He whispered dramatically, pointing along the hedge, where they could see tanks draped with camouflage, their guns pointing south-westwards, the same direction they were travelling. Several soldiers were relaxing, smoking, and talking amongst themselves, but the family remained unseen and crept back along the path, their mirth and happiness curtailed.

"What now?" asked Anna.

"I suppose we must go back and round, and cross the open fields further to the south," Nina suggested, "otherwise, if they see us, goodness knows what they'll do. If they know we've seen them they may stop us going further. So, what do we do, keep quiet and move further south?"

It took them almost five days to travel the few miles to their new home, avoiding their own soldiers and towns. All the way the sisters did not know if there would be a house for them when they arrived. Would the British and Americans have already gone through and flattened it, or had it been burnt or bombed? Would Johannes's parents be there? There was no solidity, no safety left to life any more, everyone had to live a day-to-day existence. They began to envy the Frau Wessels of the world; how simple and uncomplicated their lives seemed.

Claudia had only been to Bocholt a few times, soon after she was married. "I remember the house is only three miles from the Dutch border and it's up on a ridge overlooking the river."

Anna and Nina had the same thought: if it were in such a strategic position, would it have been commandeered? As they trudged nearer the town, through small, unsigned villages in the nearby hills, there was a noticeable increase in troops either stationed out of sight, or on the move along the narrow tracks. And always during the day the noise of battle increased. Sometimes it seemed sporadic, in one direction only and over quickly, at others it seemed to come from all directions in their path. But all the time it grew louder and louder as they approached Bocholt. How different from Hamburg where the closing in of darkness had been a signal for the bombers to begin their raids, and they had spent their nights in the cellar expecting each morning to reveal the blackened remains of their temporary home. But here no bombing raids had disturbed their sleep, only increasing fears of a sudden advance by the enemy, a push through the quiet Dutch countryside, across the Rhine, and into the low rolling hills and valleys north of the Ruhr.

From East Prussia it had taken them over six weeks, and when they finally arrived at their destination they had reached the limit of their endurance.

Thirty Five

Bocholt seemed quiet, there were few people around. Someone confirmed that if they continued through the main street they would reach the house on Aalten Strasse. "Take care, there are many soldiers up that way. If you take my advice, you'll make a noise, that way they won't think you're the enemy. They're trigger-happy up there!"

The woman who spoke suddenly realized what she had said, and tucked her head down in her scarf and hurried away, just in case they were informers.

The sisters looked at each other and their shoulders sagged. "And we thought it was nearly all over!" Nina spoke their thoughts.

It was still daylight when they saw the house in the distance. The sidewall, caught by the rays of the falling sun, looked red, though it was made of grey stone. And from the top window a rifle, lying on the windowsill pointing towards the west, glinted in the last rays.

"All right, children. This time, I want you to make a noise when I tell you," Nina said.

"I'm tired," Elsa complained. "Can't we just go inside?"

The other children agreed, no longer having the energy for shouting. Nina looked despairingly at them, then up at the sinister, quiet rifle pointing outwards menacingly, towards the enemy. How quickly could it be turned on her?

She made them all wait by the wall behind which they could take refuge if necessary, then gingerly, with great trepidation she approached the house, calling out as she did so to attract attention. She hoped that there would be no danger to her if the sniper were not alarmed. He had heard her coming and moved the rifle slightly, waving her up the eight steps to the front door. She was met in the hallway by more soldiers.

"Where are the owners?" she enquired politely, somewhat peaked to find that after all their suffering they were not to have the comfort they had so looked forward to.

"They're out the back," the answer came tersely. Under normal circumstances Nina would have commanded whistles and admiring looks from the soldiers, but now she was thin, lined and ill and her thick winter clothes looked out of place in the spring-like warmth of the west.

"May I see them? I'm a relative," she turned and waved her arm in the general direction of the road. "We're all relatives from East Prussia. We hoped they might be able to put us up."

"You're not all going to fit into the cellars, that's for sure!" The sergeant waved her through to the back of the house. "Frau Doctor Rott is in the kitchen."

Nina made her way through to the back, knocking gingerly on the door before opening it. She was pleasantly surprised at the cleanliness everywhere, there was little to show here that the house was occupied.

Wilhelmina had her back to the door, and half-turned, expecting one of the soldiers. The knife she was using to cut precious potatoes into quarters, clattered into the sink and her wet hands flew to her face.

"Nina! Nina! How magnificent! You've made it! Oh, wait till Max sees you! This is wonderful!" She hurriedly dried her hands on her still pristine apron and clasped Nina to her. Then she quickly held up a metal saucepan and banged on it with a heavy spoon, directing the sound outwards to the garden where Max was digging.

"That's our signal," she explained. "There isn't any glass left to tap on!" Max lifted his face and seeing Nina's head framed in the window dropped his spade, tore off his special gardening gloves and limped in as fast as he could.

Max was sixty-five and had been wounded in the last war when he had volunteered for active service. He had been a barrister, but had retired during the midyears of Hitler's reign, refusing to remain in practice under Hitler's orders, unable to say what he believed he ought to in defence of his clients. As a barrister, he had commanded a large salary and was now living off his savings.

When the hugs and tears were over, Wilhelmina asked cautiously "Are you alone? Who's with you, Nina?"

Nina smiled joyously, "Claudia!"

Wilhelmina took Max's hand and looked into his face, tears springing readily again to her eyes. "Oh, Max! What a day this is!"

"And Anna, too, Mina! And all the children! And a few more besides our own." While Wilhelmina wiped her eyes, Nina added, "We didn't know if you'd be here or if the house had been... well, you know." She did not mention Claudia's illness. "Is the barn intact? Will we be allowed to live in it?"

"The barn's still there, but the livestock's all gone. We've hidden some of the last chickens down in the cellar and we have to sneak them out to the barn each day so the soldiers don't take them, and Max sometimes manages to catch a wild rabbit. But even those have gone to ground or been hunted to extinction! But we're surviving!"

Max had been biting his lip and looking at Wilhelmina and then at Nina pointedly.

"I think Max wants to tell you something, Nina," Wilhelmina said and nodded to Max to show her agreement. He led her through a door from the kitchen, which led down to the cellar to show her where they lived, while Wilhelmina went out to explain to the soldiers who they were, and to ask permission for them to use the barn.

"So this is where we live now," Max showed Nina the big underground room and some of the smaller rooms and cubbyholes in the basement, more like cupboards than rooms. There was some light in the big room coming from the two little casement windows, uncluttered now. It was very cold. "We have a small oil stove, but no oil left, and we have to conserve the firewood for the evening."

"Will we all be able to stay? There are rather a lot of us ..." she involuntarily checked over her shoulder, then whispered, "Four of the children with us are Jewish." It never once occurred to Nina that Max or

Wilhelmina would have any objections to that.

"Oh, Lord!" Max took Nina's shoulders with his hands and gazed at her in admiration. "Still the same Nina, still helping others less fortunate, even when your own circumstances are dire! We have countless little cubby holes down here, and an unexpected escape route, too."

He pulled open the wooden side of what looked like an enormous, if ordinary, hoop barrel, and dimly she could see steps going down. "The steps go down to a warren of passages. You'll have no trouble squeezing yourself through there, you've got so thin, Nina! One passage goes to the barn; we've checked that one. One is supposed to go to Holland, but I've never explored that far! I don't really believe that, but one day we may be forced to find out!" He closed the barrel up carefully, putting the chequered kitchen tablecloth back over the top and placing a cup on it. "There! That looks casual enough, doesn't it? One good thing's come from the war... I've lost weight, too! There was a time when I couldn't get down there. I think we can get you all down here; it will certainly warm it up a bit to have so many bodies all together. But the children must not know of this," he patted the barrel, "not yet."

"Of course... you can't risk them giving it away."

Max showed Nina yet another small room, where the children could sleep and play, pausing yet again to look searchingly at her. "Nina, you and Claudia I know very well, very well. Claudia has stayed with us and she knows the house's secrets. But Anna? Can I trust her, Nina? I'm sorry to ask you. I don't mean any offence, you know that, but she had many Nazi friends."

"You can trust her absolutely, Max. She's looked after the children for some time now as if they were her own, taking the same risks we took. She's quite safe."

"All right then. What I'm now going to show you I leave you to decide who will know, but I think the children, except for Klaus, should not be told about it." He went quietly to one of the small rooms furthest away from the windows where in the lee of the stone chimneystack was another door, unnoticeable in the dark. He tapped on the door - three times, twice, then once, and then opened it slowly.

In the darkness Nina could see nothing, at first. There were no windows to lighten any corner of this little cupboard. She could smell the smoke rising from a recently extinguished candle. Then, as her eyes adjusted to the light, she discerned a figure slowly emerging: a thin masculine shape painfully pulling itself upright. The person hobbled towards her and into the pale light, arms outstretched, wordless. The hands were heavily bandaged and as he came out into the light Nina recoiled at the face: bruised, black and red, and twisted out of all recognition.

She looked at Max, her eyes appealing for understanding.

"He hoped you might have been Claudia," Max said gently and Nina gasped. She could have bitten her tongue rather than let out that gasp, it told them both so graphically that she had not until then realised whom the figure was.

"Be careful, Nina! He's in constant pain. Don't hold him too tightly."

Nina broke down and wept, and Johannes put his bandaged hand onto her head and stroked her hair gently until she regained some control. She took the hand and pressed it to her cheek. "What have they done to you?" she wailed, lamely. In the darkness of the little room she whispered, head down, "I want to say something to you both, but I don't know how to say it without hurting you..."

"Just tell us straight out, Nina, we've all had many pains to endure. One more won't break us," Max said for both of them.

She gently took hold of Johannes's arms and looked him in the face so that even through his half-closed lids he could see her eyes, reflecting the only light in the room. "Upstairs Johannes... upstairs there is someone... " She felt the arms stiffen in sudden tension. "Someone you want to see very much."

Johannes tried to speak, but no words came out, only strained grunts. Tears sprang to his eyes, which fixed themselves firmly on the staircase.

"But, you must hear the rest first, before I bring her down. Claudia has gone through so much she could not take any more," she tried to choose words which would hurt the least. "She hasn't spoken to us properly for over six weeks. The only time she did speak was when we met up again with Anna and the children... and Klaus."

Johannes stiffened again and pulled at her arms, trying to tell her to bring them down to him, now.

"We don't know what happened to her, she won't talk about it."

Nina abandoned the rest of her speech. Perhaps it was just as well to bring Claudia and Klaus down to see him, and as she climbed back up the cellar stairs, she reflected that it might even be a good thing for Claudia; she was a nurse after all.

Max stayed with Johannes in the main cellar while Nina tried to prepare Claudia and Klaus. She had not got the heart to stop Johannes from seeing Klaus. They would have to take their chances and hope that he did not reveal Johannes to the others, not even to Dieter. She would have to swear him to secrecy.

Everyone was crowded into the kitchen, waiting to see if they would be allowed to live either in the cellar or in the barn. The children were slumped on the floor, too exhausted to be polite or noisy, and Wilhelmina and Anna were trying to divide the small amount of food in the kitchen between everyone.

Nina took Claudia and Klaus outside, "Klaus, you know that Daddy was taken by the Nazis, the bad police, don't you? You know they torture people, and that means that they hurt them. You have to be very, very gentle with Daddy. Don't rush at him and jump on his back like you used to, or even hug him, because he hurts all over. You'll see his face and you won't be able to see who it is. They hit his face you see, and his hands are painful, don't grab them. Promise me, Klaus?"

Nina had spoken to the child, but hoped to appeal to the mother. She continually watched Claudia's face all the time, looking for signs of real understanding. Claudia had listened and understood, but she was like a machine that was plugged in, yet switched off; she had remained disconnected. It was not until Nina led them both down to the cellar and she saw Johannes for the first time in many months that she began to function normally again.

"And Klaus, you must not say anything to anyone – especially the other children – about seeing Daddy. Do you understand? Not even to Dieter!" Klaus said nothing. He just nodded in affirmation.

Nina had been right, the appeal to the nurse in Claudia stirred her as nothing else. As she held his hands and looked at the tearstained face she saw not the present so much as the past; she saw the Johannes who had loved her when she had been unlovable, with scant regard to his wishes. She saw the Johannes who had adored and played with baby Klaus and started him on the road to becoming the staunch, loyal and likeable young boy who stood before him; a miniature image of his father, having to become a man so early in life.

She had her family back again, and the chance to redeem herself.

Thirty Six

The family quietly took possession of the cellar and the barn even though they had not received official permission. The children had become so used to being quiet and obedient they were no problem, and the soldiers were virtually unaware of their presence. The children no longer played, they had all but forgotten how. The minds of the adults were on the west from where they knew that any moment the big push would come. The family slept in the cellar at night. During the day they would leave quietly through the kitchen and go out to the barn to get some fresh air. They brought in some wisps of hay still lying in the barn, to make warmer beds for everyone. They tried to catch rabbits and the hens would lay one or two eggs now and then, which were given to the children.

For three days they hardly saw Claudia. She took over as Johan's nurse, tearing up dress material for makeshift bandages. To help his fingers mend straighter and reduce the pain she bound them to pieces of wood. Silently she spoon-fed, cleaned and clothed him, grateful for the skills she had acquired. Her eyes expressed her hidden emotions. There was no need for words.

Klaus had not recognised his father and only went to him when requested to help Claudia. He felt a sense of duty towards his parents, but none of the old feelings of affection. All the children's emotions were dulled from over use. Too much had happened in too short a time, and Klaus, like the rest, was unable to cope with it all. But Claudia had learned patience; she knew that given time love would return.

During those last few days of the war, life was curiously normal, despite the soldiers in the house. Secrets were easy to keep even with so many children; they had become used to being quiet and wary of adults, and keeping their own confidences.

One morning, less than a week since they had arrived, Max crept up from the cellar to ask permission for the family to come out. It was quiet; there was no-one in the house. The sound of battle outside had intensified especially in the direction of Wesel. He checked everywhere noisily. Finally in the top room, he found one soldier crouching behind the window as usual, his rifle steadily aimed westwards. His head was half turned towards Max and half looking out the window: a sniper left to hold up the enemy, to give the others time to escape.

So the British and the Americans were on their way at last! For Max and Claudia, they could not come soon enough. Johannes could be taken to hospital.

Despite the fact that they had come so far to be caught by British or American troops rather than by the Russians, the rest of the family were more fearful than ever. If a sniper was operating from their home they could expect no mercy, whoever their enemy. They had to persuade him to surrender.

"Look, son," Max began in a fatherly voice. "You've lived in my home for weeks now. Do you really want to see it, and us, blown to pieces, right at the end of the war?"

That was a mistake. Herman looked at him briefly, and set his eyes back on the small road stretching away towards Isselburg. From the top of their house they could see as far as the Rhine; it was a perfect lookout. He could see movement this side of the river and knew, as did his fellow soldiers, that either the British or the Americans would be there within two hours. "It's my job," he scowled. "Otherwise I've wasted four years of my life. Besides, how do you know it's the end? The Führer will unleash his wonder weapon and then we'll win. Wait and see."

"Yes, the rockets have knocked London for six, killed thousands of the enemy," Max reasoned, "but their soldiers are still just over the Rhine. It hasn't stopped them yet."

"I meant his new wonder weapon, the big gun they've got now. It can knock out London and their big cities in the middle of the country and all those factories making weapons. And after that they've got plans for rockets on New York as well."

"But those are for the future, Herman. They're not working yet. Meanwhile we've got their soldiers just down the street."

"I don't care," he snarled menacingly. "My job's to stop this lot. This is just a temporary set back. Wait till the gun gets working, then we'll push them back into the sea. Now, get back down to the cellar."

Unsure if Herman simply wanted to be rid of him, or to preserve his life, Max obeyed. The cellar was the safest place.

Max had forgotten that Herman was a young man, just in his twenties. He was only nine years old when Hitler came to power. All the skill and might of the Nazi propaganda machine had been aimed at him. Herman was a proud and unthinking product of the Hitler Youth; he would never give up.

How could the poor lad be expected to trust anybody but his leader when he had no outside news, no foreign country to which he could compare his own? How could he know any different? He simply accepted everything. He had been programmed to believe.

"It's no good," Max told the others in the cellar, "he won't listen to reason. He thinks this is a temporary set back and Hitler's going to use this new weapon we've heard about. If he'd the least idea of geography he'd know differently. He's just a boy from Berlin. He's never been this far away from his home before, and has no idea how big a country France is."

"That's true," Mina agreed, "the British wouldn't have got this far unless they meant business. They're not going to give up and go back to the Channel. Besides, they have the whole might of America behind them now."

"He might have a point, though. The rockets we're now sending over the Channel make them want to retaliate and hit us hard," Nina said.

"And what about the new weapon? Is it ready to use yet..." Anna was interrupted as a shell screamed overhead and exploded in the field behind the barn.

"Look out!" yelled Max. "We've been targeted! Keep down!"

They waited fearfully, cowering under the thick wooden beams, hoping the heavy stone cellar would survive a direct hit, and fearful that it probably would not. The house shook every few seconds and dust cascaded, choking everyone.

"I think now's the time for you all to discover our secret," he gasped between heavy thuds. He quickly opened up the wine butt to reveal the steps, and said to his wife "Mina, go first and help the children down. Then the rest. As fast as you can, while I get Johan."

"Uncle Johan?" Helga queried excitedly.

"Yes. No time for explanations. Just do as you are told, there's good children." They were quickly helped down into the cold, damp, dark and frightening passage beneath the cellar to wait out the bombardment.

"Where in heaven's name did you get that from?" Anna asked as he lit a candle, impressed by his sagacity.

"We've kept candles and matches, and even tins of food and bottles of water down here for some time now. We half expected we'd have to use it sooner or later." Max's good humour was part of his character, but also partially a show put on for the children. When they had all just settled down, a thud, louder than the rest, made the house rock, and dust was shaken down into their passage.

Even so far beneath the house they could hear the squeaking metal of tanks passing close to the house. The children were shocked into silence. They had expected that all they had suffered in the past few weeks had led them to safety at last. They did not understand the geography of a war on two fronts and their journey between them. They thought their flight had ended the war for them, not begun a second. They shivered in silence for over an hour as the squeals of tanks and the thuds of mortar bombs continued unabated.

The noise grew fainter. They heard rifle fire, and the sound of voices around the house.

"British, I think," Anna suggested.

"Sounded more American to me," Max responded.

"Not French?" whispered Wilhelmina, "They don't like us hereabouts. I hope they're British."

"After five and a half years of war, I doubt if the British like us much either," Max replied cynically. "I'll plump for the Americans. They didn't sound English. The Americans haven't been involved too much, and they've not been attacked at all at home. I think I'd prefer to be captured by them."

"They could be Canadian?" Claudia suggested.

"Oh, Lord! What on earth is that noise?" Wilhelmina gripped Max's hand in the dark as the strange, wailing sound grew louder. It seemed to be coming from above. The children clung to the nearest person in terror.

"Anna! Claudia! Don't you recognise it?" Nina's voice was happy. Unseen by her family, a happy smile of gratitude and delight lit up her face. "It's a bagpipe! We're to be captured by the Scots!"

She scrambled for the steps and gingerly opened the wine butt a crack. Dust fell onto her face and she let go the door, which swung back with a bang. She coughed loudly.

"Now you've done it!" whispered Max.

"Who's there?" came a sharp voice in English. "Come out with your hands up or I fire!"

"Don't shoot!" Nina screamed in his mother tongue and opened the door again, to be roughly and unceremoniously hauled out by two pairs of hands.

"What have we here?" A dirty face leered into hers. "She must be the sniper, eh, George? What do we do with snipers?"

He turned and grinned at his mate in anticipation, still handling her roughly. Nina began to wonder if she had chosen the right enemy to whom to surrender.

Behind her, Claudia had climbed out through the barrel. She had heard Nina's gasp as the soldiers grabbed her. In perfect English and with a voice full of anger she let forth, "Take your hands off her." Like an upper class English woman, she assumed dominance over these lowly privates.

"How dare you treat my sister like that? Where is your commanding officer?" she snapped, with the implied threat to their positions.

"There's no need to take that tone," one of the men began.

"Leave it, Jack," George said quietly. He watched the people continuing to come out of the wine butt and looked uncertain of his position. "Oi, Sarge?" he yelled up the cellar stairs.

Claudia dismissed Jack's comment. "I shall take any tone I want. We have rights under the Geneva Convention and you are exceeding yours!"

"Are you lot English?" Jack asked, perplexed at their command of the language.

"Scottish," Nina offered, hopeful that coming from Scotland would help them, rather than being English.

"Where is your commanding officer?" Claudia persisted, mindful of some advice from Johannes before he had been arrested. 'Always go straight to the top.'

Even as the family all came up out of the passageway, the army was moving on. Satisfied that there were only women and children, one old man and a badly wounded man, they left to continue eastwards. They were bound for Hamburg. Others made for the Elbe, to meet up with the Russian army coming towards them, so no part of Germany would be without foreign troops on its soil, subduing its people, overseeing its future.

The family remained out of sight until the first wave had passed through the town. Before the next detachment came they had time to take stock. They emerged to find rubble and choking dust everywhere. Even those relatively undamaged rooms had lost plaster from the ceilings.

"It isn't so bad," Max announced after going over the whole house. "We've lost part of the roof and two of the top rooms will be wet when it rains, but we've still got two floors and a cellar!" He put his arm around his wife's shoulders. "And some of the furniture can be saved. It just needs cleaning, that's all."

Wilhelmina wiped away a tear. "And what's more, we'll be able to sleep in the beds soon! At least we have a home. These poor souls have lost everything."

"No they haven't, they have a place here for as long as they like." No one voiced the thought that they might never be able to return to Pomerania or East Prussia.

"Including the children?" Johannes articulated the sentence with great difficulty and waved his bandaged arms towards Heide and the others.

"Yes! Of course! All of you!" Wilhelmina hugged each one of the four bewildered orphans. "You stay here if we have to fight all the British army to keep you!"

Anna took Max aside and whispered, "What happened to Herman?"

"He's dead, I'm afraid, Anna, which means I'll need to get him down from there. Have to wrap him in a sheet. Keep the children away, he's not a pretty sight."

"We'll help you later, Max, when the children are outside."

"Two things of importance," he commanded, as if these were his troops. "Firstly, we have to clean up, see if we have water or electricity and so on. Secondly, and much more importantly, we must contact the army doctors as soon as they set up in this area and get Johan seen to properly."

Although groups of soldiers and tanks passed through constantly on their way to join their comrades at the front, for the family the war had passed them by, the fighting was over. The front line had already moved miles further east. Every day it went further away, and with it the danger of any air or mortar attacks. The Allied armies - the Americans, French, Canadians and the Russians - were spearheading straight for Berlin.

They put out their flags as everyone else did, half of a white bed sheet. As Anna was anchoring it over the windowsill so it would not flutter too much in the spring breeze, her eye caught a movement below. Dozens of soldiers on foot, one behind the other, were creeping along the walls each side of the road; they were peering into houses, trying doors, entering when they were open, kicking them in if they were not. One of them looked up and saw her. He raised his rifle and pointed it straight at her. She leapt back from the window, breathing heavily.

"Nina, come here, quickly," she screamed for her sister who was cleaning the room behind her.

"What is it?"

Anna pointed out of the window, half-expecting a rifle shot.

Nina peered out.

"Be careful!"

"It's only the soldiers checking to see if there are any more of our troops here. I'm sure they won't shoot a female."

"They'll shoot first and find out you're a woman too late, Nina," Anna suggested. "Why don't you put out your Swedish flag? They might stop waving their rifles at us if they think we're Swedish. And it might help us get Johan some treatment."

"What a good idea, Anna," Max agreed, lugging a newly cleaned chair into the room. "They must have this house down as a sniper's nest. And Johan needs urgent help."

The soldiers were still passing by when Nina put out the small Swedish flag, which Erik had made her promise to carry everywhere. 'After all Dieter is Swedish and I'm Swedish by marriage,' she thought, justifying her action. As she tied it with two pieces of string to the inside curtains one of the soldiers looked up and saw it flapping over the bed sheet, "Sarge! Come here a minute!"

Anna watched warily as Nina leaned out and yelled down in English, "We're Swedish. Tell your commanding officer."

"Is that the Swedish flag, then?" he called back.

"Yes."

Nina watched the soldier pass the information on, and an officer driving by in a jeep being flagged down by the Sergeant, who engaged him in a long conversation. Their discussion seemed to go on for ever, with much gesticulating at the house.

She couldn't understand why they didn't come in and puzzled for a while. "I know what's wrong," she gasped suddenly as the soldier pointed at the window above her head. She ran as fast as her exhausted legs could take her down the stairs and out of the front door. The sergeant held his rifle at the ready as she raced down the front steps.

"I'm sorry, I didn't mean to startle you, but we need help."

"I gather you're Swedish," the officer stated, warily. He was clearly not prepared to accept what any German woman said, even if she did speak perfect English.

"Yes," Nina answered. "But the others are not..." she was about to explain but the officer cut her off.

"I understand this was the house with the sniper. Is he still inside?" He signalled to the other soldiers to surround the house and began walking towards the steps, with the sergeant accompanying him. Their eyes never left the front of the house, not even to meet Nina's.

"No, he's dead. He was killed when your guns hit the attic. We're all anti-Nazi..."

"Now where have I heard that before," the sergeant began sarcastically.

"You're going to hear it a lot more, Sergeant. Get used to it," the officer said curtly. He knew that most Germans would deny they had ever been supporters of Hitler. But thankfully it was someone else's job to work out who was telling the truth.

"We're mostly women and children or wounded..."

"Wounded soldiers?"

"No! Not soldiers," Nina was frantic that she wasn't explaining herself well enough and they would mark them all down as Nazis. "One old man and one wounded man, tortured by the Nazis, because he was in the plot to kill Hitler," the words came rushing out in a torrent. "He needs hospital care. Please can you arrange it?"

The officer followed her into the house and after seeing the children sitting quietly on the stairs trying to make sense of it all, and Anna standing at the top, with her arm around Heide, he told the sergeant to return to his men.

"Who's in charge here?"

Seeing Max limping along the hall, Nina motioned towards him and said, "Herr von Rott. This is his house."

"Can I help you, sir?" Max began affably. It might pay to be a little subservient.

"I'd like a list of all the people living here, and their nationalities."

Max rattled off the details of the family members and turned to Nina. "You'll have to give him the other children's names, Nina, I can't remember them."

"The other children?"

"Yes, we have four Jewish children we brought out of East Prussia with us. We pretended they were ours." She gave him their names.

"That's all?"

"Yes," Max answered, "there's no-one else."

The officer motioned to the soldiers outside and two came running in.

"Check out the rooms, including the cellar. Should only be women and children, and one wounded man. Bring him to me."

"I'll get him, he's in the kitchen," Max said, looking at Nina as he passed her. Both of them hoped that Johan would be taken to the British field hospital straight away. Max disappeared into the kitchen at the end of the hall.

Nina heard the heavy boots running across upper floors and looked on as the soldiers ran past them and down to the cellar. They returned quickly, just as Max reappeared leading Johannes gently along the corridor, with Claudia on his other arm.

"Women and children only, sir," one of the soldiers reported.

"Thank you, Private." He turned to Johannes, "Your name?"

"His name is Johannes von Rott, he's my son," Max answered for him. "His jaw was broken by the SS when he was tortured. He can't answer for himself, yet."

372

The officer examined Johannes, carefully. "Private?"

"Sir?"

"Take Mr. von Rott to my jeep and wait there for me. Carefully!" He shouted as the soldier grabbed Johan's arm and Claudia made a threatening move towards him.

He turned back to Max and Nina, "You mentioned four Jewish children. We're not equipped to look after them yet. They'll have to stay here until we've set up an orphanage for them."

Max and Nina both checked the children sitting on the stairs and smiled at them. "They can stay here for the rest of their lives as far as I'm concerned," he said, watching Heide's face break into the nearest thing to a smile he'd seen. She of all the children had suffered greatly and he wanted to give her the reassurance she craved. She was safe and had a home with people she liked.

"There will be a standpipe put up soon so you'll have decent water laid on. I shall be reporting this meeting to Major Fraser in intelligence and I think you'll be hearing from him quite soon."

He saluted and left the house.

Nina and Max looked at each other, then both at the same time laughed and Nina flung her arms around him. "Mina! Anna!" Nina shrieked.

The kitchen door flew open and both women strode quickly towards the family grouped in the hall, watching Johannes disappearing in the jeep, unable to turn or wave to them.

Nina ran down to Claudia standing in the middle of the street, with the soldiers still moving past. They looked up at the flag, then at the sisters, curious to know what had been happening.

"He'll be fine now, Claudia," Nina kissed her sister, hugging her ecstatically.

"I know, I know!" Claudia was weeping with happiness. "The soldier said they were taking him to hospital."

"Let's go back in. There's nothing more we can do for now."

The children looked from one adult to another, with grins on their faces, but they had little idea what they were supposed to be happy about.

Anna caught their expressions, "It's going to be all right, children. Johan has been taken to hospital, not to prison. He'll be treated well and be back here before you've time to miss him. You're safe. We're all safe now."

"Yes," Max agreed, standing with his arm around his wife, holding her tenderly, "the war has gone past us."

"And I think they've accepted that we're not Nazis," Nina said.

For a day or so the whole house was euphoric; everyone was smiling and happy and the children began to laugh again. For the first time in years the sound of children playing was heard from the direction of the barn.

Max came down to earth before the rest of the family. One morning Wilhelmina and the sisters were busying themselves washing sheets and clothes in cold water from the new standpipe, and the whole family were working together to clean up the house when Max spoke up "We're not out of the woods yet, but keep it to yourselves. There's no point in worrying the children; they've had enough. I've been thinking, there still might be some retaliation. It doesn't matter to them that we were never Nazis; that we were in the resistance movement. They'll only see us as Germans. The British, under whom we are to live, it seems, will be especially keen to see us kept down. It's the Germans who have caused two world wars, they will say." He was fatalistic about their chances of fair treatment.

"But the British are a decent nation; they'll treat us justly won't they?" Wilhelmina asked, expecting him to know all the answers.

"Just because they're reasonable most of the time doesn't mean they'll always be so. Wars bring out great anger in people," he explained, as he brushed off the armchairs out in the yard.

Wilhelmina reached up to hang out a sheet, trying to remember the last time she had enjoyed the freedom of watching her laundry drying in the fresh air.

"The soldiers who come through here don't represent their legal system." Max persisted, "They've been sent over here, unwillingly conscripted to fight us. Don't think for one moment we're all safe yet!"

The girls listened in dismay.

"Any one of these soldiers could shoot you in cold blood, in hot blood, perhaps in anger, and still get away with it. They've seen their friends blown to pieces in front of their eyes, just the same as our soldiers have." He glanced at Nina and Anna almost apologetically. "Don't you think that would make them hate us, and want to kill us in revenge? Look at it from their point of view."

It was not what they wanted to hear. They carried on with their cleaning in silence, the light-hearted mood of the morning shattered. Wilhelmina and Nina thought Max was just being sensible, but Anna thought he was unnecessarily alarmist. A sense of caution had been brought to their euphoric state. The war was not over yet, and they wanted it to be with all their hearts.

Thirty Seven

When the front line had moved on and was already many miles deeper into Germany, the British Intelligence forces set up their enquiry centres to which each of them would eventually have to give evidence. As the concentration and extermination camps were liberated one by one and the inhumanities of the Nazi regime became public knowledge, the behaviour of the Allied soldiers towards their captives changed. They were spat at, and when the captors were drunk, as they frequently were, they would point their guns and threaten to shoot them just for being German. Rarely did they see a British face, which did not show contempt or hatred.

Johannes had been admitted to a British hospital where he had, with difficulty, been questioned by Major Fraser who was in charge of the special section of intelligence. Their house and its occupants had, therefore, come to his attention early and Nina and the others were 'invited' individually to an interview with the Major at his headquarters.

After their preliminary introductions he asked Nina, "Can you prove that you are Swedish?" She surveyed him as carefully as he had studied her before answering; trying to pick up clues about his attitude towards her; but his face was impassive. She handed him her papers, which she had kept sewn into her lingerie.

"So, you were German, but you married a Swedish man. Name?" His manner was brusque. He saw, stretching out before him, hundreds, perhaps thousands of interviews with all kinds of Germans. He expected most of them would try to excuse their conduct, deny their part in history or pretend that they were someone else. Here already was one woman saying she was Swedish. But here, also, was the proof in his hands. The name was vaguely familiar to him.

"I'm only Swedish by marriage, but my son is Swedish by both blood and birth. It was for his sake that I put the flag outside our house. He must have a chance to get back to his grandmother in Sweden."

"And to whom are you married? What does your husband do?"

"His name is Erik Larsson. He used to work for the Swedish government, but then he became an art dealer in Warsaw." She hesitated for a moment, on the verge of breaking down at the very thought of him. "He was in Warsaw for most of the war. I don't know where he is now," her voice dropped to no more than a whisper and she could barely control her throat muscles. She did not dare dwell on whether he was alive or not. That part of her life all seemed so far away. She could barely believe that she had once had a life with him, an ordinary life where no one had been frightened to say what he or she thought, where lights were left on without the curtain needing to be drawn or blackout put up at the windows. A life where you could buy almost anything you needed or wanted in the local shops, where everyone said hello and chatted openly to you without weighing you up to see if you were safe or a government spy. How far away all that was now.

"Did your husband once work in London?" the Major enquired, a thoughtful look crossing his face.

"Yes, when he had just begun his career. That was where I met him." She relived again that moment when she had slumped inelegantly against his door, and saw again the tall, handsome figure and gazed again into his green eyes. She forced back the tears that were pricking her eyes, trying to swim down her cheeks.

"I believe I met him once... some debutante's ball or other, probably. Describe him to me."

To Nina it seemed an odd request, but she complied unwillingly. To picture him was to remember him, and she did not want to focus on those memories, they were too personal and too painful. She briefly described his appearance, his work and some of his friends, including Thomas.

"Ah! That was where I met him then, at the good pastor's house. So you know Thomas Dietermann?"

"I knew him, yes. We knew him very well." She looked up, startled.

"Did you know him?"

"Knew? Is he dead?"

Nina winced at his tactlessness. "He was taken by the Gestapo and we were unable to find him. We don't know where he was taken, to which prison, or what happened to him. Johan, my sister's husband, was taken, too... around the same time, and he's still in a terrible state after they tortured him."

The Major had already seen Johannes and the extent of his injuries. "Why were they tortured?"

"Thomas was thought to be involved in the plots to kill Hitler. Johan was in the Abwehr, and he gave us vital information to help our escape line. The Abwehr was eventually disbanded by the Gestapo and most of the members were imprisoned. That's when he was taken and put in a concentration camp, but he escaped."

"Escaped? I thought no one escaped from those places."

"He was being transferred from a camp in the north to one near Frankfurt on the Main, and he was temporarily in an ordinary prison overnight, waiting for transport to the new camp. Your planes came over and bombed part of the prison and he escaped through the hole in the wall." She smiled ruefully at part of his story. "He was going to send a telegram to Field Marshal... Tedder? - is it? - in London, to thank him for bombing Germany! When you see him you'll know why he didn't."

The Major busied himself looking through his notes, comparing their stories. "Tell me why he didn't."

"He can't write. They tore out his fingernails and stubbed out their lighted cigarettes... " She couldn't bear to even think of what they had done to Johan, what might have happened to Thomas, and what even now Erik might be enduring. "If you want to interview him, I'm afraid you'll have to wait. He can't talk either... they broke his jaw and... did other things..."

"What was it that you all did that made you the targets for the Gestapo? You've told me your friend Thomas tried to take Hitler's life, but what did..." he looked back through the notes he had made, "Johannes von Rott do? You said something about him giving you 'vital information to help your escape line.' What was that all about?"

"It was set up in East Prussia by ordinary people who were in positions where they might be able to help Jews to get out of Germany. Later we hid them and we also hid a British airman and Russian soldiers, too. Johan told us about changes in administration - in stamps or signatures - so we could forge the right sort of papers for them."

Nina gave him only the minimum of details. She began to feel as though she were somehow betraying Germany. She was feeling very unwell, and several times during the interview she felt hot and dizzy. She had eaten so little for so long; they were very short of food and, far too often, she had given her meagre ration to the children.

"How did you get the Jews out?"

"We sent some to Sweden to my mother-in-law or Switzerland to my cousin. Her husband is part Jewish so they had to leave Germany or be arrested. They sent others on to America to another cousin." She hesitated for a moment then continued, "We still have four Jewish children with us. We need to find their families, though I think they're all dead."

"And what will you do with these children if their parents are no longer alive?"

"Look after them, of course! Bring them up! In Sweden if I can, in Germany if I must, though they will hate the Germans when they are old enough to understand what happened to their families."

"I've often wondered; what was it like to live under a regime that you disapproved of? How did you manage to come to terms with it?"

Nina wondered how far she could trust him with any of their secrets. Should she just stick to name, rank and number? But she was too tired and too ill to care, she wanted the interview to be over as quickly as possible. "Hitler was voted into power by a majority, but was disliked by many. Can we be blamed for accepting his democratic," she emphasised the word, "election into power? Can we be blamed, because those who tried did not

380

succeed in ousting him from power? I used to be a pacifist, someone who did not believe in killing, but now, after what I've seen, what we've all been through, I think if Hitler were brought in here I would kill him myself. Thomas and I used to argue about the merits and demerits of killing. He was right," she added quietly, almost to herself.

"What was it that Thomas called Hitler? The Antichrist wasn't it?"

Nina looked up at the Major in astonishment. How could he have known that? Who was he? Before her she saw the Major looking fit and healthy as all the British did; how different from their own troops who had once been the envy of the world. He could not be much older than she, yet so very different. How dingy and miserable it made her feel to see his clean, neat, well fitting uniform whilst she had been reduced to borrowing Wilhelmina's clothes - what was left of them. She no longer had cotton to mend the clothes with, or polish to clean Wilhelmina's ill-fitting shoes, and there had hardly been any water this morning to have a well-needed wash. She found it hard not to cry with shame and embarrassment.

"Yes, that's what he called Hitler. He argued that the army shouldn't wait until he did something against their code. 'Whilst he's winning, leave him alone,' was the army's motto, or seemed to be. Thomas said 'No, Hitler was evil and...' "

"Therefore he should be killed anyway, regardless of any terms to be gained from us when he was dead. 'Kill him first, then talk to Britain,'" the Major finished her sentence.

"How could you know that... unless you were one of those that Thomas met to discuss terms with? Did you know him?"

"Yes. I met him both in London and later in Stockholm when he tried to convince the British that Germany had a kind of shadow government waiting to take over if Hitler were deposed. He asked for our help."

With the last ounce of her strength she leapt to her feet. "Why, in God's name why did you refuse it? Why didn't you accept what he said?" she cried, knowing that there would be no response. "If only you'd believed him! How many good people would still be alive, how much misery might have been avoided. This waste, this... carnage, might never have happened. How could you have ignored his pleas, our pleas?" She stopped, neither condemnation nor entreaty showing on her face, only a world-weary sadness. The weight of the horrors that had been unleashed on Europe seemed now to be sitting on her solitary shoulders. She sank back into her chair. "I sometimes feel that men simply want to fight each other - to see who is the best, the toughest. It's all dressed up with ideals and reasons, but at the end of the day it's just a good scrap to see who's going to be the top dog. Why did you go to war?" She directed the question at him personally.

He ignored her question, as she knew he would. "Why did you want to save Jews?" he asked her bluntly.

She visibly recoiled from the question. Was he no different from the Nazis after all? Were the British the same? "They're people! In Nazi Germany they lost all their rights, even to exist. I could not accept that. Everyone has a right to live whatever their race, colour, beliefs... and until we understand what that means for us, we'll go on fighting each other."

"What does it mean, Frau Larsson? What does it mean to you?"

"It means that we must accept the differences between people. We have to learn to live alongside someone of another colour, race or religion. If you look at America, white and coloured soldiers exist alongside each other without fighting; we have to learn to do the same. There are historic fights between nations that we've just got to put aside. The League of Nations tried, but it had no teeth."

The Major looked at her hard. He was dimly aware that there were some Germans who had not accepted Hitler wholeheartedly, but he was not sure yet that he believed what this woman was telling him. Her clothes were torn, she looked filthy, even her face was smudged with dirt. Her shoes did not fit her feet and she had what appeared to be rolled up paper behind her heels. How could he trust someone who looked like that? But - if it were true, she might prove to be useful.

He tapped his pen on the desk thoughtfully. Earlier in the war he, like most others, had simply wanted to defeat this arrogant, powerful nation. No country should have the power to cause wars as Germany had done; they should be beaten into the ground and never allowed to rise up again. Since then he had risen to his present position in Intelligence and had to plan several steps ahead. He would be partially responsible for the future of Germany; and he would have to help in the running of the new country when hostilities finally ceased. To do that, they would need the help of Germans who were used to positions of power and could wield authority and organise. "And can we, Frau Larsson? Can we ever learn to live together?"

"We *must!*" she stressed urgently. "Otherwise it's all been for nothing! All those deaths for nothing..."

The Major got up, picking up his papers, "Frau Larsson. Germany will need people, its own people, to help with the reconstruction of the nation when the war is over. I may need to call upon you and your sister's husband in the near future to help in some way. Would you have any objection?"

"I think I'm too tired, and hungry, to help anyone at the moment, even myself," she said, and immediately could have bitten off her tongue. He represented the enemy.

He could see that she was weak and helped her up from her chair.

"My husband once said that we owed it to the next generation to finish the fight as quickly as we could, so that they had a future Europe worth living in. I can't let it have all been in vain. There has to be something I can do for their future. When I regain my strength, I'll do everything in my power to rebuild Europe, not Germany, or France, or Britain, but a unified Europe where all nations live together and we never ever go to war with each other again. All my strength will go towards achieving that. If you have a job I can do to that end, then you have my pledge that I'll do everything I can, whoever I have to work for. Providing we are all working towards that aim together."

"So! What now, Nina?"

Anna and Nina had learned to lean heavily on each other, Anna, because by nature she preferred someone else to do the difficult thinking for her and then she would decide on the merits of the decision. And Nina leant on Anna, because she was at the end of both her physical and mental strength. Throughout the war, even up to their arrival at Bocholt, she had led the others; given them ideas or orders; run the escape line almost single-handedly since Thomas had been arrested; and she had tried to organise their own escape. Now she wanted to rest, she wanted others to do the thinking. Her body was telling her to relax, but she kept pushing it to its limits.

"I don't know, Anna. I suppose the war is over as far as this part of the world is concerned, that's one blessing. But I don't know what the peace has to hold for us, what further problems we're going to have. We've no water, no food, no money, and no jobs. What can we do?"

For the first time in her life Nina had ceased to care what happened to her or her family.

"What did he say to you Nina? The Major, I mean?"

"Something about... after the war, after the war... I don't remember, something about needing people to help..." Nina's answer tailed into oblivion. She stopped talking and looked at the floor.

She sat there for a long time, her head leaning back on the wall behind her low backed chair. She was asleep with her eyes wide open.

"Nina? Are you all right?"

"I don't feel well, Anna. I'm hot and I'm so tired, and I was dizzy once or twice during the interview." Then she started to cry, "And I can't remember what he said! I can't remember! What's wrong with me?"

Nina's thin, frail body, refused to allow her to continue; it shut her down and she remained ill and inactive in bed for many days, feverish and delirious.

Her interview had reminded her of the days, now gone forever, when she had talked to Erik and Thomas, and she could no longer push those thoughts aside. They demanded attention. While she seemed to be thinking of nothing, or half-asleep in a twilight world, she was buried in the past, remembering what was best left forgotten.

Ruth's prophetic words now returned to haunt her. 'Many of us will have to make that ultimate sacrifice' echoed over and over in her head, tormenting her. Alice whom she had left behind, and who might now be dead in one of the shipwrecks in the Baltic. Thomas's certainty that Hitler was the Antichrist. In her dreams, waking or asleep, her talks with both Thomas and Erik sped through her mind.

She lay sometimes speaking incoherently or moving her arms or legs involuntarily; inside her head, life was pulsating. Once again she walked through the trees with Erik, her arm tucked in his, and gazing lovingly at his face, radiant with happiness. There was her mother-in-law's home, glowing with light in the semi-darkness as they came out of the woods towards it, lit up with the sun as its setting rays transformed the western windows into little squares of fire. How wonderful those days had been! Had it simply been youthful ignorance of what was happening in the world, or had it been like that for everyone? And the talks they had had, the discussions, the arguments with Thomas over the moral aspects of resisting Hitler's government, "Whether 'tis nobler to suffer the slings and arrows of outrageous fortune..." Thomas had quoted Shakespeare at them, and Erik had completed it, "or by opposing, end them." How prophetic all that now seemed to her.

She lay immobile in one of the bedrooms undamaged by the bombardment. The whole household was stricken by her illness. For the first time in her life Anna took a chance, and went to visit the Major to ask if there were any assistance to be had.

After his interview with Nina, the Major had been impressed by her intelligence and the work the whole family had done. He visited the house twice while she was ill and suggested that she had the civilian equivalent of 'shell-shock'. "She's had to take too much. The body can only go so far, then it will stop completely, or it will close down some of the functions while it makes its own repairs. The doctor says she'll come out of it, but I've no idea how long it will be. I've taken the liberty of bringing along a few army rations. Please see that she gets them and doesn't give them to anyone else."

"She won't even know they're there, let alone give them away," Claudia answered. The doctor recommended sleep, rest, and quiet, especially from the children. "Time will heal her," he said.

Claudia now had two patients and spent her whole time with either Nina or Johannes who had returned home from the hospital. But at least she now had Wilhelmina and Anna to help her.

It was two weeks before Nina came back to life. She had been remembering a discussion about what the world would think of them after the war. Thomas had compared their situation to the old witch trials, 'If, when we are judged, we are dead, then we must have been good Germans, because we were prepared to die for our beliefs. But if we live, well, you remember how they judged the witches? If they drowned, they were human and innocent. If they survived, they were witches, because they had saved themselves. If I die, then they will believe in my credibility. Only then will they accept that I am anti-Nazi. If I live, they will argue that I was 'planted'; I was not a genuine representative of the resistance movement. Whatever we do, we cannot win!'

Nina woke, startled back to life, and screamed out, "No! No! Erik, don't die! Thomas!" Her voice tailed off as she realised she had been dreaming and Claudia was gently shaking her. "Claudia? I was dreaming about Erik and Thomas. I won't let them believe that two such good men were not really anti-Nazi. Oh God! Let them live and I'll persuade the British somehow that they were reliable. I'll force the British and Americans to realise that they were wrong to ignore them, and their proposals for peace." She sank back into the pillows. "You don't know what I'm talking about, do you?" She smiled wanly at her sister. "If I ever told you off for leaving Johannes and becoming a nurse, I take it all back! I couldn't be more grateful for having a real nurse in the family."

Claudia smiled, kissed her sister's forehead and without a word left the room.

She came back with Johannes.

"Johan! You look so much better. Can you speak yet?" Nina leant forward to grasp his hands and then remembered.

"As long as you hold them gently," Johannes whispered slowly and held his still bound hands towards her. She took his arm carefully and he bent slowly down to receive her kiss on his cheek.

"I'm so glad, Johan. So glad. You must get better soon, the Major said they'd be looking for well-qualified people to help rebuild the town. You'll be needed, Johan and you'll earn good money and we need it so much."

"Don't worry, Nina. Max and Mina are already helping to reorganise the local government structure, along the lines they want, of course," Anna told her, "but it won't last for long. Once the war is over, we'll be in a good position to rebuild a new Germany, the way we want it to be."

"We must be careful or they'll accuse us of arrogance and of trying to dominate the new Europe. How are we managing for food and water?"

"Stop fretting, Nina! You'll kill yourself with worry. There's a tap organised in the street. We send the children to queue up. It keeps them busy and they feel useful. Then there's a soup kitchen in the town and we're beginning to get some Red Cross parcels. And the Major has sent some to you especially," Anna told her.

"For me? But why?"

Anna looked at Claudia and they grinned, a sisterly conspiratorial smile.

"Well, come on, tell me. Is he trying to build me up for some special job?"

Claudia laughed, the first for many months. "No! We think he rather likes you, that's all!"

"That's all? Nice man or not, I'm not fraternising with the enemy."

"That's rich, coming from someone who hid all those Russians!"

"That was wartime. This is peace... well it's almost peacetime. Did I tell you he knew Thomas?"

"You didn't have time to tell us very much at all before you collapsed, but we've spoken to the Major since then and he knows what you did, what we all did. I think he was very impressed, especially with your part, Nina."

"He might be, but I'm not. I lost three children, two Russians and an Aunt on the way to Danzig. Poor little things. We've never even had the time to pray for them or give them a memorial service. That's the first thing I have to do, as soon as I can get out, I must go to the church and light candles for everyone, especially Mother and Father, and Nanny... and... "

Claudia patted Nina's arm. "How do you think we all feel? We've all failed someone, haven't we? We still haven't found out where Aunt Alice is. I thought I'd put her on a boat, but it seems she's lost, too. It isn't possible to always do the right thing and you're only human, Nina, like the rest of us. But look at what you achieved! The children would have been captured, probably killed. We saved them from a horrible painful fate. Even though we lost the others through the ice it was a much quicker and easier death than they might otherwise have had."

"I saved the other four. I should have been able to save them, too," Nina interrupted.

"Yes, you saved the others. You saved Anneliese, too, remember? And how many hundreds of other Jews? You can't go on blaming yourself for things that didn't work out the way you wanted them to. I did that for too long until, thank God, I had Johan to look after and I learned through him to live with my past mistakes."

"It isn't so much the errors as the guilt over things I ought to have done. I can't get used to second best. Do you remember when the Steiners' shops were closed down and every Jew had to wear the Star of

David? I thought later, too late, all of us should have worn it. If everyone had sewn it on how could they ever have known who was Jewish?"

"That's the point at which they won, didn't they?" Claudia agreed. "As soon as we all made the distinction, as soon as we admitted being Jewish mattered. We should have refused to answer that question."

"Yes, You're right, Claudia! I hadn't seen it before. As soon as we filled in the forms and said Christian or Jew they had us. How dumb we were, how stupid!"

"Listen!" Anna said, holding up her hand for quiet, "What's that?"

"It's a church bell, isn't it?"

Outside the children's voices had ceased as they, too, listened. Did it signal the start of another air raid? They ran inside and up to the bedroom for reassurance.

"I thought all bells had been melted down."

The children's shouts and their noisy footsteps clattering up the uncarpeted wooden stairs drowned out the sound of a car door slamming. Politely saluting, the Major stood in the doorway unnoticed.

Over the last two weeks of Nina's illness he had taken the opportunity to interview the adults, and one or two of the children unofficially. This was a German family capable of becoming a building block for the future.

He knew, and politicians had said it, that when the war ended, they would have the Russians to contend with and they would need a strong Germany as a buffer state between Russia and the western nations. There was to be no revenge, no impossible reparations placed on the Germans as there had been after the last war at Versailles, no Diktat. Reconstruction was to begin immediately.

Here was a family with six well-educated adults - all speaking perfect English and other languages, who could act as translators or clerks - who desperately needed the money they would be able to earn. They had lost almost everything, but would they accept? Would their pride prevent them from taking anything from their conquerors? He had tried conscientiously to put himself in their position; how would he feel in their place?

He had worked hard for this family and, as he was about to show them, he wanted them on his side, working for the new system whatever that was going to be. They represented the good, older values of Germany that coincided with his own educational background.

He looked at Johannes sitting on the bed, with his arm around Nina's shoulders, his fingers still bandaged, but his mouth now pulled back in a smile. He and his father were the potential mayors of local towns. He had tried to find the previous incumbents of many town halls, but where were they? They seemed to have fled and the Major was left with the task of filling the posts with non-Nazis.

When Johannes had fully recovered he would offer him such a position. He believed it would be accepted when it was understood that the occupation of Germany was to be temporary and they would eventually be left to run their own country. He was glad to find them all together in one room, where they had gathered when Nina came back to 'life', because he had some news for them.

He made his presence known with a slight cough. "Gentlemen, ladies," he laughed with them, and made a flamboyant salute to the children. He nodded to Nina, "I'm glad to see you looking better, Frau Larsson."

He then addressed the gathering; "Everyone looks pleased so I assume that you have heard the news?"

"What news should we have heard? We were listening to the bells."

He took off his cap and smiled. "The war in Europe is over!"

A shocked silence greeted him. Too much had happened to all of them for great demonstrations of joy, too many had died. There was only relief.

"Thank God!" Nina whispered fervently, and closing her eyes she prayed silently, tears pouring down her cheeks. The children had been promised that when the war ended they could make as much noise as they liked, but they discovered that it was not so easy. They had become used to quietness, making a lot of noise had lost its appeal. Little Joe went over to the Major and gave the British salute and Heide gave him a polite handshake and said, "Can I be called Hannah again?"

"Children," Anna suggested in order to clear the room. "Off you go and spread the good news to all the neighbours."

No one noticed the Major hold Dieter back and take him from the room separately, and return alone. Patiently he waited for the right moment to give them the tidings they all wanted to hear, and which he had worked diligently and swiftly to achieve.

"Anna, help me up, I want to see what's going on outside. Oh, Claudia, Johan," Nina breathed in deeply as the four of them stood at the glassless windows, surveying the balmy spring day. As they supported her still weak frame, she hugged each one tightly, even Johannes, who bore it bravely. And kissed them affectionately. "I wonder what it will be like, this brave new Europe of ours? We owe it to the children to make it a land worth living in. Do you remember who said that?"

"I did."

Slowly Nina took courage and turned to confront the new speaker in the now quiet, motionless room.

He stood by the door, only a little changed from the last time she had seen him. His blond hair greying at the temples, the lines on his forehead now friendly and distinguished rather than signs of age or inner torment. His grey flecked green eyes fixed on her, twinkling as they had done the first time they met in London. At his side, holding his hand and looking up happily and trustingly at his father was Dieter, already reunited.

Nina stood transfixed, one hand clutching Wilhelmina's dressing gown to her heart, the other pressed at her open mouth, trying unsuccessfully to stifle the ecstatic cry that broke from her throat. "Erik!" In an instant she and Erik were in each other's arms, both openly weeping with joy.

The Major observed the touching scene from the doorway, then, with a courteous salute to Anna, he turned and left as unobserved as he had arrived.

Rosie

by

Mark Carter

ISBN 1904278 41 2

After living in an enclosed order for twenty years, dressed in ordinary clothes, Sister Marie Rose was sent to Medjugorje, Yugoslavia, to find out more about the reported miracles. There she met Bill who was, also, not who he seemed.

When she agreed to visit London and her natal land of Wales with Bill, Rosie thought she would be spending a few quiet days in the outside world before going back to St. John's Abbey, but events were to take a completely unexpected turn…

A few exciting months later, Rosie's mind is in turmoil. Should she obey her Revered Mother's order to return to the convent? She was married to Christ, how could she break her vows?

And what about Bill…?

LOST IN FRANCE

by

Gillian Ogilvie

ISBN: 1 904278 50 4

In the Sarthe region of France, during a horrendous storm, a young woman had been dumped, battered and bruised, on a farmhouse doorstep. Her past and her identity are a complete mystery. Did any one wish her harm? Why had no one searched for her? Where was her family?

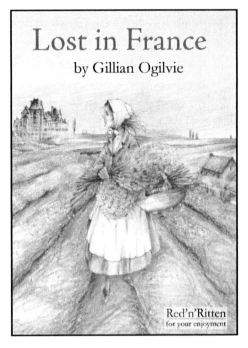

Five years on Marie-Anne can only remember the time she has spent with the Dubuis family. She loves a local farmer and her lack of official papers threatens to deprive her of the longed for status and security he can offer. Desperately and urgently she seeks answers to her many questions. But what will such searches reveal? What will the truth bring with it?

Meantime, in England, another woman has also found the man of her dreams and a new family...

Each character is happily making plans for their future when a photograph causes a ripple of events that enmesh all four. Will each of them eventually emerge from a tangled web of past tragedy and misunderstanding to live happily...?

Other Autobiographies published by Red'n'Ritten Ltd.

Three delightful childhood memoirs
set in Sussex, London
& Hampshire

Autobiography:

The story of an RAF Armourer, 1939-1946.

ISBN 1904278329

by Eric Gardner

Eric Gardner grew up in Frome on a small family farm. The *Introduction* to this book is his account of the farm itself, daily routines and the animals with which he shared his childhood, and paints an engaging picture of rural life in 1930's Somerset.

At the age of 19 he joined the RAF. His witty observations of day-to-day life as an Airman in

Red'n'Ritten
for your enjoyment

wartime Britain and Canada give a fascinating insight into the life experienced by many ordinary men and women, from all backgrounds, who were brought together by World War Two.

Like many of his generation, Eric Gardner did not receive a higher education, and was unable to fulfil his obvious potential. In later life he often commented that the RAF had been his university.

Eric thought his wartime experiences would be of little interest to anyone else, because he did not see any active service. His family did not agree and encouraged him to commit his memories to paper.

He finished the manuscript for *A Somerset Airman* just days before his sudden death at the age of 82 and so, sadly, Eric never saw it in print.

BAMBY

The story of a Swiss girl who becomes a Section Officer in Photography in the WAAF

ISBN 978 1904278 481

Born to a German actress mother and Swiss artist father, Barbara (Bamby) Dallas's life, (née Schmidbauer and Bamberger) was destined to be anything but straightforward.

by Barbara Dallas

Part One (1921-41) tells of her rural life in Upper Silesia; and then her school days, after her mother's second marriage to a Merchant Banker of Jewish origin, in a Pestalozzi school in the Reinland and a finishing school in Switzerland. When the Nazis took over the Bank in 1938, her parents fled to England, and Barbara joined them travelling alone via Berlin and Amsterdam just in time for World War Two …

Even though her parents were Enemy Aliens, she joined the WAAF as a photographer, and met her Army pilot husband. **Part Two** (1941-45) is a transcript of Bamby's diary, written whilst serving in the WAAF. She met an Army Pilot during the war and they married just after VE Day. Ian's family insisted he join the family firm of Insurance Brokers, but it enabled them to bring up a family in comfort. In **Part Three** (1945-2005) we see that Barbara's life was never going to be problem or adventure free…

We also learn more about her very young childhood from her stepmother and stepbrother, and the fate of those who did not escape to or stay in England.